THE BEST
THING FOR YOU

THE BEST THING FOR YOU

ANNABEL LYON

National Library of Canada Cataloguing in Publication

Lyon, Annabel, 1971-
The best thing for you / Annabel Lyon.

ISBN 0-7710-5397-5

I. Title.

PS8573.Y62B48 2004   C813'.6   C2003-907171-5

We acknowledge the financial support of the Government of Canada through the Book Publishing Industry Development Program and that of the Government of Ontario through the Ontario Media Development Corporation's Ontario Book Initiative. We further acknowledge the support of the Canada Council for the Arts and the Ontario Arts Council for our publishing program.

Typeset in Janson by M&S, Toronto
Printed and bound in Canada

This book is printed on acid-free paper that is
100% ancient forest friendly (100% post-consumer recycled)

McClelland & Stewart Ltd.
The Canadian Publishers
481 University Avenue
Toronto, Ontario
M5G 2E9
www.mcclelland.com

1   2   3   4   5   08   07   06   05   04

THE BEST
THING FOR YOU

NO FUN

The landscapers wake me up. It's five o'clock and they're leaving for the day. They're dragging their shovels along the gravel path under my window, back to their truck, which bristles with implements.

I pull on a robe and go downstairs in my bare feet. Outside I catch the older one coiling my garden hose. "I've been rethinking the patio."

"Good morning to *you*," he says. My hair must be sticking up.

"I work nights. What I was thinking, instead of concrete, maybe stone? With plants growing in the cracks."

He nods. "The old wild-thyme-amongst-the-stone-flagging trick. The aged look? You step on it, it smells nice?"

I nod.

"Tuscany, am I right?"

"I've never been." Although, okay, yes, this is one of my plans for a perfect future. Maybe when my son is old enough to fall in love. It would be a gift his parents could give him, taking him to a place like that to fall in love. Olives and wine and wild thyme in the flagging. Olives and bicycles, summer.

Back upstairs I'm pulling on my running gear when I overhear the older one telling his assistant about my idea.

3

"Tuscany?" the assistant asks.

"Not yet."

"Funny," I say to no one. If I keep moving, I just have time to make supper, go for my run, shower, and still make my shift at the hospital.

My husband, Liam, comes in and slumps down behind me while I'm on the floor lacing my runners. He puts his arms around me and hooks one leg over mine and starts kissing the back of my neck. "Hi," he says.

I give us a couple of minutes of this. Then I say, "Where are the boys?" Our son, Ty, this summer, is inseparable from Jason-from-swimming. This summer they are "the boys." We like saying this, Liam and I. We're distantly thinking of another baby, when life settles down, the renovations and my shifts and his tenure. It's not too late, although Ty is fourteen and it might look a little weird. But it might look cool, too.

"Look." Liam points out the window. Down in the yard Jason is holding three white tennis balls and looking over Ty's shoulder. Ty is reading aloud from a book. He's wearing basketball shorts and a white vest with great loops for armholes, showing a lot of thin brown chest. He's just started putting muscle on his back and shoulders, and he's almost as tall as I am, but his face is still smooth. Jason is blond to my son's dark, with a backwards baseball cap and a black T-shirt with white lettering on it, cut for someone fifty pounds heavier. His elbows flex in and out of sight in this T-shirt. He clutches the tennis balls to his chest like eggs. When he drops one we hear his thin, unbroken voice say, "Sheet."

"They're going to learn to juggle from a book," Liam says.

"Ty's idea, sounds like."

"Who else?" Liam has told me he finds Jason a bit dull, also shifty. He's not wrong. We go downstairs, holding hands.

"Fish for supper," I say.

Liam lets go of me and snatches open the fridge door. He spreads his arms like an opera tenor hitting a high one, waiting to be impressed by the contents. "It's all mocha yogurt with you people, isn't it?"

I grind a lemon on the juicer, pinch cilantro, fork oil in a dish. One of my half-hour marinades. The door opens and Ty sticks his head through. "Can Jason stay for supper?"

"Nah," Liam and I say together. He grins. Jason appears at his side and he starts smiling too, although he doesn't know what at. "Is it okay?" he asks. "We'll do the dishes."

This is too sweet, even for them. "It's okay if you go home and tell your mother and change your T-shirt," I say. Liam comes over to have a look so he stands up tall and pulls it straight with his hands. I'VE HAD SEX, the T-shirt says.

Ty is smiling at the ceiling. Liam bites the inside of his cheek and turns away quickly. He starts humming, ducking to look out the window. He's holding his breath, humming, eyes closed.

"Now," I say.

While the fish marinates, I go for my run. My route takes me along a few quiet streets of big old houses and maples, down to the gravel beach path. At twenty minutes I turn back. When I turn the last corner I stop to walk, to cool down and admire our house – gables and dormers, an upstart thirties' baby but trying to blend. Now it's a character home. When we bought it, it was acid yellow and the yard was somebody's scorched earth policy. We threw a party for all our friends. "That's going to go," we said, pointing at the paint. We gestured at the yard, expansive gestures. "It's all going to go." Now it's the prettiest on the block: Nantucket blue, climbing yellow roses, lawn like jade, basketball hoop nailed to the garage. And we're having the back done, finally – sunroom, greenhouse, patio. I stand, hands on my hips, breathing hard, and admire.

Ty is sitting on the front steps, using a stick to prise pebbles from the treads of his new Nike Shox. He begged me for those shoes. I've seen him wash them with shampoo.

"Jason gone home?" I ask.

"He's coming back."

"That's what I meant." I ruffle his hair as I pass. Soft hair, like his father's. He jumps up, sock-footed, and opens the door for me with a courtly bow.

I shower, bake the fish, and we eat. Liam, professor of film studies, explains to the boys why we won't let them go see *Summer of Sam* at the second-run theatre.

"It has violence," he says, taking salad. "Violence and sex and penises."

"Yech," Ty says.

Jason says, "It does not," and looks expectant. He now has a flannel shirt buttoned over the T-shirt. He holds his fork in his fist and his knife in his other fist, like a toddler. But he says please and thanks and washes his hands before he comes to the table. I asked Ty once about his parents and he said, "They're really nice."

"Still, no," Liam says.

Jason loves Liam. He watches him, waiting to laugh.

"What are you boys going to do tonight?" I ask.

"Get into trouble," Jason says promptly.

Ty says, "Pillage."

"Not on my watch." Liam stacks our plates. When he gets to Jason's, he squints at it. Jason has scraped all his cilantro to one side, a green wad. "What in hell is that?"

Jason looks at me, embarrassed. "I wasn't sure."

"It's okay," I say softly, and smile. "It's just a herb."

"It's grass from the lawn," Liam says, and Jason smiles.

"I gotta go." I stand up. "You've got ten hours to do the dishes."

Liam follows me out to the garage and presses against me in the dark. "Wake me up when you get in," he says. He's serious.

"Wow, no kidding."

"This is nothing," he says. "I'm waiting for you."

I'm a doctor at Charity Eagle – a tiny local hospital with an even tinier Emergency that strictly ought not to exist, except that we're a wealthy riding. I spent years pulling strings to get here, a ten-minute drive from home, which is why I'm temporarily on nights, filling in for the Emergency resident who's on stress leave. What stress? is what I can't help thinking. Not a stabbing, not an overdose, not a severed spinal cord in sight. I keep thinking, hit me. I can take it.

There's no vending machine. Once an hour or so, the nurses make everybody tea.

"Dawn," I say, greeting the nurses. "Daisy."

"Hi, hi, hi," they say.

It's a quiet night. An MI, a dog bite. "What kind of dog?" I ask, as Daisy prepares the hypodermic.

The victim, who looks golf, shakes his head. Fifties, rueful. "Terrier. My own damn dog. I thought we were playing."

"Little guy probably thought so too," Daisy says.

It's a ripping bite, not deep, but messy. "He hung on," I say. I get him to bend the knee a few times.

"Sure, what do you want, he's a terrier," the man says.

Dawn sticks her head through the curtains. "Doctor," is all she says.

Outside they've got one on the table. "Okay, yes," I say.

The ambulance man reads from a clipboard. "Concussion, fractured rib, fractured jaw, broken nose, bruising to face, back, shoulders, shins, severe bruising to genitals." He looks up. "A beating."

I look at his face. Down syndrome. He's awake.

"Hey, buddy," I say.

"He's not, ah, receiving you," the man says, tapping his ear.

"Don't be a jerk."

"No, I mean they found his hearing aid nearby. Looked like someone stepped on it. Here's his jacket. Wallet, Care Card, provincial ID. In case of emergency contact."

"Okay." I point to reception. "Dawn?"

"Sorry," she says, hustling back. "Paul Malone."

"Who found him?" We're busy now.

"In the parking lot behind Silver Video. At Eighth Avenue?" I nod. It's our local. I have a card for Silver Video in my wallet. "Employee locking up. Said he'd been in the store an hour and a half before, returning videos, wanting to chat. Apparently he's a regular."

"What was he doing round the back?"

"I guess getting the crap kicked out of him."

We send Paul Malone off for X-rays and a scan, an orderly wheeling him. He's awake this whole time. He's cleaned up and we've got painkillers in him but his face is looking worse, puffy and darkening.

"Who would do that?" I say, watching him go, and Dawn says, "Lord, I know."

I pick up his jacket, a navy blue shell from Coast Meridian Sports. It's pretty scuffed up, and square in the back is a footprint, so clear you can see the pattern on the sole – Nikes.

Dawn spans her hand next to the print.

After about twenty minutes his people start coming. By this

time I've got a baby. I'm telling the parents, your baby eats talc, your baby's going to vomit talc. Keep the lid on the talc. They're nodding.

"Doctor," Dawn says.

I shake hands with a white-haired woman, the supervisor of Paul Malone's group home. I explain about the tape on his ribs, the jaw, the nose, which will need surgery but not immediately. No apparent brain damage or internal damage, although he's going to have pain talking and especially urinating. I explain he might not recognize her right now, with the Demerol, and we'd like him to stay at least until tomorrow for observation.

She asks for a list of his medications, goes and takes a look at him, then sits down in the waiting area and starts making notes.

A family with food poisoning – shellfish. Even the two-year-old had clams. I would never give my two-year-old clams. The next time I look over, there's a weedy man with a honey-coloured moustache sitting next to the supervisor. They're conferring, I would say. He goes over and makes a call at the pay phone, referring to some papers she's given him. Then he tips her a little salute and leaves.

It's about three a.m. "Pastry?" says Julie at Reception, when she sees me heading for the double doors with my water bottle, and holds out a plate.

I take my break outside, in the dark cool, like a smoker. I chomp my Danish and suck my water. The sliding doors sigh and two people come out, the supervisor and another woman. They don't see me. The supervisor lights up. When she sucks, her cheeks go black in the white fluorescence from the EMERGENCY sign over the doors. They wander off the grooved rubber mat and the doors sigh closed. They sit on the edge of a box planter.

"I'm guessing kids," the new woman says. "Teenagers."

I bite my Danish quietly. It's good.

The supervisor taps ash, looks away. "He shouldn't have been out so late on his own. The videos were overdue. The night staff told him, first thing tomorrow morning, you go take those videos back. I guess he was trying to get the job done. Nice warm summer evening and all."

"Elaine, I'm not blaming you, I guess," the woman says. "But I just think someone has to take responsibility here. He could be dead."

The supervisor tucks her cigarette into the bark chips in the planter behind her. "Let's go back in."

"Somebody's at fault," the woman says.

The rest of my shift is medium busy. It's the weekend, so we get a few extra drunken stupidities, nothing major. In a quiet moment I pick up Paul Malone's jacket again and look at the footprint on the back. I'm thinking, *teenagers*. The print is kind of small.

"See what I mean?" Dawn says.

Pink light, filtered through the smoked-glass doors, hits the floor in an orange pool. It glows fiercer and fiercer until it disappears – sun's up. Julie's phones are ringing silently, red lights winking and twitching, fibrillating.

I take a last look at Paul Malone. His face is purple, lip stitched, jaw wrapped. He watches me move around the bed. The woman from outside sits beside him, holding his hand. Someone's put a hearing aid back in his ear.

"Is this your sister?" I say, and he nods.

Six a.m. I go home.

The neighbourhood is bathed in summer dawn, the trees are weighed down with it like syrup. In this light even the cars are tender and lovely, although the damp salt cool off the ocean, tangible blocks up from the beach at night, is already fizzing dry under the blue heat of the sky. And people hate our neighbour-hood, elsewhere in the city, hate it, they talk about us on the radio call-in shows because our old trees are saved at extra expense during road repair, because Charity Eagle thrives when other hospitals are closing, because this is where the lawyers live. Liam and I shouldn't be here, even with our incomes. There was a blip in the market, a window, and we jumped; otherwise we'd be bitching it out in the suburbs and hating us too. In fact, most of our good friends, people we went to university with, live else-where. In fact, we only know one lawyer, and she is shy.

A police cruiser is parked in our driveway. As I pull up along-side it backs into the street. The officer waves at me before he drives away. Moustache, sunglasses. He looks like a prick.

"Fuck was *that*," I say to no one. My heart is beating. I put the car away. In the house, I go straight up to Ty's room, but he's not there. His weights are lined up under his Steve Nash poster, his plaid sheets are on his bed, his computer is on his desk, but he's not in any of his places. I can't see his shoes.

I go to our bedroom. Liam's in bed, asleep, naked. The note on my night table says, *Kid's sleeping over at Jason's.*

The room is white, light-swollen, awake.

"How was work?" Liam says. So he's awake too, just not moving. I sit beside him on the bed and tell him about the very first one, the one I lost, the MI.

"Again?"

"Heart attack. He was hanging on when they brought him in, but there was nothing we could do. I wish those guys would die at home sometimes."

"With their martinis and their chicken-fried steaks and their hippo guts and their stressful stockbroking careers."

"All of that," I say. "Why was there a police cruiser in the driveway just now?"

The phone rings. "What the hell?" Liam says. "It's not even seven. If that's Ty wanting to be picked up, tell him he's on his own."

I let the machine down in the kitchen take it. "Liam."

"We're having words when he gets home, anyway. The pair of them took off last night without telling me. Then he phones from Jason's, by the way Dad, I'm staying here tonight. Not asking, notice, telling. *And* they left me the dishes, which as we all know is women's and small boys' work."

"What time was this?" I say. "Approximately."

"It's that Jason, I think." He's up on an elbow now. "There's something kind of morose about that kid."

"Liam."

"Ty's a bright boy," my husband says, sitting up. He's getting excited. "He should have bright friends. That Jason gets on my nerves. I want to sock him."

"No you don't want to sock him."

He cups my face in his hands and looks at my hair. "Yes, I honestly do." He makes a fist, draws it back, slow-mo, lets his knuckles kiss my jaw in a pretend right hook. "Bam! Like that. And that T-shirt."

I bite my lip.

"He's repugnant. A sniggering, repugnant little boy."

"Which you never were."

"I was a prince," Liam says. "My son is a prince. The lower life forms, we're not accountable."

"Liam, why were the police here?"

"I'm just coming to that." He stares at me for a minute before saying, "Nope. Can't think of anything funny. Was there really a cruiser in the driveway?"

"There really, really was."

"Let's have a baby," Liam says.

We get into position. Then I say, "What if there's something wrong with it?"

He hesitates over me. "You mean, like, it turns out closer to the Jason-end of the spectrum?"

"I mean, like, a condition, a deformity or a – syndrome, of some sort."

"That's horrible," Liam says. "We're making love and you're thinking about things like that? I guess it could be a racist bigot and a psychopath too. Why do you want to think these things? Do you want to jinx us?"

I tell him my idea about the flagstones. "That's more like it," he says. We stop talking and start enjoying ourselves. "Be noisy," he says. "Kid's out of the house. Be noisy."

As he ruts away I tell myself I'm not, not, not going to worry about a child that isn't my child. I should know better than to try to peek behind the scenery: it always snaps back before my eyes have time to adjust, and I'm left with the props and the big lights and the goody-goody goodness of my life. I have the house, the job, the world with the bright, neat-edged colours of a cartoon. My blood twinkles in my healthy veins. My husband is a prince. My son is a prince. The prick in the cruiser was just turning around.

After he comes, gasping and shuddering like he's wounded, I send him down for orange juice. "Newspaper, bagels!" I add. I want to eat, but I also want to be asleep before the landscapers arrive or I'll just lie there listening, needing to supervise. Lying on my back, knees up, I think of the war soup going on inside me, hopefully. "Girl," I say, poking myself in the belly. "Hey you. We want a girl."

"Pulp?" Liam calls. "Or no? Kate?" But it's pleasant to ignore him, lying here and thinking I know where Ty's mobile is, elephants rounding to Brahms, and his little suits. I kept everything. I'm letting consciousness go, moment to moment, like pruning out a handful of helium balloons. Red is a good colour for a baby's room, I'm thinking, brass elephants, candles, a carved wood chest. Darkness and textures, a warm cave. I'm going in.

The next few days pass as some days will, water through glass pipes. The beating makes a small worrisome item on the local news as a probable hate crime, then goes under. The landscapers bring us stone samples, big as pizzas, which we do gravely consider. Marble is not out of the question. Ty seems sleepy, out of it, which I attribute to a late-summer growth spurt, a little too much computer, the imminence of school. Still, we manage to have the following conversation:

Us: Would you like a sister?

Him (face lighting up): No.

At the hospital are painters, men responsible for the term "hospital green." When I ask, they tell me it's known in the trade as "herb." And I like it, wet or dry – the world being made new for Labour Day, the sticky creak of wet paint coming off the roller. I discuss with Administration certain possibilities, a shifting of shifts, to which they proclaim themselves open. There's a spot in the out-patient clinic next door, which I covet, and I let them know. We look each other in the eye, Administration and I, and neither of us has to blink. I go days at the clinic.

Late afternoon, Sunday before Monday before school, me still a little groggy from the turnaround, there's a message on the answering machine from the Parmenters, Jason's parents. Would we go round this evening and bring Ty? Liam phones back three times to confirm but all he gets is tape.

"I doubt it's supper or they'd have said supper," I say. "Let's take a bottle of wine. If they feed us, great. If not, takeout."

"Can we eat in the car?" Liam says.

We've been having an awful lot of sex lately. We're both feeling a little puffy with it, a little silly and bruised.

"Ty!" Liam shouts, even though he's right here, leaning in the doorway like we've taken his crutches. "Who are these people? Are these Merlot people or Chardonnay people? What exactly are we dealing with here, son?"

Ty shrugs. When I take his chin in my hand to make him look at me he scowls. "What?" I say.

He mumbles about not wanting to go.

"Well, hell," Liam says. "I'm just going so I can throw spitballs at Jason. Your mom's just going so she can administer CPR if people start choking on their own boredom. You know? Maybe they'll let us watch TV. How bad can it be?"

I say, "Did you and Jason have a fight?"

Ty inarticulates.

"Enunciate or I'll belt you," Liam says.

He doesn't smile. "Can I have a shower?"

Shocked, we stare. He looks miserable.

"Yes, god," we say, and he turns away.

At ten past seven we're heading up the garden path. It's not a great house, pretty bad house, in fact. Stucco, rusted railings, crap for grass. "Uh-oh," I say softly to Liam, nodding at a tealike stain spreading from the eaves to the front window.

"In and out," Liam responds under his breath. "One, two –"

"Mom," Ty says.

The door opens. "Hel-*lo*!" we say.

It's just barely possible to imagine Jason ever replicating the big piece of meat that is his dad. He's got a gut and hands like beefs, but also his son's hair, that same straw-blond I associate with virgin farmboys. Without a word he gestures us into the house, while managing not to take the wine (a decent enough Cabernet). Ty trails. In the living room are Jason, who stares sullenly at the floor and doesn't look up when we come in, and Jason's mom, who's obviously been crying.

I grab for Ty, to protect him from the big man behind us.

"Have you seen the evening news?" the big man says, and then I see he's been crying too. His eyes are red and he's biting down so hard he can barely talk. "Our boys have something to tell us." Except that isn't exactly what he says. He says, "The evening newsh." He says, "Shomething to tell ush."

"We haven't seen the news," Liam says idiotically, yielding, it seems to me, some pretty basic ground. But I look at Ty and Ty is crying. He hasn't cried in years, that I've seen. He's had no call.

"Liam," I say sharply, the way I speak to my nurses sometimes, and everyone looks at me. I look at Jason's dad, Mr. Parmenter. I look him in the eye. "Say what you've got to say."

"It wasn't me," Ty says.

"It was the two of them together," Mr. Parmenter says. Mrs. Parmenter opens her mouth and cries soundlessly. "We're going to the police," Mr. Parmenter says.

"No," Ty says to me.

Liam says, "Don't say anything."

Mr. Parmenter says clearly, "Animals."

And now I can see it coming: like a fist, like in slow motion, I can see where it's going to hit before it hits – a meteor closing in on its own shadow. Pinned, fascinated, I let Liam do the talking. "You are fucking out of your mind," Liam says.

"Do you want to know what they've done," Mr. Parmenter says.

I can feel Ty start to shiver like he's cold. A big dirty yellow dog walks into the living room and falls to the floor at Jason's feet like it's been blackjacked. When Mr. Parmenter talks its tail thumps, grooving on the sound of the familiar voice.

"Do you want to know what they've done," Mr. Parmenter repeats.

"Don't fucking tell me anything," Liam says. "Look at your family." And, indeed, peripherally, I've been keeping an eye on Mrs. Parmenter, who is now smiling fixedly at her hands. She's got a dozen years on me, more, with the perm and the house dress. The smile is shock. Beside her, Jason is watching Liam. Probably, it occurs to me, he's never heard anyone talk to his dad the way Liam is talking to his dad. Probably Liam is just going up and up in his little head.

"Our boys beat up a retarded man," Mr. Parmenter says.

I walk out of the house, then, with my son, and no one tries to stop me.

In the car, I watch him strap in, next to me, in the front. Liam is still inside.

"I know about it but I wasn't there," Ty says.

And I love him, I can't help it.

Instead of asking questions, I tell him I know about it too. I tell him about the tests we ordered, the injuries. I use terminology. Inessential details come back to me as I talk – dandruff, how the fingernails needed clipping – but I leave those out. While I'm talking I put the key in the ignition and turn it to Battery so we can play the radio while we wait for Liam. I'm unafraid because I have seen and believe in mistakes.

"Will he be all right?" Ty asks, when I finish talking.

"Yes."

We sit in silence. Finally Liam comes out the front door, closes it behind him, and jogs down the path. He gets in the back. The first thing he says is, "We need a lawyer." I put the car in gear and pull away from the curb. The second thing he says is, "How about a drive?"

"Dad," Ty says, but Liam puts a hand on his shoulder.

I drive us to the parking lot of Ty's school, Carter High. I know what Liam's thinking: they could be there, waiting for us, cruiser in the driveway. And if our son's time is suddenly valuable, it's most valuable to us. We get him first.

I back us up against the green chain-link fence and cut the motor. We watch a pair of older boys, shavers, go one-on-one in the court. Ty watches too, his eyes alert, even managing a brief wry smile at a goofy one-hander that shouldn't sink but does. I wonder if he knows them.

"So what happened," Liam says.

Ty keeps his eyes on the game. He's thinking. To help him, I repeat everything I just said for Liam. For those moments, when I'm conscious of him knowing what I'm going to say before I say it, it's as though he's my husband and Liam is our son.

When I'm done, Ty says, "Jason and another guy did it. He bragged about it after, but I didn't believe him."

"Where were you?" Liam says.

I try to see my son's shoes but he's got his feet stuffed up by the heater vent, the way he always does, out of sight. Have I mentioned our car, a Jetta? And his legs are getting long?

"I was tired," Ty says. "It was like ten, eleven? Jason went out but I stayed in bed."

"His parents let him do that?" I say.

"Which was it, ten or eleven?" Liam says.

"His mom went to bed early and his dad had bowling league. I think ten."

"Bowling league," Liam says.

"But they knew you were in the house."

"Well," Ty says. "No."

I do ironico-skeptical: lean back, chin down, eyebrows up. "You're never in bed by ten."

"Well, then, eleven."

"Ty, which," Liam says. "People are going to ask you this stuff." He's fiddling with the dash vents, flicking them open and closed. "I don't look at the clock right before I fall asleep."

"You go to a sleepover and he goes out and you stay in?"

"Mom, god," he says. "Sleepover."

"What your mother is saying," Liam says, "and we're together on this, okay?, is we don't quite believe you. We want to believe you, we're trying, but our feeling is you are fucking around. You're not even looking at us when you talk. Look at me." Ty turns around. "I don't believe what Mr. Parmenter believes, which is that you and Jason did something together. I don't accept that. But you're acting tricky, son. Did you watch?"

"Jesus Christ of course he didn't watch," I say.

"I once watched a group of white kids beat a black kid," Liam says. "You know, beat him up. In high school. When I say watched, I was a distance away. I was aware of it going on, okay? Most of the school was aware of it going on, I would include some teachers. So I'm asking, did you watch?"

"No."

"Why didn't you say anything when you heard about it on the news?"

He shrugs.

I ask, "Who was the other boy?"

"What?" Ty says.

"You said Jason told you he did it with another boy. Who was that?"

"I don't know," Ty says. "Somebody he met. Some kid. He might have been someone Jason knew but I didn't know. Probably that's who it was."

"Why didn't you go out with Jason?" Liam asks again.

Ty yawns. This time he says: "I wanted to use his computer."

I squint at him.

"I pretended I was too tired so I could play on his computer while he was out. Like, how far away were you, Dad?"

"What?"

"From the black kid."

Liam looks out the window for a long time without answering. I don't realize he's actually looking at landmarks, gauging distances, until he says, "Basketball court."

"What were you doing on the computer?" I ask.

"What?" Ty says.

"Tyler."

He looks at his lap. He digs a finger under his sock to scratch an ankle and I see the shoes, the Nikes, and the Indiglo watch on his left wrist. It's exactly eight o'clock and some split seconds. "I was looking at this web site," he says next, softly.

"What Mr. Parmenter told me," Liam says later, "is that our son was the other boy."

It's 10:10. We're sitting in the kitchen, drinking the Cabernet. Ty is up in his room. We've got a call in to our shy lawyer friend to ring us when she gets in, no matter when. "I shouldn't really be drinking this, in case," I say, pouring us more wine.

"Do you believe him?"

I raise my glass, hesitate. "Have to."

He touches his glass to mine and I wonder what we've just decided, just done. "You?"

"I believe the part about the dirty web site. Would he have told us that if he didn't have to?"

I take a deep breath, like I'm about to say something, and then I exhale.

Liam taps his mouth with his fingers, thinking. Minutes pass.

"Healthy curiosity," I say finally, which is the succinct kernel of everything I want to say. I'm drinking faster than Liam. "At his age of fourteen." The phone rings. "Finally."

"Shut up," Liam says, and answers it. It's our very good shy lawyer friend, Isobel. "Yeah, not so," he says. "Our son might be looking at an assault charge."

What an amazing sentence. I shake my head. Assault charge, that's the nut of it, right there. I'm blasted and I know it, but still I'm acting like I'm blasted. "Amazing," I say.

"Kate, quiet." Liam looks at me while he listens to Isobel. Then he looks away. "Well, you know. You can pretty much guess."

"Hi, Isobel," I say loudly.

"She says hi," Liam says to me, relaying. "She says she knows a great criminal lawyer."

"Great!" I say.

I go upstairs to Ty's room. "It's me," I say from outside, and then I go in. It's dark except for the liquid crystal light of the computer screen on his face. He's playing a green game. He plays a lot of games because we don't let him have the Internet in his room. I lean in the door frame like he's taken my crutches.

"Mom." He doesn't look up, joylessly savaging the joystick.

"You're gonna be a pilot," I say, and then he looks at me. I lean down to pull the plug out of the wall and the room goes dark. The computer takes a few last seconds to die, strangely lifelike with its falling whine.

"Ah, Mom?" he says. "You could wreck it that way. You could have just wrecked it right there."

"You shouldn't be playing games right now," I say. "Go to bed." I drop the plug on the carpet and go back down to the kitchen.

"Isobel says we're looking at the Young Offenders Act," Liam says. "I guess I knew that without knowing it. Also there are some changes pending in the legislation, apparently."

I take my wineglass out to the front step. I stand in the doorway, looking at our street. It's warm. There are stars and cars and rags of cloud.

"Let's drink inside." Behind me, Liam tries to get my elbow. I walk down the steps so he follows. I sit on the grass so he sits on the grass. "Almost done?"

"You made that up about the black kid, right?"

"No."

I look at him.

"I didn't make it up," he says defensively, like I was accusing him of something. "You never watched somebody do something bad?"

I go down on my elbows.

"Oh, don't do that. Don't settle in."

I toss the rest of my wine behind me into the bushes so it won't spill and set the glass on the grass. It falls over. I lie down and tell the stars, "I think it's hitting me."

I feel Liam lie down beside me.

"Can you imagine what they must be going through?" I mean the Parmenters.

"You just knew the dad was going to be at bowling league, or something," Liam says. "I don't want to imagine what they're going through. I don't want to think about their ugly lives at all. Do you think it's obvious we don't want Jason coming over any more, or should we spell it out?"

I ponder. "I think it's obvious."

Across the street, a light goes out in an upstairs window. Liam says, "The neighbourhood is watching us." He sits up. "Ah, Jesus. How're we going to keep this quiet?"

"Not by talking about it on the front lawn."

"My point." He tugs at me but I don't give. I think of the backyard – plumbing trenches, plastic sheeting, rock dust – a dark, crowded disorder we're paying for but don't totally control. I don't want to go back there.

"There's nothing to hide," I say. "He didn't do anything."

Liam picks at the grass.

"So they beat the shit out of the black kid," I say.

"On the playing field at recess. Someone went after him pretty much every day. That day was just a little worse. I wasn't even watching, it was going on in the background kind of thing. I was sitting with my friends talking about the Canucks or whatever. I only remember because the rumour was he went to hospital after. He was back in school the next day, though. I'm saying that was one tough kid. And his name just came back to me, how's this for weirdness: Taylor. Okay?"

"High schools don't have recess."

"You're right, they don't," Liam says. "What am I thinking of?"

My stomach gurgles. "That child ate food in our house."

We lie quietly for a while under the constellations. I get the Big Dipper and Orion's Belt and then I'm stumped. For a while my ignorance frustrates me, but then I think: I'm urban. Is there any reason why I should know these things?

"Well," Liam says, and waits.

"I was going to take him shopping tomorrow."

"Well, do that," he says.

"Are we hungry?"

"We are. Wow. Now that you say it, I realize."

"Kind of like the Young Offenders Act."

The day is pretty much over. Our voices are the only voices around.

"Maybe do the shopping in the afternoon," Liam says. "I forgot to mention, Isobel figures they'll probably drop by in the morning."

"They."

"They, them. You know who I mean."

We hear the front door and Ty's step on the porch. I can't see him, but he must be looking down at us. "Hey, you guys are lying on the lawn," he says.

"I already told you to go to bed," I say. "They're coming for you in the morning."

"Did you come out here to lecture us on deviant behaviour?" Liam says.

We hear the door close behind him.

"I think I've handled this pretty well so far," Liam says.

Isobel is right. The next morning I breakfast on toast and water and ibuprofen, and then I tidy up the dining room. I move both laptops, clear the table, dust. At eight-thirty I take a mug of hot milky coffee up to Ty's room. He wakes up all at once, alarmed. "Isn't it Labour Day?" he asks.

I sit beside him on the bed while he drinks his coffee. His room smells a little – strong, but not bad. For my eyes, my head this morning, the filtered light is just right. I just want to sit here and look at him for a while.

"Hi, Mom," he says after about five minutes.

I go back down to the kitchen and put out his breakfast: whole-grain cereal and an orange. This way, if anyone asks what he ate this morning, it will be something normal.

Last night we had a salad before we went to bed. I lay on my back too long, in the shoals of consciousness, drifting in and out of nightmares. Fully awake again by four, I spent the next couple of hours rehearsing my defence of my family: *We've always been more like three adults than parents and child. When Ty was a toddler he used to give his toys away. We've never hit him, ever.*

Everything I recalled seemed incriminating. Beside me, Liam slept. "How can you sleep?" I demanded once, aloud.

Now my mouth is dry and I promise myself ice cream, soon, later. I follow the muffled sound of gunshot and tires to Liam's office – movie posters and coffee air. One wall is painted black to deaden reflection on the big-screen TV. French doors swathed in double layers of black cotton lead into the backyard. Unshaved, Liam sits at his desk, making notes. His eyes flick from the screen to his pad to me. Utterly unrecognizable is the movie to me, as most of them are: black and white, I would say forties, which is odd since he pretends to be over film noir. He wrote his Ph.D. thesis on Raymond Chandler but lately everything with him is Russia, Russia, Russia. I wonder what he's thinking.

"Livia Claire." He points at the screen.

I look, but it's a big Irish cop in a trench coat setting his gun down to light a cigarette.

"Shit," Liam says. "Lemme rewind."

"Have you eaten?"

He's prodding at the remote. "I want you to see this." He looks up, catches my eye. "You want them to think we're sitting here waiting for them?"

"Why not?"

He turns the TV off – a tick, mild static crush – gone. "I had an apple."

"How do you suppose it started?"

He flips his spiral-bound notebook closed with one hand. "Maybe some protein and coffee."

"Listen," I say. "I'm trying to get my mind around this. What happened in that parking lot? How did it start? Maybe they bumped into each other and it turned into a shoving match?"

He looks at me. "Shoving match."

"Jason must be so – angry, about something."

"The beauty of the situation," he says, "is that I don't have to think about Jason, because he's not my kid."

"Our son's best friend does this Nazi thing and you're not curious?" I glance down at the carpet, a low, honey-coloured weave, and think: must vacuum.

"I don't share your fascination with deviance, no."

That word, again. "What's that supposed to mean?"

"Forget it."

"I should have known this would be my fault."

Liam says, "Absolutely. I distinctly remember saying that."

"You implied."

"I suggested," he says, closing his eyes in a show of saintly patience, "that, with your past, you might have more insight into the situation than me."

"Jesus Christ. I was politically engaged, once upon a time, which is more than you can say about yourself."

"You had green hair." He's smiling, not nicely.

"Why that so endlessly amuses you, I will never understand." The room feels warm, as though someone has been nudging up the thermostat, notch by stealthy notch.

"All I'm saying is, the rebelliousness, he doesn't get it from me," Liam says.

I could push on at this point. I can see the ghost of the conversation stretching out into the future, all the old insults and accusations. Instead, I try to pretend this isn't about us. I reset, rewind, take it from the top. I say, "Our son's best friend does this Nazi thing and you're not even curious?"

"See, that's an excellent word to describe it – *Nazi*," Liam says. "Because it captures the two essential elements of the act. First, it's sick. It's fucking nasty." He stands up, rests the heels of his hands on the edge of his desk, and leans forward, like he needs to stretch his back. "Second, I don't get it. You don't get it. But the thing is, that's fine, that's all right, because we're not supposed to get it. If we could get inside that kind of thinking and understand where it comes from, we'd be Nazis too. It's inherently incomprehensible to the person of average, I mean not even above-average, average, or even slightly below-average morality. So no, I'm not curious. Plus, I've already told you what I thought of Jason. Something not right there all along, I mean, we've had this discussion, right? But the key is, whatever it is, it's inaccessible to me. I was thinking about this last night," he confesses.

"So you *were* thinking about it."

"I analyzed it. I didn't torture myself."

"Well, words." I wave them off. "I *analyzed* it too, okay? Did you notice how much older than us the Parmenters were?"

Liam shrugs.

"And Jason is an only child?"

He looks out the window. He does bored.

"I'll bet there's some stuff there if you scratch the surface, abuse or serious unhappiness at a minimum. Mrs. Parmenter, remember how she looked so fragile? Remember how Ty said she went to bed so early? I wonder if she works. I'll bet you anything it all comes back to her."

"As I keep saying, I have no desire to scratch the surface. I lust for coffee and peanuts."

"Ew."

"Yep." He rubs his hands together with relish. "Ty up?"

"I think." He follows me out to the kitchen. Ty's breakfast is still sitting there; above our heads we can hear the shower rain. "We haven't really told him what to expect."

"Do we know what to expect?"

I J-cloth some clean counters, thinking. "Some discomfort," I say finally.

Liam's already deep into yesterday's newspaper.

I pour him coffee, make myself decaffeinated black tea. It's my day off. After a few minutes Ty comes down in jeans and last year's Vancouver International Film Festival T-shirt. Bare feet, damp head. Hesitating: "I had a shower."

Liam turns a page without looking up. "Magic."

Still, the tea is helping. I watch him sit opposite his father and start to eat, our cub. The cereal spoon looks too big for his mouth. He's a young fourteen, thin and smart and good, so far sneaking under the radar of the girls at school, but not for much longer, I suspect. He's started talking about basketball tryouts. He's started talking about coming running with me, and the cross-country team, and clothes. He's coming into his father's height and looks; another year and he'll slay them. An error of judgment is all you can accuse him of here, and it won't stick. This little thing won't show on his resume.

"They're here." I watch out the window as the cruiser pulls up the middle of the driveway and stops, blocking both sides of the garage. I wait to see the cop from two weeks ago get out, the prick with the moustache and sunglasses, but nothing happens. I tell Ty to run upstairs and put some socks on. I tell Liam, "You should have shaved."

"It's fine," he says. "We're all fine."

The doorbell rings. "Should we act surprised?"

Liam says no. "We're not guilty."

"Do we say we've talked to a lawyer already?"

"No. If we get a lawyer, it isn't going to be Isobel, so talking to her doesn't count."

"But maybe we should ask to have a lawyer here, now, for this. Although I guess they'll tell us if we need one?"

Liam smiles – faintly, sad. "So trusting."

The doorbell rings again. "They can't take him anywhere without us, can they?"

He touches his jaw. I feel it against my own fingertips: sandpaper. "I don't know."

We answer the door together. The officer is a Chinese woman named Veronica Stevens. We take her into the dining room and introduce her to Ty, who has this moment appeared in socks and shoes, hair combed, T-shirt tucked into his pants. Liam explains about the "bizarre scene" with the Parmenters the night before. "So we've been expecting someone since last night," Liam says. "Of course, we're glad you're doing your job."

"Uh-huh," she says.

While she questions Ty, I try to imagine her aiming a gun. She's a solid little thing, good skin, looks calm. She's probably a crack shot. "What was that web site?" she's asking.

"What?" Ty says.

Somewhere nearby a lawn mower starts up. She pushes a pen and a slip of paper across the table to him. "Why don't you write it down for me, okay, buddy?"

Flushing a little, he writes, folds the paper, and hands it back to her. She opens it, reads it, and tucks it in her notebook. "All right then!" she says.

We all stand up.

"Here's my card," she says. "You might want to get in touch with us again. We might want to get in touch with you."

"Yeah?" Liam says.

"Yeah, probably." We see her to the door. "Beautiful day!"

"It's a good one," Liam says.

"We're going to need him to come in for a formal statement. We're doing pretty good so far, though. Hey, is that a bay laurel?"

I say, "Yes, it is."

"I'm trying to grow one of those," she says.

Next door, Brill is mowing and watching us. The three of us watch Veronica Stevens get into her car and drive away. No one waves. Brill stands there idling, without the toupée he wears to the investment firm where he works, chewing some kind of little cigar. When she's gone, he cuts the motor. "You folks have a break-in?"

"Nothing like that," Liam says.

"Some kind of trouble?"

"Isn't your grass already pretty short for mowing?"

"Don't get snotty with me, Mick." Brill has already complained to us twice about the noise from the landscapers, whereas I've sunk bamboo kebab skewers amongst the delphs to stop his cats shitting in my beds, so this is a pretty typical exchange. Still. "That brat of yours been shoplifting?"

"Ignore." I pull Liam inside, closing the door.

"Shoplifting, yeah, shoplifting," Liam says.

⬦

"You need anything?"

High noon and Liam is back in the black room with his movie. I'm key-fingered, key-twirling, ready to take Ty on our annual last-minute school-shopping excursion. Normal is how I'm going to act, I've decided. Frozen yogurt, maybe a T-shirt for me; binders, jeans, socks, diskettes, dividers, sweaters, and what-all for him. Without looking at me Liam says, "Colombian Dark Roast and a quarter of espresso."

"Coffee is the rust of the human body," I tell him. "It eats out your insides."

He doesn't smile, instead looks moody, worried. I decide it's the talking-to we gave Ty after Officer Stevens left. Primarily we dealt with the not coming forward after it was reported on TV, although we also touched on Jason-avoidance at school and elsewhere. "Yeah, I know," Ty said humbly. While I tactfully went upstairs to make the beds, Liam riffed a little on the exploitation of women in the context of pornographic web sites, and then we were done. I came back down, hugged him, and we sent him off for half an hour of recuperative MuchMusic so we could debrief before shopping.

"Just don't be too nice to him," Liam says now. "We want him to learn a lesson from this."

"I'll buy him ugly clothes. I'll push him into walls and stuff, in the stores." But he still doesn't smile. "I was thinking, why don't we all watch a movie together tonight? So he knows he's not alone and we love him."

"He knows," Liam turns back to his notebook.

I touch his shoulder but he shrugs away.

Ty's waiting in the car. At first he doesn't want to talk, but after a while he pops back into his old self, maybe a little speeded up. He tells me funny stories about people in other cars and on the sidewalk, what their names are and where they're going and how they decided what they were going to wear today. It's a game he's learned from Liam, who talked just like this – nervous, compulsively funny, painfully afraid of silence – on our first date. "That's Edgar," Ty says, nodding at the man in the Lexus next to us at the intersection. "Edgar is eagerly awaiting his mail-order salad spinner to distract him from his marriage."

"What's wrong with his marriage?" I zip closed all the windows and put on the air conditioning as a dump truck pulls in front of us.

"Ass," Ty says to the dump truck. I give him a look. "Ass means donkey. It was in *Julius Caesar*."

"What's wrong with his marriage?"

"His wife is Isis, who is, like, goddess of cats. She's right over there." But I'm taking the dump truck and can't look. "Way to kill us, Mom," he says, as I scoop around three cars to catch a left on yellow. Someone honks.

"It was yellow!" I say.

"Park close to the doors, like Dad does." We're in the mall parking lot now and I join the cruisers. It's packed. Suddenly Ty wrestles out of his seat belt. "You can let me out here and meet me inside." I power-lock the doors. "Dictator," he says. I park in the back lot behind the food court and delivery bays, the mall's rear end, where the air smells of french fries and garbage, and seagulls pick along the curb. Ty groans.

"You have leg problems?"

"Dad always parks by the doors."

"That's part of what makes Dad, Dad," I say. "I'm Mom."

Clearview Mall tries for festive. At the entrance, a girl on Rollerblades hands us coupons. From the height of her blades she is haughty, freckled. "Hi," Ty says reflexively, stuffing the coupon in his pocket. When she ignores him, he blushes. Inside are streamers and roaming clowns with whistles. There's a lineup at the frozen yogurt place.

"Just a minute," I tell him, but he ignores me. "Ty, what flavour?" I have to raise my voice, he's moved away.

"Not for me," he calls over his shoulder.

"Strawberry," I tell the girl.

"Cone or cup?"

I've lost Ty. One hand on the counter to keep my place in line, I'm on my toes trying to see his head amongst the heads. What's he doing? "Cup, cup, cup," I say.

After that, she's slow on purpose. Looking at her, I can't imagine having a daughter like her, sly-smart to Ty's dumb-smart, cat to his dog. Her hair is French-braided and clipped with little glitter butterflies, but she's done her eyes with fuck-me black eyeliner and her mouth looks delicately cruel. Still, paying for my cup of pink, when I inadvertently touch her hand she flinches and I think: there's someone trapped in there.

"Enjoy your yogurt," she says.

Following Ty, I pass a toy store, a joke underwear store, a Gap, and a Dream Jeans. The Gap slows me down – they're doing those fall harvest colours I like, they're playing the Clash – but then I see my son standing with some other boys, up between Sam's and the Nike store, so I take my yogurt to a bench to wait him out. I cozy up to the fake palm so I can watch through the fronds without embarrassing him in front of his peers. Every now and then I glance into Dream Jeans like into a tropical fish tank – blond Asian kids in platforms and stripy Wicked Witch of the East socks with skateboards and Tweetie Bird knapsacks – and then back to Ty. The boys with him are tall strangers to me, in enormous jeans with loops of chains and hooded sweatshirts. Next to them, in his sandals and tucked-in T-shirt, Ty looks like a little dork. I wonder how he knows them, what he's done to earn their respect. I watch them laugh. The bigger one leans forward and shakes both arms from the shoulder, like he's loosening up for a free throw. He cuffs Ty's head lightly and they split up, the tall boys into the Nike store, Ty back towards me. Right away when he sees me I hold up my frozen-yogurt cup and say, "I want to finish this and then I want to go to the Gap," so he won't think I was spying. He shrugs.

The rest of the day does not go so well. Ty is sullen and shy, the toxic brew of adolescence. He wants me to buy him clothes, but he doesn't want to come out of the change room to let me see them. Hell, he doesn't even want me in the store, and this is distressing to me, new. I wonder if the interview with Officer

Stevens this morning and then jazzing with the bigger boys hasn't gone to his head, made him over into this grunting, slouching creature who thinks he wants this T-shirt with skulls down the sleeves. I say, "You are kidding, right?"

"No."

I hold the T-shirt up to my own chest, check the arms. It would fit me, actually. "Actually," I say.

"I changed my mind." He walks right out of the store, so I buy the T-shirt. "Who's that for?" he says when I catch him up.

I decide to fuck with him. "Me."

He shrugs again. It's getting annoying, a tic. Maybe he suddenly wants to try being a teen instead of a person, but I don't have to play.

"Untuck your shirt," I tell him. "You look nine."

"I think they're playing Bing Crosby now, at your favourite store."

Steaming, we do Wal-Mart. The drive home is icy silence. "Thanks, Mom," I say, getting out of the car. I make him wait before I pop the trunk. Maliciously, while he's grabbing his crinkly bags of stuff, I lean over to kiss his head.

He goes in, leaving the bag with the skull T-shirt in the trunk beside my purse; so I take it into the kitchen, saw through the plastic-threaded tags with a steak knife, and pull it on to cook – wok food. Dicing vegetables, I walk myself slowly through the forensics of the beating – the bruising, the fractures, the probable number of blows. I've been doing this all day, to anaesthetize myself to it. I wear the T-shirt through supper and Liam, looking from Ty's face to mine, doesn't ask. Nobody says anything, so I leave it on to vacuum. I get to like it, sweeping paths and swaths of paler carpet, variegating the pile, pushing and pulling with my new black arms.

"Nice shirt," Liam says bleakly, startling me when I cut the motor. He's been standing behind me, watching. "I take it you guys had a good day." I roll my eyes. I reach for a hug but he dodges me, won't meet my eye. "Come see what I bought while you were out."

I loop electrical cord around my shoulder and follow him with the vacuum cleaner. "Yeah, yeah," he says when I pause to plug it into the outlet outside his office door. Ignoring him, I recline the handle and trundle it ahead of me into the room.

"Ta-da," he says.

"Looks like a coffee maker."

"It *is*. It *is* a coffee maker." He's got it on his desk like some museum thing newly unboxed, still half-clad in packing.

"We have a coffee maker."

"Yeah, in the kitchen. You're going to take that thing off soon, right?"

"This?" I do a little dance from the hips, snake my arms up and down like an Indian goddess. "No, I like it. Think I'll keep it. Think I'll wear it to work. Think I'll revert to my true, former self, okay with you?"

"You're a bad influence on your son."

"Damn straight," I say. In the weird pause that follows I realize he was serious. I say, "I'm what?"

He says, "You need to grow up."

Nodding, I press the big plastic button on the vacuum with my foot. Now I can see his lips move but all I hear is noise.

Now, here comes school: radio in the morning, to me, is school. Red apples, red leaves, blunt scissors. Ty and I are shy with each other, this morning, poison past – we slept it off. "Sleepy," he says over his waffles. He looks it, too, but Liam looks worse. He came to bed last night long after he must have thought I would be asleep.

"Are you growing a beard?" I ask.

"He's growing a fur," Ty says.

What he looks is tragic, there at the sink, sunlight doing an outrage when he cracks the blinds – he winces, has to look away. Khakis, black sweater, his work clothes. "Unh," he says, and doses himself with more espresso.

"Dad's epitaph." I make bunny ears with my fingers. "'Coffee.'"

Liam claps his mug on the counter and we jump. "Don't talk to Jason at school."

Ty freezes.

"Okay?"

He hesitates. "Yeah."

"Yes, Daddy," Liam says.

"Yes, Daddy."

"I don't –" I start to say, but Liam's already out of the room. After a minute we hear the rumble of the garage door, the chunk of the car door, ignition.

"Bye, Daddy," Ty says.

"Doctor."

And of course I drop everything – clipboard, swab jar, paper cup of water – because I'm doing what I shouldn't: staring at the gardener through the one-way glass, some college kid the clinic has rented, watching him shave the evergreen bushes with sweeps and licks of a power trimmer. Kneeling for the mess, I pet the water stain on my knee as though it might brush off. "I was going to drink that," I say wistfully, blotting at the damp cloth with my sleeve. I look up. It's Calvin, one of the day nurses. "Hi."

He goes, "Hey," eyes on the gardener.

"We're having the yard done," I explain quickly. "I was looking at him with those evergreens and I had this revelation: holly. For in the winter, when everything else is dead."

"Okay," Calvin says cautiously, like there might be more. "What's up?"

"Mrs. Lowe is in seven. She won't let me take her blood pressure. She wants you."

"Calvin."

"She hates me."

This is hard to imagine. Calvin wears jeans and, under his smock, a T-shirt with a picture of the Grinch on it. He's twenty-four, maybe, tall, with nice arms, and the pierced eyebrow, and the sleepy, slightly worried face. Handsome isn't it, but endearing, yes. Probably he has a great stereo and a girlfriend he can't get enough of and not much else. I know the type. Appealing, to me, in an itchy old way.

I take the cuff and knock on seven. I go in and right away, there's your problem. Mrs. Octogenarian Lowe is wearing a turtleneck dress. "That's right," she says when she sees me. We get her out of the dress. I wrap the arm, pump the bulb. "Now, do you know the origins of Velcro?" she asks brightly.

"Yes," I say, and then we talk for a while about her arthritis. When it's time for her to go I tell her, "Remember, next time, short sleeves."

"In November? I'll die."

"You won't die."

"Ah, ah, ah," she says, shaking her finger at me like I'm a naughty girl.

Calvin is waiting in the hall with another paper cup of water. "Do you have a real job?" I say, and he smiles. No one smiles as little as Calvin.

"He has a crush on you," May says later. She and Calvin are the pediatric nurses; they give shots.

"Funny," I say. We're having lunch together in the staff room. She sips Chinese tea from a four-ounce can. I'm fiddling with the pull tab, dabbing at bagel crumbs with a fingertip. "That stuff any good?"

"I'll bring you one tomorrow. I'm serious."

"She's serious." I throw the tab at her. "You're hazing the new girl."

"You should be flattered. He barely says hello to me any more."

"Aw."

May shrugs and offers me a moon cake. But one bite and I'm retching so badly I can't see. I'm actually passing out. "Doctor," May barks, not at me, and someone grabs my elbow. They haul me over to the sink, where I heave and heave until I'm sure there's going to be blood. I hear May say something about sesame seeds.

"Too sudden." A male voice, Doctor Gagnon. "That's no food allergy."

"I'm fine." Sweating, cold, but breathing. I feel much, much better.

"What was that?" they ask. Doctor Gagnon, grandfather, ex-army captain, has his hands on his hips. He was on my hiring committee; he sounds like he's wondering if it made a mistake.

"I've been feeling a little off all morning," I lie. I don't tell them about the image I had, of the man in the parking lot not knowing which way to turn.

The afternoon pours slow and even after that, gold in the trees, colds and sprains, big-eyed babies taking me in. I'm floating, I'm healing the sick, I'm drifting through Reception when Calvin, phone clamped between ear and shoulder, gives me a message to call Liam on his cell. It's from an hour ago.

"Calvin."

Expressionless: "I didn't take it."

I decide I'm going to have to ask about him.

May tells my next patient I'm running five minutes behind and follows me to my office. "Problem?"

"Is Calvin slow?"

She sees the message slip in my hand and colours. "The receptionist gave it to me. I had a patient so I asked Cal to give it to you."

"When was this?"

"Five minutes ago."

I squint.

"It was in my pocket for a while," she says softly. "I apologize. The mistake, it was my mistake."

I see she's ashamed. "Look, no," I say hurriedly. "It's no problem. I just – I'm sure it's nothing. I didn't mean to – I'm not accusing you, I just thought that since Cal, Calvin, gave it to me – May, it's all right."

She nods and leaves. "Ah, shit," I say. No tea for me tomorrow, I'll bet.

Liam's number yields Liam's recording. I leave something terse and go back to work, last patient of the day. May hands me his folder in the hall. "Mr. Resnick is feeling breathless," she says, poker-faced. I cross my eyes at her and go in.

Mr. Resnick is obviously a walk-in: the brand new folder, the attitude. "I'm not paying for this," is the first thing he says. I get this a lot.

"What seems to be the trouble?" I hear myself say.

"Are you going to search me?"

I look at him again: long white hair, dirty suit, scaly shoes. Sixty, sixty-five. Blue eyes. "No."

"Usually I see a man."

"Do you have a regular doctor?" I ask.

"Usually I see a man."

"At this clinic?"

"This clinic, the other clinic. I can't afford to pay."

"That's all right," I say. "How old are you, Mr. Resnick?"

"Today's my birthday."

"Well!" I say. I ask him if he knows the year he was born.

"Nineteen-thirty," he says. "I'm a Jew." I ask him about feeling breathless. He says, "I feel like a paper bag."

"Do you smoke?"

"Cigarettes." He shrugs. "I like cigarettes."

"Are you on any medications right now?" He doesn't answer. "Do you have pain?" I ask. "Or just discomfort?"

"Did my landlady phone you?"

"No, sir," I say. "Can you show me if it hurts anywhere?"

"I'm not sure." He stands up. "I'll come back tomorrow."

I say, "Well, but you're here now." I reach around for my stethoscope.

"No." He backs away from me. I put the stethoscope down. "I never even got married," he says.

I look at his hands and take a deep breath. "I'm glad you came here today," I say slowly, trying to make eye contact the way you're supposed to. "It's good to come see a doctor when something feels wrong. You did the right thing."

"You're not a doctor," he says.

"There's my certificate." I point to the wall.

"Did my landlady phone you?"

"Sit down, Mr. Resnick," I say firmly. He opens the examining room door. "Mr. Resnick."

"Goodbye," he says loudly.

I follow him a little ways down the empty hall. "Excuse me,

excuse me," he says. He turns left and I hear him tell the receptionist, "I don't have to pay this time."

"You come back and see us again, Mr. Resnick," the receptionist says.

The examining room, when I return to it, is tainted with a
rancid piss-and-gravy smell I'm afraid will get into my clothes
and hair.

Outside, textbook Indian summer: taut blue sky, leaves
crisping, but blood-warm, bathwater-warm. Something about
the staff parking lot pleases me intensely: altitude, maybe. You
can't quite see the inlet but you can see the open sky above it and
the mountains, eye-level, on the opposite shore. My Jetta is
parked between Dr. Gagnon's Lincoln Continental and a little
cartoon Mazda, red as lips, all rounded and low. I throw my
jacket and bag into the back seat and punch the radio – news.
I punch some more. One of Ty's stations – lustful, lustily amped
teenagers – will do me for the ride home. I think about calling
Liam again but decide I can get there as quick as calling. I
wonder where Mr. Resnick lives, because he surely doesn't come
from this neighbourhood unless someone's letting him fester in
a basement.

When I pull up to the house, I see Liam standing in the drive
with his jacket on. Before I can cut the engine he's getting in the
passenger side, strapping in. "Finally," he says.

"What?"

"Drive, please," he says. So I back us back into the street.
"Where do you want to go?"

"Me?" I say. "Where do I want to go? I don't want to go.
What's going on?"

"Can I turn this off?" He means my radio. He reaches for the
dash but hesitates. We listen to the rest of the song, some serious

bewailing and bemoaning and guitar-wrangling, before he kills it. "Like that," he says grudgingly.

"We're old," I remind him.

"Know where I was today?"

It's a sunny day. I'll play straight man. "Class?"

"First I was in class. Yes. This morning I was in class. This afternoon I was in a police station with your son while they interviewed him."

"*My* son."

"Me, the police, our lawyer, and your son in a room with wire on the windows. I wanted to kill him."

On the avenue, I parallel park in front of the *phô* place. "Where is he?"

"In his room."

"You sent him to his room?"

"Too right," Liam says.

"He didn't do anything." No reaction. "Hey."

"He's scaring the hell out of me," Liam says softly.

I'm trying to box the information as he gives it to me, break it down into manageable pieces. "Ty's okay?"

"They went to his school to get him. Ah, hell, Ty's fine, only his classmates are going to know pretty soon if they don't already, and then their parents will know, and so on, and so on. You know how it goes."

"There's nothing to know."

"Yeah, but. That shit gets twisted."

"This lawyer, this was the lawyer Isobel recommended?"

"Are we getting *phô*?" Liam says.

We go in. I hold up two fingers. "Two beef," I tell the girl at the counter.

"To go?"

I look at Liam. "You want soup in the car?"

"To go," Liam says.

The girl, in a crisp white man's shirt, writes it on a pad. "Ten minute," she says. We sit on chairs of straight-backed cherry-wood laminate to wait, our backs to the window, arms touching.

"When did you tell him he could come out of his room?"

"When we get back."

"Liam."

"He has the computer. He'll be fine."

The girl withdraws into the depths of the empty restaurant, leaving us alone. Steamy heat reaches us from the kitchens, fogging the windows and seeming to nourish a palm in the corner beside Liam's chair, so big its trunk grows sideways where it hits the ceiling. I'm sleepy in here, I'm starving. Minutes melt. My husband, legs crossed, wrists crossed over his lap, has his eyes closed. He opens them when he feels me staring at him.

"Why didn't anybody call me?" I ask.

"I left you a message."

I explain about that. "I meant the police. Presumably it's our right to be there. Why did they call you and not me?"

"Apparently they did what Ty asked them to."

"Oh," I say.

On the counter is a bowl of mints. Liam gets up, takes one, sits back down, and pulls on the plastic-wrapper ears with both hands. The candy falls into his lap. With his right hand he puts the candy in his mouth. His left, holding the wrapper, trails beside the chair. He lets the wrapper fall to the floor.

"Why didn't he want me?" I ask.

"Hello, your order," the girl says, coming back with two big Styrofoam tubs. "Ten ninety-five." She pulls two plastic-wrapped packages from under the counter, which from past experience we know to contain paper napkins, plastic spoons, and balsa chopsticks. "You want a bag?"

Counting coins, I dismiss the bag.

"So, is hot." She blows on her fingers and gives Liam a smile.

In the car we bite open the packages, snap separate the chop-sticks. Rush hour and the street is lined with parked and moving cars. A sport-utility vehicle hovers, seeing us sitting, but we wave him on: we aren't leaving yet. He fingers us. Our tubs of soup are lidded with more plastic, like coffee cup lids but bigger. We toss them on the dash. Liam dives straight in with his chopsticks and extracts a tongue-shaped piece of pink meat, while I spoon. I say, "This lawyer."

"I phoned him on my way to the station. He told me we should sit tight until he got there, I should tell the police we had a lawyer on the way."

"Did they seem surprised at that?"

"I don't think so. Ty and I sat in somebody's office while we waited. He told me the assistant principal pulled him out of English class and walked him to his locker for his jacket and when they got to the office there was a cop waiting there. The cop drove him to the station and told him he could phone whoever he needed to before giving his statement. He phoned me."

"Thank god you were there." I spoon-slice some noodles. "You could have been in class."

"I *was* in class. Ty told the departmental secretary it was an emergency and not to hang up the phone until she found me. She called Campus Security. I had to tell a hundred and fifty first years to go home."

"Wow," I say. "I guess we should be proud of him. That's pretty together."

He shakes his head. "I don't know what I'm going to tell the Dean tomorrow."

With my chopsticks I transfer a piece of beef from my cup to his. "Sounds like they were trying to scare him, coming to the school." Together we watch a Camry parallel park in the space which has opened up in front of us. Eyeing us, she takes her time. The *phô* place is hopping now, takeout mostly. "Was Officer Stevens there?"

"Yes." Liam slurps up some noodles. "It was just like when she came to the house, all the same questions."

"That's good," I say, meaning it as a question.

"The lawyer thinks we're not done. I made us an appointment for the day after tomorrow."

"Have you paid him yet?"

"Some."

"Some," I repeat. I re-lid my soup, prop it between Liam's knees, and start the car. "Can we go home now?"

"Seat belt."

I hesitate. "You don't think he was there, do you?"

He shakes his head.

At home, I knock on Ty's door. "Minute!" he says.

"No, now." He opens the door, a little flushed. "Am I bothering you?"

"Can I come out now?"

Instead, I go in and look around. Bed rumpled but made. Window open so things are smelling good, better. On the computer, his screensaver – a multicoloured, gyrating webbing, expanding and contracting like something vaguely undersea – tells me he hasn't been on in at least five minutes unless he's changed the settings I fixed for him when we last upgraded, three months ago. I give the mouse a flick to see what he's doing and get an empty page of Word.

He's watching me from the doorway. "Way to infringe my privacy, Mom."

"Have you eaten?"

"You have." He makes a face. "You smell spicy. Did you bring me any?"

"No." I figure he was masturbating. "How was your field trip today?"

He flushes.

"Come for a run?"

Amazingly, without hesitating, he says, "I gotta change."

Downstairs I find Liam surveying his office. "Something's missing," he says.

"Air?"

"A sofa." I tell him Ty and I are going out for a bit. "Take your time," he says.

Ty's waiting for me in his basketball gear. He waits while I lock the front door and tie the key to my shoe. So far we've run together maybe half a dozen times this year. He's got good intentions and a good clean form, fast, but my endurance pisses him off, discourages him, so I say, "I just want a small one today," and hope I'm not too obvious.

The beach is crowded with strollers and runners, good citizens released from work, bankers in singlets, girls with their girlfriends and dogs. Ty and I, I'm thinking, make a nice pair, a nice picture: healthy lifestyle, healthy relationship, nice clothes, smooth. The business with the police gives us an urgency, an aristocracy the people around us lack. We pass them like cattle.

"Scary day?" I ask.

He waggles a hand.

"Talk. If you can't talk, you're going too fast."

"I wasn't scared."

"Was Jason at school today?"

He's speeding up. "No."

"Was anybody talking about him? Like, asking where he was?"

"No." I point to the next fountain, meaning: let's make for that. "Mom, Jason's not very popular. Kids wouldn't really be curious about where he is. They wouldn't notice."

"Are you?"

"Curious?"

"Popular."

He's matching me, stride for stride. He's growing up. "I'm all right."

"What does that mean, all right?"

A clot-calved biker is filling his water bottle at the fountain with one hand, talking into a cellphone. We prowl, waiting. When he's finished we take turns. The water is icy. Ty gargles.

"You haven't answered my question."

"I'm extremely popular." Then, startling both of us, "I'm the love god." The biker, who in his Mao-collared spandex shirt had retreated to lean against a nearby tree, grins and toasts my son with his water bottle.

"Hail," I say.

"Were you popular in high school?" We start back, loping gently now. It's the kind of question that makes me suspicious. I can see wanting to change the subject after that love god crack, but it's a little too sitcom for him, too sweetly earnest. Though perhaps it's no different from me enjoying the image of the pair of us, imagining people must look at us running together and smile. And today can't have been a good day, by high-school standards: he drew attention, which is never good. So I try.

"I was a brainy girl," I say. "My friends were not the trendiest, but I wasn't lonely either. We went to dances and stuff. Is that what you mean?"

"What about Dad?"

"Dad and I didn't go to the same high school. We met in university. You know that."

"I know. I mean, was he popular?"

"Listen to me carefully," I say. "Your father was a geek and I took pity on him. Anything he tells you different is an evil lie."

"Did you have other boyfriends than him?"

"Zillions."

"Did you really have green hair?"

I sigh. "You know I did. Long ago in a land far, far away, when I was very angry about things like greed and insincerity and classical music and world hunger."

"Mom Vicious," Ty says.

"I was very big on breaking the bonds of convention. I was very big on destroying illusion in all its manifestations. The illusion of good manners, the illusion of capitalism, the illusion of responsibility to an irresponsible government, the illusion of beauty –"

"But you became a doctor."

I poke him in the arm. "Stop listening to your dad so much, okay? The two are not incompatible. I cared about people and about making the world a better place. That's what I *did* care about. I was extremely young. Do you know the origins of Velcro?"

He doesn't. I tell him. "Is that true?" he says.

"How come, at the police station, you called your dad and not me?"

He hesitates. Then: "Your job is more important."

And he's right, though I can't say so. "Walk," I instruct. We're back in the streets, approaching home. "Do you worry about people liking you?"

"Dad says Jason is sick," he says instead of answering. "Is that what you think too?"

"As a doctor, you mean?" He nods. "What do you think I'm going to say?"

"You'd need to examine him?"

"Well, that," I say. "What do you think?"

He presses his thumb several times against the side of his index finger, as though pointing a remote at my head, and says, "Click. Click." This is family code for when someone changes the subject.

"I don't understand what he did," I say to placate him. "I don't want to judge him before I've tried to understand. I don't think calling someone sick is a good excuse for ignoring his behaviour or dismissing it. Maybe there are some categories of people who are just hopeless, but the thing is, it's really difficult to know for sure who they are. It's not, you know, printed on their faces, usually. Sometimes you have to give people the benefit of the doubt."

We're standing in the front yard, vaguely stretching. I stand on one leg and grab my ankle behind me, pulling to work my quad. Ty says softly, "Is that why you believe me?"

"Who doesn't believe you?" I say sharply.

He shrugs and for the second time in years I see him bite hard, trying not to crumple. "I don't know."

"Dad believes you."

"Okay."

"Ty, he does."

"Okay."

"He gets mad when he gets surprised, that's all." When he doesn't say anything I touch his arm. "What are you thinking?"

Really, really quietly he says, "I'm so hungry right now."

We're in the kitchen grating low-fat cheese on multi-grain toast when Liam comes to tell us the police charged someone this afternoon with the beating, but they can't release the accused's name because he's underage. So far he's the only suspect.

"So," I say. "Jesus. I guess they phoned?"

Liam tells Ty, "Just now, on the TV news."

Later, after we've both showered and Ty's gone to bed, I find Liam in the garage breaking his new coffee box down for the recycling. We keep a neat garage, generally – lit, swept, lawn chairs hung up on nails, stainless-steel garden tools arrayed on the funky-functional storage modules, space to walk entirely around each car, just like in a magazine – but Liam is struggling, making a mess. There are Styrofoam chips in a spray on the floor around him, and the box he's simultaneously pushing and pulling at will just not give. The box's guts – more foam moulding and assorted plastic, snow-white twist-ties, a booklet or two – are strewn in widening disorder as he shuffles around, kicking at them, trying different tactics with the box. He tries holding it down by his knees for leverage, then up by his chest for power. He pulls and pulls. He stops, takes a deep breath, and wings the box at my car with a shout of frustration. It bounces off and lands on its side, back by his feet. The passing breeze of it has sent a few more of the foam peanuts skittling away under the car. He stands with his eyes closed, breathing heavily through his nose.

I turn to go silently back into the house but my foot dings against one of three or four rustic-style aluminum pails I use to store my spring bulbs in. He turns to look at me.

"You have to pop the tape," I say.

He looks like he's afraid to move, like whatever action he intends will be expressed as violence, which he can only prevent by standing absolutely still. I make myself go over, pick up the box, score a break in the packing tape with my fingernail, and flatten the box with a quick pull.

"You have to pop the tape," I say again.

"Kate," he says. I can see he's working up to something so I stand there for a long time, waiting for him to let it out. But all he comes up with is, "I can't."

"Can't what?"

He won't say. I put my arms around him, tentatively, put my head on his shoulder. He hangs on pretty hard. I rub his back and stare at the box on the ground, which shows a crisp photograph of a full pot of translucent, chocolate-coloured coffee. It could make you cry, the steam alone is as delicate as art. The writing is in Italian.

"Come to bed," I say.

I make a move to step backwards but he doesn't let me go. We stand like that for a few more minutes. He swallows, once, but I can hear his breathing slow.

"Come to bed," I say again.

"Soon," he promises, letting go this time.

It is midnight before I stop trying to stay awake, waiting for him.

Isobel's great criminal lawyer works on the thirty-first floor of one of the glass bank towers downtown. His firm is green leather and brushed bronze, Supreme Court Reports, art. I think I recognize a Jasper Johns in the lobby. I nudge Liam. He and Ty, in ties, look identically miserable.

"On the other hand, lots of people have interpreted the number eight," Liam says.

"Our retainer is insuring that."

"Nah, that's just a print," Isobel's great lawyer says, startling us. He came from somewhere behind. "Your retainer keeps me in golf clubs." We shake hands. I know his name to be Joe Leith.

He doesn't look like Sam Spade, too neat and tall, but I like that he's a prick, at least. At least he doesn't have one milky eye and fingerprints on his glasses and nervousness. I had a bad experience once.

His office is around a couple of Persian-carpeted corners. Secretaries with Dictaphones word-process in softly-lit nooks opposite their bosses' doorways. I tell Ty to stand up straight. In the office, Joe Leith touches the back of a couple of chairs, meaning for us, before crossing behind his desk and seating himself. Liam sits right down and wings his spiral-bound pad open with one hand, the way he does. I hesitate, studying a poster next to the guy's professional diplomas: a Japanese silkscreen of a sumo wrestler, robed, with that pixie hair. It says, "Sumo Bashô 1998."

"I *love*," Joe Leith says, following my gaze.

Ty, too, is standing, waiting for me. He sits when I do.

"You know there's a witness, right?" This Joe Leith has a file open in front of him now. "This is how they identified Jason Parmenter. This individual, the video-store clerk, claims he looks out the window and sees some kids roughhousing in the parking lot. He can't see them too clearly, doesn't think anything of it. Then one of the kids comes in to rent a movie. But, later, when the police come calling, he can check the computer –"

"What an idiot," Liam says.

We all look at him. I can tell he was criticizing it like a movie. I know him.

"Jason, I mean," Liam says.

"The good news is, our clerk cannot identify the exact number of individuals he saw in the parking lot," Joe Leith continues. "However, he thinks more than two. The only one he can describe is the little one, who came into the store."

"This would be Jason."

He bows to me, a sitting bow. "This would be Jason."

"Well, so, good."

"So, now. If Tyler is charged," he says, "and personally, if I were the Crown, I would charge him, you're going to have a first appearance in a few days."

"What do you mean, you would charge him?" Liam demands.

"I would charge your son because it might be enough to make him confess, if he was there, and if he wasn't or if I can't get sufficient evidence I can just drop the charges later. Costs me nothing. If he's charged and it sticks, you're looking at the actual trial in another couple of months. The system is not fast but juveniles have priority. If something opens up it could be as soon as one month."

Ty tightens his shoulders in his jacket. It's not a shrug any more.

"Now, Tyler," he says, smiling, and for the next twenty minutes or so Liam and I watch him extract details from our son, getting the events of that evening lined up like dominoes. Ty mumbles syllables, he won't make eye contact, but what he says is credible enough. Jason went out; he stayed back, feigning tiredness, so he could watch naked girls on the Internet. He's not sure of times. He didn't see or speak to anyone else in the house while Jason was out. When Jason got back, they went down to the rec room and watched the movie he had rented, *Anaconda*.

The lawyer takes notes. Liam takes notes. I'm thinking about a phone call I got last night, after Ty was in bed. When I answered the piece of meat at the other end hesitated. I heard him say, "No, man, it's his mom." Then, to me, "He's got my math homework, right?"

"I doubt it," I said.

"No, yeah, he does. Is he there?"

"Do you shave?"

"Course I fucking shave, fuck," he said. I hung up.

Now this Joe Leith says, "That's us." He means we're done.

I ask him if I will have to testify since I was the first person to examine the victim. Ty and Liam look awed – they had forgotten.

"Nah," Joe Leith says. "Written reports are all they'll want. Just as well, eh? We don't need the whole family up there."

In the elevator, on the way down, I ask Ty where he'd like to go for lunch. He grunts.

"Skip it," Liam says.

"Well, I want lunch," I say. "Maybe I should have asked Joe Sumo up there. Maybe he would have had lunch with me."

"So, so, go back," Liam says. He looks slapped.

"I could, I might," I say. "Costs me nothing."

"Shut up," Ty says, grabbing his head, choking on tears. "Could you both just shut up?"

When Ty was a baby, we shared a house with some of Liam's film-school friends. I was still in pre-med. Liam had taken a year off to work nights as a security guard so we could live. We barely saw each other, barely knew each other, and Ty, this little scrap in a soft blanket, was already wearing us down. Occasionally the film students liked to watch themselves babysit: they would eat Cheesies in front of the TV, taking turns cuddling the little guy and holding him up so he could watch *Taxi* reruns with them while Liam and I went out to a real movie and Chinese food afterwards, staring warily at each other across plates of guy ding and won ton, under the paper lanterns. I have to say it was a bad time. Tyler was a good baby, sucking your fingers and peeping when he was hungry; but I had only recently taken the safety pins out of my ears, and Liam was beginning to refer cynically to his unfinished Master's thesis, and for a time we behaved like animals, fucking and hissing at each other, and feeding the baby in silence, trying to shield him from the toxic thing we had for each other. For a time, too, Liam moved back to Nova Scotia. When he came back he re-matriculated, got a job as a teaching assistant, found, painted, and furnished a one-bedroom apartment, marched me down to City Hall for a marriage licence, and enlisted Ty in the University's daycare program. There were still problems: Liam's family, for instance – mother and aunts and a couple of brothers – who knew me by reputation and a few photographs Liam had unwisely shown them, who continued to phone at odd hours, their mosquito voices whining down the phone. There were my own attitudes – towards school, assorted authorities, my new in-laws, the world – which I could not shed as quickly as my old clothes. There was Liam, who at times still seemed as repelled by me as he was attracted, staring at me like he was trying to bore holes, like he was trying to understand why he couldn't let me go, while I raged and taunted and still tried (in my new, whole Levi's and happy cotton sweaters, bizarrely brunette, child on my hip) to shock us down below the surface of things, to some reality that was not, in my estimation, a big shiny lie.

But we were trying, and you could say that was the important thing.

"No," I say, waving off whoever it is in the washroom doorway. I've got my head in the sink again. My day hasn't even started. When I straighten up, I see it's Calvin. I spit once more, on purpose, and grab the tap.

"That was terrible," Calvin says.

The soft clean stream from the low-pressure faucet is annoying. I cup my hand, scoop water around the basin, try to clean up faster. I duck my head to drink and rinse my mouth. "Morning sickness," I say briskly, ripping off a waffly piece of paper towel.

"Well, sure. You should try Gravol."

"And you would know?"

"You are so fucking unfriendly," he says.

We stare at each other.

Later that morning a child's screaming pulls us into Reception. "CALVIN," he's screaming. His mom is trying to hold him but he's a big boy, maybe seven, big and kicking, trying to twist away from May, who's kneeling beside them. "CALVIN CALVIN CALVIN," he screams.

"There you are," May says.

"Hey, Davey," Calvin says. He takes the boy from his mother and carries him back to the examining room, bouncing him a little the way you do with a baby. The boy has his head on Calvin's shoulder and his little arm around his neck.

"He likes Calvin," the mother says apologetically. She glances at me, then May.

"Everybody likes Calvin," May says. She smiles at her feet and I think, Oh.

At noon she takes two cans of tea out of her lunch bag and hesitates. "I'm afraid to give you this after the last time," she says.

I touch my can to hers, a mock toast. "Liam and I want you to come over for supper, you and your husband. How's Saturday?"

May puts two fingers to her temple and stares at the tabletop. "Saturday, Saturday, Saturday."

Calvin comes, hesitates, pulls up a chair. "Friend of yours?" I say quickly, meaning the child from this morning.

"Autistic. May thinks he likes my voice."

"The reverberation," May explains, tapping her chest.

"When my son was a baby we couldn't put him down unless his dad sang him a lullaby first," I say. "When I did it, he would just scream. To appreciate the perversity, you have to have heard Liam sing."

"He's that bad?" May asks. I cover my eyes, shake my head.

"Can you sing?" Calvin asks.

"I sang in a punk band for a while. Put myself through a couple of years of school."

"But does that answer the question?" May says doubtfully.

I sip my tea. "Am I being friendlier?" I ask.

"Somewhat friendlier," Calvin says.

May stands up. "Can I get back to you about Saturday? I should just check it out with Jupiter."

Inadvertently, I look at Calvin.

"Jupiter, my husband," she says.

"Jupiter," Liam says.

"I'm telling you now so you won't laugh when I introduce you. They're Taiwanese, okay?"

"I might still laugh, though," my husband says gravely.

Upstairs our son is playing CDs, turgid and feedbacky, much guitar. The bass seems to drip from the ceiling. "I'm afraid to ask him to turn it down," I say, because he's had a lousy first week of school, cumulative troubles. I rap my knuckles on the counter. "I know that *song*."

Liam nods. "Schubert."

"Are you going to wear that?" I ask. Black pants and a black silk shirt, open at the throat – matte, but still. "You look like a dance critic."

"That would be a euphemism?"

"May's the only person at the clinic who doesn't seem to be judging me because I'm new. I just want to make a nice impression."

Upstairs, Ty bumps the volume another notch. "Mercy, grace, faith, hope, charity," Liam says. "We should have drowned him before his eyes opened." He goes to the foot of the stairs. "What the fuck is your problem?" he yells up into the din.

In the kitchen, I check the food: pots of curry and rice, dishes of nuts and condiments. "Should Ty eat with us?" I ask when Liam comes back.

"Okay, yes," Liam says, like he's been expecting this. "Yes, because I am not just going to let him turn into this thing he wants to turn into. If we let him eat in his room we're sending these terrible messages, that it's okay to be anti-social, that he's not welcome, maybe even that we're afraid of him, of letting these people meet him. If he starts to think we're afraid of him all hell is going to break loose."

"He had one bad week."

"He's not the one that got arrested."

A pot on the stove spits and seethes. I turn the burner down. "Are we being too hard on him?"

"You mean me."

"I do, actually, yes."

We're looking at each other, squaring off for round one, when the doorbell rings. Liam clears his throat. "Settle down," I tell him.

"Doctor," May says, when I open the door. Grinning, she hands me flowers. Her husband has a brush cut and round glasses behind which his eyes are tiny as raisins. He's grinning too. He hands Liam a bottle of wine, looks at the ceiling, and says, "Wow." He means the noise.

"You have kids?" Liam says.

"Is that what that is?"

I say, "He's had a bad week."

"Jupiter, my husband," May says, and we do introductions.

"Jupiter," Liam says, shaking his hand.

"Pretty good," he says to May, cocking his head at Liam.

"Really good," May says.

"My name," he explains. "You didn't react at all."

"Kate warned me."

Jupiter laughs. "There was a vogue for it in the late sixties, okay? I know a tax accountant named Pluto. I used to go by Jay but in law school my mentor told me I should use it so people would remember me."

"Wow, you had a mentor," I say, moving us into the kitchen.

"We all got assigned one," Jupiter says.

"Law school." Liam's pouring wine, keeping his voice even. "What kind of law?"

"Civil lit." We listen to the seepage from Ty's music, an icy, thrashing crush, like a speeded-up record. "What do they call this stuff?"

I say, "Jungle."

Liam says, "Schubert."

"I'm looking forward to meeting your son," May says.

Liam hands her a glass of wine. "You're a brave woman." We all raise our glasses. "Crime," Liam says.

Jupiter and May touch glasses. "Crime!"

"Settle down," I say.

We lay places in the kitchen, where it's warmer and friendlier than the dining room. The dining room is also where Ty had his interview with Officer Stevens. "Is it true, what you told Calvin about being in a punk band?" May asks.

"Who's Calvin?" Liam wants to know.

"Kid at work. Yeah, it's true." I stop, uncomfortable.

"Always the quiet ones," Jupiter offers.

"The first time I saw her," Liam says, setting a fork down, "at this party, she had a Mohawk hairstyle and war paint. Like, red and black slash marks here." He touches my cheekbone with his thumb. "And this ripped-up dress, and safety pins through her fingertips, the soft part, the pads."

"Painless." I shake my head. "Can we talk about something else?"

"Kate, no," May says, looking concerned.

"She was with these two other guys dressed similarly. I later learned this was her band."

"We had this idea of sending up traditional Native American costume," I say apologetically. "I don't know what we were thinking. It was very rude."

"I ask around, I find out she sings, she plays guitar, she's honours pre-med. I fall in love."

"Love," I say. "You stalked me."

"It worked." Liam rolls the stem of his wineglass between finger and thumb. "Smokin' good wine, Jupiter, by the way."

Jupiter bows.

"Stalked me," I say.

"I had a case not long ago," Jupiter says. "Now, you tell me what you think. Here is this young woman, single, living alone in her apartment. She has a job, has some regularly scheduled activities on evenings and weekends – a fitness class, some volunteer work. Her routine is pretty predictable, okay? Next door to her is a retired man, widower, nice guy. They say hello coming and going, he shows her pictures of the grandkids. He gets to know her schedule and takes to sticking his head out the door when she leaves in the morning. Same thing when she comes home at night. Doesn't phone her, doesn't knock on her door, doesn't follow her down the street. Twice a day he goes a little out of his way to say hi, that's it." Jupiter pauses. "Question: is he stalking her?"

"No," Liam says.

Jupiter looks at me. "Well, I mean, no," I say.

"All right. Now, imagine the man a little differently. This is a younger man, university student, also single. Big guy. Very good-looking." May, who has obviously heard this before, is lifting up pot lids and smelling the food. When she sees me watching her, she gives me a thumbs-up. "Exact same behaviour as the first man. Instead of the grandkids, he shows her pictures of his horse. Gradually she starts looking forward to seeing him there in the hallway every day."

"All right," I say.

"They fall in love."

"All *right*."

"Is he stalking her?"

"No," Liam says.

I put my hands on my hips and squint at Jupiter, mock-tough, half-smiling. "What's your point?"

"Last scenario. Same, identical situation. Only this time the man is paranoid schizophrenic. He's on permanent disability. Rarely leaves the apartment. He's taking his meds but sometimes she hears him talking to himself, he wears the same clothes every day, he seems nervous of everyone except her." I start placing plates on the table, now that I know what's coming. "Is he stalking her?"

"Yes," Liam says.

"Oh, come on," I say. "You're going to walk right into that one?"

"Walk into what?" Liam says. "It's totally different. There was no reason for her to be afraid of the first two. Here, a reasonable person would be apprehensive. How does she know he's not going to have some kind of – episode?"

"Hey, May," I say. "As a woman, wouldn't you have been a little apprehensive about the second guy, the cowboy? Jupiter said he was big."

May nods. "Big, yeah. Big can be intimidating."

Sheer nonsense, of course. Calvin, for instance, is big. So what?

"You had the man?" Liam asks.

"I had the woman. She couldn't get any kind of criminal charge brought, so she wanted to sue for infliction of emotional suffering." Jupiter looks at me. "My point is, you can make the same act right or wrong just by changing the variables. There's no such thing as an evil act, murder as an act or stalking as an act. The evil lies in the person who's doing the act, and our perception of that person."

"So you're saying Liam didn't stalk me?"

"Hell, I don't know," Jupiter says. "That's my party story. You just gave me a lead-in."

"I didn't exactly stalk her," Liam tells May.

"So on your theory, the victim's identity is also relevant."

Jupiter, chewing pappadum, nods frantically. "Sure, crucial."

"If she's very ugly, for instance."

"Okay, I know where you're going." He makes a stop sign with his hand.

"Not exactly?" May asks.

"I went to see her band a few times."

"Twelve times," I say. "In one month. Plus he hung around outside my house a lot. Look, all you're talking about is motive. Same act, different motive, depending on the individual. And to determine motive, you rely on stereotypes. No, piss off." Liam's trying to stick a pappadum in my mouth. He and May are laughing at me. "If he's schizophrenic, we assume he's motivated by a desire to harm. That's like saying if the victim's ugly there's no harassment, because who would be motivated to harass a dog?"

"So how do you want to get at motive?" Jupiter asks. He's not laughing. He's interested. "Hate crimes, for instance."

"Like stalking isn't a hate crime?" May says.

"It's a love crime," Liam says.

"That's disgusting," I tell him. "I was scared of you."

"I know," he says, so only I will hear.

May makes busy, stirring one of my curries. "I love being a nurse," she says. I realize we're embarrassing her. She's a tidy package, May, in her black tights and black cord jumper and stretchy denim headband, with her smart talky husband, and I want her to be my friend.

"Is anyone allergic to nuts?" I take a Tupperware container from the fridge and shake it. "I have coconut for the chicken."

"Stand back," Liam says. "She's gone hostess."

Abruptly, the music above our heads stops. I'm thinking it's the hurricane eye between songs but the moment stretches until we're all cringing.

"See, my view," Liam says, frowning, "and Kate and I have had cause to discuss this recently, is that motivation is basically opaque. What motivates a Stalin or a Charles Manson? Don't know. What motivates my son to torture us with that noise? Don't know."

"'No Fun,'" I say.

They look at me.

"That song," I tell Liam. "That song I recognized, it was a cover of an Iggy Pop song called 'No Fun.'"

"How old is your son?" Jupiter asks.

We say, "Fourteen."

"That can be a difficult age," May says. "That was the year I decided to give up the violin. My parents were very angry but I was so stubborn, eventually they had to give in. I was a brat."

"I was a ping-pong *champion*," Jupiter says.

May frowns at him. "I was good too," she says, looking troubled.

"May, Jupiter." I touch the backs of a couple of chairs.

At the stove, Liam is jerking rice onto five plates. The rice comes off the paddle in sticky shaped clumps. I transfer the curries from the stove to three toasted-looking cork pads on the table. May rearranges my settings to help make room. "Here," she says, handing Jupiter a saucer of mint condiment, keen and pretty as poison. He studies it, head bobbing faintly like he's revving up for something, until she takes it back and sets it in a new place. "Did you say your son was having trouble at school?"

Liam and I glance at each other. "He's also having trouble at school," Liam says.

"Just a fight," I say. "He's a boy. He's never had a fight before, now he has. He's just going through the monkey stages."

"What was the fight about?" Jupiter wants to know.

Liam and I are doing the same thing, looking around the table to see what's missing. "Basketball."

"Calvin plays basketball," May says. "Plays or played. I think he used to be really good."

I say, "Here's Ty."

Ty looks pretty good, looks not bad, in a button-down plaid shirt and jeans, skinny wrists and hips. The clothes seem a little big on him. The puff on his cheek, the boxer's eye from school two days ago – the work of his new bad-boy friends – I'm almost used to. They make him look hardy, wry. I watch him shake hands with May, watch her hang on to him while she ducks her head automatically for a better view of the damage.

"Mr. Chan, Ty," Liam says.

"Jupiter, please!" Jupiter says.

"Okay, hi." For the first time, probably because I'm trying to see him through the eyes of our guests, I notice a deeper note in Ty's voice, the first light bow-strokes of a cello.

Jupiter seems disappointed. "I was named after the planet," he's saying.

"Is Borneo a country?" Ty takes a chair between Jupiter and me. "Homework," he explains. This is the old Ty: little, affable, honour roll Ty.

"First week of grade nine," Liam says grimly. "Is that a rock and roll curriculum or what?" He isn't looking at me now.

"Borneo, Borneo, Borneo," Jupiter says.

May takes a half-spoonful of each curry, setting them at equidistant points on her plate so they won't touch or mingle. "I bet they have that on the Internet."

"Don't encourage him," I say, and he scowls at me. This is the other Ty, the changeling.

"Ask me some trig," Jupiter says.

For a while we eat, and I'm distressed because May and Jupiter are eating little, slowly. When May asks Ty what his favourite subject is at school he rolls his eyes. "Tyler," I say sharply.

"I'm not currently enjoying school, Mrs. Chan," he says. Liam puts down his knife and fork. "I guess it's the curriculum." May and I start to laugh, we shouldn't but it's not a choice. Jupiter, lenses of his glasses flashing, is grinning at his red shirt. Gingerly, ignoring us, Ty fingers his bruised cheek. I guess he was trying to be rude, not funny, and we let him down.

"You hear they made an arrest in that beating case? That retarded man?" Liam says.

I start taking plates.

"May I be excused?" Ty asks. Liam says no.

"I heard it was a teenager," Jupiter says. "Maybe a couple of teenagers?"

"They've only charged one so far."

"Dad," Ty says.

Liam's leaning back, hands in his lap. He's left some odds and ends on his plate – gravy-dirty rice, a bit of skin, chickpeas – like he's in a restaurant. "Speaking of hate crimes."

"It's a weird phenomenon, these violent kids," Jupiter says, nodding. "Predatory. It's not like, you play dirty on the basketball court, I call you on it, we throw a couple of punches." He winks at Ty. "But teenagers going after a disabled man in a deserted parking lot, it's like they think they're hunting moose or something."

"Like sport," May says. "Where are their parents?"

"Please Daddy may I be excused from the table?" Ty says.

"So what do you think, Kate?" Jupiter winks at Liam this time. "What motivates these kids?"

"Tea, coffee?" I count heads.

"Kate," Liam says.

"We weren't there," I say. "There may have been reasons. We don't know how it happened, what he did or what they did. But I agree with May. If the parents are good people, the children will be good people. Good kids will not get involved in things like that, and I believe that. A kid who's been good all his life does not suddenly turn on a man with Down syndrome just because there's an opportunity. You look at the kid who did this, you look at all the circumstances of his life, and you'll find a straight path back from this act to other acts, to the upbringing, to the parents. I'm talking about patterns of behaviour, established predictable patterns. A thing like that doesn't come out of a vacuum."

Jupiter's waving his hand even as I'm talking. "Chicken and egg, fate!" he says, getting ready to argue.

"Down syndrome," May repeats. "Was that on the news?"

"Daddy, please," Ty says.

"Come here," I say. He comes over to where I'm scraping bits into the garbage disposal. "Are you really doing homework up there?" He shrugs. Liam is pouring the rest of the wine, saying something to May, who's smiling again. I lower my voice: "Borneo?"

"I was making conversation."

I walk him to the foot of the stairs, my arm on his shoulders. "Quit pissing him off."

He touches his face again. "He's pissing *me* off." But sick, not insolent, is how he looks.

"I'll tell you something," I say. "When you came home from school looking like that? He started crying. After you went to bed."

Ty doesn't say anything.

"He loves you so much," I say.

"Ty," Liam calls. Startled, he flinches.

The kitchen smells of coffee now, that bracing, roast smell, and I see Liam has ferreted a bottle of liqueur from the cupboard under the food processor where we keep the kirsch and other undrinkables we seem to have acquired over the years.

"Sit," Liam tells Ty, holding the bottle up against the light and tilting it. Liquid rolls thickly inside. May and Jupiter look content enough but there's an edge to Liam I'm not liking. "We need to work on your conversation skills," he says. "You can start by telling us about your real, actual homework."

"How about he just goes and does his real, actual homework?" I say. I haven't let go of Ty's shoulder.

Liam puts the bottle down.

"I have a biology lab," Ty says quickly. "We're doing a genetics unit and the parts of the cell. You want me to tell you the parts of the cell?"

May and Jupiter have gone still.

"Yes," Liam says.

"No," I say. I put both my hands on his shoulders and turn him to face me, so he can't see his father. "I want you to go upstairs now and finish off what you're doing. I'll bring you your dessert up in a little while. And not so loud with the music, we're trying to hear ourselves think down here." I give my eyes a Nixon-flick towards our guests, hoping he'll pick up on it.

"Good night, Mrs. Chan, Mr. Chan," he says. "It was nice to meet you."

"Good night," they say. Their voices sound small and quiet.

"Go," I say. I turn him away and give him a push towards the stairs, a little harder than I mean to. He goes.

"What you see here is a difference of parenting styles," Liam says when the sound of Ty's light step on the stairs has disappeared. "On the one hand, I'm trying to raise our son to be a moderately decent human being. On the other hand, Kate here doesn't care what he turns into so long as she gets to be the good cop. Brandy?"

Jupiter quickly lifts a flat palm, dismissing the bottle. May, blushing, shakes her head. I see them exchange a glance, see Jupiter straighten up in his chair, preparatory to leaving. I know if they go now there'll be a rent between May and me that no amount of bubble tea and friendliness will repair. "Coffee, dessert," I say, eyebrows raised, nodding encouragement, trying to make it a question and a statement at the same time.

May looks at Jupiter. "I would love a coffee," he says. "Could I just use your bathroom?"

I lead him out of the kitchen and down the hall. "Should we go?" he says, when we're out of earshot. I like how he does it – unembarrassed, matter-of-fact. His manner makes it easier to respond in kind.

"Not at all," I say, reaching in for the light and stepping out of his way at the same time. "I'm sorry about that back there. Ty's always been a great kid, great grades, nice friends, cleans his room, you name it, and suddenly these past few weeks it's just been one headache after another. It's just – caused a few tensions, lately. It's just karma, right? I guess now we have to pay for all those years of him eating his vegetables and so on."

"I like the alien abduction theory." Jupiter squeezes past me so that now we've traded spots – him in the doorway, me in the hall. He lowers his voice to a cheesy intense whisper and wiggles his fingers by his ears to be spooky. *"That's not really your kid out there."*

"That's not really my husband out there. This isn't really me, for that matter. We must sound pathological to you."

He does a double take and a smile, and puts one hand on the door. "You seem like slamming parents to me, Kate. I know May thinks the world of you."

"But?"

He grabs his belt and does a little collapse at the knees with a frazzled look on his face.

"Go," I say, laughing, turning away. "I'm the good cop. I'm not stopping you."

In the kitchen, May and Liam are talking about the clinic.

"It's a problem," May is saying. "Salaries here just aren't competitive with the States. It's almost impossible to keep new nurses in the country."

"You stayed, though, for instance." Liam doesn't look at me.

"My family is here, my life." May smiles up at me when I hold a cup of coffee out to her. Liam's I set down in front of him.

"I wouldn't have minded the opportunity to travel," Liam says, staring at his cup without touching it. "San Francisco, Saint Petersburg. At certain points it would have been extremely beneficial to my career. I found having a family quite limiting, in fact."

"Financially," May says, frowning and nodding at the same time, trying to understand.

"That too," Liam says.

"Thanks so much," I say, as though this is just another of our routines, as though this is a line he's used before and I'm not rocking, reeling hurt.

"Calvin's travelled a lot, I think," May tells me. "Thailand, Vietnam. Did you know he's a Buddhist?"

I nod gravely. "You can just tell."

"Tell what?" Jupiter's in the doorway, pulling at his cuffs. He gestures I shouldn't get up, he'll help himself to coffee.

"Calvin, at work," May says. "I told you about him. He's kind of cute, too, in a sad sort of way." She giggles. Jupiter rolls his eyes and puts his hands round May's neck like he's going to strangle her. Then he sits down and sips his coffee.

"Kate's fitting in, then, at the new job," Liam says. "Everybody loves Kate, as usual."

May giggles again, inadvertently, then stops, like she's stopped a bottle of bubbles. She's not stupid, she has radar. She glances at Jupiter again and this time it's not a question. He holds up his cup for a fraction of a second which I take to mean, I know. Just let me finish this.

Liam must have seen the signals too, for he puts the brandy bottle away and makes some more conversation about nursing shortages and government cutbacks, but May and Jupiter are wary and within a few minutes they're on their feet pleading an early morning. We hug, and the men shake hands again, and May says, "See you Monday."

"They don't even work weekends, I'm pretty sure," I tell Liam when we've closed the door behind them.

"Lucky them," he says.

We spend some time in the kitchen cleaning up. Silence makes the house feel like a decompression tank down under water. Liam starts taking chairs out into the hallway so he can sweep. "Let's move the fridge," I suggest. We grapple the fridge out of its nook until we can see the precise dimensions of its absence: a square patch of dust and a couple of Cheerios.

"May has a crush on this Calvin guy from your work, wouldn't you say?" Liam says. "Did she talk about anything else all evening? I can't remember."

"He likes her too," I say. What the hell. "He tries to hide it but he can't. It's kind of endearing."

"Poor Jupiter."

"Yeah," I say. "It's always worse for the husband, isn't it? So *limiting*."

He gives me a look from the old days: misery. Then: "I'm going to Mass tomorrow."

"Oh, great," I say.

"I have to do something."

I cap the Pine-Sol with a sponge and flip the bottle upside down, then back. Kneeling in the gap between fridge and wall, I make passes over the floor. The dust collects on the sponge in black lines. The linoleum shines wetly. The fumes are the best.

"I want to go to confession," he says.

"Why?" I take another shot of Pine-Sol on the sponge and hand it to him. "Now what have you done?"

Drainage ditches bisect what used to be the back lawn; it's rumpled as a rug now, creased and flipped back. The yard is a lot of bumps. I'm thinking it looks worse than when they started. Pushing aside some tarpaulins protecting the glass, I go into the greenhouse, a stuffy orange ten-by-ten space, and remove a Coke can and a MMMarvellous MMMuffins bag of cigarette butts. I can't imagine why they take their lunch in here unless it's not to be seen. But why?

A few days ago I suggested the thing about the holly. The older one said, "That your boy out front?" We could hear basketball sounds – spaced slaps, the backboard rattle. It was a rhythm.

He knew. I said sharply, "Why?"

His eyes shifted. "Glossy green sprigs tucked around the house at Christmastime. Sure, I'm seeing it. You know the little cute berries are poisonous?"

The assistant, shovel in hand, stood slack-shouldered, slack-mouthed, as though what we were talking about changed everything.

Now, late-September sun sparks off the mud, tangles in the trees. I look for a conspicuous place to leave the can and the bag. Maybe it's not so bad: five evergreen bushes, roots balled in burlap, line the fence we share with Brill. You see a bird here, every once in a while, a pigeon, wings snapping the air with a sound like laundry. Eventually it'll all heal over. Newness and all that, new green growth.

I drop the garbage in a wheelbarrow and pace over to the black-curtained French doors to Liam's office. I tick on the glass with a knuckle. "Open," Liam calls. I slide the door but there's a new wrinkle: a sofa barring my way. As usual my husband is watching a movie. I let myself slide over the back of the sofa, landing with my spine on the seat and my feet in the air. I could have managed better but there's mud on my sneakers and the sofa looks new.

"This is not good." I stare at my feet in the air. "In my condition."

"You have a condition?"

"Officially."

"Well," Liam says. I can't see him – I'm upside down, I'm in the sun, and he's not. "You going to close that door?" I kick my shoes off and close it with a sock foot, sliding us both back into the dark. "Come here."

I go stand behind him and put my hands on his shoulders. He puts his hands on my hands and we watch his movie together for a while. Gangsters are planning a heist; they talk fast and mean. In the background a pretty moll fixes drinks and slips a baby revolver, a gunlet, in her garter when no one's looking. She has a white face and black lips – the movie is black and white. Liam uses the remote to squiggle through a few scenes. We watch an interview between the moll and a detective, him struggling to light a cigarette, her looking bored. Liam freezes the frame on her heart-shaped face. "Livia Claire," he says.

On an impulse, I reach down between his legs. He's hard.

"Where'd that sofa come from?" I ask.

"Bought it," he says, swallowing. It's a futon on a pine frame, with a black cotton cover on the mattress. "Lately I want to nap."

"Tell me she's dead."

"If she weren't, she'd be older than my granny. It's 1941 in there."

We watch a little more. "I'd question your placement," I say finally. "If you're ever planning to use that door again as, you know, a door."

"Never." I wander over for my shoes and try to tug straight some diagonal creases in the futon cover. "Leave it."

From the bookcase I collect a dirty coffee mug and the lifestyle section of this morning's paper. "You jerk off in here, don't you?" I gesture with the shoes, but he doesn't answer. "Just like old times. I'm telling Ty about the baby, okay?"

He shrugs.

I find Ty up in his room with some kid I've never seen before. Ty's sitting on the floor and the new boy's ape-limbed all over the bed. The window is wide open.

"This is Carl," Ty says. "He's the one who hit me in the face."

"Don't like you, Carl," I say.

"It's all right, Kate. We worked it out."

Ty giggles. After a second I place it: the meat-voice of the late-night phone calls.

"Tyler, sweetie, it's almost time for you to go watch your favourite shows, okay?" I say.

Carl tells me he loves my T-shirt.

"Get your fucking shoes off the quilt." Downstairs the door-bell rings. "And put those cigarettes out!"

On the doorstep are Officer Stevens and another officer, taller, a man. "Dr. Clary, is Tyler home?" Officer Stevens asks.

"Hi," I say.

Their cruiser is parked in the driveway.

"He's home," I say. "Will you wait just a minute?"

"We have a few more questions. We're going to need him at the station."

Liam looks up when I come into his den. "I can't stand this," he says. "I'm unhappy. We need to talk."

I tell him police are here, and go upstairs for Ty. "Carl, I'm afraid something has come up and I'm going to have to ask you to leave now," I say. "Ty, shoes."

"It was me smoking, not Ty," Carl says.

"Officer Stevens is here," I tell Ty. "Carl, *now*." I pause on the stairs, wondering if I have time to change out of the skull T-shirt.

"What the fuck did you do, man?" I hear Carl ask Ty, laughing.

Downstairs, the officers have stepped into the hall. They step aside to let Carl pass. "Hi," he mumbles, leaving.

"Hello there!" the male officer says.

Liam hurries in, telling us the lawyer will meet us at the station.

Outside, Brill is belly-up to the fence separating our properties. He's seen the cruiser, the uniformed officers: he can look now, he can take his time. The male officer has his hand on Ty's shoulder. None of us says anything.

The deal is, I ride in the back seat with Ty, and Liam will follow in the Jetta.

⬥

"It's a mistake," I tell Joe Leith. "Will you please look at him? He's a child. It's a dirty mistake."

It's after; we're in the car. They've charged him. They've *charged* him.

"Like I told you," Joe Leith says. He's an outline to me – a voice and some thick lines. He's got no face. "They're trying to flush out the undergrowth. It's what they do."

He says he can make the charge go away. He says, give him a couple of days. "They've got no substance," he keeps saying, waving his white hands. "It's all very thin."

"They can't raise him, can they?" Liam asks.

I look at him, can't look at him.

"Not at all," the lawyer says soothingly.

Liam has the papers. When you get charged, there are papers. I say, "Raise him?"

"To adult court."

Joe Leith is centring the knot of his tie with three fingers and a thumb, firming it up.

"Raise him?" I repeat. "You've already got the fucking jargon?"

"Isobel brought it up. I'm just telling you what Isobel said."

"Isobel," I say.

"How is dear Isobel?" Joe Leith says.

When we get home we have a fight with yelling. After a while Ty goes to his room. Liam and I end up in our bedroom with his laptop, trying to figure out if this web site our son claims to have been cruising that night is real.

"Slow," Liam says impatiently as we wait to get on-line. It's after-dinner homework time, high-use time. The connection fails and fails again. There's spit on the windows, the first of the fall rains. We hear the modem crush. "Read me that site."

"I don't have it."

"In the Information," he says. "The sheets, the sheets." I hand him the papers from the police. He turns the pages back gingerly, my husband, afraid to make a crease at the staple.

"That witness only saw Jason up close," I remind him, but in my speaking voice this time. "It's Jason's word against Ty's. I know who I believe." I read off the name of the site, something that sounds innocuous enough. He types it with all his fingers, like a pro. "Got it?"

"Got it." Liam hunches, then leans back. "Christ, this is going to take forever."

I look over his shoulder. So far the site is scaffolding, a lot of empty boxes with ripped corners and tricolour balls. The computer grinds, working on it.

"Graphics," Liam says.

"I can't." I look away.

I can hear him breathing while he waits. I lie down on the bed.

"You fucker." Liam hits a key. "Lost the connection."

"It exists. How much more do you need?"

He fires up the modem again. I leaf through the papers. "How are you doing?" he says grudgingly. It's the first time he's asked, the first kind word of the evening.

"We're fine," I say.

"Isobel says it would be illegal for the media to report his name. She says in the court documents they'll refer to him as T.C."

I'm reading.

"Kate."

"T.C."

"Here."

He's got the site. I stand at his elbow while he jumps us through a few screens.

"Mammal," I say, pointing.

After a few more screens, Liam clicks on "Go," clicks on "Home." The image of the three entwined girls is replaced by our preferred home page, a site maintained by a local TV station, with its familiar layout of advertising logos on scrolling banners, search engine, weather (a cloud with digitally sprinkling rain), sports stats, and news headlines: SECOND TEEN CHARGED IN ASSAULT.

"Oh, no," Liam says, surprised. "No."

I take the mouse and click on the headline. "'Police are releasing few details,'" I read. "'They confirm that a second fourteen-year-old has now been charged in last month's vicious attack on a mentally handicapped man in a video store parking lot. The trial is set for November.'"

Liam makes a breathy noise, a laugh or a gasp.

"That's commendably fucking prompt," I say.

We stare at the little words, which by rights ought to be as private as our own blood.

"Don't let's tell him about this tonight," Liam says suddenly. "It's going to be everywhere tomorrow. Let him get one more night of rest before it all starts."

I think, *This is love?*

"Maybe we should pull him out of school," I say.

"We're not pulling him out of school."

"What do we do now?"

"Nothing," he says. "Wait."

He says he wants to sleep in his office for a while.

The next morning, Ty won't go to school. He won't get up.

"You know we almost named you Gordon?" I tell him. I'm sitting on the edge of his bed, looking at the neatness of the sun, the orderly rows of glow between the blind slats. Ty's curled away from me, facing the wall. "It was some stupid idea of your Dad's. Look at me, I'm talking to you."

"Go away," he says.

"So the plan is I phone your school and say, Ty's going to be absent today because he's facing a criminal charge and he needs some quiet time? Something like that?"

"I keep throwing up."

I look around. "Where?"

"Last night."

I put the back of my hand on his forehead. "Were you there?" I say suddenly.

He looks at me, horrified.

I stand up. "I'm going to work now," I tell him. "I love you, but I am so sick of this. You look after yourself today."

By lunchtime I'm also sick of everyone at work, of May and Dr. Gagnon and the nice receptionist and all the sneezy, achy people waiting in Reception like a lot of weeping sores. I decide to take my lunch out into the air, walk away from them for forty-five minutes or so, find a pocket of park and a bench under a pine tree with a view of the sea – me, my soup Thermos, my water bottle, my red pepper and my banana. Calvin follows me.

"Go away," I tell him.

Insufferable is the silence between us. I eat while he stares at the sea.

"You are poison," he says finally. "You're a goddamn toxin in my system. I don't even like you all that much. You're not a good or decent person. You don't care about your patients. You condescend to May. You torture me. Are you really pregnant?"

"Yep."

"Get rid of it," he says. "Oh, please. Oh, god."

"No."

"Are you laughing?" he asks. "This amuses you?" I screw the Thermos cup back on the Thermos and tuck the banana peel through the Thermos handle. "I didn't choose this," he says.

"You're okay, Calvin," I tell him. "You're going to be fine."

He gives me a look of hot, ragged hatred. I look at my watch.

"Five minutes," he says, so I sit there for five more minutes, looking at the view, bouncing my Thermos on my knee, and then I go back to work.

We take to clipping articles from the papers, Liam and I, after our son has gone to bed, dating them, and keeping them in a file called "Parmenter." Over the next couple of weeks we collect a dozen such articles from local and city papers, even a couple of smug Letters to the Editor ("Perhaps now our revered politicians will emerge from their labyrinthine circumlocutions around what has become the one premier issue of our time, television and copycat violence –"). Nothing so far in the nationals.

"Who writes these, you know what I'm saying?" Liam says one night.

He uses scissors. I use an X-Acto knife and a breadboard. I say, "Nobody. Tea drinkers."

"ESL students," he says. "'Dear sir, I wish to register my utmost outrage at a system who fosters the pernicious scourge of peer violence between our children –'"

"Here's one. This woman's a homemaker. As she watches her little ones get ready for school, shrugging on their little knapsacks –"

"Fuck me, poetry," Liam says.

"– she worries about what's waiting for them out there in the world. She knows she cannot be with them every step of the way, but she also knows that she has filled them with the great tide of her love which they will carry in them always as a talisman against evil."

"Her point?"

"People should stay home." I scan the remainder of the article. "People should just stay home with their stay-at-home mothers and feel the great tide of love sloshing around inside them all day."

"Maybe we don't need *all* of these."

"The lawyer said."

"I tell you what," my husband says. "The amount we're paying him, he should be doing this."

"We can afford it." I square some pages, fold them away for the blue bag.

"I can't afford it. I've got tenure review coming up in a few months. Imagine if this gets out."

I say, "Yeah, imagine."

"Which reminds me," he says, ignoring me and talking to me at the same time. "Faculty party next Thursday, okay?"

I say, "No, not okay."

"You have to come. Other spouses come. We have to act normal."

"In case of what?"

"Exactly." He slaps the file closed like it's settled.

"Last order of business," Dr. Gagnon says. "The parking lot."

Everybody groans. Dr. Gagnon grins and shows us his fists – asymmetrical, like a boxer. Around me doctors are starting to push back their chairs and collect their papers. It's the clinic's monthly administrative meeting, my first. "Whoa, whoa!" Dr. Gagnon says.

"Cut it out, Paul," says Dr. Silver, a curly-haired blonde my age, tough and tiny as a gymnast. "We did this last year. You lost." She's gone.

"What did we do last year?" I ask my neighbour, Dr. Li.

"Voted not to expand the parking lot."

"This is not about trees," Dr. Gagnon is saying. "This is about access."

"This is about sap on your Lincoln," someone says.

"I like the parking lot," I tell Dr. Li.

"Dr. Clary likes the parking lot," Dr. Li says. Everybody looks at me.

"The view," I say quickly, but they're staring too long. Most of them don't know me, have probably never heard words from my mouth before, but still. The next thing I know the meeting's over and Dr. Gagnon's asking me for a word. We go to his office. "Am I in trouble?"

"How're things working out for you so far?"

I tell him fine.

"Everything okay with the staff?"

"Is there a problem?" I'm thinking, if he knows about Ty, if they all know, he should come out and say it. He shouldn't do it like this.

"On the contrary." He raises his eyebrows. "Your nurses love you."

"About the parking lot?" I say, but he laughs and waves me off, waves me right out of his office. I understand the issue isn't dead but I'm not a player here, not yet. He'll use me when I'm useful. In the hall I close my eyes, exhale, open my eyes. What does he know?

"Keep in touch, Doctor?" he calls after me.

"I never know what to wear to these things."

"That," Liam says.

I've got clothes all over the bed. In my underwear I'm standing, hands on hips, surveying all my worldly goods here on the bed. I hold a skirt hanger to my waist, trying to picture myself in the article – a little flippy wool job, almost a skating skirt. "I must have bought this," I say.

"Wear what you wore this morning."

I almost could, too – the sharp black suit, the bracelet, the black shoes. Only this has become my outfit for visiting the lawyer's, and I don't want to be reminded. "There's going to be drinks, right?"

"The Dean will be there, the tenure committee," Liam says.

"Yes, Mom."

On the way up to campus we drop Ty at Isobel's. He doesn't especially like it. He says, "Suddenly I need a babysitter?"

We tell him Isobel needs help moving some boxes.

"I don't like bullshitting him, but I don't like leaving him alone either," Liam says. "And Isobel doesn't have TV, which is amazing. I think he could use a quiet evening to think about Monday." Monday, Jason's trial.

"Those were some pretty tough questions this morning," I say. "I thought lawyers weren't supposed to do that. Coach the witness." I feel stupid saying the phrase.

"He didn't tell him what to say."

I wait, but he doesn't say anything more. "You don't want to talk about this, do you?"

"See, only because I'm driving."

He parks at a meter near the Fine Arts department. The wind is pushing leaves down the street. It's gone cold. A nearby tree is red. "Witness for the prosecution," I say, now that we're out of the car.

He gives me a look.

"Fall," I say, pointing. I'm thinking: six weeks already.

"You're here!" Cheryl, the departmental secretary, says when she sees us. She seems surprised, concerned.

"Shouldn't we be?" Liam asks.

She makes her eyes go big.

"Hi, Cheryl," I say, and she grabs me in a hug. We have never hugged.

"You look –" Instead of a third word, she makes a big gesture.

"Fat? I look fat?" I whisper, as Liam steers me away, into the common room. We nod and smile. People are turning toward us. "Let's get out of here."

Liam is smiling. "You are paranoid," he murmurs.

"Dr. Clary." A great tall man puts his hand on my husband's arm, staying us. He means Liam, but I don't laugh – practise. "I've been going through your grant application. We should talk." He says this darkly, peremptorily, like an actor doing a surgeon. This is the Dean. I smile ten thousand watts and excuse myself to the makeshift bar.

An hour and a half later, this:

"Sudan, Mauritania," a bearded man is saying. "I'm saying, slavery in our time! I'm saying, right now! But will people believe it? Until someone goes in there with a camera?"

My group shakes heads.

"Y'all hear about that beating a ways back, outside that video store?" Where has this Texas accent come from? How did it get in my mouth?

"You mean that thing back in the summer?" someone says. "Should you be sitting down?"

"No, why?" I say.

"This world," someone says. "Slavery, Jesus."

"Video is over," someone else says.

Everyone starts talking at once and gesturing with cheese. I go find Liam. "Bad," he says, taking the wineglass from my hand. He's flushed; instead of putting my glass down he drinks from it. "The Dean thinks he can get me funding for my book."

His book? "That's great, honey," I say. But he's barely looking at me. Restlessly he scans the room, bounces in his shoes.

"I think we should both be there on Monday," I say loudly. "For Ty's sake."

He smiles again. "Jesus fucking Christ," he murmurs. "Of course we'll be there. Can we talk about this later?"

"I just wanted to make sure."

"Liam," someone says. "How's the little book coming? On the little starlet?"

"Brian," Liam says, shaking his hand.

They call this work.

"Katherine, you look amazing," this man, this stranger, says, and he hugs me too. "My sister had the same procedure a couple of years ago and she's fine."

"Okay, what is going on?" I ask Liam in the hall.

Ty, when we collect him, is in a mutinous mood. "You told her," he accuses us. He means Isobel.

"Did you talk about it?" I ask, because my Liam is driving.

"I knew it," Ty says. "She was being nice to me."

"And normally, god knows, she's very mean."

"Who else knows?"

"Look, idiot," I say. "We had to get a lawyer somewhere. Isobel referred us. Should we have picked one out of the phone book? You know what happens when you pick them out of the phone book?"

"You're going to tell me," he says, so then I don't. Instead I ask Liam about his little starlet.

"You know," he says meaningfully.

When we get home he goes straight into his office and shuts the door. We hear the TV go on, the now-familiar screech of tires and sting of music signalling the start of *that movie again*. I tell Ty to get the hell into bed.

"Sieg heil," he says, and I slap him.

We stare at each other, sharing disbelief. He reaches for, but doesn't quite touch, the reddening mark of my hand on his cheek.

Before this, the worst thing I ever did was vandalize a car. That ended badly, as you'd expect – getting caught, going to court with the sweating, stuttering, milky-eyed phone-book lawyer, facing my parents – but the core truth was it was fun and I'd have done it again. The car belonged to Liam's aunt, though I

didn't know that at the time; I thought it was Liam's car. Nor did
I know that she lived with Liam (or rather he with her); that she
was watching me through the window, phone in hand, blue
lights already on their way, while I tried to let Liam know how I
felt about him pursuing me. Love was a disease I was immune
to, for a while anyway.

"Just so you know," I tell Ty. "Your father's been telling people
I had a biopsy, to account for all the work he's having to miss,
because of you."

"I don't know what that means," he says. He's crying, again.

Stuffed in the bike courier bag I use as a purse, in my office at
the clinic at the end of another endless day, these gifts: the
twenty-fifth anniversary reissue CD of the Sex Pistols' "God
Save the Queen" and a travel-size vial of chewable Gravol. No
card, no note, no mystery either.

Sunday night, end of the line. Rain hemorrhages. In our basement, what the Parmenters call the rec room, a window no
bigger than a shoebox lurks near the ceiling. A watery black eye:
rainwater makes sheets and swags of unclarity on the glass.
Beyond I can see the wavering lines of the iron grille we bolted
over the window after a rash of neighbourhood break-ins last
summer, but not the low-down, grass-in-your-face, cat's-eye
view of the garden you get during the day. The garden is gone,
the street is gone, the city is gone, and it is just the three of us,
alone together in this cave carved out of the empty black stuff of
night. Dark-red tones I had chosen for a colour scheme down
here, and grouped before the single flickering light of the TV we
could be prehistorics before a flickering fire, holed up in the

false, ruddy safety of our den. We have adopted the following attitudes: myself at one end of the sofa, Liam lying with his feet on my lap, Ty between us on the floor, leaning half against the sofa, half against my leg. The movie is a soother of Liam's, Alan Ladd and Veronica Lake with the sound turned low. A few hours ago we told Ty we loved him. Then, not knowing what else to do, we suggested movies. He asked for popcorn, but the bowl sits full and untouched on the chair he abandoned to sit nearer to us. Now, touching, we are still and separate as three photographs. The rain rains, the movie moves, and the hours roll away like weights that kept our lives from blowing away. The trial starts tomorrow.

The plan was that we would meet Joe Sumo in the courthouse cafeteria, but where we find him is in the underground parkade, jogging toward us, waving his cellphone.

"Good morning!" he calls, his voicing echoing off the cars and concrete. "I'm glad I caught you. Jason's going to plead guilty. No trial, that means. For us that's the bluebird of good news, or whatever. I just got the call. They'll go straight to sentencing. You can watch, if you like."

We ride upstairs in the elevator, the four of us, three of us dead numb. He explains Jason finally admitted to the beating, an hour ago, only, and if anyone was with him he wasn't saying. Joe Sumo speculates there will be some psychiatric testing. When we step out into the courthouse lobby, he excuses himself to catch up with some character in a black robe and white dickie who greets him like a cowboy, pretending to draw guns from his belt and fire. They laugh.

I can't breathe right. I say, "Let's go home," and my voice is loud in my ears.

Liam shrugs. It's Ty who says, "I want to see."

From a distance, Joe Sumo points us toward the right room and makes some hand signals meaning he'll catch up with us inside.

Waiting for the judge to hand down his verdict, we watch him deal with a girl caught shoplifting K-Y jelly from Wal-Mart.

"What I'm going to do now, I'm going to suspend your sentence," he says. "What that means is, I'm not going to punish you. Everything you've had to go through with the store security and then coming to see me here, I know this has been pretty embarrassing for you and I think that's enough. I think you're not going to be stealing again, right? Contraceptives or what have you?"

"Will this go on my record?" the girl asks.

"Yes," the judge says.

When they're finished, the girl comes and sits right in front of Liam and me, next to a tousle-haired woman in an Adidas warm-up jacket and matching tearaways. "Wake up, Mom," the girl says. "Time to go."

"I just want to watch this next one," the woman says.

Jason is led in from a side door. I haven't seen him since the night we took wine to his parents' house. He wears leather shoes, dark dress pants, and a dark shirt buttoned up all the way, but no tie. He notices us right away, can't not – the courtroom is not much bigger than a school classroom. I see him nod at Ty, next to me, who bobs his head. Shame? Liam's seen, too; on my other side, he nudges me, but I'm not ready to react. Jason and his lawyer stand while the clerk reads the name of their file, and sit with their backs to us while the judge reads the charge and then the verdict. Jason's lawyer talks a bit about Jason's grades and behaviour at school – apparently he was having troubles – and about his little personality generally, and then the judge hands down his sentence: a year in juvenile detention. Jason doesn't flinch, doesn't look up as he's led back out the way he came in. Ty, beside me, exhales.

"All rise," the clerk says, and then it's time for lunch. Just like that.

"Mr. Leith," Crown says to Joe Sumo. We follow them out of the courtroom along with the general throng. The Parmenters are nowhere to be seen. We watch the two men walk a little ways up the hall together, then shake hands. Crown hurries away while our lawyer comes stepping back to us, a costly peacock. "He's dropping the charge against Tyler. You'll get formal notification tomorrow the latest."

"That kid was psycho," the K-Y girl is saying, a few feet away.

"I'm just phoning your Dad." The woman pulls a cellphone from one zippered pocket and bends over to dial, stretching the shiny fabric of her pants over her hams.

"I'm not talking to him," the girl says. "I don't want lunch. I hate the cafeteria here."

"Did I say you had to talk to him?" the woman says.

"You're not smiling!" Joe Sumo tells Ty.

"It's grotesque."

"But good, for us."

"Great for us."

"Animal, though. Jason."

"I know who you meant."

We're giddy as moonlight here in the backyard in the sliding late afternoon sun, still trying to process it all.

"That's basically it," Liam keeps saying. "Right? For us?"

I start picking dead needles off the cedar deck. "It's excellent," I tell him. "It's the bluebird of good news."

"We're lucky, though, hey. If you think we let Ty play with him all summer long."

"We weren't to know."

"But that's basically it, now, isn't it?" Liam says.

Behind us we hear the latch. Ty steps through the kitchen door, carrying a mug of something hot.

"Hi, baby," I say. "Is that my tea?" He hands me the mug. I tip him my gathered handful of sticky needles. "Smell," I say, but he dumps them on the ground.

"Come here, son," Liam says. "I'm sure that was the worst of it, today."

Ty looks at the greenhouse. "I'm sure."

"What?" I follow his gaze.

The tarpaulin-sheathed door opens from the inside and the landscapers come out, blinking. The younger one won't look at us. The older one does a double take, a cartoon stagger. "Folks!" he says.

"Son of a bitch," Liam says.

I say, "You're still here?"

"Well, I guess so," he says, setting a boot up on my deck like we're the trespassers.

Getting ready for bed, I can't relax. I walk around the bedroom, picking things up and putting them down, while Liam uses the ensuite bathroom. He keeps wandering out to check on me – brushing his teeth, popping floss. I do sit-ups, feet hooked under the end of the bed, then remember not to. "Adrenaline," I explain. The faucet rushes. I mumble, "Psycho."

"Do you sleep at night?" Liam's voice is muffled. "I have trouble."

I hesitate. I decide to say something, to listen to the sound of the words. It's a curious, strict feeling. "He could still be lying."

Liam doesn't answer. I wait, on my back, until I hear the toilet flush, the bedroom door open, and his padding footsteps on the stairs, heading down to the dorm room he's made of his office.

This time, a note, a missive I skim but can't bring myself to read. I shred it and take the pieces into the staff washroom, where I flush them down the nice clean toilet. The bits of paper swirl and dissolve like sugar candy.

I don't remember how Liam and I met. One night at a party I realized I'd seen him around before, and that's the night I remember, looking at his face and thinking, *Him again*.

When he started phoning a few days later, I said no. He didn't look like anything to me.

For a while I sang and screamed with this band. We all lived together in a house in Jericho, not far from the University, and it was exhausting. We would get home at two or three, haul the gear in, and everyone else would go to bed while I tried to stay up and eke out another hour of study. We had cash floating in and out of our pockets and people were scared of us because of what we did to ourselves, but for a smart girl trying to hang on to a scholarship it was not a good way of going around in the world. Had I been less cranky and pissed off I might have been lonely; but people spitting at me in the street and ignoring me in shops and trying not to sit next to me in buses and lecture halls made me believe I was better alone.

Shaving half my head did not deter Liam, though. Curses and spit did not deter Liam. Can you picture how it was? Him down there in the street and me up in my room, wondering when he would give up and go away? And then when I started to let him in? Oh, we had ourselves a romance for a while, sparks flying everywhere. We were young.

⬥

"I'm flattered, I am."

He rolls his eyes.

"Cut it out," I say, as though he's my son.

Banquettes of blood-coloured vinyl, white paper napkins in tarnished chrome dispensers, tiny round tables like dinner plates on poles, jolting hot cups of coffee in a cool whitewash of early November sun. Morning sickness past, the smell of coffee is a balm again. The café I've chosen for this sun-up showdown used to be a favourite of mine, my old study hangout before Ty, before Liam. They were nice to me here, quiet me with my textbooks, even in all my finery. It's been sold a couple of times since and gone upscale, in that rather self-conscious, retro-funk fashion that passes for cutting edge these days – clapper lights in the bathrooms, so witty – but it still beats the hell out of Starbucks.

"What I don't get," Calvin says, "is how you went from being a girl in a punk band to –" He waves his hands, pulling in my clothes, my hair, my car, my practice, my life.

"A yuppie," I suggest. "Acquisitive. Consumer-oriented. A sellout."

"Regular," he says.

Calvin's pre-work clothes are skate shoes, jeans, and a T-shirt advertising some band I've never heard of. He looks sleepy, and hunches over his coffee like it needs protecting. He also watches me the way Ty used to when he was a baby, unable to take his eyes off my smallest movement. It's unnerving. That he knows nothing of the troubles of the past few weeks, of Liam, of Ty, makes this all the more unreal, inconsequential, a game I can play any way I want. Still, I try to do right.

"The devil came to me at the crossroads at midnight," I say. "What do you want me to say? I had a child. After that, sometimes a safety pin is just a safety pin."

"You've used that line before."

I have, too. I try again. "Things changed. I had more responsibilities and less time to do my hair in the morning."

He tilts his head to one side. "Why can you only tell it like a joke?"

Because it seemed like a joke, I want to say. Putting on civvies and going about without turning a single head, as though someone had come down with a giant eraser and just scrubbed me out. Because of how easy it was to become a child again, with a child of my own; how easy it was just to give up and fit in, and how good I was at it. Because if you don't laugh you'll surely cry. "What do you want from me, exactly?"

He looks surprised. He looks around the coffee shop, as though some crucial new information that changes everything might be written on the walls. He looks back at my face. "This," he says, as though it's obvious.

Morning, coffee, talk. Us together. "Calvin," I say. My voice is nicer than I mean it to be. He nods. "You have to stop with the little notes and gifts and things. It's too much right now."

He asks politely if that might change later.

"Really, really not."

Outside, traffic is picking up. I take a last sip of coffee and reach behind me for the coat I've arranged over the back of my chair. My watch says 7:38, past time to be leaving. I hold out

my arm to show him, but he's still staring at my face like something's written there.

"You should see us at home," I say. "You'd see how normal we
are. We're so normal it's sickening."

He reaches over to brush my cheek with his fingertips. I lean
back, out of reach.

"The punk girl," I tell him. "That's what it is, isn't it?"

"Partly."

"No more. All gone. Normal, normal, normal."

"Never," he says, with that look I thrive on – nervous, hopeful,
hurt.

⊰◈⊱

"Nobody *needs* therapy," Liam says.

I'm in my office at the clinic. He's in his office at the University. I picture him with his feet on his desk, looking down over
the quad, shoulder-holding the phone while he plays with his
letter opener or flips paper clips.

"He's fine," he says.

"He wouldn't get out of bed again this morning. Then, when
I get back from lunch, there's a message on my machine from
the assistant principal saying he's done no homework for any of
his classes since school started. She says she understands he's
been unwell for the past week, but maybe we could have a
meeting to arrange for drop-off and pickup of assignments until
the leg is healed."

"The leg."

"The leg, yeah. He's been cutting for the past *week*. Where
does he go?"

Calvin walks by my open door, hesitates. Since our talk in the
café, god help us, we've made a game of it. I make my hand into
a gun and hold it sideways, the sexy way they do in the movies

now, palm to floor, and point it at him. He grabs his heart and staggers away.

"I want Ty to have a couple of sessions. Maybe after that the three of us –"

"No fucking way."

"– therapy. I thought you said you were unhappy."

"Unhappy. Not unstable."

On my desk are Bakelite photo cubes from a swish store called Industry. I have Ty in the green one and Liam in the blue one. And they're tiny, tiny. "What *do* you want, then?"

"Jesus," he says.

He goes to different places, he says. Sometimes the mall, sometimes the beach. Sometimes Granville Street. Granville Street is CD stores and cinemas, but further down it's also arcades and sex shops and teens in pyjamas begging for smack money. We are aghast. We say, "Granville Street?"

"Mostly the beach," Ty says.

Each of us has staked out a piece of kitchen turf: Liam is pacing in front of the stove, Ty leans against the fridge, I'm sitting at the table squaring up papers and magazines. We're maintaining a certain distance. I got a referral through the office, went ahead and made the appointment with a therapist, and that's what's keeping me calm, numb. I watch my hands sorting and leafing, setting aside some flyers I want to look at later. I'm very capable.

"Sorry," Ty says.

Liam asks him what he's sorry for.

"Forget it," Ty says.

"No, I want to know," Liam says. "For skipping school or lying to everyone or what? It couldn't be about that beating, because you weren't involved in that, were you? Were you?"

Ty says quickly, "About skipping school. But everyone knows about it at school. Everyone knows why Jason isn't there, why he isn't coming back. Can I go to a different school?"

"You may not," Liam says.

"How does everybody know?" I ask. Ty shrugs. "No, not good enough," I say.

"I don't know how they know. I don't have friends any more. They – nobody will talk to me."

"I knew this would happen," Liam says.

"What about Brad and Matt?" Liam rolls his eyes like I'm changing the subject. Ty doesn't answer. "Come here." Ty pushes off from the fridge and comes to sit beside me. I reach over and pretend to pick a piece of lint from his hair, an excuse to touch. "If they know about Jason, they know you weren't involved. Right? They know you weren't there. I don't under- stand – no, baby, look at me. I don't understand why people would treat you this way. Are you maybe exaggerating a little?"

"No!" he says.

"I mean, I can see it's probably awkward. I can see that. You were his friend, the police came to the school. But it's over now, isn't it? And if it's over, if there's no more to it than that, doesn't that mean some of this must just be in your head?"

Ty closes his eyes.

"Your mother asked you a question," Liam says.

"It's not in my head."

"Then why would your best friends treat you the way you say?"

The question hangs in the air like something sharp and shiny suspended from a string, turning slowly, allowing us to consider all its angles. Why, indeed?

"Son," Liam says.

Ty opens his eyes.

"I think it might be in your head," I say. "I think you might be feeling some things you don't really know how to talk about right now that are making you want to avoid your friends at school."

"No, Mom," Ty says again, but I keep going.

"Maybe it would be easier to talk to someone other than us. What do you think?" And in my best soothing voice I tell him about the therapist.

He says, "No way."

"Son," Liam says again.

"No freaking way. No fucking way."

"You," Liam says, pointing a finger at him.

I start talking again about the therapist.

"Shut up," Ty says, and starts flipping through a Safeway flyer on the table in front of him.

I grab his chin and jerk his head around, forcing him to look at me. "You lied to me."

"I said sorry."

"No," I say. "You lied to *me*. That is more important and bad than anything you may or may not have done to anybody else, ever. I didn't fuck my life up having you so you could spend your fourteen-year-old days pissing around the beach feeling sorry for yourself. If you have something you want to say, say it. Otherwise you're going to school tomorrow and you're going to the therapist after that and you're going to get back on that fucking honour roll. Do you have something you want to say?"

"No," he whispers, and looks from Liam's face to mine, back and forth, to see if this is the right answer.

"Maybe a different school isn't such a bad idea," Liam says later. We're sitting in the living room, in the dark.

"There's Larkin. Larkin's a French immersion school."

"French is good," Liam says. We hear something get pushed through our mail slot. "I'm thinking also, it might be good for him to wear a uniform. I had to wear a uniform."

"You went to a parochial school."

He points at me. "There's St. Thomas."

"Ty isn't Catholic."

Liam looks at the wall.

I get up to see what was just delivered. It's an old newspaper clipping, one of the first: SECOND CHARGE IN SILVER VIDEO BEATING. It's neatly snipped, a three-column box with a single-column tail. Ty's name, of course, isn't mentioned in it. I take it to Liam and click the halogen lamp next to him, which turns the front windows black. One glance – we have it in the file – and he's going for the front door.

Outside, of course, no one – just the street, the houses, the familiar spread. "Goddamn it," he says. "Isobel said no one would find out his name. T.C., she said."

"Kids."

We're both shaken. He crumples the clipping in his fist and takes it to the kitchen. When he steps on the garbage canister pedal the lid pops up and he drops it in. "I could *make* him into a Catholic pretty damn quick," he says.

The phone rings. I grab it and bark, "Hello?"

"Is Ty there?" Through the tinny reverb of a cellphone I recognize Carl.

"No, he's not," I say.

"Shoot," Carl says. "Aw, shucks. Darn."

I hang up.

"Aren't you lucky?" I tell Ty the next morning. We're in the car. "Other kids walk to school with their actual feet."

He says, "All *right*."

I overtake a dawdling fish-silver Saab. I tell him his father might ask him to go to Mass on Sunday and he should at least consider it, for his father. He says he doesn't remember how.

"You do too remember how." He asks me to let him out, but we're still two blocks from the school so I say no. "I want to watch you enter the building."

"Mom!"

I park across the street from the front entrance, around the corner from the basketball courts. Kids are sitting on the steps, smoking. The girls greet each other with hugs and wan smiles; the boys' eyes dart. Everybody looks tired. "This is where I'll pick you up. You're sure the library's open until six?"

He says, "I hate this."

"Dr. Gross is a busy and expensive man. Your appointment is at six-fifteen. Keep me waiting and I'll come inside to look for you. Kiss your mother." And because he's still a child and doesn't always recognize sarcasm, he does.

They hear the car door slam; pale faces turn. Do they draw themselves up? At this distance I can't tell. Ty threads on through the scrum of them. A girl with long swinging yellow hair turns her back as he passes, but what does this mean? It's a catwalk spin, surely – showing her clothes to her friends, jiving and teetering on her platforms. She's just a lollipop. I'm hauling on the wheel, pulling out, when I glance over one more time to see one of the step-sitters swing around and plant a foot square in the centre of his back, sending him sprawling up the last couple of stairs. Around him kids start to applaud. Ty doesn't turn around; he picks himself up and carries on through the doors, out of sight.

Fear takes me like love, heart pounding, dry mouth. I go to work.

"Doctor," May says. She hands me a file and says, "Number seven." She looks harassed.

"Where's Calvin?"

"He called in sick."

"Bastard. Who?" I gesture towards the examining room.

"Mr. Resnick."

I say, "Fuck," and she looks away. I say, "Sorry," but the damage is done.

Mr. Resnick registers me with his pale blue eyes. "Are you going to charge me?"

"What?" I say, rattled. "Charge you with what?"

"Charge me money."

I grab my stethoscope and advance like a monster. "Open your shirt."

"It's all right." His hand flutters at his throat.

"I need to examine you. I need you to co-operate with me right now. Goddamn it," I add reasonably.

"You're not having very good luck with that one, are you?" the receptionist says a minute later. I've followed him out to the lobby but stopped there, had to let him go. He's gone so fast the silk trees are swaying and swiping the windows.

"I think he's afraid of me."

"He asked for you when he made the appointment."

She's fat and calm, this receptionist. Every smile is a light question.

"I have to leave early today," I tell her. "I promised my son something. Say, five-forty?"

"Hokey-pokey," she says, consulting the big book. "No problemo. How old is the little guy?"

I don't hesitate. "Six."

"Aw."

"Yep," I say, turning back to my office.

⌘

I'm sitting in the therapist's grey-and-teak reception area, six-teenth floor, waiting while he talks to my son. I've read a *National Geographic* article on St. Anselm's deer and a brochure on talking to your children about schizophrenia. I have a flaming cork-screw of a headache. On the drive over I had told him I saw what happened on the school steps and he said, "Good for you." I put my hand on his shoulder but he shrugged it away. We didn't speak after that. In the underground parking lot he tried his first full-on mutiny, refusing to remove his seat belt.

"Get out of the car," I said, slowly and deliberately, as though I was talking to Mr. Resnick. And then, as though I *was* Mr. Resnick: "Get out of the car. Get out of the car. Get out of the car. Get out of the car. Get out of the car. Get out of the car." He did, too, exploding into motion – belt whipped, door slammed – as though suddenly he couldn't get away from me fast enough. He ignored me all the way to the elevator, and, as the doors began to close, darted out, leaving me alone in my slowly, deliberately ascending cage. By the time the doors opened he was already at the nurse's desk, still ignoring me, coolly giving his name and particulars. He had taken the stairs. I felt smug, knowing he still lacked the confidence to defy me outright, but frightened too at his willingness even to pretend to leave me behind.

Now, when he emerges, we're both elaborately casual. He yawns and stretches. I toss my magazines behind me, non-chalantly slopping up the pile. I touch his hair briefly, warily, a question he can ignore if he wants, and – remarkably – win a frail smile.

In the car on the way home, Ty volunteers that he likes Dr. Gross, he'd like to see him again. He seems drained, head on the headrest, breathing through his mouth, but he looks at me when he talks, which he hasn't been doing lately.

"What if we all went to see him together, you and me and your Dad?"

"First, me," Ty says.

I try not to look at him. I look at him. He's calm, staring at the sky, or the green glare strip on the windshield.

"I've already made an appointment," he says. "I can figure out how to get there on the bus."

"Crush me," I say. I'm afraid to say more, to ask what happened in there, afraid I've dreamt up this amenable little boy I just barely remember from what seems like a lifetime ago.

When we pull into the driveway, Liam is painting the front of the house. In his everyday black clothes he's slapping blue paint on the blue siding, stroking savagely. When he sees us he flinches, speeds up.

"Please go inside," I tell Ty. I cross the grass to Liam and confirm what I thought I saw, a blurt of red, tail of a graffito, which Liam is erasing with the wet blue. "What did it say?" I ask.

He won't tell me. Instead, after supper, he proposes taking Ty to stay with his mother in the Maritimes for a week. "Someone is gunning for us," he says, looking at his hands.

"What did it say?"

He smoothes the cloth of his pants.

I reach under my sweatshirt to pull my T-shirt straight. It's got rucked up on one shoulder. "Kids."

"Again."

"But maybe not directed specifically at Ty, though. Could just be vandalism, some random –"

Liam's shaking and shaking his head, brushing down his sleeves now. "I walked up and down the block. Our house was the only one. Plus, the clipping."

"Okay, the clipping," I say. "Fine. But Nova Scotia? What about me?"

"I was thinking maybe we could all use a bit of a break from each other."

He won't meet my eye after he says this, and I'm left studying his face, his person. He looked a little Christly, once upon a time, my husband, with the longish hair, pale skin, dark eyes, and all that hunger. Now, though, he just looks tired. He looks like what he is, I guess: pretty cool for a professor, which isn't the same thing as cool itself, despite what he thinks; not old, not young, definitely a four-square citizen with a couple of cars and a mortgage, with a dental plan and a teenager, with cares.

"You've never really told me about your book," I say.

He looks away.

"The little Irish starlet," I say. "The one you have the thing for."

He checks to see if I'm being sarcastic. I'm not.

"She died young," he says. "Lived a pretty wild life. She made some very odd films."

"What is it about her?"

He looks at me then, and doesn't look away.

"You know we still haven't told Ty about the baby?"

"When we get back," he says.

In the lunchroom, May is quick to move her bag from the chair next to her to the floor. I'm grateful. When I ask politely what she's eating she says, "Are you all right?" I open my mouth to say something else. "Tired," I hear myself say. "I'm tired."

"You look it."

I don't mention the baby because I haven't told Dr. Gagnon yet. I do allude to Ty and his ongoing troubles at school, though I omit the therapist and the graffiti. I mention his and Liam's impending trip to the Maritimes. Her smooth brow wrinkles with concern. By the end of lunch she is patting my hand and inviting me over for supper while my men are away.

"Who's going away?" Calvin asks, joining us.

I explain again. May, I notice, has immediately withdrawn into herself, tidying up her lunch remains, saying little.

"She has a crush on you," I tell Calvin after she excuses herself, leaving us alone.

He says, "I don't think so."

"Well, it wouldn't kill you to be nicer to her."

We smile, then, can't help it, because we are something like friends now, and understand each other.

"Hey," I say. "Hey. Would you help me with something?"

The next morning there's a knock on the door. Liam is in his den; Ty is sitting on the carpet with a pile of padlocks and rings of tiny keys, trying to find fits. Their suitcases are in the hall. I pause to heft one and yank my bicep. "What the hell?"

Ty doesn't look up. "Dad's movies."

On the doorstep, Brill. "I have a right to know what's going on," he says.

"Liam," I call over my shoulder.

"Never mind trying to scare me. I am getting craziness about you people in the mailbox with my mail, warnings, okay? Also there are messages on the front of your house."

"Again?"

We walk down into the yard. Liam's paint job has dried thin and the words show through.

"No, that's from before," I explain.

"What's that boy done? I've seen the police in your driveway. Is he a danger?" I take a step towards him and he jerks back. "I consider that a threat," he says.

"Good. Get the fuck out of my yard."

"You rude woman. We have a right to know. We've had a meeting."

"What meeting? Who?"

"You've got to use a thinner on that." He backs away, pointing at the siding. "Don't you even know that? You people are bringing down the neighbourhood. We know what he did."

"That was you," I say, pointing at the house. Now we're both pointing at the house.

Liam appears on the porch, shoeless, holding his coffee mug.

"It was not," Brill says.

"Morning, neighbour!" Liam calls.

"What meeting?" I say.

"You people are cheap," Brill says.

We go inside. "What meeting?" I say. I hammer my fist on the wall facing Brill's house. "What warning? What messages? What meeting, you Nazi?"

Ty says, "Mom."

"Shut up, Kate, just shut up for a change," Liam says.

"Daddy," Ty says.

We yell, "What?"

He looks at each of us in turn. "I phoned the fucking airport the way you fucking showed me," he says. "The fucking plane's on time."

The landscapers, the landscapers.

By now the situation is this: the evergreens are in. The terrace is in. The paving stones are down. You can walk a little walk from the kitchen door past the place for the herb garden to the greenhouse door and your feet need not touch God's green earth. The guys have unswaddled the greenhouse. Now, my own men days gone, it is time to pay them.

"Thank you for choosing Green Garden Landscapers," the older one says. As far as I can tell, he and his assistant are Green Garden Landscapers. "We came in a little over budget, but I think you'll see that's because of the marble."

"It's fine," I say, writing a cheque against the side of the house. "It's very handsome."

"I bet you'll be glad to see life returning to normal after all this palaver."

He has the tan, the squint, the inscrutability of all outdoors. He could be as old as my father. He's sent his assistant to wait in the truck, in the passenger seat, where I can see him staring fixedly at the front of our house.

"What do you mean by that?" I ask softly.

He doesn't answer. Maybe he didn't hear me. We walk around front, him gently waving my cheque as though to dry the ink. You can see the clean blue patch on the weathered blue of the house, under the front windows where the graffiti was, and where I've been adding coats to Liam's paint job in the days since they've been away.

"Been doing some painting, there, I see," the older one says.

I say, "A little."

"Spot work." He folds my cheque twice and puts it in the pocket of his overalls. "Covering up a bad spot."

"Something like that."

He hesitates, my landscaper. Then he says, "It's that big one, isn't it. That friend of your son. I saw him one time shoving things through the mailboxes around here. He the one giving you the trouble?"

"Yes," I say fervently.

"You know the one I mean?"

I nod.

He nods too, looking towards the horizon, like he's bored already.

"Thank you," I say.

"I don't like to rat on a kid," he says. I half expect him to pluck a blade of grass to stick in his mouth while we talk. "On the one hand, boys will be boys. On the other hand, some boys grow up faster than others. You're nice people. Your son is a nice boy. You've been looking pretty spooked."

"No," I say.

"It's nothing to be ashamed of." He looks straight into my face, briefly, and says, "Good luck." Then he gets into his truck.

"What do you mean by that?" I say again, but he's started the engine, he's driving away. The assistant raises his arm through the open window in a wave – a single, decisive movement – and they're gone, these naïfs, my well-wishers, racks of tools bumping and rattling like something donkey-drawn, like they're off on their way back to another time.

That night, I do what I should have done at the start: I hole up in Ty's room and *look*.

He's made the bed, so I start there. I strip it, unsack the pillow, mound the linen in the hall in a colourful punky-smelling pile; throw open the window to give the air a rinsing. The night sucks at the blind, making a light clatter against the sill. It's raining. I sit on the bare mattress, elbows on knees, feet braced, and consider. My intention is to take the place apart, brick by shingle, as it were, poke a flashlight into the dark places in his baby head and see what he thinks he's been hiding there. *He's still mine*, I keep thinking; *he still belongs to me*. Who does he think he is?

Who does he think he is? I go to the computer first, putty-coloured CPU tucked inside the desk leg. I kick it a couple of times, trying to cross my legs in his child-assed swivel chair. My first bring-it-home discovery, then, about my son: *he's smaller than I am*. I make a mental note to buy him a new chair for Christmas.

I check his files, school work mostly, letters to his grand-parents from Christmases past, and a list of web addresses salted away for when we let him get Internet access in his bedroom. It's inevitable, only a matter of time. He wants NBA.com, Sports Illustrated, Mars-Hubble (bless him). The unsavouries I'm sure he's got memorized. I go back to the bed and heft the mattress – nothing. But *under* the bed, now, are some items. Not a trove, but it's a start. For instance, a stuffed dog. For instance, liquorice Twizzlers: red, my flavour. They're a little stale but gummy sweet, just like I remember. Also a pair of corduroy pants, almost new, which (I guess) didn't make it past the fashion masters at school, but which (he knows) won't make it past his mom to the Sally Ann either. I add them to the pile in the hall, then change my mind and put them back so neither of us will have to explain. A broken telephone he liked to play with as a tyke (I intuit a sturdy, Boys' Own resolve to fix it one day with tweezers and string and use it to lobby us for his own line); some sci-fi paper-backs with textured foil covers, guys in robes staring up at three moons. But no drugs, bloodied clothes, neo-Nazi paraphernalia, girlie magazines, cigarettes even. In his pencil kit, a single wrapped prophylactic; but the district nurse could have passed these out at school. In fact, didn't I read something about this in the local paper, some Condoms in the Classroom fuss? Isn't this a standard part of their kit now? I leave it in there with his Pink Pearl eraser and his Extra-Fine Black Felt Tips. I start to wonder if my son is maybe a bit of a prig.

Downstairs the doorbell rings once, a quick shot, like I ought to know.

"So, here I am," Calvin says.

He's big, this Calvin, with that big dog shagginess, the sad eyes and the rare grin. When I don't say anything he looks crushed: the slumping shoulders, the hung head. The sex would probably be terrific. But he doesn't frighten me, and that's a grave deficit; it guts the temptation, leaving a sweet shell with nothing inside.

"This was wrong, wasn't it," he says. "I should leave, shouldn't I."

I squint at him. "When you were a teenager, where did you hide stuff?"

He gives me a look not unlike Jupiter's frazzled look in the bathroom doorway.

"Yeah, yeah, yeah," I say, and let him in. I click on the outside porch light, illuminating the long panes on either side of the door.

He looks around like he's memorizing. He lifts his hand like he's going to touch me, then lets it drop. "Where did *you* hide things, when *you* were a teenager?"

"In my head."

The next thing I know, I'm telling him the whole thing – the beating, the Parmenters, the police, the lawyer, the therapist, the graffiti, even Brill. I'm even telling him how Brill has rallied the neighbours against us. I've wanted him, I realize, this Calvin, this big shaggy dog; I've wanted him right from the beginning, for just this. The relief is like surfacing.

"Let's see his room," Calvin says calmly. So far, I haven't let him past the hall.

I point automatically. "Shoes."

Upstairs he toes the pile of laundry in the hall. Ty's room is cooler than the rest of the house, cold actually. When I turn back from closing the window he's sitting on the bed. I say, "No way."

"Jesus Christ," he says, shaking his head. He goes and kneels in front of the desk and runs his hand along the underside of the single drawer. Then he opens the cupboard door and starts feeling around inside Ty's old sneakers.

"Ew," I say.

"We count on that," Calvin explains, handing me back a crumpled pack of Players.

"Well, that's not so bad."

I sit on the bed, holding the cigarettes, watching him work his way through the room. I can see he's taking more care than I did, trying to leave things looking unruffled. He pokes his finger into the rind of a deflated basketball, shakes it, then puts it back the way it lay. "Basketball player, huh?"

I flip-flop my hand.

"Not a skateboard punk like his mom?" Grinning.

I look down at the skulls on my biceps. "I've got to stop wearing this."

"Suits you." He comes out of the cupboard. "I bet you were a scary kid."

I shrug. "Lonely. Like everyone. It was fun finding a tribe."

"I was a jock," he says from the dresser. "In high school, I dated a cheerleader. But she refused to sleep with me and I became very morose. Does your son have a girlfriend?"

"No."

He tosses me a satin bra, baby blue. "Fucking hell, that's *mine*," I say, and he laughs. He comes over and sits beside me on the bed. "It's the desperate age," he says. He takes the bra out of my hands and gives it a wry look.

"What do I do about Ty?"

"Believe him." He gets up and leaves the room and for a moment I think he isn't coming back. Then I realize he's gone to throw the bra on the laundry pile. On his way back in he turns off the overhead but leaves the door open so we've got the hall light to see by, a bright triangle that just touches the bedpost.

"Give it up. From all you've told me, the lawyer, the therapist – have you seriously considered he might be telling the truth?"

"Not for a while," I admit.

"This is very bad for me, just being here," Calvin says.

"But how do I do that, decide to believe or disbelieve? You don't decide a thing like that. You have feelings and instincts. It's like the choice is made before you have a chance to think about it."

"I guess lawyers do it all the time. Presumption of innocence, right? Acting in your client's interests? Maybe you have to act like you believe him, and eventually the acting takes over and becomes the true thing. You start to believe your own performance."

I think about that. "So pretend you hate me."

He shakes his head. "Tried." He leans over in the dark to kiss my cheek but misses and gets my ear instead. We sit like that for a moment.

"You know I have to kick you out now?"

He sighs. "I know."

I walk him down to the front step, watch him walk away down my street. Like a movie star, he doesn't look back.

May and Jupiter rent the top floor of a house owned by a retired couple who used to have something to do with the film industry. The vanity plate on the couple's BMW, parked out front, says 2REEL. Last week the postman accidentally left one of their Christmas cards, from someone named Lauren Bacall, in May and Jupiter's box. We argue about that one for a while.

"I bet you there are at least ten people in the United States right now named Lauren Bacall," I say.

"Ten? A hundred," May says. "I would bet. Maybe more."

"O ye of little faith," Jupiter says.

The walls, painted sunny blues and yellows, slant with the roof. The resulting spaces are awkward, interesting, nooks and corners. Small. A skylight sloping over the kitchen table lets an open grey light onto our dinner: a stringy lasagne, Safeway garlic bread, and an indifferent salad. I wonder why they didn't cook Asian. Maybe, like me, they were trying to do ethnic.

"Did you see the return address?"

"LA," Jupiter says.

"Proves nothing," May says. Jupiter sticks his tongue out at her and she kicks him under the table. They are less inhibited in their own house, more physical, jostling and affectionate, squabbling like – squabs. When I arrived they each hugged me gently, me with my tender new girth. May asked, girl or boy.

"Boy," I said. "You could see his package on the ultrasound."

Jupiter asked after Liam and Ty while May put my hothouse designer daisies in a vase.

"Coming home day after tomorrow," I told him, trying to sound brisk, pepped.

"May says there've been some issues." She turned from the sink and threw a leaf at his head. It stuck. "I was bringing it out into the open!" he protested.

"No," I said. "It's all right. We decided, Liam and I decided, Ty needed some time in another – milieu. To think about –"

There was a space I couldn't seem to fill.

"– things," Jupiter offered.

"The house must be so quiet," May said.

I used that as a cue to ask for a tour of their place. From the kitchen you stepped off the lino onto carpet and then you were in the office: desk, ergonomic chair, computer, reading lamp, and melamine bookcase of texts and files, presumably Jupiter's. The bathroom was white and immaculate, with a lot of fruity products from The Body Shop in a basket on the counter next to an inhaler and a sealed hypodermic, part of an allergy kit. "Mine," Jupiter said, seeing my glance, holding up his hand like I'd asked him a question in school. "Shellfish."

"He cramps my style," May said.

The single bedroom was dominated by the bed, covered by a faded quilt with a watermelon pattern, and the TV, a seventies model complete with rabbit ears. I guessed those two were socking their savings away and would be retiring – cleverly, quietly, without fuss – at forty-five.

"Liam would know," I say now. "Whether she lives in LA, the real Lauren Bacall, I mean. He's full of trivia like that."

Jupiter starts to clear the table. May, to my surprise, doesn't even gesture toward helping. I wonder if this is some standing arrangement between them. She cooks, he cleans?

"How long have they been away, now?" she says in her soft voice. For the first time I notice the trace of an accent, a lingering on the "o" in "long," a brusque clipping of the final "a" in "away."

"Just a week."

Jupiter is speeding up, stacking plates precariously and trying to carry everything at once over to the sink, to absent himself from this conversation. I'm beginning to understand.

"Have you spoken to Liam?" May asks. "Does this trip seem to be helping Ty?"

"He's got his homework. It's not hurting him."

"You've spoken to Liam?"

"May," I say, reaching for her hand. "Thank you. But we're not separating. It's been just one week."

Blushes upon blushes, predictably; as usual, I have been too blunt. Jupiter smiles apologetically and goes into the bedroom, closing the door behind him. I hear the TV go on, the groan of bedsprings. He's done his bit for the evening, then. May is apologizing for her concern, which she calls her rudeness. "Only you haven't seemed well, lately," she said.

How much to tell her, without corrupting her just by making her listen? "You have to understand, with Liam and me," I say. "It's always been this way. We go through these cycles. Would you believe me if I told you this was the eighth time in fourteen years he's gone home to his family when we weren't getting along?"

"I, too, am very close to my mother," May says.

She gets up to fill the kettle and I pray for a Chinese dessert, sweet rice dumplings, maybe, or lychee nuts in syrup.

While she makes coffee our talk drifts to work, scheduling and such. "How long has Calvin been at the clinic?"

"Longer than me." She brings milk and sugar to the table. The coffee gurgles. "I've been there three years. I think for him it's closer to five. Are you getting along better with him now? I know at first there were some problems."

I'm caught off guard. "No, no problems," I say. "Just a misunderstanding."

She sits back down beside me, hesitates, then says, "What you have to understand about Calvin is he's the same with everyone. Before you, it was me. It's sort of a joke. The other nurses told me. He used to write me letters and leave gifts in my coat pockets. One very nice Jascha Heifetz CD after I told him I used to play the violin. After you came he started all over again. After you, it'll be someone else. That's just the way he is."

"Oh," I say.

"No, it's nice," she says. "Don't be hurt. It's flattering." She laughs again and I feel ashamed. I thought I had been swimming in water where I could stand up if I chose, when really it just goes down and down. Of course I'm also thinking about Ty.

She brings the coffee to the table, also cups, spoons, and a pastry box – biscotti, custard tarts, a few chocolate truffles in tiny foil cups. "Jupiter, sweets," she calls.

Ty, I'm thinking, but what I say is, "Yummy."

⊸◇⊷

At the airport, as Liam and Ty wait for their luggage on the carousel, I tell them I've put on six pounds.

"So, run," Ty says.

"No, six pounds is good," I say, and we finally tell him about the baby, there in the airport.

Us: You're getting a sibling.

Him (dully): That's great.

I insist on hugging him until he hugs me back a little. "Missed you," I say, then turn away – I tell myself – so he won't have to respond.

This is my new son, the revised Ty, the reserved Ty, the Ty who treats his parents with a kind of delayed formality, as though we are communicating across a vast distance where words travel slower than meaning. This is the Ty who wakes one morning with a spray of acne on his forehead, disappointing me terribly. This is the Ty who defiantly cancels his last few appointments with Dr. Gross and routinely bolts his dinner to go out in the dark and play three-on-three with his new basketball buddies, including, I strongly suspect, Carl the vandal.

"Carl the *vandal*," I tell Ty.

"Yeah, yeah, yeah," he says. "Yeah, yeah, yeah, yeah, yeah, yeah, yeah."

Probably the clippings and graffiti were some kind of rite of passage, something he feels he has survived, something he now has no intention of discussing with his mere mother. Probably Carl the vandal was a sweet child who loved milk and shared his toys.

When the Nova Scotia cousins send a crop of photographs from their visit, he and his dad sit on the sofa going through them, trading names and reminiscences like a couple of old women. They demand lobster and roll their eyes at each other when I object to the cost. Liam even takes to asking after Carl in a fake German accent, which the two of them seem to find hilarious. I wonder if Liam's star is ascending in Ty's little galaxy, even as my own falls. I wonder if I shouldn't be more grateful for small mercies. Brill, for instance, still won't speak to us, but Mrs. Lindstrom from across the road brought us a stollen at Christmas so we knew his hold was slipping. Now, early January, a For Sale by Owner sign appears on his front lawn. We see couples unlatch his gate and trundle up the path, often pausing to point at our house, as though to say: wish it were *that* one. I get a kick out of this.

We start to use the dining room again, the night our shy lawyer friend Isobel comes for dinner. We talk about careers, vanilla talk; Isobel asks Ty what he wants to do. "Law," he says.

We gape. He takes his plate into the kitchen for seconds.

"Picked your school?" Isobel asks.

"Dal," he calls from the kitchen. Dalhousie.

While he's out of earshot she asks us about the thing. Liam says, "It blew over."

Before dinner Liam put on the Bach Solo Cello Suites for background music. Now I say, "I always think people who love the cello aren't getting any. The vibration, you know?"

Isobel says, "Well, I'm glad to hear that."

My husband looks weary.

"I'm just so sick of this *reverence* for the cello," I say.

The dining room, I am seeing now, could in fact use some work. The walls are a blended hue, ochres and umbers we sponge-painted six years ago, that looked subtle and Mediterranean, hot-cool at the time, but now seem effortful, amateurish. Ty returns from the kitchen with a plateful of treats: rice crisped brown from the bottom of the pot, blackened rinds from the roast, a puddle of sweet meat gravy, and, because I have taught him to eat in groups, a single sarcastic bean. I watch him slice and fork his meat, grind his molars, and after a while he becomes aware.

"What," he says.

"No, not *what*," I say.

The evening swoops along like this, conversation blossoming and curling back on itself, arabesques of good feeling tipped with tiny barbs. I ask Isobel about her experience at law school, earning an earnest account of her love for competitive moots and a scowl from my son, who I can tell is wishing he himself had never confessed to anything so earnest as an ambition. Liam serves dessert and talks about his own collegiate passion, film noir, discovered one rainy undergraduate night at the Cinematheque, during a James Cagney / Aldo Ray double bill. He does his Cagney impersonation, which I find particularly endearing when he's wearing his glasses, as now. Isobel and I laugh. Ty murmurs, "Fucking bullshit cunt crap," I'm pretty certain, and gives me a smile like a seraph. I see Liam has heard too but he won't bite because we're in company.

"I was a chemistry major at the time," he tells Isobel, looking at Ty's head bent studiously over his plate. "I was very discontent. It was my eureka moment. I thought, you love this! Do what you love!"

Ty snorts.

"Chew nicely," I say.

Even Isobel catches a scratch, as Liam helps her into her coat and we gather at the door for goodbyes. She invites Ty to spend a day at her office, to see what a law firm is all about.

"I'm not really interested in tax law," he says to this good, gentle woman who has known him since he was a baby. Her mouth twists briefly, laughter or hurt, or both.

After Liam closes the door he gives me a look as though to say, do you want to do it or should I?

"Come for a walk?" I ask Ty.

He says no.

Liam takes his glasses off.

"Fine," Ty says. When he knows he must obey us it pleases him, lately, to act as though he does it under coercion, if not the threat of outright physical harm. Whereas it pleases Liam and me, we agreed the other night, that we are both still ever so slightly taller than our son.

January in Vancouver is not so bad. It's a balmy eight degrees or so, raining lightly from a nine-o'clock sky. Black sky, slick black street, babbling in the gutters, German metal in the driveways, windows of buttery light. Trees, reaching nudes. What it is to be safe again.

"Where are we going?" Ty wants to know.

"I feel like a movie."

Our footsteps neither ring nor crunch, but are simply themselves on the wet pavement. Ty shoves his hands in his pockets like he wants to pop the linings. Liam turns his face up to the sky and walks a few steps ahead of us, leaving me to it. I pull the zipper of my jacket up over the blob of my belly, five months' worth. Five months, I'm thinking, is long enough. I expect Ty to object and he does take a single breath deeper than the others, a mouthful of fuel for speech, but nothing comes out. I chafe the pad of my index finger against the corner of the laminated Silver Video card in my pocket. I know he's also expecting a dressing-down after his performance at supper tonight, and pick my words thoughtfully.

"Isobel wears too much lace and tax law is very boring," I say. "But she means well."

"Fine," Ty says.

"Look at me. She is a dear old friend and you are going to phone her and apologize."

"I said fine."

Up ahead, at the crest of the hill, we can see Silver Video, between the cheesecake place and the dry cleaner.

"You want to know what is not fine?" The baby flutters. I say, "Ho!"

"What?"

"Baby's moving." I grab his hand and clamp it to my belly. "Feel that?"

He angles his head, listening. After a moment sullenness melts into curiosity and he lets his fist relax into an open palm. He lets me move it around.

"That," I say, and something flickers on his face. He felt it. He leans down and I can hear him breathe.

"Helloooo," he says, stretching the word out like someone trying to make an echo.

"Baby," I say. He takes his hand back, but nicely.

We catch up to Liam at the top of the hill, across the street from our destination. It's a raw moment – awkward, intimate – with a few sparse raindrops pegging us on the head and shoulders like something personal. Silver Video, from this vantage point, is a fish tank. Through the glass wall I see a lone customer bopping one video off his thigh while he reads the back of another. Then he sets both cases down and limps over to the Used / For Sale rack. Outside, the parking lot is empty, shiny black, the parking spaces delineated by yellow lines worn pale and grainy as fingerprints.

We cross the street. I walk over to a garbage can by the bushes where it happened, pretending to empty the crud from my pockets – a couple of tissues, peel from a roll of breath mints – half expecting a change in temperature or a whirring like insects, but it's cool and damp and unremarkable, a blank page again. Ty and Liam hang back, waiting for me by the doors. Liam has one foot up on the concrete barrier meant to stop cars from rolling through the plate glass windows. Ty, leaning his bum against the window, with his hood up and his hands still in his pockets, is shaking his head at something his father is saying, shaking his head and then smiling, grudgingly, as Liam punctuates his monologue with a duck-like waddle, one hand on his belly. Now they're both laughing, smirking a bit, glancing to check where I am. Out of earshot, is where; they're safe from me.

In a perfect world, I would look down at this moment and see a winking twist – my son's MedicAlert bracelet, say – half-buried at my feet. Instead there's a new-looking, extra-large drink cup from a local convenience store, complete with lid and straw, abandoned on the lip of the asphalt. I kick it into the bushes and turn back to rejoin my men, but there is only Ty, standing by the doors.

"Dad's inside," Ty calls, and we both roll our eyes and smile a little because he couldn't wait.

"Poor Dad," I say, and I'm conscious, as I cross the last few metres separating us, of my walk, of my hand on my belly. "He can't help himself."

We don't go in yet. We watch Liam through the windows for a while, Liam the scholar, frowning and tapping his fingers against his lips while the overhead TVs blare their silent promotional dreck. We watch him pick up one video, put it down. We watch him drift to the DVDs. Working hard.

"Are you okay?" I ask Ty.

He says, "I'm good."

We look at each other for a second, have to look away.

"Is this too weird?" I ask. "Being here?"

A car pulls into the parking lot, a navy Mini, a new one. My verdict on these cars is I would like them more if everyone else liked them less. Ty and I step apart to let the driver and his passenger, a tall, thin man with an expression of long-suffering good humour and a woman whose hair is a voguish rat's nest of streaks and straws, into the store. "You've seen everything!" the woman is saying.

"No," Ty says.

"You understand why," I say.

He says he does.

"We believe you," I tell him. "We're trying really hard."

"I know."

Through the window I watch Liam glance over his shoulder, checking out the woman with the hair. He sees me and waves his arm in a big corralling gesture, mouthing, Come in.

"What's he got?" Ty says, because Liam's also holding up a DVD.

"Something violent," I say. "I mean, my god, I hope."

Ty pushes off from the window.

"Boom, bang," I say. "Pow. Pow."

I watch him go inside, join his dad. We pretend Liam needs supervision, Ty and I. Through the window I see Liam show him the case and they study it together, just like old times, like Ty is a visiting expert whose opinion he has gravely solicited. He plays us both, our son, and we let him get away with it. There's nothing you can't forget, in the end. I step up onto the curb, reach for the heavy door. Inside, the familiar three-pronged turnstile and the bee buzz of the lights complete the world as Ty comes toward me with the movie in his hand, hoping this is the one we will agree on, the one that will take us home.

THE GOLDBERG METRONOME

The metronome had been hidden in the bathroom, under the counter, taped to the pipes beneath the sink like a bomb taped to the chassis of a car. Fanciful, Anika reprimanded herself, though she did not reach to touch or remove it right away. She knelt on the tile floor and held the cupboard door open with one rubber-gloved hand, studying the package so plumply swaddled in brown paper and packing tape, so firmly affixed to the crook of the black PVC pipe. Once, in the old house, Thom had pulled off some of the wood panelling to get at a mouse nest and had pulled out a pair of child's pants filthy with mould and rice-like black scat, the same as they had been finding in their pots and pans and even in the burners on the stove. For a vibrant moment they had stared at each other, down in the gloom of the unfinished basement, wondering what could possibly come next – a small body or bodies, police, newspapers, television cameras on the front lawn, inevitably a move, away from the horror of it – but had quickly realized the pants, and blanket, and other, assorted children's clothes stuffed behind the panelling were simply old rags used in place of insulation. Which only went to show, Anika thought, staring at the package under the sink and simultaneously recalling the tiny trousers, perhaps some child's very first pair, you never knew what some people would leave behind.

Thom, she called.

Frustrated with their landlord's apathy – about the mice, the insulation, the water that pooled in the basement every time it rained, the black, indelible paste of mould around the tiles in the bathroom where the caulking should have been – they decided to move anyway. They had thought the East Vancouver house a find, at first, with its eleven-foot ceilings, abraded hardwood, and lushly overgrown garden. Later, jaded, they pursued the search fitfully, defensively. *Character*, they had learned the hard way, meant rot; *cozy* meant stifling low ceilings, *fenced yard* meant more dog shit than dirt. They bought newspapers each weekend for the classified ads and spent precious Saturday hours poring studiously, instead, over the crossword. Sunday morning outings to neighbourhoods they felt they could afford degenerated into Sunday afternoon walks through neighbourhoods where they really wanted to live: Dunbar, Point Grey, the West end. They drank innumerable small, strong, expensive coffees in casually smart cafés, pretending they lived just around the corner, trying to postpone the inevitable return home. They both freelanced – he as a graphic artist, she as a photographer, neither entirely by choice – and their finances, while often good, were always precarious. Even coffee was a luxury over which they lingered, budget-conscious, for hours. One would read the paper while the other stared out the window. A moment would come, the lighting of the lamps that would knock the street outside into deep blue darkness, or the arrival of some other, better-dressed couple their own age, regulars greeted more warmly by the barista than they themselves had been, and they would rise and pull on their coats, leaving behind half-finished papers and empty cups, and find their way back to the car, an ugly and reliable 1980 Civic.

On one such occasion, driving back through the tree-lined streets of apartments between Denman Street and Stanley Park, she had ordered him to stop. A small white For Rent sign stood staked to the lawn of a modest low-rise. It was the twenty-ninth of the month, October, just before the newest vacancies would be advertised in the paper. They called immediately from a pay phone and got an appointment for the next day.

What is it? Thom said. He had been unpacking boxes in the second bedroom, what they called the study, which would also do for a baby's room in another year or two, though they had gingerly avoided putting this into words.

She pointed to the package under the sink.

Drugs? he said.

He, too, hesitated for a moment, and she knew they shared the same thought: that finding this apartment had, after all, been too good to be true, and that this object, whatever it was, was surely the reason the previous tenant had left. It encapsulated whatever would be the next trouble in their lives. Trouble, Anika thought, was not too strong a word, though they argued rarely and always with an honest, distressed perplexity that each could not see the other's point of view. No, it was not arguments so much as distance, a polite remoteness that had led to more and more meals taken in front of the television, and a gradual lessening of regret over the hours they spent apart. The first bloom was off, that was all, Anika told herself. They were steady mates now, no longer clinging and foolish fond. But the sense of unease, of a wrong turn taken, persisted. People split up this way, quietly, without fuss; people drifted off into their own orbits and never snapped back. It was almost a scent, like bitter orange, the knowledge that they did not absolutely need to be together. She came to wonder if the disappointment of the East Vancouver house was not the cause but the effect of the widening space between them, the high drafty rooms and wet cracked floors the embodiment of the creeping absence she sensed. She wondered how long they would last.

Hold on, Thom said.

She held the package firmly with both hands while he reached awkwardly around her shoulder, trying to get at the tape. She felt his breath on her ear, felt, too, the warmth of a muttered oath.

I have nails, she said.

They traded positions, he holding the package with one big hand while she picked at the tape with her fingernails.

It's light, he said, when she had freed one end and he had the weight of it in his hand.

They tore the package free, leaving a wind of tape and a flare of beige paper stuck to the pipe. Thom tore the rest of the paper away, less cautiously than Anika would have, letting it fall to the floor in drifts. Under the paper was a layer of cotton batting, and inside that was a black wooden box, roughly coffin-shaped, with a simple geometric pattern inlaid on the diagonal up each side, its symmetry marred by a small brass knob halfway down the right side.

It's a metronome, Anika said. She took it from his hands and removed the cover, revealing a metal face with the numbers all but worn away, and a delicate brass needle and pendulum. She set it on the counter next to the sink and gave the needle a push, but it fell with a heavy finality to one side and stopped there.

Wind it, Thom suggested, but the brass knob was stuck, and she hesitated to apply much pressure and risk snapping it off.

Broken, she said. Well, it looks old.

They took it into the living room to look at it in better light. Thom stroked the high sheen on the lid with his fingertips while Anika pushed the needle back and forth a few times, hoping to elicit a tick. The sun came out from behind a cloud, sending a sudden dust-teeming shaft through the window and across their hands, and at the same time each said, It's blue.

What they had taken for black was in fact a deep indigo.

We should give it to Phyllis, I suppose, Anika said.

It was Phyllis who had answered their call about the apartment. Phyllis was, first, a voice: old but not frail, deliberately slow, with mannered good manners. Boston, smart. Phyllis in person (when they showed up the next day to view the apartment, overdressed, their references in an anxious manila envelope) was charmingly matter-of-fact, in a sweater with the sleeves pushed up and a pair of faded blue jeans. She described the building with disparaging affection, confessed to having managed it for thirty years and lived in it for forty, confessed to being seventy herself, all the while tossing out bits of information about laundry and parking and utilities as though they really were prospective tenants and not the objects of some particularly cruel practical joke.

We won't get it, Anika whispered to Thom when the elevator reached the fifth floor and Phyllis marched off ahead of them down the hall, shaking out a ring of keys.

I know, Thom whispered back. It's too good.

Listen to the dulcet tones of our doorbells, Phyllis said, pressing a button beside the door that yielded a failing rasp, ending with a distinct clank when she released it. The three of them laughed. Thom and Anika were by now painfully excited.

You know, Phyllis said. It's old-fashioned, like I told you. Not modern enough for the other couples who came through. David, she called, rapping on the door. When no one replied she opened the door with a key.

Cupboard here, she said. The management company will see to whatever painting needs doing, of course, before you move in. Bathroom behind you, there. Master bedroom. Please, please.

(She gestured for them to precede her.) Look around. The blinds are necessary, as you can see there's a lot of sun. Cupboard. This is the smaller bedroom. Immaculate tenant, as you can see. The pine floors are original, yes. Please. Kitchen. Not large, obviously, but *so* clean. David is a lovely man. He's in the diplomatic service, just been posted to Trinidad, I think, or thereabouts.

Yes, Anika said politely.

Now, the living room. This is one of the nicest suites in the building, I think, because of this room. The ocean view, as you can see, and quite spacious too, compared to the bedrooms. You'll be spending a lot of time in here, I imagine.

Yes, Thom said, looking at Anika. I guess we will.

That's settled, then, Phyllis said.

Phyllis will know where to send it on, Anika said now.

It doesn't really look like he wanted it, though, does it? Thom said. It almost looks like he left it behind deliberately. Wrapping it up that way, and hiding it the way he did.

They spent some time trying to construct a personality out of the furnishings they had seen when they first walked through the apartment – Gabbeh rugs, spare teak furniture, Naipaul novels on the shelves. A large bureau dominated the smaller bedroom (art deco, Anika thought, coveting it), and a single black and white photograph of a nude male torso graced the fridge.

Gay, Thom suggested, and she shrugged, not disagreeing. There was a large gay population in the West end. Early for their appointment, they had stopped in to a busy coffee shop two blocks away, only belatedly realizing that the other customers were all male, and Anika was drawing wry half-smiles. It had been excellent coffee.

Not poor either, Anika suggested now. I guess diplomats do all right.

Maybe the drugs are inside, Thom said, peering at the metronome's base.

Anika smiled, half at their own tired furniture on these honeyed floors, half at Thom's doggedness when he found an idea he liked.

You have that little screwdriver for your glasses, he said.

She fetched it from its sleeve in the silk lining of her glasses' case, but when he got the back off there was no cache of pills or baggie of white powder, only the machine's tiny mechanism, shiny and oiled and apparently in order.

I give up, Thom said.

That evening they took it down the hall to Phyllis's apartment and explained where they had found it.

No, he didn't leave a forwarding address, I'm afraid, she said. She tapped a wrinkled finger against her lips and turned the metronome over in the light of a table lamp. Blueness came and went in the dark wood like an illusion, or a bruise.

It's pretty, isn't it, Phyllis said finally. Very David. He collected antiques, as you saw. Exquisite taste, he had. Only the best.

It's broken, though, Anika said.

Drugs, maybe? the older woman suggested, with no hint of excitement or the least loss of poise. Thom punched Anika lightly in the arm.

We thought of that, Anika said gravely. Thom unscrewed the back but there was nothing inside.

No, I wouldn't have thought it of him, Phyllis said. David was a decent, hard-working man. But you never know. Taped to the pipes, you say.

Taped to the pipes, Thom said. Would you like it?

Oh, I've no room for more clutter, she said brightly, fluttering her hands at forty years' of possessions – books and tables and lamps and chairs and embroidered cushions and potpourri pots and china and plants – her two-bedroom layout the distorted mirror image of their own. You keep it, she said. It's a pretty thing.

She knows we don't have many pretty things, Anika said that night. They lay in bed, wide awake, adjusting to the traffic noises, not overly invasive, and the unfamiliar quality of the darkness.

Yet, Thom said. (This was a fixture of their conversations, as window shopping was a fixture of their weekends.)

He adjusted a pillow between his shoulder and her head and pulled her legs between his. They had not lain this way, just awake and talking, Anika thought, in a long time.

It's like he wanted us to find it, Thom said. Let's keep it, for a while anyway. Maybe get it appraised.

David, Anika said experimentally, as though the feel of the name in her mouth might yield a clue.

David, Thom repeated.

⊰◆⊱

David had stepped into a little shop in the Village, musical antiquities, and was standing before a locked glass case of metronomes when he heard a voice behind him say, Are you a Jew? Because I will only sell to a Jew.

David turned and said, Are *you* a Jew?

No.

Then what's wrong with them?

The woman was in her fifties, probably, with fashionable clothes (tight pants, blue leather jacket, scarf of some mottled, bronze, filmy stuff) and hair (Roman emperor), dramatically plucked brows, a deep slash of a mouth, and a harsh, guttural accent.

You have every right to ask me that, she said. Nothing is wrong with them. And I am somewhat melodramatic. It depends on the piece. You like this one?

She selected a key from the ring on her belt, unlocked the cabinet, and withdrew a tall, pear-shaped wooden metronome with a lovely symmetrical grain on either side, on an elaborately carved scrollwork base.

Eighteen thirty-six, Vienna, she said. Twenty-five thousand. Maelzel. The case is signed on the inside. You could buy this one.

What about the blue one?

Maelzel, she repeated. The inventor of the metronome. Believe me, when I was a girl, I loathed Herr Maelzel.

Piano lessons?

She didn't answer. David could not decide whether he liked her or not; splintery women could go both ways. He watched her wind the metronome, set it down on a nearby table, and let it go.

Hear it speak with its velvety throat, she said, and he decided she was monstrous, and the only possible thing was to enjoy her enormously. The tock was rich and round (definitely not a tick), evoking a lost world of stone and wood and firelight and horses and cream. But it was not James, somehow, and like a vessel he was filled, this trip, with thoughts of James, and returning home to James. He needed something leaner, more astringent, elegant but a bit stark and forbidding, too.

What about the blue one? David said.

The woman had apparently taken a liking to him, and began to show him around her store. The carpets were dark red, and the walls – turquoise – were hung with instruments on nails: lustrous horns he did and didn't recognize, strangely tortured shapes, flutes straight and curling, a family of saxophones and another of strings, a bitty inlaid guitar. A grand piano, a Steinway, was clearly queen of the room, but there were also a harpsichord, a daintier clavichord, and the sheer, tempting sheen of a gong. In glass cabinets built in around a cold fireplace he counted fifty metronomes, coffin and pear. The bookcases held hundreds of scores. She walked around touching lamps, casting spoons of light and shadows onto the walls. All these gypsy colours and noise-makers, David thought: is this what it's like inside her head?

Now this, she said, taking down a score and opening it for his perusal. His mouth quirked briefly as he bit down a smile. He was a little afraid, in his laughing way, to confess to her he couldn't read music.

First edition? he asked politely.

She laughed, and showed him the cover – torn, chartreuse and cream, with enormous fading letters in an almost illegibly ornate gothic type. German.

Bach, she said. *Die Kunst der Fuge.*

So she is German, David thought.

She opened to the title page and pointed to a signature, also illegible.

Artur Rubinstein, she read.

She flipped through the pages, stopping every now and then to draw his attention to pen marks on the score.

Annotated, she said.

Valuable?

Clearly not to you.

She closed the score and put it back on the shelf.

I was just looking for a gift, he said. For a friend.

A musician?

No.

Bravo, she said, and he turned to leave.

But where are you going? she said. All day long, musicians. Their big scarves, their little gloves. So respectful, so knowledgeable. May I confess to you my horror of musicians? Of students? They like to carry their instruments on their backs. The tips of their noses are always pink, like mice. They like to buy my scores. They like to stand in my store and stroke the pages. They think they can catch talent like the clap, though even the most talented of them has no talent. Even their arrogance is false. They carry water bottles like athletes, they grow their hair long to suggest untameable passions, they practise until their fingers bleed, they close their eyes when they perform. We live in the culture of the orgasm, the pursuit of the orgasm. The Juilliard School, Carnegie Hall, the Tchaikovsky competition, these are the orgasms they strain and strain to achieve. Their teachers are no better, they are old panders, merely. What I say is nothing new. The true artist venerates nothing. I tell you, I despise them all.

What about the blue one? David said.

Are you a Jew?

He decided the woman's business must be failing, and she was probably deranged.

Why do you keep asking me that? he said, genuinely curious.

I owe the world a moral debt, the woman said. We all do, of course, but mine is bigger than most. It is not a debt I can pay in cash. I cannot write a cheque to this organization and that organization and then I am free. I must *live* in the right way. You understand the difference between spending and living?

I hope so, David said, genuinely again, though she might well have meant to insult.

I will explain why I keep asking you this question, she said. But it is a long story. If I make some tea, you will have some?

I'd love some tea, David said.

In the back of the store, through an archway, was a sitting
room with a couple of velvet chairs, a settee, and tea things on a
low table. Here too were a desk, a laptop computer, and the
props of a business, ledgers and files and pigeonholes of invoices.
One corner was stacked floor to ceiling with boxes of various
shapes and sizes.

My business is quite complex, she said, returning – from
what he guessed was a bathroom, in a cupboard behind a bead
curtain – with an electric kettle. She set it on the table and
plugged it into the surge protector that also served the computer. Delicate, she continued, and not always strictly legal. Aha,
I have interested you. You think, she speaks so highly and might-
ily of morals, yet she deals in stolen property?

Goodness, David said agreeably, taking one of the lemon
cookies that she, in a nice Bohemian gesture, offered in the
paper drawer they had come boxed in rather than on a plate. He
wondered if they learned this sort of thing at finishing school,
when to *stop*. He wondered why he suspected her of having
attended a finishing school. She poured the tea, Earl Grey, and
answered the unspoken question in what she said next.

Her name was Ulrike Weber, and she was born in Tübingen,
a famous old university town in southwestern Germany, a couple
of years after the end of the war. Her mother was gentle and
calm, clean and pious, a thrifty woman who loved Schiller
and Christmas and attended free lectures at the *Musikverein* with
her friends. Her father she knew as a formal, distant man who
worked long hours at the University (he lectured in medieval
history), yet with a streak of indulgent silliness he reserved just
for her. She was an only child, and for her first decade or so
a good girl, the best – quiet, studious, affectionate, obedient, a
little dreamy. (Milk? she offered, proffering a china jug, and
when he declined she let three drops fall in her cup, three

twirling ribbons in the clear liquid.) The three of them lived in a two-bedroom apartment, a little small, perhaps, but filled with nice things: comfortable chairs and books and a tiny fireplace with a blue-tiled hearth that was her special place to sit. There were a few *objets d'art*, too – an ancient Greek clay wine-cup, a couple of icons, an empty, iridescent perfume bottle, the blue metronome – pretty things that were put away when guests came to visit because, as her mother explained, it would be sad to see them handled casually, and broken.

One day in her early teens (the century's early sixties), a truck stopped in the narrow street in front of their apartment, and a piano was winched up on a crane and gently swung through the empty window frame (a glazier had been called the day before), to alight in the middle of their front room. From that day on her relationship with her parents began to deteriorate. Her mother, it turned out, had ambitions. A teacher was found, and Ulrike began the arduous business of mastering an instrument for which she had little natural affection and no aptitude whatso-ever. She managed to muscle through her first couple of years on sheer determination; progressed, in fact, at a speed that was not unusual given that most beginners were a half or even a third her age, but that her teacher and mother misinterpreted as talent. But by her third year she had had enough. Mother sat in her chair, daughter sat on her bench, score sat on its ledge, and metronome sat queen of all, reproving an increasingly rebellious Ulrike with her sternly waving finger and strict regulation of every moment's action and thought.

I won't! Ulrike said, flinging the score to the floor because she dared not touch the blue metronome itself, once so precious and delightful.

You will, her mother said, picking up the score and replacing it in front of her, while the metronome made dispassionate comment on the seconds and minutes and hours and days and months and years they had spent trapped, together, in these newly hateful little rooms. When her father returned home from the University he, too, offered stern reproof.

Your mother and I have discussed your music studies, and it breaks her heart that you are so opposed, he said. You have become argumentative, unpleasant, and disobedient, even violent, your mother tells me. You need discipline. Music lessons – lucky girl! If all men had the opportunity to learn discipline through music lessons!

Now, Ulrike had never had many friends; had not needed them, as close as she was to her parents. But as the hateful lessons dragged on and the mood in the house turned from grey to black, she began to pay closer attention to the outside world. Her schoolmates, she saw, were all fighting their own wars of attrition with their own implacable, tyrannical elders; but instead of giving in, they had found an unthinkably obvious way of shifting power.

Papa, Ulrike said one suppertime, after a particularly brutal session that afternoon had left both her and her mother tense and pale, where were you during the war?

You know I was in Berlin, her father said.

What did you do?

You know that too, her father said pleasantly. I worked as a translator. I translated the London papers, and other English and American propaganda. Sometimes I transcribed radio broadcasts.

From his war work conversation turned naturally to an upcoming language conference at the University where he would be giving a paper, but Ulrike nevertheless suspected she had touched a tender place. After supper, cleaning dishes in the kitchen, her mother reminded her of her father's favourite boast: in six years of service he had never carried a gun.

The next night she tried again.

Are we rich? she asked.

Her parents exchanged a glance she could not read.

We are comfortable, I think, her father said.

But are we rich?

Enough, her mother said. Eat your supper.

But her father saw what was in her face.

Where are you going, Ulrike? he said.

We have so many nice things, she said. The icons and the – the metronome. I wondered where they came from.

Nonsense, her mother said.

I bought them, her father said.

Where?

In Berlin.

Her mother set down her cutlery, though her plate was still half full.

During the war?

During the war.

Who did you buy them from?

A collector, her father said.

A Jew?

Not in my house, her mother said, rapping her knuckles on the table. I will not have this in my house.

Her father shook his head. His smile was cold and thin.

In every house, my dear, he corrected her. It was inevitable. Why not in ours too?

And was the collector a Jew? David asked the woman in the shop in Greenwich Village, for she had stopped speaking and was staring at the air in front of her.

Oh, yes, she said, rousing herself. Yes, of course. How could my father have afforded such expensive things otherwise? He was a Corporal during the war, never more than that.

They sat for a while in silence, then, as darkness fell, outside and inside the shop too. The tea was long cold. After a while David got up to turn the sign on the door from Open to Closed. Then he sat down again, and waited for the woman to continue.

I thought that was all I would get from him, she said. Her face was lost in shadow, but her voice, in the crowded backroom, seemed especially intimate and near. My parents' faces were so terrible that night, I could not bring myself to take the next step, the step I had planned, which was to blackmail them into letting me quit piano. Can you imagine? That was all that had been filling my head. But when I saw their faces I could not bring myself to do such a trivial thing. I felt guilt, the famous German guilt, and I said nothing more. I even practised harder than ever, though my mother no longer supervised me. When I came home from school she would disappear into the kitchen, to avoid me.

The next weekend my father asked me to accompany him on one of his country walks. I had taken great pleasure in those Sunday hikes when I was younger, long hours of my father's undivided attention, but in the last couple of years I had avoided them to punish him for my musical studies, and he had long since stopped inviting me. This time, however, he asked me quite formally, out of my mother's hearing, and something told me not to decline.

David waited again through a long silence. In the darkness he could smell that she had lit a cigarette.

There was more to it, of course, she said. He thought I would forgive him once I had the full picture. I will tell you the story as he told it to me, and when I am done you will tell me if I was not justified in doing what I did next.

⊰◈⊱

In the year 1932, in the city of Berlin, Hannah Goldberg fell into love and riches, goods that forced her out of herself like an orange hull thumbed concave, forcing out the fruit. She was seventeen, serious, not shy but cautious, a listener rather than a talker. She had been playing the cello since she was seven – a scaled-down child's model first, later the sumptuous old Italian instrument her father bought her when it became clear she had both the passion and the gift for a career. A series of competition wins yielded the riches: a promised concerto performance with an orchestra (which fell through for mysterious reasons but did not disappoint her terribly, as she intended to debut memorably and knew she was not quite ready) and, more importantly, a scholarship to the Conservatory for the following fall, when she would turn eighteen. It was winter now, not quite Christmas. The scholarship was not strictly necessary – her father would willingly have paid her way to the Conservatory and anywhere else she might have wanted to go – but she was pleased to be able to contribute, finally, to what she knew had been a very expensive education.

A change of teacher yielded love.

But why? she asked Herr Jacoby, who had taught her since she was a child. He was by now more than a teacher, more like a beloved uncle, who ate with the family on her lesson days (two or three times a week) and stayed in one of the guest rooms if the night was particularly cold or wet, or if there was any rowdiness in the streets. There he would be at the breakfast table the next morning, in one of her father's silk robes, lifting his coffee with a shaky hand and beaming at Hannah with rheumy eyes.

This particular afternoon found them, as usual, in the music salon, a long, carpeted room with a concert Steinway and tall windows overlooking the garden, sitting opposite each other with their instruments.

I should have insisted before now, Herr Jacoby said. I've been selfish, *Liebling*, keeping you to myself for so long. From every teacher you learn something new, something valuable. You mustn't allow your teachers' limitations to become your own. At the Conservatory you'll be exposed to many new influences, and you'll face so many – challenges. I thought, a little bridge from here to there, a little preparation, so you'll be ready to adapt when the time comes. I'm explaining badly, he added, seeing her face.

Hannah understands, her mother said. (It was her practice to sit in on the lessons, silent and invisible in one of the big stuffed chairs at the far end of the room. She said the music soothed her headaches, which were increasingly frequent and debilitating.)

There's a young man I know, Herr Jacoby said. From the symphony. His name is Herr Bernhardt, and he's agreed to take you on.

Did he study at the Conservatory? Hannah asked.

In Vienna, Herr Jacoby said, looking at her mother.

Vienna! her mother said. See, Hannah.

Is he strict?

Strictness, of course, did not bother Hannah at all – she worked hard and well and had nothing to fear from other people's standards, which were never higher than her own. But she feared for Herr Jacoby and what would become of him when he no longer had an excuse to come to their house, no longer had a favourite student to look forward to. Hannah wondered, indeed, if she was not his only student, for whenever her mother sent him a note he would come right away, and always on foot, never in a taxi. She wondered if none of this had occurred to her parents, or if perhaps they had made other arrangements. Her father was always making arrangements for people, the servants, employees at the store, even vagrants on the street.

Yes, I believe he is quite strict, Herr Jacoby said. If Monday afternoon suits you, Frau Goldberg?

Hannah will be at home on Monday, her mother said.

After tea she and her mother and younger brother (Paul, fifteen) sat by the fire playing desultory hands of cards, while outside it turned cold and luminous, an odd light, threatening snow.

How's that moustache coming? she asked her brother.

Paul ignored her. He had decided, these past few months, he was a man of the world in a family of dreamers, and had taken to reading the papers in the morning and economic philosophy at night, and cultivating a heavy down on his upper lip. Now he was angry about Herr Jacoby, and had said at least three times in the last hour that they were "throwing him to the dogs."

Maybe we could persuade him to start your lessons again, Hannah said gravely. One month when you were twelve was not much of a try. I think you have matured a lot since then, anyway.

She heard her mother sniff delicately, trying not to smile.

Music is for women, Paul said, making them both laugh out loud. He frowned ferociously.

Schätzlein, Hannah said, leaning over to kiss him, but he squirmed away, upsetting the cards. The maid came in.

Please, she said. The tree is here.

The Goldbergs went to the entrance hall, where three delivery men were erecting an immense fir tree by the staircase.

Two hours late, her mother murmured. And it's dry. Look, you can see the needles falling already.

It's fine, Hannah said.

Getting ready for Christmas, are we? one of the delivery men called, glancing at them over his shoulder.

Her brother disappeared back into the depths of the house.

Her mother pressed some money into her hand and followed him, massaging her temples and calling for the maid to bring some vinegar.

When they presented her with the bill it was half as much again as what her mother had arranged on the phone, but Hannah merely smiled and paid and watched them go. It was how her parents had taught her to deal with problems, always to smile, never to argue or insist or show any discomposure.

The maid returned and asked if she should bring up the decorations.

It's nice, isn't it? Hannah said. Maybe we can get it done before my father gets home.

It's dry, the maid said. Look at the needles all over the floor. I'm afraid they've cheated you.

No, no. It doesn't matter, Hannah said. We'll make it nice.

By the time her father's car pulled up, at six-thirty, they had hung the tree with glass balls and wooden deer and stars, and soldiers in red felt uniforms with shiny black boots and gold sequins for buttons.

Isn't that pretty, he said, taking her hand, and together they turned their backs to it and walked into the house, while the maid collected the last of the empty ornament boxes and swept a few stray sprays of tinsel from the floor.

By Monday afternoon the house had also acquired a wreath on the front door, paper snowflakes on the windows, and numerous candles set in nests of holly cut from the garden on mantles and in front of mirrors. Hannah sat in the music room, playing a few velvety scales on her cello, waiting for her new teacher. Her mother sat in her accustomed chair with sheaves of white paper, a pair of sharp scissors, and a few more finished snowflakes in a basket at her feet. Distantly they heard the doorbell and the approaching commotion of footsteps.

He's late, Hannah said, setting down her bow.

Hush, her mother said. He probably just had trouble finding the house.

Herr Bernhardt, the maid announced.

A tall young man with a shockingly battered cello case stood in the doorway, surveying the room thoroughly before turning his gaze to the women. He wore a tweed jacket and grey flannel trousers, baggy at the knees. His blond hair showed the plough-marks of a fine-tooth comb.

Herr Bernhardt, we are honoured, Hannah's mother said. Herr Jacoby spoke so highly of you. I'm afraid perhaps you had some trouble finding the house?

None at all, the man said.

Hannah stood to introduce herself. He advanced into the room to shake her hand. His grip was dry and gentle, even soft. Close up, she saw his eyes were grey.

Is that yours? he asked, meaning her instrument.

Next he shook hands with her mother, and then he asked her to leave the room.

My mother generally stays, Hannah said.

The new teacher said nothing, only smiled and remained motionless until her mother slowly rose, gathering the basket and bits and pieces from her feet, and excused herself with a tremulous, formal bow.

You will stay to tea, afterwards, I hope, Herr Bernhardt? she asked from the doorway.

Perhaps.

For the first half hour the lesson progressed almost word-lessly, as Herr Bernhardt put Hannah through her paces, asking for exercises and slowly circling her while she played. He did not remove his own instrument from its case, though he would occasionally play a brief figure on the piano to show her what he wanted. Once or twice she felt the circumference of his circle round her widen as he examined the room itself, bookshelves of scores, her childhood cello, Paul's violin (of the single month's acquaintance), the metronomes (she had three), and all the accoutrements of her art: rosin, cloths, music stands, a spare bow, and so on.

You're quite the thoroughbred, aren't you? he said finally.

She stopped playing.

You're good, he added negligently. Not quite as good as Jacoby would have it, but that's hardly a surprise. You know I keep a studio in Kreuzberg?

Hannah did not know.

I generally teach from there. Your mother was quite insistent, however, that you should take your lessons at home. Why was that?

My mother doesn't like to go out, Hannah said. She's happiest when we are all at home, together. She likes to know where we are at all times.

How gruesome.

She shrugged.

I can see that for a man it might be so, she said, thinking of her brother.

She saw he had pulled a few scores from the shelves and laid them open.

You will learn these for next time, please, he said.

Bach, mostly. She realized she did not like him well enough to confess she had already been playing most of the pieces for years.

Goldberg, eh? he said at the end of the hour, as she was putting her instrument away. She had reiterated her mother's invitation to tea and he had accepted with an ironic bow and a bitter rind of a smile. Goldberg, he repeated. Any relation?

There are Goldbergs in Bremen and in London, she said, not sure what he meant. Cousins of ours.

He laughed, and played on the piano a famous phrase, the opening of Bach's Goldberg Variations.

Oh, that! she said, laughing with a relief she could not have explained. My father says yes, in fact. You know the story, the count with insomnia who commissioned the variations to be played to him in bed, to help him sleep. Goldberg was the count's musician, who had been a student of Bach's. It was he who asked his old teacher to write something for his patron. My father says he is the great-grandnephew of the Goldberg who was Bach's student. I never quite believed him, though. I always thought he told the story to humour me, and make me feel special. Even when I was a little girl I thought that, I'm not sure why.

Herr Bernhardt was watching her with a curious fixed expression.

It could be true, though, she added. I would like for it to be true.

So it talks after all, the little Goldberg, he said, this time with a smile that reached his eyes.

They took tea in the sitting room, she and her mother and the new teacher, with her brother and his English tutor, Herr Asbury. Accordingly, they spoke mostly English, though Herr Bernhardt's competence in the language was feeble. He offered little in any tongue, in fact, except to refuse plates of bread and cheese and cold meat and pickles. In the end he accepted only a cup of tea and a single jam tart. Hannah felt obscurely ashamed, as though she were somehow responsible for him and his odd behaviour.

After tea, after Herr Bernhardt had been paid and left, she and her mother returned to the music room so she could practise.

It's up to you, her mother said. But I didn't like him at all. He was – well, impudent sounds such a trivial word, but I want to say impudent. Not rude outright, but –

I know, Hannah said quickly.

Her mother opened her eyes and sat up straight.

He wasn't rude to you, was he? she asked. During your lesson? Because that I won't tolerate for a minute. I didn't like leaving you alone with him, I didn't like that at all. Shall we ask Herr Jacoby to find someone else? I'm sure he must know many qualified teachers. Berlin is such a musical city. He can't be the best, can he, with those trousers?

Hannah pictured the trousers and the hair and the eyes and the queer changeable temper of the man. Also, he had slighted her playing, something she was not used to at all.

Perhaps we should give him a chance, she said. I mean, wouldn't Herr Jacoby be offended if we didn't trust his judgment for at least a month or two, after all these years?

Herr Bernhardt was twenty-five minutes late for her second lesson. Fortunately it was one of her mother's bad days, and she was not present to witness this impertinence. Neither were Paul and Herr Asbury, who had gone to the Pergamonmuseum for the afternoon.

You play like a child, he told her.

He worked her harder than she had ever worked in her life, and deep down, in the part of her mind that was still cool, she wondered if he was trying to bring her to tears. She realized, too, that Herr Jacoby had never worked her as hard; indeed, these last few months, he had not worked her at all, only let her play and play while he smiled and nodded. She felt a spasm of irritation at Herr Jacoby.

Again, Herr Bernhardt said. Again. My God. I suppose those metronomes are ornamental?

No, Hannah said. They all work.

Then why do you not use them? he asked, in apparently genuine anguish. It's Bach, not Chopin. Why do you play in that disgusting mincing way? Why do you move your body so much, and take so many liberties? You think you're being emotional? Your emotions interest no one. Not me, not your audience. Your mother, perhaps. Where is she today?

In bed, Hannah said. She has *migraine*.

She seems sickly, Herr Bernhardt said. He sat down in the chair opposite her for the first time and began to open his case. Yes, yes, he added, seeing her uncertainty. Take a rest.

She set her bow on her music stand and watched him remove his cello.

Yours is nicer than mine, isn't it? he said, with the smile she disliked. She said nothing.

Watch, he said, and began to play.

Discipline, he said, when he was done. Purity, precision. You lack all these things. Not surprising, really.

Really, she whispered.

The same teacher all your life, I mean.

You don't play with the symphony, do you?

Herr Bernhardt laughed.

Is that what Jacoby told you? he said. No, I don't play with them any more. Jacoby may not exactly know that. How is he, anyway? Do you see him still?

My father visits him, she said, hoping this was true.

Tell me, he said at the end of the hour, as she rang for the maid to see him out. I see all these Christmas decorations. Which holiday does your family celebrate?

A moment, then, a ripple across the clear surface of things.

We celebrate all the holidays, Herr Bernhardt, Hannah said.

That evening at supper her father asked how she was getting on with her new teacher.

Your mother seems to find him a little rough around the edges, he said, when she hesitated.

He plays beautifully.

She found she was thirsty, and drank from her water glass until Paul laughed.

Hannah's in love, he said.

Stupid, she said, setting her glass down with absolute composure, and her father smiled.

He's scruffy and a snot, Paul said. He pulled himself up tall in his chair, waved at a dish of peas, and said in lisping English, No sank you. No sank you.

Strongly influenced by Herr Asbury, her brother had adopted dandyism with his politics, and had once informed Hannah in a voice of languorous boredom that poorly cut trousers gave him pain.

You only dislike him because he's poor, she said now. You're afraid he might contaminate you with his poverty.

Hannah, her father said, sharply for him.

He shouldn't be poor, if he works for the symphony, her brother said.

Both of you, her father said, with a rare strain in his voice.

Brother and sister looked at each other, and between them quickly turned the conversation to Paul's visit to the museum.

At the end of the meal Hannah took a tray up to her mother's room.

Is that my soup? she asked from her bed.

Hannah helped her sit up. Her face was haggard, her eyes sunken with pain.

Well, this was a silly day, she said. I'll be much better tomorrow.

But after a few mouthfuls of consommé she said the weight of the tray was too much, and she had no particular appetite anyway.

It's all right, she said, seeing the worry in Hannah's face. The doctor came today, while you were having your lesson. He said not to worry about the loss of appetite so long as I keep taking fluids. He said the body tells one what it needs. If I were to crave grapes, for instance, or quail.

Her eyes drifted closed.

And do you? Hannah asked.

Her mother opened her eyes again, with obvious difficulty.

Crave grapes, Hannah said.

Downstairs, in her father's study, she asked him what was wrong.

Worry, he said simply. There is nothing physically wrong with her, the doctor says. The headaches, of course, but he says those could be cured with fresh air and relaxation. She must get out more, but she gets so anxious, and then the pain comes.

They sat in immense leather wingback chairs before the pleasantly cracking fire, her father sipping his whisky and soda. Earlier he had touched a match to a crumpled newspaper and the fire had opened up like a mouth while they talked of the department store he owned, his pressures and successes there. Hannah knew if her mother were feeling better it would be the older woman sitting in her place, while she played chess with her brother in the nursery upstairs, or squeezed in a last half-hour of practice before bed. She flexed her bow hand a few times, unthinkingly.

Molehills are mountains for your mother right now, her father said. Will he do, this new teacher?

Hannah nodded.

Perhaps, then, let it stay at that. Your mother doesn't need every detail. The less worry the better, you see what I mean.

The fire snapped and bit at the air.

I see, Hannah said.

So her mother did not hear about Herr Bernhardt's chronic lateness, nor about his displeasure with every aspect of her playing, his sarcasm, or his almost anthropological interest in her family (did they observe the Sabbath, did they keep kosher, had Paul had his bar mitzvah, and so on). When she, emboldened, tried to respond in kind by asking unexpected questions about his training or his career, he replied with bitter, oblique comments about the power of rumour. When she did well he would turn his face away so she would not see it soften. And when, one Monday in February, he did not show up for her lesson at all, her mother did not hear about Hannah's frantic, inexplicable tears.

There were other troubles in the household by then. Herr Asbury, disgusted (he claimed) by the recent elections, had given his notice and was preparing to return to England. Paul, who for all his fashionable clothes and self-confidence had few friends, was despondent. Privately he confessed to Hannah his fear of becoming a prisoner in the house ("like you"). Their mother had trusted Herr Asbury, but he suspected she would not trust his next tutor as far. It was not a trusting season.

He's invited me to come visit him, though, he said, brightening a little. He says I may stay as long as I like. I know he had a long talk with Papa about it, too.

Papa will let you go, I'm sure, she said. In fact, their father had grown so distracted by work, lately, she knew he would have consented to just about anything that spared him tension at home. Nervously she traced a crease in the lap of her skirt, over and over, a line and a loop: P, for Peter. She had seen it on the calling card wedged in the lining of his cello case, and his address too, the week after his unmentioned absence.

Then, in the spring, just as the first blur of life was appearing in the naked branches of the linden and her mother had begun to come downstairs for meals again, calamity. One Saturday morning her father called the maid into his study.

There is a new law, he explained to Hannah, who had encountered the sobbing maid in the hall ten minutes later and gone to him immediately, indignantly. (Käthe was her own age and the two had grown up together, playing with their dollies in the kitchen while Käthe's mother cooked and gossiped with Hannah's mother.) A Jewish household may no longer employ a single German girl under the age of forty-five as a domestic.

Nonsense, Hannah said. She might even have laughed, a little, in disbelief.

Be quiet, her father said.

By afternoon the house was in deep gloom. Paul had locked himself in his bedroom with the previous day's papers and would not come out. Her mother had suffered a relapse and returned to her bed. Käthe was already gone, and her father had already spent two hours on the telephone trying to find a suitable, legal replacement. Hannah sat in the music room with her Bach and her metronome, willing herself to practise. Her father found her there, still silent, at tea time.

You like the most stylish one, he said, sitting beside her and gesturing at the metronome. Like your mother.

She's been vomiting, Hannah said in a low voice.

Her father took the bow from her hand and laid it carefully across the music stand. He pulled his chair as close to hers as he could and awkwardly put his arm around her. She laid her head on his shoulder.

You would not believe the difference, he said. You would not believe the girl she was when she was young, so carefree, always laughing. She was a musician too. When I met her she was mad about the piano. This little fellow –

He picked up the metronome.

This was my first gift to her. Have I ever told you that story?

No, Hannah said, a lie. She knew the story well enough. But so consumed was she with the whirling, shameful troubles of the house – the loss of the maid, her brother's palpable fear, her mother's illness, Herr Bernhardt's constant abuse, and above all, the despair of the intervening hours and days until she would see Herr Bernhardt again – that she didn't mind letting her father talk, as a way of filling that void.

❖

May 10, 1915

Dear Mr. Newbery,

It is now my extremely unpleasant duty to write to you about the events of yesterday evening, events which it appears shall pre-cipitate our departure from Walberswick. I feel it is my obligation to inform you first, as it was your great kindness and hospitality that brought us to Suffolk, and until this last day or so had been such a refuge for us from our troubles at home. I would not like to think of you hearing of these events from some other source.

As you know, Margaret and I had intended to stay on at the Millside house instead of returning to Glasgow. We found much that was congenial here – the house, the beach studio, our friendships with other visiting artists, and the easy acceptance (we thought) of the local people – and so much to avoid at home – a grim, provincial city, a lack of commissions, even an outright hostility to my own work especially that wounded me deeply, as you know. If Glasgow found us bizarre, queer, deca-dent, and long past fashion, well then, we thought, Walberswick was for us, so be it. We were so pleased to accept your invitation to share the house at Millside last summer, and (I confess it now) enormously relieved when, returning to Glasgow yourselves, you so kindly permitted us to stay on for the winter. Glasgow does feel less and less like home.

I am writing to you now from a jail cell in the Walberswick police station, where I am being kept overnight, like a rowdy. The charge, I fear, is in fact far more serious, though the absurdity of it would make one laugh, were one able to watch from the distance of the stars. They have been kind enough to provide me with a little chair and table, at any rate, and have permitted me to write letters to pass the time. Sleep is out of the question.

Last night, as is our custom, Margaret and I took a stroll around the village. Returning to Millside at around half past seven, we were stopped by a soldier with a bayonet fixed at the gate, and informed that military police were searching our rooms. Finding some letters with German and Austrian postmarks – from a Viennese architect inviting me to work with him in that city, a possible commission from Berlin, a German publisher interested in a book of watercolours, and so on – they accused me of being a German spy and took me into custody. One of the constables who knows me from the Anchor let slip that my habit of walking at night and my "strange" Highland accent raised suspicions with some of the locals, and thus was I "tipped off" to the authorities.

My work has always been more accepted on the Continent than at home; indeed, were it not for the present war, I dare say I would have more work in Germany than a man could comfortably handle in a lifetime. Yet my contacts and connections with that country have always been of an artistic nature, and anyone who knows me knows there never lived a stauncher Scottish patriot. On top of all the indignities I have suffered these past few years, this disgrace truly is more than I can bear. I am resolved to take my case to the House of Lords just as soon as I am able, to clear my good name.

Meanwhile, I am told I will be forbidden to live in Norfolk, Suffolk, Cambridge, or anywhere along the coast, near main roads, or railway lines. I cannot now see us returning to Glasgow, or rather I can see our reception there all too clearly, and have no appetite for it at all. That leaves London.

I hope what I have written here will not cause you to doubt for a moment our gratitude for all your many kindnesses and your hospitality. Margaret and I have no regrets about coming to Walberswick; I only wish we were leaving under happier circumstances. Please accept, too, my apologies for any future embarrassment you may suffer in the village as a result of my having been a guest in your house at the time of these unfortunate events.

> Yours very sincerely,
> Chas. R. Mackintosh

May 10, 1915

My dear Margaret,

I am compelled to write to you, though I imagine you will never read this, or if you do, it will be with me at your elbow reading over your dear shoulder, apologizing for the anger, the haste, the untidiness, the bitterness of this screed. I imagine a warm fire in the grate, the tea on its tray, and our bags packed and waiting, in the downstairs hall, for the morning train. We must leave, we will leave, we will start again in London, that is if you think that you can work there; for I have said before and I say again that I have talent, but you have genius, and it is your work, above all, that matters.

Your face, my dearest, when the soldier met us at the gate last night (only last night! it seems years ago now), when he put his hand on my arm and we realized he would not let it go; your face

when I stumbled and had to ask him to slow down on account of
my limp: eyes like jewels and hair like embers. No, my dear,
don't be afraid. Remember we had just spoken of the garden,
and the warmth of the nights now, and of our watercolours?
Remember we had just decided to look for forget-me-nots to
paint in the morning, and how you thought you had seen a
cluster near Mrs. Thomson's house? The soldier thought I had
been too long at the Anchor, but you know my dear that was not
true, not last night at any rate. They have all seen "Old Mac"
about the village often enough to know my gait. That soldier
was young and himself intoxicated, I think, with his own
uniform and important business, there at our garden gate. He
reminded me of the students at the College now, so young and
proud and pleased to dismiss their elders like flies from the feast
table, to show them their own irrelevance.

Now you will say I am moaning, and you are right, it does not
suit a grown man. But, Margaret, have we not suffered a little,
we two? Have we not seen our work ignored, where once we
were respected; have we not gone from comfort and success to
this exile's life, forced to be grateful for what crumbs of work
still come our way? And you, my dear, have you not suffered
even further in putting up with my melancholies and my noc-
turnal ramblings always ending at one of two places, places you
know all too well though you have never set foot inside either?
Ah, Margaret, let us moan a little, just this once, and get it off
our chests.

When I was a young man I lived a kind of double life, a day-
life at the architectural firm and a night-life at the art college,
and my greatest dream was to reconcile the two, the straight
line and the curved, the leaf and the bloom. Now it seems I am
cast in that role again: puttering old flower painter in a deerstalker
muttering over his pint, and German spy, as swift and stealthy

and deadly by night as I am lame and harmless by day. There's a frightful flower from an unlikely seed, wouldn't you agree?

One cannot of course control how one is seen by others. One can never in fact hope to control the totality of anything; I think that has been one of the greatest disappointments of my life. I never desired to be an architect, or a painter, or a designer of fabrics or furnishings, but rather some grand embodiment of all these, creating houses whole with a new way of living already complete inside them. Perhaps I am not so very far off the level, as far as the Germans are concerned, now that I see the words written, for the Germans are a people who admire discipline and control, and can be as inflexible in their way as is a certain Scot in his. No, don't chide me, I am not all straight in my head tonight and am mixing ideas like colours on a palette, though my hand is clumsy and everything comes out a muddy kind of grey. They have me in a cell, Margaret, a room of such unremitting dreariness I think even you and I together could not salvage it. I spent some moments trying, if you can believe it, the first minute after they showed me in, my mind not yet caught up to my eye, which raced ahead as is its custom – a frieze rail perhaps, a wheat-coloured rug, a simple square light fixture in one corner, one of your large gesso panels above the cot – but our old accustomed lightness ill suits this gloomy place, and when I caught myself playing with pale colours and spring-like visions I reproved myself sternly, as a schoolmaster might reprove a dreamy pupil, and set about in full consciousness to give the place, in the mind's eye, its due – dark wood panelling, a sombre bare floor, and minimum of ornamentation. None of our old curves and ovals, but something harder and more geometric, balanced, spare, slashing through any pretence of prettiness. A new style, one we shall forge together, for your own eye has ever complemented and perfected my own.

And forge it we shall, because here is news, dear Margaret, news that in its prematurity I had been keeping from you. Amongst those letters on my desk that have caused us such grief tonight was one from a new client, a German businessman, an admirer of the Mackintosh style (his words) who covets (and offers a small fortune for) a trinket with which to woo a young lady. Very well! But the gentleman further lets drop he is heir to a prominent Berlin department store, and that when the store passes into his stewardship he would be honoured to consult us on the refurbishment of the premises, and perhaps on two or three as-yet unbuilt stores, if the German economy should one day prove favourable to an expansion into the suburbs. Of course I have not met the young gentleman, but his letter impressed me, with its mixed modesty and enthusiasm, and I intuit that we would understand one another completely, and he would not seek to dominate or impress upon me his own ideas. Money, he says explicitly, is no object.

As for the trinket, well Margaret it is a metronome. It seems the young lady in question is an amateur musician, a pianist, and the gentleman from Berlin writes feelingly of how the object will mark the time between their visits together, and make that time more bearable by emphasizing its "finity." (His English, have I mentioned, is delightful: very elegant and startled by more rules – each absolutely logical in itself – than have ever, I think, yoked the language before.) Apparently the lady is not unwilling, though the father is dead set against the marriage. It is a matter of religious difference, which is certainly an impediment though not, I think, in these modern times, so great a one as it once was. He is a romantic, I suspect, in that high, hopeless German vein, and I do not like him the less for it. I understand the innards are very like a clockwork's so the construction should be straightforward. For some reason, when I imagine the casing, I keep seeing the Necropolis at the end of Firpark Terrace, where we lived when I was six, with its headstones and monuments and mausolea like little houses, where a small boy could play hide-and-seek for hours. I see the metronome like a little dark house, though I can hear you telling me I am wrong, for love is light and beautiful, not a queer, dark, boxed ticking. It was not so for us, at any rate, was it, my dearest? We always knew how to be together, we matched like right and left, like the palest silk gloves.

It is the needle that fascinates me, the swing of the needle from left to right, from ill to good, from misfortune to fine red-headed luck. We are no longer young, and our own little houses will only ever be for two, yet I feel the pendulum has begun to swing back to us, and we will find a way out of this present unhappiness, to a place of love and work and calm where everything we do shall be the product of two souls so entwined that no one shall know what was yours and what mine; and we shall laugh at the confusion, as we ever have, and never care.

> I am always,
> Your loving
> Toshie

May 10, 1915
Dear Herr Goldberg,
Many thanks for your letter. I have never heard of a lady wooed, let alone won, with a metronome, but the challenge is one that appeals to me very much. So you remember my drawings for the *Deutsche Kunst*, for the House of an Art Lover competition. I think you must have been very young, for they were published in Germany well over a decade ago. I am not averse to attempting a design in that style, as you suggest, though I have moved

on significantly since and would prefer to put some of my more recent ideas into practice. The whites and creams and pale gem colours I favoured at that time would at any rate not suit the project you suggest. The metronome is a symbol, is it not? I was thinking, rather, blue.

The fee you propose is generous; indeed, I could design a flock of metronomes for the sum, and probably persuade them to fly, into the bargain. There remains the small matter of the present war, which I fear might delay delivery of the finished article, but let us cross that bridge when we come to it. Perhaps I shall fletch the object after all, and send it on its way to you independent of all postal systems, checks, borders, customs, stops, searches, suspicions, or prejudices of any kind.

Your letter has given me the greatest pleasure. What higher calling, after all, could art serve, than the pursuit of love? There is nothing like a lady's hesitation to spook a man; believe me, sir, I have served in those trenches myself, and I know. Thus I wish you all happiness and Godspeed in your suit, and will do my all on this side of things to further a victory of the heart. I am,

Yours very sincerely,
Charles Rennie Mackintosh

Herr Professor Gerhard Weber met Daniel Goldberg for the first and last time in the winter of nineteen forty, when brown ice candied the puddles and street corners cut sharp as paper against the cold air. The go-between, a former university colleague who had turned to the black market in antiquarian objects when the race laws cost him his teaching position, had chosen an address in a part of town unfamiliar to Herr Professor Weber. Many of the storefronts were boarded over and scrawled with more and less official graffiti, and on the sidewalk glass crumbs crunched beneath his shoes along with ice. The streets were virtually deserted. He passed a girl in a felt coat with a paper pinned to the lapel who averted her face when he neared, and a pair of men who pulled their hats low, pushed their hands deep in their pockets, and finally crossed the street and disappeared down a narrow alley to avoid any proximity to him. He himself was stopped by a greatcoated soldier who requested, in the charming accents of the Black Forest, his papers, returning them with a polite word or two when he saw that all was in order. The Herr Professor would not have minded chatting a moment with the soldier, who was young and seemed friendly enough and whose accent reminded him of his new wife's, but his breast-pocketful of cash advised caution.

Have one for me, the soldier called after him, and a moment later, in a starburst of wit: Have two! For the Herr Professor had confessed, as instructed, to being on his way to a pub far from his own neighbourhood, where no spy of his wife's would report him. There was probably only a slim wedge of years between himself and the young soldier, but at the mention of a wife he saw the boy's eyes deepen, as if in contemplation of a vast abyss. Deference, envy, awe: a wife! Beer, the Herr Professor guessed, was still his newest friend; women were probably a scuffle and sparkle and a handful of marks in a dim doorway. Wives were still distant as the sun. But he did not seem unhappy, the Herr Professor thought, raising a hand in world-weary benediction as he walked away, playing the role. Barracks life was probably more exciting, for the moment, than whatever the boy had left behind, school or some apprenticeship. The thought was not condescending. The Herr Professor was thankful for the extra start of years that had levered him into a profession, and then this wartime translation work, before the army could fix him up with his own greatcoat and gun. He had loved his studies, loved the arcane logic of medieval law (his area of speciality), loved his sweet, sensible wife and the life they had embarked on together. It was that future life, and an urge to insure it, that had brought him to this neighbourhood with all the cash money he could reasonably muster and an address he had sworn not to write down.

The air, dark blue now, smelled of smoke, rank creamy garbage, and fried potatoes. So there was life hidden in these buildings after all, cautiously cooking in the innermost, windowless rooms. He was glad.

Weber, a voice said from somewhere quite close, though he saw no one.

He had arrived at what had once been a chemist's shop, saw the three numbers inscribed in his memory realized in pale, unvarnished wood on the otherwise lacquered black door, ghostly absences where the ornate ironwork of the original fixtures had probably been pried away for scrap. The windows were nailed over with boards. He closed his eyes in sudden, immense fatigue. The voice spoke again from his feet.

Weber.

He looked down and saw through a grating in the brickwork the face of his former colleague.

I come, he said, and vanished with a jerk. The Herr Professor guessed he had been standing on a chair by the high basement window and had jumped off to scurry away, around and up, through the dark, to the door. He caught the metaphor and reproved himself. His former colleague had specialized in religious architectural history, wrote several books on the building of Gothic cathedrals, and had a particular fondness for gargoyles, which he delighted to sketch. On weekends he would ride his bicycle for miles to remote villages and monasteries,

looking for specimens like some frog-besotted botanist. Also he
had a deep voice and liked Russian caviar.

Quickly, he said, opening the door.

The Herr Professor ascended the three steps to the threshold
and felt another wave of fatigue. His former colleague was
already at the back of the store, a dim impatient figure holding
back a heavy curtain, trying to hurry him through the chaos:
a smell of mildew and char and something cloyingly floral, a
broken perfume bottle, perhaps. Cardboard advertising displays
– lipstick, chocolate, foot powder, tonics – littered the ground
underfoot. An apothecary's counter had been picked clean,
probably before the fire. Broken glass and rags still lay in a
black-white drift of ashes someone had swept to one corner, and
left. The Herr Professor had had time to see that his former colleague's coat was dirty, and he had lost weight.

You weren't followed?

The Herr Professor shrugged.

In the basement his former colleague introduced Herr
Goldberg. They shook hands. The icons, wrapped in oilcloth and
hidden in a butter crate, proved first rate: Saint John Chrysostom
and a gaunt Saint Peter, both looking pinned, afflicted with gilt.

Only the two? the Herr Professor said, feeling inside his coat
for his money.

The older man spread his small hands.

We sold the third last week, he said. I have, if you like –

The Herr Professor shook his head, not wanting to know.

For your wife, Herr Goldberg said, producing a tiny glass
perfume bottle, clear, yet with a pink and blue gasoline sheen.
The Herr Professor thought of his wife, of her fine hair and large
hands, and the way she shaped the pillows, warm and plump as
loaves on the bed each night. He had had to leave her behind, in

Tübingen, when war duty called him to Berlin. He had not seen her in some months.

Not expensive, the older man whispered.

There was a clay wine-cup, too, and a metronome by a famous designer. The Herr Professor began to bargain zestily, as if in a fever-dream, to drown out the voice of his conscience. There was a story he remembered from childhood, something about a boy in a chocolate shop, who glutted himself and ended poorly. His former colleague, who had resumed his watchful post on the chair by the high grated window, glanced back over his shoulder from time to time. The deep shadows near the ceiling seemed to cast his features in grimaces of leering approval, or disgust, or both.

How many of you are there? the Herr Professor asked finally.

Herr Goldberg had been watching him count bills off the roll. Four.

Four, the Herr Professor said, reckoning the cost. Where will you go?

England.

And where do you live meanwhile?

The older man shrugged. But seeing the question had been posed without malice, he appeared to change his mind, and gestured for the Herr Professor to follow him. In the very rear of the basement he pulled aside a curtain strung up across an archway. In an alcove lay a woman on a cot, clearly a sickbed. Beside her sat a girl in her mid-twenties, thin and wan, dandling a small blond child on her knee.

My son is already in London, with a friend, Herr Goldberg said, letting the curtain fall back. We hope to join him there.

That evening the Herr Professor locked the door to his little apartment and imagined showing his wife his purchases, telling her about Herr Goldberg and his family, in the basement of the burnt-out pharmacy. Long into the night he talked to her ghost, about what he could have done, should have done, whether to return the articles, whether to resell them on the black market (for surely a German could extract higher prices than a Jew) and return the money to the little family. She would know Goldberg's department store from the advertisements in her sewing magazines. The Herr Professor told his absent wife he had liked Herr Goldberg, who throughout the transaction had showed great courtesy, dignity, and tact.

The curtains turned from black to grey; and, as he pushed himself up from the table with the extra effort of anticipation (after a sleepless night, a long day at the Ministry blackening his hands with newspaper clippings, trying to recall a vocabulary from his student days in England, coyly tucked in the landscape of his mind behind the looming hills of more recent experience, and frightened to still deeper cover by the approaching footsteps of his immediate superior, who had the authority to demote him from intelligence to infantry if his work turned slow or sloppy), his eye lit upon a tin of sardines on the counter next to the hot plate, and he remembered he had seen the same brand of sardines on the table in the alcove behind the curtain, a tiny detail from the Goldberg family tableau. And the knowledge that they had this in common, he and that poor family, a meal of sardines in the near future, warmed and comforted him; for in preserving himself was he not thereby preserving a part of them, too – a shred of shared humanity – if only in memory? The thought bore no great weight, was like a rickety wooden bridge across a roaring gorge fit for one man to cross once before it collapsed in splinters and shards. But it got the Herr Professor across the gap – narrow, but impossibly deep – between night and dawn (the curtains were rosy now), got him into a clean shirt and off to the Ministry in good time, got him through a morning of exceptional industry and accomplishment (earning him a hand on the shoulder from his superior), got him all the way through to the end of the day, that anticipation of a meal he had eaten a hundred times before, yet never savoured with the proper gratitude and humility until now.

⊰◈⊱

Now, Ulrike Weber said.

There was more to the story, she said, but at a certain point she had stopped listening. That her father had paid more than he could easily afford for the objects, and far more than their owner asked for them, did not interest her. That her father had liked the man and felt a kinship with him, equally, she disdained. He had profited off a Jew during the war, and that was the bridge that had broken under her father's weight, the bridge she could not now cross.

She quit the piano, cut off her hair, and read the newspapers in her bedroom, holding her cigarette out the open window and tapping ash onto miniskirts and Beatles and that whole era, so juicy-ripe and dripping with fun. The sixties waned, and she went to university. Marxism and demonstrations, all that campus blather, did not entirely suit her either, though the fit was slightly better. She dated a series of angry young men and found herself to be angrier than any of them. But she was also terribly calm and pale and smart as a cliché, as a whip as a tack as a trap, and her classmates began to fear her a little, even before they had reason to.

One day, on the steps in front of the library, she was approached by anarchists.

Piss off, she said, because she was enjoying her cigarette and her book and the rare February sunshine, and because the anarchists were two boys and a girl she vaguely recognized, sporadic, unwashed presences in her Chinese history class. The girl, a mousy creature with bum-length brown hair, a pot-addled stare, and a childish, piping voice, doggedly held hands with both boys, one arrayed tweedily, with a dirty football scarf and dirtier hair, the other – a loudmouth in class, soft-spoken here – clad more conventionally in denim.

Come to a party, they said.

Bored, she went. The anarchists lived in a newer house on the outskirts of town, with great maps of water damage on the stucco and a yard scorched by dog piss. She herself lived as she was accustomed since childhood, in a small, well-kept flat in the old town, within the keep of the old medieval walls. This was not Tübingen but another university town, half a day away. Secretly she was house-proud, and making her way up the front walk she felt an alloy of contempt and shame. She would hate to live here as much as the anarchists (this one that greeted her at the door, say, who smelled of onions and bolted the door behind her, locking her into a distinctly un-party-like gloom) would hate her flowers and first editions and WMF silverware. They might have a record or two in common, she thought (propelled up a dark staircase by a firm hand in the centre of her back), Janis Joplin, the Stones, but the area of overlap – the penumbra, as they called it in her semiotics seminar – ended there. In the time it took for her eyes to adjust to the black hall at the top of the stairs, and to discern a thin smear of light beneath a single door, she wondered if it was not childishness that made her covet pretty things, shame that made her hide them (she never invited friends or lovers over, never, telling herself her flat was her sanctuary), and her parents' persistent, pernicious influence that made her so afraid of dirt and disorder, so reluctant to look chaos full in the face.

Weber, a voice said.

From the darkness she was pulled into a room of harsh fluorescence, the windows taped over with black cloth, where half a dozen people were at work with typewriters, paper and scissors, glue brushes, and a mimeograph machine. She shifted the bottle of wine she had brought from one hand to the other and caught the eye of the soft-spoken loudmouth, who acknowledged both her presence and her error with a wry eyebrow and a quirk of the lips. This was no party; she was being recruited.

At first she had trouble adjusting to the new lifestyle. Though they talked a fierce line, the group's political activities seemed restricted to issuing a rather demented left of left newspaper, handed out free on street corners, and indulging in the occasional bout of shoplifting or public urination in the name of insurrection and free love. The loudmouth boy refused on principle to keep regular hours, even when fatigue made him puffy and petulant, like a child; he would rise throughout the night to work on articles, returning at dawn to flop heavily on the mattress they shared and ruin yet another hour's sleep, snatched in his absence. He chided her for sleeping at night, all nine hours in a row; for eating three meals a day; for going to class; for her refusal to deface library books; and for her insistence on proper spelling and punctuation in the newspaper, which she had undertaken to copy-edit. She had also made herself the laughingstock of the house, somehow, by purchasing a bottle of iodine when she noticed several of the anarchists seemed to suffer from an inordinate number of cigarette burns on their hands and arms; she later learned this was a kind of game with them, the finer points of which she refused to allow them to explain.

Yet for all their wilful squalor and childish melodramatics, Ulrike began to like herself in this new life, to like her own toughness and leanness (she lost the last of her baby fat away

from her cozily stocked little apartment), to like the narrow
focus of their ideals, that rendered the usual student occupations
– studying, drinking, music, fashion, falling in love – irrelevant.
She began to write articles of her own for the newspaper, cold,
tight, reasoned pieces that earned letters to the editor in the
major papers. Attention of any sort bewitched her comrades,
and soon they were looking to her as a leader. As silliness became
notoriety, the group began to look for ways to leave a larger
mark on the world.

At Easter, Ulrike went home to visit her parents.

They met her at the train station. In the eight months of her
absence (she had not gone home for Christmas) her parents
seemed to have aged years, and stood both frail and lumpish,
peering nearsightedly down the platform. When they caught
sight of Ulrike her mother's face contorted in a spasm of
emotion, while her father offered, then cautiously withdrew, a
half-dozen red and yellow carnations in a paper cone. She was
aware of having left in jeans and a black turtleneck, with a man-
icure and an icy determination to succeed, and of the picture she
now presented: a chop-haired beanpole dressed in army fatigues
liberally defaced with ballpoint pen.

Is it you? her father said, the flowers hanging slack at his side.

She wanted to show him the book in her knee pocket, as a link
between now and then – a paperback edition of Aristotle's
Nicomachean Ethics – but turned instead to walk between them,
silently, back to the apartment.

After a lovingly starchy meal, her father enquired about her
grades. She admitted she had no idea.

Ulrike? her mother said. She noticed they both used her
name frequently, as though to reassure themselves she was still
their own child and not some changeling.

There followed a predictable acceleration of hostilities, during which Ulrike refused to account for her allowance (though "feeding anarchists" seemed a suitably anarchic response). Her mother wept, while her father said she must be under the influence of some dangerous cult, and threatened to take her down to the local hospital and have her committed for psychiatric evaluation, frogmarch her if necessary; at which last suggestion Ulrike, unpardonably, laughed. It was the knowledge – joyous, blasphemous, tragic and comic too – that she was too big and strong, finally, to be contained, and if it came to a physical struggle her white-haired father would inevitably come off the worse. She had wanted to cry, and had therefore laughed. Still, had she not laughed, her mother would probably not have slapped her, and her father would probably not, in the same instant, have ordered her out of the house "forever" (the word must be hobbled this way, in quotes, as anger usually hobbles forgiveness, that is, harshly but temporarily). In the scuffle, as the two of them together plucked at her arms, in a last desperate exertion of parental authority – to chastise, but also to touch – she would probably not have shaken them off to collect her knapsack, and in so doing spotted the metronome, still poised on the piano lid, and – seeing several problems align like monoliths on a midsummer's eve, allowing a single solution, like a single shaft of light, to penetrate them all – slipped it into her knapsack and left her parents' smug, narrow, comfortable, corrupt home forever.

On the train, on the way back north, she got the metronome's back plate off with a penknife, and compared the guts of the thing with a diagram in one of her books, a thorough, thoughtful work on the construction of elementary explosives. Like a clockwork: good enough. As for a target, that would not be difficult: every family had a skeleton in the closet, everyone knew of this or that official who had somehow stayed on in the very job he held during the war, like those bell-bottomed wooden dolls that rocked and rocked and didn't fall over. Someone would know a city counsellor or administrator or doctor or perhaps even a judge who had signed a paper or looked away, it would not (to stoke Ulrike's heartbreak and rage) need very much.

When her comrades weakly protested that the metronome was unreliable for a timer, a self-indulgent choice, she stood firm. The raised arm, the swastika, the yellow star: had it not also, she argued, been a war of symbols?

You take it personally, said Lucas, the gentle loudmouth, watching her pack her knapsack with clothes and books. As well as an anarchist he pretended to be an aficionado of Eastern religions, and was always espousing transcendence and the dissolution of the self. He was also sick with love for Ulrike, and hid it rather badly.

Six weeks at least, we agreed, she said. Don't come looking for me and then say you forgot.

No, he said.

She slung the knapsack over one shoulder and put the package containing the metronome rather more gingerly in her coat pocket.

Walk me to the courthouse.

He nodded and swallowed and reached to embrace her but she pushed him away, saying, Stupid. The metronome.

He nodded again, and they went out.

They took the subway to the courthouse, an imposing stone building with lions on either side of the stairs. They stopped in the shadow of a paw and made a huddling business of lighting cigarettes.

There, Ulrike murmured, nodding at a line of sleek black sedans parked out front. That one. See the licence plate.

Kiss me, Lucas Loudmouth said huskily. She refused.

I'll make a distraction, he said.

Lucas, no.

Watch, he said, and pulled from his own pocket a contraption she immediately recognized as a cruder version of her own.

Idiot! she said, but he had already pulled away and was running out into the square, whooping and waving the wiry tangle over his head. Heads turned, cars slowed. Ulrike shrank back into the lion's shadow. She saw him stop, seventy or eighty yards away, and raise the contraption to his lips as though to kiss it. Afterwards she realized he must have been lighting some part of it with his cigarette.

The explosion was not loud, from that distance, nor were the screams of passersby, nor even the impact of two cars whose drivers both veered away at the same moment. The flash did not seem big and the smoke dissipated quickly, but foolish Lucas Loudmouth did not get up from the ground. The doors of the courthouse opened and people began to emerge, tentatively, to see what had happened. Many more leaned out of the windows. Shouting she heard, and sirens, but distantly, as though on the other side of a huge glass wall. A man rushed down the steps, brushing against her, and ran over to where the body lay; when he got close she saw him turn away to retch. She began to walk back to the subway station. On the way she stopped in a café to use the washroom. Locked in a cubicle, she disabled the device in her pocket, flushed some parts, deposited others in a sanitary napkin disposal box, and walked away clutching the maimed metronome in her hand. She already had her passport and a couple of thousand marks tucked inside her Aristotle. She had planned to go to Switzerland until the police lost interest, or perhaps Italy.

At the airport she set the metronome on the ticket counter while she counted out the cash. Her hearing was slowly returning, but the scarfed, blond-beehived ticket seller still had to speak twice before Ulrike understood her.

You are a musician? she repeated, smiling curiously, nodding at the metronome.

Ulrike nodded.

The ticket seller booked her on a flight to Frankfurt almost immediately, but cautioned her there would be a four-hour wait for the next flight to New York.

Luggage? she asked brightly.

It was sent on ahead, Ulrike said. Then added: To Juilliard.

Ah! the ticket seller said.

In Frankfurt Ulrike bought juice and a pretzel and a postcard showing the Staatsoper. Fortunately she had dressed well for her first terrorist act, in heels, a dark wool suit, and a beige trench coat, and drew little attention. Her plan had been to walk briskly down the street past the line of cars, stopping beside her target to remove an imaginary stone from her shoe, while slipping the package from her pocket and sticking it to the inside rim of the front wheel.

She tried to write a note to her parents on the postcard.

Years later she would imagine she had been spotted outside the courthouse moments before the blast, by a security guard who thought the loitering conjunction of the well-dressed young woman and the scruffy, animated young man suspicious. After the explosion his eyes would have returned to the young woman, who, after a moment's hesitation, walked briskly away from the chaotic scene without once looking back. He noted carefully what she was wearing and notified the police, who traced her as far as the airport, even found the unwritten postcard abandoned on a plastic seat in one of the lounges, but never located the woman herself.

He *died?* David interrupted.

It was probably a fuse, the woman said. He probably thought he'd have time to run away, and while everyone was looking at the explosion I would have time to get the bomb under the car. You don't want to hear the rest? she added, because David had stood up.

You're sick, he said unhappily. You're making this up.

There isn't much more, she said. In New York I got a job with an import-export company, because of my German. Then with an auction house, where I learned the antiques trade. I never married, out of respect for Lucas. I started my own business fifteen years ago, and here I am. Would you still like the metronome?

Something curious happened in David's brain. For a brief, swirling, neurochemical moment he believed everything she had told him; and in the next moment he found himself smiling at the fabulous story he had found, this souvenir from New York, about an old German lady in a music shop, mad as a hatter, who thought she'd been a terrorist the way other women thought they'd been beauties, and both flattered and tormented themselves with the memory.

Very much, he said.

Are you a Jew?

And because he felt tender towards her now, because her mind had clearly gone lacy over the years, he told her he was.

I tried to find the son in London, she said. To give it back. I wrote letters to several Goldbergs, but either they didn't respond or they responded too eagerly. I didn't trust them. I just put it here on the shelf, finally, with the others.

You'll miss it, David said, while she busied herself behind the counter with tissue and tape and wrapping paper. To crown her dementia, she had insisted he accept the metronome as a gift. No other transaction, she said, was ethically possible.

She shook her head.

It ticks like a bomb, she said, and for a moment he saw every-thing it had come to mean to her, over the years, all the horror – whether real, suspected, or purely fantastic – in the starkness of her teeth, the taut deadness of her skin, and the frail out-standing bones of her skull.

James, back home in Vancouver, had trouble accepting the story as part of the gift, and told David that the woman had lied to him, that the metronome was worth only a fraction of what it would have sold for had it still worked.

You had it appraised? David repeated, incredulous.

The relationship limped on for a few more months, but by the end there was no point even pretending they might have a future together. James insisted, quite formally, on returning David's gifts, including the metronome, whereas David refused to give up the cherished half-dozen books and the silver cufflinks he had received in return. They parted on the worst possible terms. When David received the promotion that would take him away from Vancouver, possibly forever, he gave his notice and packed his belongings and spent an inordinate amount of time pretending to himself he wasn't sitting by the phone waiting for James (who would surely have heard by now) to call. On his last night in the apartment he retrieved the metronome from his briefcase and wrapped it elaborately in some cotton batting and leftover kraft paper. A gift it had been, and a gift it would remain.

David had kept the apartment well, the white walls unscarred, the wood floors shiny and smooth. By the time he had finished cleaning the existing cleanness the next occupants would not be able to guess who had lived here before, though they would find the metronome and they would try. They would try, he thought; and, if it amused them, would it matter if they got it wrong?

Wait, Anika said. That can't be right.

What?

Maelzel, she said. The metronome. I'm sure it's older than – what did we say? Eighteen thirty-six?

I didn't say anything, Thom said. You're the one who had all those piano lessons.

Eleven years! she said, making her eyes big and staggering a little in the elevator to express the burden of it. He laughed.

They had moved in on the first of December. Now it was the eighteenth, dusk. The elevator drifted slowly upwards. Their arms were full of shopping, gifts and groceries, and some library books. They had continued to elaborate the story of the metronome, begun their first night in the new apartment, as a kind of entertainment to get them through their first days in a strange place. But already the strangeness had worn away, and they felt as though they had never really lived anywhere else. Already they had their favourite shops and haunts – a particular deli, the gay coffee shop, the library on Denman. Still the story of the metronome stayed with them, curling and flowering around each of these bricks that was finally falling into place in their new life. Thom had got a couple of leads on jobs from a man he met in the elevator and was working almost full-time. Anika got a job interview with a newspaper the day after they moved in, and was set to start in January. She spent her last days of unemployment taking black and white photos in the park and cooking elaborate meals. When Thom got home they would pick up the story wherever they had left it off the day before. The distance between them was shrinking and Anika thought they were slowly being restored to their old selves, laughing, affectionate, pleased with each other. They touched more.

Inside the apartment they busied themselves, lighting lamps, stowing food in the fridge, stacking the library books next to the sofa. A book on Germany in the thirties, a biography of Charles Rennie Mackintosh. They had traded off portions of the story – Ulrike and Mackintosh were Thom's, David and Hannah were Anika's – and delighted in pouncing on each other's inaccuracies. Baader-Meinhof was the seventies, not the late sixties, Anika would say, and Thom would respond by touching on some detail about the Nuremberg Laws she had sketched in only vaguely, unsure of herself.

Where is it? Thom asked now, as she squirted soy sauce in a bowl and unwrapped a plastic tray of California rolls. Outside the carol ships glowed on the dark bay. Oh, but their lives were delightful now!

What? she said.

The metronome.

Then they were putting their coats and shoes back on and hurrying back downstairs, because Anika had taken it to the library with them, had almost invariably left it in the stacks, sitting on an empty shelf where she had pulled it out to compare to an Aubrey Beardsley drawing Thom had found. But by the time they got back to the library it was closed.

That's just as well, Thom said. The staff will have found it and put it in the lost and found. We'll get it back tomorrow.

Stupid, Anika said, not really meaning it, tapping herself on the forehead.

They did not open the library books that night after all; it seemed pointless without the metronome as touchstone.

The next day, after Thom had left, Anika went back to the library, but none of the librarians remembered having seen a blue metronome on the shelves. The lost and found, a wooden milk crate, contained only several umbrellas and a pair of child's rubber boots.

Never mind, Anika said, and thanked the librarians for their trouble.

Since she was out anyway she decided to do her shopping for that evening's meal, and to make up for the disappointment of the loss of the metronome she decided to go all out, with flowers and wine and an expensive cut of meat, something cooked slowly, to a heady succulence. As she moved through the morning, constructing the meal in her mind and moving from shop to shop, she found she was in a particularly good mood. They had moved from one phase of their life to the next, perhaps, that she could contemplate such a meal without agonizing over the cost and wistfully settling for something less; that she could lose an antique, valuable maybe, and care so little. The irony of having money was that you thought less of it, cared less about it, mourned its loss a little less.

When Thom got home that evening she waited for him to ask about the metronome, but the question never came. He told her about his day, spent consulting with a team of web designers. That was the future, he said, talking as much to himself as to her. There was money there, and all the work a person could want. He would take some evening classes, pick up some new skills. Most Web designers were techno-brats with no graphic ability at all, he said. He was eager to get on the computer, even before she had served dessert, and show her examples of their work, and explain how he could do it better.

As his computer skills blossomed and her wallet grew swollen with paycheques, they began to fill the apartment with the nice things they had always craved, books and rugs and pictures, better clothes in the cupboards, better food in the fridge. Anika grew brisk and efficient, with her new job and newly moneyed life; the days of aimless wandering and elaborate, painstaking meals she consigned, privately, to an underemployed and slightly depressed past. Thom became cool, the one with the newest sunglasses, the tickets to movie premieres, the fastest computer, the latest CDs, the loudest laugh. He met interesting people, he did stylish things for them, and they rewarded him. He never asked about the metronome. Sometimes Anika imagined it ticking away – someone would have found it and fixed it, surely – marking off the days and weeks and months until he remembered it, their talisman. Eventually she gave up waiting. She watched him drink his martinis, swear at his computer, criticize her clothes, kiss her hands. She saw that her feelings for him would swing from patience to impatience, liking to loathing, closeness to distance, and there was nothing she could do about it. Nothing but wait, and wait, and wait for the needle to swing back, and hope that their love would not prove so delicate, so ambiguous, and so easily, irretrievably lost.

THE BEST THING FOR YOU

$$\left(1\right)$$

The idea first came to her one limpid yellow morning toward the end of the war, as she sat across the breakfast table from her husband, watching him chew with toast-textured jaws. The minutes were falling down like dominoes, and she had a full day planned once he had left for the eight-fifteen, so that the idea had at first seemed negligible, a silver coin of a lake glimpsed from the window seat of an airplane, easy to forget.

When do I expect you tonight? she asked, turning back to the immediate clutter of her coffee, her magazines, on the table in front of her. Grape nuts, Victory Bonds.

And he, across his plate and paper: Late. Tanner's invited everyone for drinks. How's eight-thirty?

Well, that's fine, she said.

Make lamb chops.

All right.

Kiss me.

Shave.

Kiss me anyway.

She moved to his lap and closed her eyes and there it was again, a long way off yet winking deliberately. She had planned

a day of work and errands, and wondered if this funny little
fantasy would accompany her through the sequence.

Our lady of the dry cleaning, she murmured. Our lady of the
cold cuts.

I'll bring you a present, he said thickly.

Hm.

He was big but helpless: these were the first and last things
she had learned about him. Do you like this? she would ask, after
they were married and she no longer had to play shy. This?
With a single finger she could belabour his breathing, tip him
past speech. But just now her mind was elsewhere, on the day's
goals, and on this funny bright bauble her fancy had produced.

Oh, that's good, her husband said.

She got up and went to the bedroom to dress.

After he had gone she marked her mouth with lipstick, gathered her keys and pocketbook, and locked up the little bungalow
their four parents had helped them buy. On the sidewalk her
heels ticked nicely. She was twenty-two and cute, pale plump
skin and blackish curls, tarry-eyed, small. Her husband, ten
years older, was gross and blond, a prairie boy, cheerful and
dairy-bland. He worked for the Vancouver *Daily Province*, not
writing but with the equipment, the presses and type, though
he was hoping to get into photography. They had been married
for two years.

She joined the queue for the streetcar, behind a handless man
and a girl and another man in uniform. Carnegie Library, please,
she told the driver when it was her turn.

I know, the driver said.

She spent the morning in a chair in a block of sun in the cold
stone library, working with a notebook and a French grammar,
occasionally distracted by thoughts of the handless man. He had
kept touching the girl with his stump, once even smoothing her

hair with it while he and the officer talked about baseball. Towards the end of the morning she set down the grammar and picked up *Le jeu de l'amour et du hasard* by Marivaux. She wrote in her notebook, in a rather round, childish hand:

Silvia: Are we not pleased with Léandre when we see him? But, at home, he says not a word, nor laughs nor growls, his soul is frozen, solitary, inaccessible. His wife does not know it, has no relations with it; she is wed but to a figurine from a cabinet, who appears at the table to stifle with apathy, with chill and boredom, all that surrounds him. Is this not a delightful husband?
Lisette: I freeze before the story you tell me; but what of Tersandre?
Silvia: Yes, Tersandre!

At noon she closed her notebook, returned her little books to the shelf, and walked into a day that had turned warm and dull. Gulls like paper gulls tipped and looped between the buildings, through the soft, soiled cottony sky. In a café on Hastings she ordered bread and butter and tea and ate slowly, staring at the window. She was trying to remember how many pairs of intact stockings she had. The idea came again, bright as a gewgaw, beginning to annoy her. Stockings were expensive, and she decided to make do for another week or two. Perhaps, anyway, this was the gift her husband had spoken of: a single expensive pair of stockings. That would be an intelligent gift.

The streetcar deposited her on a tree-lined street equidistant from her home and the food store, an edifice so new they had only just finished laying the parking lot tar. Inside she tarried. They were offering a home delivery service now, she noted, but it was more than she could afford.

At the meat counter she waited patiently behind four other women, watching the butcher scissor off half a dozen sausage links and wrap them in brown paper, watching the woman in front of her sweep her baby's mouth out with a finger and wipe what she had found on her coat, watching the door to the back swing open just as she stepped up to the counter and a boy of sixteen or seventeen appear in a clean apron, glancing at his similarly aproned father and receiving a nod.

Hello, Stephen, she said, smiling gently.

Ma'am.

What a clever boy, she thought, as he wrapped her chops and ham, weighed the neat packages, and wrote sums on them with a pen. She didn't like the way he rushed through everything, racing his father and beating him to the single set of scales, slapping her purchases, her food after all, on the counter. He had learned the business but not the manners of the business. He had also propositioned her once, three months ago now, scribbling a note on the underside of one of the brown paper flaps for her to discover when she got home and started to cook. He had not yet grown into his nose and ears but was not terribly unpleasant either: hair dark like her own, eyes a pretty, lashy hazel. He had an inch or two on her and probably weighed less. Skin angrier some days than others, lips a bit thin. She never considered shopping elsewhere, simply appropriated the name he had penned, using it each time to show him his own youth.

Anything else for you? he asked, not meeting her eye.

No, thank you.

Though if I were to do it, she thought, walking home, mightn't a boy like that be useful? Mightn't he be just the one? She swung the string bag of apples and purchases by her calf, smiling at how quickly the little silver crime had overflowed its banks, eroding a river, a bright thread through her thinking.

❖

That night, when her husband got home, she was in a good mood. She turned up the radio and made him dance with her in the living room, still in his shoes and overcoat. This was the kind of thing he liked. She had cooked carefully and he praised the meal, his favourite, and the candles and the shiny windows and her good housekeeping generally.

You're high, she said.

What? he said, laughing. A little. No, listen, though, I got an assignment. That Bonner trial on Monday, you know, they want me to wait in the alley behind the courthouse and get the woman as she comes out. They think she'll come out the back way.

She'll have a veil.

He laughed again. Is that what you'd do, baby? Wear a veil?

No. But she will.

I'm going down there tomorrow. Saturday there won't be too many people around. Just check out the lighting, the angles. Figure out where this goddamn back door is anyway. Then there's this bar on Granville, Peretti was telling me, where a lot of them like to go. I thought I might look in there. He said he'd introduce me to some –

Will you be late?

Well, yes, he said patiently. I've got to see the place at the same time of day, under the same conditions. That'll be late afternoon, so I guess I'll just grab a bite out, then this –

Just that I might go to the pictures.

Sure, sure.

She washed the dishes and he dried.

Peretti was in Spain, he said after a while, as though the sentence clinched something in his thinking. He set a pan on the counter.

Hey, not there, she said. Next to the stove. Hey, where's my present?

Hey, her husband said.

Please.

What have you done to earn a present?

Nothing, she said immediately.

He hung the tea towel, with its chickens, on the back of a chair.

Nothing, she said. I've been bad, actually. I've had terrible, shameful thoughts all day long. Dead nuns are weeping for me. I should be punished.

He stared at her. She hesitated.

It's a game, she said. Just a game.

Still staring, he lifted his hands to his face, fingers stiff around nothing, as though framing a shot of her as she stood there at the sink.

The next day, Saturday, opening the paper packet of ham to make sandwiches for lunch, she found a second note.

Up from the basement, where he kept his photographic equipment, came her husband, in a pair of corduroy pants and an old wool sweater. When he saw her he said, Do they fit all right?

Her present, he meant. She extended a leg toward him, toes pointed, so he could see.

I've been thinking, he said. You can't say no right away. Only I was thinking it might help me if you came along this afternoon.

Me?

You can be the woman. Stand by the door where she's going to stand so I can work out the details on my own time, nobody rushing me. Like a dress rehearsal. I don't want to get there on Monday surrounded by pros and realize I've got the wrong damn lens.

Of course not, she said. All right, I guess. I'll feel like a fool, though.

Now you're talking.

Will I miss my show?

Shouldn't, he said. I shouldn't need more than an hour.

I mean, you don't need me to come to that bar?

He laughed. Baby, no.

I might be late too, after, she said. If I meet some of the girls.

Paint the town, he said, biting into his sandwich.

He didn't like her hat. It's in the way, he said.

It's because of people like you she'll be wearing it. Think about it. She doesn't want her picture taken.

How do you know so much about it?

A couple passing the mouth of the alley paused to look.

Trust me, she said.

He was taking readings and scribbling in a notebook.

Are you sure this is the right door?

His flash bathed the alley in a sudden milky light.

Buddy!

Just a couple of real ones.

A small crowd had stopped to watch. Hey, mister! someone called. What's it for?

He couldn't resist. *The Daily Province.*

Who is she?

It started to rain again. That's it, he said softly to himself, and the flash exploded again, showing everything.

Who is she?

Hold this one, baby, he said, handing her a lens. She shielded it in the breast of her coat while he packed up, hurrying against the rain. His touch with the equipment was getting more confident, she thought. Gently he took the lens back from her and zipped it into a thickly padded pouch that fitted into a hollow in the camera bag he wore slung across his chest.

Who is she?

Who *is* she? her husband said, as she tipped her hat lower over her face. He took her elbow and steered her firmly through the crowd, out of the alley. Well, I like that!

On the corner they kissed. Don't wait up, he said.

You neither.

Stay dry, he added, as the lights changed and she stepped into the street to cross. They were going in different directions. Belatedly he called, What's the show?

She waved without looking back, acknowledging his voice over the rain and the traffic noise.

The picture was a silly one, something about a housewife who secretly supported her family by singing in a seedy nightclub. Her husband, a blind man, thought she went babysitting every evening. A neighbour who noticed the long silver dress under her drab coat thought she was having an affair. Then one night at the club the housewife witnessed a murder. She knew she should go into hiding, but her husband needed her help. She decided to stay with him, relying on her meek housewife persona as a disguise. When the hit man tracked her to her neighbourhood, he was stumped. I'm looking for a real glamorous dame, he told the grocer, the florist, the vicar, but no one knew who that could be.

Is this seat taken? a man asked.

The movie was half over. He must have been watching her from somewhere else in the theatre.

But I'm in love with you, the neighbour, an artist, told the housewife. He had followed her to the club one night and discovered her secret. Come to New York with me. They will adore you in New York!

I won't run away, the fervent housewife said. My life is with my husband.

Oh, for Christ's sake, the man in the next seat said as she squeezed past him. I was only –

Outside the sky was rain-cool, rain-cleared. She walked for a while to clear the nonsense out of her head, then turned into a long, narrow café with a velvet cloth hanging like a thought across the door. He was sitting in a booth at the back. She walked over, sat down opposite him, and said, Why are you bothering me?

Bothering you? he said. Jesus, if that's what you want to call it. An invitation, a polite –

You wrote on my meat.

You know why, he said. Obviously.

She looked down then and saw his hands on the table were trembly.

Aren't you having anything? she asked.

I was waiting for you.

Of a single accord they studied the items arrayed on the table between them – spoons, salt and pepper, and a tall glass sugar shaker – collecting themselves.

You were pretty sure of yourself, she said, more kindly.

No I wasn't.

She signalled the waitress for coffees.

I'm an existentialist, he said.

She said something in French.

All right, he said, flushing darkly. All right.

She took her notebook and a pen out of her purse and wrote down what she had said, then tore off the page and handed it to him.

One must imagine Sisyphus happy, she said in English.

He folded the note and put it in his shirt pocket. Cigarette? he asked, conjuring a pack.

No, thank you, Stephen.

He put the pack back in another pocket. The waitress set their cups in front of them and left. The coffee tasted smoked.

Nietzsche says history is circular. Do you believe that? What's your husband's name?

Buddy.

Buddy? he said, laughing. Buddy?

What did you think was going to happen here?

His hands started trembling again, badly.

Chicory, she said. I remember real coffee.

You're not so much older than me.

I am, though.

No, he said, for she had risen and was pulling her coat back around her. On his jaw, like a rash: sweets plus shaving.

She said, I have to go.

Jesus, you don't.

They were both standing. She thought: look at us, each with something big and clear and important to say, but he starts his in the middle and I manage nothing at all.

Aren't we the pair, she said.

Anna. Anna!

Coming.

Here she is. Hello, love.

What's wrong with the car? Anna asked.

– under the car. Let the men.

This is new, Anna said, not quite touching her mother's silk scarf.

No.

It is.

No. Oh, sweetheart, his trousers.

– the car.

Let me hug you.

Hello, Mummy.

Aren't his legs long.

Buddy! she called, and one of his feet waggled where he lay in the street.

Nothing major, sir, he said, pulling himself out from under the car and sitting up. His hands were black.

I'm glad to hear it, sir, her father said.

There followed the regular Sunday roast and talk of war, its stringencies and sacrifices. In this they were marshalled by her father.

After they left her husband said, He never lets me forget, does he?

He doesn't mean it like that.

It's not my fault.

Of course it isn't.

He thinks it is.

They took it to bed with them, the bad feeling he had with her father.

I want to fight.

He knows that.

No. He wonders how it is I can bang you every night and still claim a weak heart.

She had wondered the same herself but said nothing. He was rarely crude. She was the one. At the dance the night they met he had asked her what she wanted from life. A mate and a litter, she had said, and felt herself in his gunsights from then on. He told her later she was like a coin toss: heads nine times running, but then came the tenth.

It's not my fault, he said again. All my father's family have it.

I know.

It's an inherited condition.

I know.

I know you know. I just wish someone would explain it to your father.

She was imagining a coin toss, a spinning silver chip. It could fall this way or that way.

I never asked about the show last night.

I left early.

She felt him go up on an elbow to look at her.

You never do that. You get mad at me if I suggest that.

I couldn't concentrate.

Why not?

My life is with my husband, she said dramatically, striking her brow like an actress.

She wrote in her notebook:

I had the fault of being excessively timid and easily disconcerted; but far from being hindered by this weakness, I advanced on the mistress of my heart. . . . It was to spite her that they were sending her to the convent, to arrest no doubt her penchant for pleasure, which had declared itself early and which would cause, in what followed, all her sorrows and mine.

She was at home, working from one of the books in her small library. Rain assaulted the windows like shot.

Her spirit, her heart, her sweetness, and her beauty formed a chain so strong and so charming that I would have staked all my happiness on never escaping it. Terrible transformation! That which forms my despair could have fixed my happiness. I find myself the most unhappy of men, by that same constancy through which I should have expected the gentlest of all fates, and the most perfect rewards of love.

Her mother had taught her to translate when she was still a girl, as a way of keeping herself intelligent. Together they had laboured over the fables of Aesop; with pains she had graduated to Voltaire and the other marble men. Then, in the first sweetness of marriage, she had struck out a little on her own and found a vein of classical indecency that, rich though it was, became her staple diet.

I was to spend six whole months in my prison, during the first of which my condition changed little. All my feelings were but a perpetual alternation between hatred and love, hope, and despair, depending on how she appeared to my spirit. At times I saw her as the most attractive of women, and languished in my desire to see her again; at times I saw but a weak and perfidious mistress, and swore a thousand oaths not to seek her except to punish her.

Downstairs the front door slammed and her husband called her name. She suppressed a flash of guilt and went down to the kitchen.

Why's it so dark in here? Don't you want to see?

The paper, he meant. He looked pale and a little ill with excitement, flicking on lights and spreading the paper across the table. You should have seen it down there. They had cordoned off the whole block and then all these flashbulbs going at once when she came out, if you had seen –

Did you get near her?

Pretty near. I had to be pretty aggressive.

What was she like?

Small, like you. I don't know if I'd have done for her what he did, though.

Why not?

He didn't answer, leafing through the big pages.

Was I right about the veil?

He grinned. Just about.

Did you get her face?

I don't know. I just grabbed it and came straight home. Bonner trial, here.

But that's me, she said.

White-faced, he made a phone call, then went out and brought back this Peretti, a brown-eyed American with more newspapers under his arm. Very nice, ha, he said as he shook her hand.

The men took their sandwiches down to the basement. After a while she followed. They had the papers all laid out on the work table.

Come, come, Peretti said, waving her over. What does she think of this?

Obediently she went to his elbow.

His thick finger touched one photo after another: the *Daily Province*, the *Daily Colonist*, the *Globe*. The pictures were similar.

It's raining in mine, she said, pointing. You can see the puddle. That silvery bit.

Good girl.

What happened?

I'll tell you, Peretti said. The excuse me cunt in the darkroom is what happened. You didn't develop these, did you, Pass?

No. I just gave in the roll.

He just gave in the roll. Peretti spread his hands, appealing to her as to a judge. So there were some other shots on the roll.

Do we call Tanner?

Hell no we don't call Tanner. We don't call anyone. No one's going to notice. But if anyone notices –

The guy in the darkroom? her husband said hesitantly.

The cunt in the darkroom, Peretti said. That is correct.

She understood Tanner was one of the editors and Peretti, as well as a photographer, was a teacher.

How's she doing? Peretti asked, thumping his chest.

Buddy –

No, I'm fine. Better now.

We don't need casualties over a little thing like this, Peretti said, watching him.

It's fine – but hand to heart, unthinking.

To distract Peretti from her husband's distress she turned back to the photographs. Her hat's a tiny bit different too, she said. But you have to look really closely to notice.

Peretti folded one of the pages, with a professional neatness, so he could lay the photographs side by side. Two women in the same alley doorway, big hat, dark coat, heels. Her own face was the clearer of the two though the focus was softened by the poor quality of the newsprint. Maybe it was enough. When she looked closely the differences mounted. But who would look closely?

Our coats are almost identical.

Peretti silently pointed to a piece of garbage that appeared in one shot but not the other. An intimate gesture – a secret from her husband under her husband's nose, an acknowledgement of her strength to his weakness. Something he wanted her to know he knew, though he kept his eyes studiously on the page.

Does this happen? her husband asked.

All the time, Peretti lied. We got lucky.

Her husband seemed consoled.

Do your own developing next time though.

Sure, sure I will.

That's me, she was thinking.

Leave the wife at home next time, too.

He grinned. Sure thing.

Peretti started to read the story under the picture.

That's me, she said aloud, experimenting.

And look what a bad girl you were, Peretti said, addressing her directly for the first time.

As he was leaving, he clapped her husband on the shoulder and said, I guess you're not a virgin any more, are you, Pass?

The phone call came late that night. She felt herself dragged up from the salt depths of sleep, hooked and hauled by her husband's voice saying: Hello? Hello?

The clock on her night table had phosphorescent green arms that doubled and wavered in her sight, but after a sentence or two she got up and started to dress. She pulled out clothes for her husband too and laid them on the bed.

No, he said, still on the phone, looking up at her in surprise. She's right here with me.

In the end they drove not to the hospital but to his mother's house.

I don't blame you, her mother-in-law said, by way of greeting, on the doorstep. I don't know what happened, but I don't want you children to think it was your fault.

Her husband took his mother's arm and walked her into the living room. Make coffee, would you? he said over his shoulder.

Driving through the empty streets, they had seemed buoyed

in an obscene bubble of sound and motion and the sensation persisted even in the house – she felt the stylish white kitchen watching her as she moved through it, setting off ripples of disapproval that bounced off the hard surfaces and interfered with each other in silently crashing patterns. Her mother-in-law was a clean, cold woman and their mutual dislike, she knew well, was probably rooted in the fact that they were so similar. See the swept counters, the chrome fixtures polished to a liquid sheen! Only the table was heaped with dry husks of newspapers.

A glass lay on the floor in the corner behind one chair and when she went to pick it up she stepped in water. She realized her father-in-law had collapsed here, died here. She looked down at the papers then and saw, with a shiver of pure physical pleasure, the photograph of herself.

They looked up as she came in, looked away as she set the tray on the coffee table and began to serve.

He always loved you like a daughter, her mother-in-law said. Cream?

She's in shock.

Sit down, Anna.

I've forgotten the sugar. No, please let me get the sugar, she said, hearing her own voice rise.

She's trying to look after us, she heard her husband say.

In the kitchen she reversed the paper back along its spine and tucked it into the middle of the pile, leaving on top the cinema listings. He too had liked the pictures; they had even gone together, once or twice, just the two of them. Perhaps those afternoons had made it easier for his meek mind to make the leap to depravity. The things that woman had done!

She had no doubt he had recognized her.

She found the sugar bowl and took it back into the living room where her mother-in-law was saying: I'm frightened,

Buddy. This big old house, the car, the funeral, I don't know how I'll manage a thing. Your father always took care of everything. I'm already frightened of you leaving and me being all alone in this house and not knowing where to put myself. I'm frightened of going to bed and waking up in a silent house and knowing I'm all alone. He's dead, Buddy. How will I live?

Her husband looked exhausted. She guessed it was the effort of not crying.

I don't know a thing about money, her mother-in-law said. I swear I don't.

But won't you come stay with us?

Her husband looked at her gratefully and she saw she had restored a derailed train. Talk of money was not appropriate but families closing ranks was appropriate. He had a child's mind, schooled in right angles.

You won't stay on your own a minute, she added soothingly. Not if you don't want to.

Her mother-in-law was crying. You're a lovely girl, she said. He was shouting something about you just before – oh, I'm sorry! But it's weighing on me, I simply couldn't understand it, he always, always loved you. Why would he say such things?

About Anna? her husband said. You misheard.

I don't know, she wept. I just don't know.

Dawn came. They took her husband's mother home with them and put her to bed in the little room that would one day be their baby's room, down the hall from their own.

Anna, he called.

She found him by the bedroom window, staring into the branches of the neighbour's maple.

I want you to lie down too, she said.

He didn't resist, saying only: Call Peretti. His card's in my wallet. He can let them know at the paper.

She pulled the blankets back over him and touched his hair.

You haven't cried yet, he said.

I can't seem to.

She sat and held his hand for a while, then kissed his cheek. Downstairs she sat at the kitchen table and began writing names on the pad she kept for grocery lists. It was five to eight.

Hello? she said. Hello. This is Mrs. Pass. I have some sad news.

She picked up the receiver and began to dial.

After the funeral there was a tea. Funeral meats, she remembered: that was an expression. But her mother-in-law had wanted it catered. She watched the mourners greet her husband with a special tenderness, knowing as well as he did what he had beating in his chest, while a hired servant circulated with trays of tidbits. She herself was stationed on the sofa behind a silver tea service laid out on the coffee table. It was her mother-in-law's service, brought over specially, her own being china – too frail and pretty.

He was a wonderful man, they told her, and she responded feelingly, I'll never forget him.

Her parents came, and embraced her formally. Her mother exchanged pecks with her mother-in-law and even gave her husband a hug, their first. Her father shook hands all around, straightened his cuffs, and then they left.

Peretti came. He kissed her mother-in-law on both cheeks and shook her husband's hand and then he came for his tea. He sat beside her in his overcoat on the low sofa, stirring his tea with a tiny silver spoon, and told her in a low voice that the paper would be willing to give her husband some more assignments and maybe she could let him know at a time when she thought it might help, some time before his two weeks' leave

was up. They had been very impressed, Peretti said, with the
Bonner assignment.

But that was a misunderstanding.

Peretti shrugged and said, predictably: No one noticed. It's
not as though he was passing off work that wasn't his. Don't you
want him to have this break?

Anna? her husband kept saying. He seemed dazed, but of
course everyone understood.

After the last of the mourners had left and his mother had
gone up for a lie-down he wanted to make love again and that,
too, was predictable, life in the jaws of death, what have you.

Her father-in-law had been a salesman in sporting goods and had
died at a bad time. Young men bought sporting goods, but most
of the young men were at war. As commissions dropped he had
suckled down his savings and his pension too. The upshot was
that Buddy's mother would be staying with them indefinitely
while her husband and the lawyers decided whether to put the
house on the market. It all came out in the reading of the will.

I will never leave you like that, he said that night, over and
over in the dark.

Bernard Pass?

She and Buddy followed the secretary into an office.

Now, the agent said when they were comfortably seated, life
insurance is always an excellent investment, but particularly for
a young couple such as yourselves.

She had finished at the meat counter and was back in the aisles of canned goods when he caught up with her, in his butcher boy's striped cap and apron, and said, I thought you'd started going someplace else.

She told him about the funeral. We had all this food left over, she explained. Little pastries. It lasted days.

Meet me.

Don't be silly.

Meet me.

I can't.

He began to speak in a low, fast voice, trailing her down the aisle. An old woman turned to look.

When she got home, her mother-in-law was sitting at the kitchen table reading *Candide*. She had not realized her mother-in-law read French.

Oh, yes, dear, she said, watching purchases emerge from the string bag. My parents had a *bonne* before the crash. I adored her. You've spent a lot today.

There are three of us now.

Oh, I eat like a bird. What's that?

Cake.

In a tin, her mother-in-law said. Is it English? My goodness. Imported cake in a tin.

It was a moist chocolate cake in a tin the size of a soup tin with so few nuts inside they were like mistakes. It had been her treat when she was a child.

It's not dear, she said. Just a little. She stopped, unable to say, just a little treat.

Buddy never liked sweets, her mother-in-law said. Nor did his father. She bit her lip.

Let me make you some tea.

You don't really remember the crash, do you, and after? So
many luxuries we just take for granted now.

The tin caught the light, flashing like code as she lifted it
into the cupboard. She decided against tea. Instead she said, I
was thinking. I was thinking I'd go over to your house tomorrow and air it out, do a bit of dusting. It's good for a house to
seem inhabited.

There was a moment, then, when her mother-in-law might
have said no. Instead: How thoughtful.

It was Buddy's idea.

But how thoughtful, her mother-in-law said more warmly.

Upstairs in her little sitting room she found the empty slot on
the bookshelf where *Candide* had been. Her hands were trembling like the boy's had. But it's all right, she told herself. You
hate *Candide*.

Her notebook lay open on the chair. She couldn't remember
if she had left it that way. She had of course written:

*One must not anger old women; it is they who make the reputations of
the young.*

⟨◈⟩

On her knees, then, in her kerchief, scrubbing a clean floor. She
had the whole afternoon. She was going to dust the cabinets and
beat the mats and strip the beds too, if there was time, remake
the house into something her mother-in-law might want to
come back to.

There was a light drumming on the windowpane.

You're early, she said, squinting into the backyard. It had
recently rained and now the sun was out, striking a painful glare
off leaves and windows. It took her strange seconds to find him,
standing colourless against the back wall of the house, his feet in

the wet muck where the sun never touched. She said, Shouldn't you be in school?

I cut.

Well, hurry up.

He ambled into the sun. His skin was awful but he had a slow smile she realized she was seeing for the first time. He was nothing now but she saw he might grow into something. Closer, he said, Are you always going to boss me?

Take your shoes off.

She sat him at the table and tried to keep working. Finally she said, Stop staring at me. Go find something to do.

Like what?

Go strip the beds upstairs and bring the laundry down here to me.

Now, alone, she could think more clearly. She recalled the last time she had seen her father-in-law, the previous month, a day that had seemed to pour thick and endless as syrup. She had been shopping in a big department store downtown, purpose-fully approaching each escalator though she wanted nothing, picking fretfully through racks of cheap blouses on two, hefting skillets on three, sitting in upholstered chairs and squeezing the armrests, though for what quality she didn't know, on five. Closing her eyes briefly she realized she was waiting to go to bed, the hours stretching out like an immense acreage between her and sleep. When she opened her eyes again she saw her father-in-law. He was one department over, showing hockey sticks to a couple of businessmen probably returning from a long late lunch. She watched them, in the middle distance, like a play: her father-in-law trying to demonstrate the correct grip, the businessmen mocking him for what he was, a servant, their faces shining with good health and innocent liquored malice. When they were gone she crossed the broad aisle separating furniture from sporting goods and greeted him warmly, kissing his cheek. So like her husband, the way his face lit up! They chatted briefly, not too long so she wouldn't get him in trouble, and then she bought a box of golf balls, for her father she said. For the rest of the afternoon she had thought, He is still up there – as she made her escape, down one escalator after another, out onto the street, golf balls in a trash can, onto the streetcar, walking under the absurd trees – he is still up there, working, while I am free in the world.

Half an hour later he had not come down.

Here you are, she said.

He lay on the stripped mattress of her husband's parents' bed, curled away from her, pants around his knees, the belt still in its loops. Bedding lay on the floor like a mound of egg white. He mumbled, Is this your bedroom?

She didn't answer but leaned on the door jamb, watching. I could help, she thought as he sweetly laboured; but if I were to touch him or show him a breast he might die, and then I'd be back at zero. I'll wait.

A rarity, an argument. They had to do it in whispers.

I am not neglecting her.

She says –

She says what? That I'm too busy cleaning our house and her house and doing the shopping and the washing and the mending and heaven knows what else to sit with her while she tells me everything I'm doing wrong?

She says you invent excuses to get away from her and I just about believe it. You're always trying to get off on your own with some book. I would have thought you'd have a little more com-passion. Put yourself in her shoes, why don't you? What if I died?

He looked up at her with an oil-and-vinegar blend of satis-
faction and uncertainty. They were getting ready for bed. Her
mother-in-law must have taken him aside while she herself was
doing the supper dishes, given him this bone to worry, and now
that he had slobbered over it for an hour alone he must needs
drop it at her feet. Self-pity was a trait he had, a boyish trait like
the freckles in his ears, that needed scouring away.

If you died I wouldn't want somebody's child wife fidgeting
over me every minute. Somebody's spoiled child wife. (Her
mother-in-law had called her this once, behind her back but not
out of her hearing, and she was deft with it in argument.)

He made a movement, a chop of the hand dismissing the stuff
of the quarrel, as though it was a game he played for her sake
that he had now tired of and wished to end. I'm asking you to
spend more time with her, Anna. Maybe she's being a little irra-
tional right now but she's grieving. Surely you can forgive her
that. Baby, please.

Just don't accuse me, that's all.

The boy had lain on the bare mattress after, panting and staring
murder at her. Finally he had said, You didn't have to watch.

She could think of nothing to say that was not wildly pornographic and sad.

You bitch, he had said. You cockteaser. He had stumbled past
her to the bathroom, gripping his loose pants with one hand
and cupping himself with the other. She heard the water
run, and then he was out again, done up, pushing past her and
crying, calling back, I was nice to you!

Be patient with her, her husband said. You can be sweet when
you want to. Take her shopping with you, let her teach you a few
things. Honestly, I don't see why you get so worked up about it.

They got into bed.

Now you're sore, he said.

I'm not sore. I'm thinking of something wonderful for us to do tomorrow.

As he had padded down the stairs, shouting and crying, she had surprised herself by laughing aloud. Pursuing him, inside the house at least, laughing and calling his name. Oh, I've been so bored, she thought. He hadn't stopped, had fled, but at least they knew where to find each other now.

Her husband said, Tell.

None of your business, you bully, she said. You're not invited.

The next night her husband brought Peretti home for supper.

What have you two been doing all day? her husband demanded right away.

He can't tell, she said to her mother-in-law. I'm insulted.

The older woman struck a pose, one hand behind her head, the other on a canted hip, and swivelled slowly like a mannequin, staring big-eyed into space. They laughed.

Anna took me to the beauty parlour, she said. In Kerrisdale. Very old money. We were the youngest clients there, weren't we?

Did you get the full service? her husband asked. Shave and a hot towel? Short back and sides?

A beauty parlour couldn't improve Mrs. Pass, because she's already a perfect beauty, Peretti said. That's why we didn't notice. He gave Anna a cold, appraising look and said: You, I think the hair is a little curlier.

They laughed again, Peretti most of all, but she realized then he was keeping an eye on her.

Look, Buddy, her mother-in-law said, and together they fluttered their varnished fingernails for him. He grabbed his wife's hands and pulled her giggling onto his lap while her mother-in-law watched and Peretti sipped his drink. It was a performance.

Supper was fish. They spoke of the war, as they had done when her parents came to visit, but this time the conversation had an illicit quality because each of them ventured opinions and her father was not there to correct them. When the meal was over and she was removing plates, Peretti rose to help her. In the kitchen he said, Are you getting along better with your husband's mother?

So he has a confidante, my husband, she thought, or a confessor. A best girlfriend.

Is that your business? she asked.

Excuse me.

She saw he was amused and hesitated, weighing her words.

The younger Mrs. Pass is also very pretty, he said quietly into that space. With or without the beauty parlour. But she's not so sure about her husband. Is she?

I don't know what you mean, she said.

He works hard now, the long hours. He doesn't have so much time for her any more.

Buddy always worked hard.

She isn't lonely?

In the dining room, her mother-in-law laughed at something her husband had said. His voice reached her too, low and amused, baritone brown. She could hear Peretti's breathing, quite close, and the want in it. She turned away.

Your face, he said.

I really don't know what you're talking about.

She says she doesn't know, Peretti said, as though appealing to an invisible audience. Do I believe her?

The door opened and her husband, all the tall warm friendly bulk of him, came in with an empty unwashed platter and handed it to her, grinning at some joke he had left behind him in the other room.

What's going on? he asked when he saw her looking at him and the other man turned away.

Mr. Peretti was just telling me how hard you've been working.

Please, he said. Michael.

Michael Peretti began to come to the house, once a week or so, and for a long time they both acted innocent. Soon he was calling her mother-in-law Cora and bringing small gifts for the house, and her husband, misreading the situation entirely, wondered aloud if he wasn't quite taken with the older woman.

He's a flirt, she could have said, or, I don't like him, but she didn't. She wondered herself if the question was disingenuous or truly stupid. She watched her husband more closely these days – he did seem more distant – and became irritated with him more easily. Michael Peretti, she knew, was watching too, and biding his time. Only her mother-in-law seemed more relaxed lately, pinker in the face, and she regularly found the older woman staring at the window, pretending it wasn't a mirror.

Regularly, too, she returned to clean and air her mother-in-law's house, but the butcher's boy didn't come back. Once or twice she thought she heard his step by the back door, thought his shadow flicked across her body as she went by a window, thought he was spying on her, maybe, but it was all a trick of the wind and the trees and clouds miles up.

There was a day when she fell ill, a rare day when she was alone in the house, her mother-in-law having gone to sew baby things for the war with some of her hen friends, a day too when their visitor was expected for dinner and she had not the strength even to do the shopping. She lay in her cool bed as the light lengthened (it had hit her after lunch) and wept in frustration at the pain in her head and the uncontrollable shivering, at her helplessness now fully manifest. After a long time she went down to the kitchen and phoned for sausage and potatoes and some other things as they occurred to her. Slowly she found her purse and sorted out some money and sat back at the kitchen table and waited. After what felt like a long time she got up and unlocked the door and then returned to her chair. She dreamed then, a waking dream of great comfort and beauty, that someone had come to take her away, had simply walked into the kitchen and picked her up and carried her out of the house and out of her life entirely. Unlocking the door had been the sign – so simple, yet she had never guessed it.

When she woke she was ashamed, of course, that such a crude symbol had seemed so ravishing.

They found her glittery-eyed and feverish, the three of them returning at once, laughing and talking and sending the air crashing around her. They kissed her and petted her and held their palms to her brow and made her sweet tea and said how good she was and suggested remedies, bed foremost, but she was too weary to move. She could hardly speak.

Drink, drink, Michael Peretti said. His voice was soft and insistent, a thread.

There was a knock at the door. Her husband answered it.

Anna? he said. Baby, did you order this food?

Past him she saw the boy Stephen in a delivery boy's clothes, with a brown paper bag and a bill. He looked shocked.

The money she had laid out, it seemed, was not enough, so her husband invited the boy into the kitchen to wait while he found some more. He fumbled with his wallet, his rush making him clumsy; he hated embarrassments over money. She tried to apologize but they hushed her.

She didn't want us to go without our supper, her mother-in-law told Michael Peretti in her public voice. As sick as that and thinking of us.

The boy stood still as a cat, perhaps thinking, cat-like, if he didn't move they wouldn't be able to see him. She could see the outline of a cigarette pack in the chest pocket of his uniform.

I'm sorry, she said, louder. I wouldn't do it again.

He met her eye then, and she saw she had him.

There you are, soldier, her husband said, handing him some bills and change.

The boy looked him over once, then stood as tall as he could, squaring his shoulders. Thank *you*, he said.

The agency was on Davie Street, downtown, on the third floor of a four-storey brick building on the hill's crest with a spanking view of the ocean – there at the end of the last intersection, white and shining weakly. When she had come the first time her husband had taken pleasure in ushering her into the elevator cage, but this time it was stalled halfway to the first floor. A repairman had swung the cage back and prised the doors open and stood staring at the mess he had on his hands. The floor of the familiar red and gilt compartment was at eye level, poised above the black shaft, in which she recognized another cheap metaphor. She wondered how delicate the situation was.

When she had recovered from her illness and came down to breakfast a few mornings before, her husband and mother-in-law had greeted her as a team, the former with such frank shame and worry and eagerness for her to immediately sit down that she realized the latter had been filling his ear with silliness again. As she came to understand the nature of their fears, or rather hopes, she could only marvel at the breadth and variety of her mother-in-law's grotesquerie. That, of all things, now! And of course it was possible. *No wonder she's fretful*, the older woman would have said. *And so hungry all the time. Haven't you noticed?*

Imagine, she thought now, staring at the elevator shaft.

Stairs, please, Miss, the repairman said.

The secretary smiled the same slightly withheld smile, even wore the same poplin suit she had rather coveted the last time, with the nipped waist and neatly squared-off shoulders. Tall as a man she was, when she stood behind her desk to lead Anna back down the hall to the office that was beginning to feel as illicit and familiar as a favourite cheap room.

Now then, the agent said. What can I do for you today, Mrs. –

Pass, she supplied, smiling.

Mrs. Pass.

Yes, she said. Yes. I've come to pick up our policy.

Of course. We could have mailed it to you, though. Saved you the trouble.

Well, it's no trouble. Also I was wondering, she said. If you couldn't explain to me some of the terms.

Well, sure.

He bent over a drawer, rifling through some files.

Is that your son?

He glanced over his shoulder to flash her a sweet sudden smile, then reached across the desk, turning the framed photograph with his fingertips to face her. This is a couple of years old, he said. John's fourteen now.

What a nice boy.

He's a terror. This said equally, to amuse. You've none yourself?

Not yet.

Pass. Here we are.

He took her through it slowly. Gradually she became attuned to the office sounds around them – the mannish secretary's quick biting step, the outer door opening and closing, a deep-voiced man laughing and bullying someone on the telephone in the next office – and the building began to seem warmer, a place you could come to work in every day and not feel lost. But there really was no decent way to ask the questions she had in mind, and she saw it would be foolish in any case because he would certainly remember later.

How is your son a terror? she asked instead, at the door, buttoning up her purse.

Oh, you know. He held a hand out, conducting her exit. He's at that age. Everything embarrasses him, his old parents most of all. He thinks he's very misunderstood.

He sounds like a dear.

He caught the layer beneath the layer of words. She saw it in the sudden unhappy look he gave her as he said, Sometimes he's a very sweet boy, just like when he was little. Sometimes he's a complete stranger. There are moments when I truly believe he hates us. Can you remember being that way, when you were his age?

Can't you?

Fourteen, the agent said, shaking his head. At fourteen I spent a lot of time outdoors.

He smiled broadly then and she saw he had withdrawn his attention from her, had gone back inside himself like a turtle, though he continued to joke and chat as he showed her out.

In the days that followed she went through her memories like a woman going through a pouch of coins, trying to reckon what exactly she had:

Sitting with him, side by side on her parents' couch. Shame

made her despise him. When he placed a hand flat on the cushion between them, reaching but not touching, she wanted him dead.

My daughter tells me you're a journalist, Mr. Pass.

She let nothing show. She had told her father exactly what this boy she'd met did, but he was determined to put everyone in the room in his place. Privately he would call her suitor a mechanic. Overnight he would grow chary of touching her, with a pointedness that said she had changed hands, how did she like that?

Well, not exactly, sir. He shot her a sheepish sideways smile as though realizing she might be dumb after all. Actually –

You might as well know we think Anna's too young, her father said. Eighteen is too young for what you have in mind, her mother and I agree.

No, no, no, he said. I mean, sir, there'll be chaperones. My whole family will be there, I don't guess we'll have a minute to ourselves all weekend. I have sisters, he said, appealing suddenly to her mother.

Sisters, how nice, her mother said.

Anna doesn't ski, her father said.

The lodge belonged to Buddy's uncle, a hearty roguish twenties type with slick hair who called his nephew Bernie and pretended to have a heart attack when he met Anna. She would remember the weekend as a collage of hair and gloves and teeth and coins, for sleigh rides and hot cider, dropped and gone in the snow. Buddy's sisters were both cheerful plain tomboys with good skis who had brought assorted girlfriends and boyfriends and country cousins, a noisy athletic crowd that treated Anna with a kind of amiable deference, like they would an exotic, expensive cat. They had cast her as the rich city girl, the catch, the juicy Juliet with the pretty muff and the useless boots whose parents almost didn't let her come. Finally, the friendly little cousin she shared a room with told her she was Buddy's first serious girlfriend and they were all keeping their fingers crossed.

Buddy himself grew ruddy in the wintry air, horsing around with snowballs and taking her for walks in the woods. On one such walk he jokingly said, You might as well know I intend to marry you.

You do?

Sure. He scooped up some snow, packed it with excess attention, and popped it at a tree trunk. That all right with you?

She thought of home, her parents' closed kingdom. She noticed how his mouth stayed open as he concentrated on his aim. It seemed a small enough thing to get used to.

The wedding was a swell affair and a strange procedure. She remembered it in the black and sudden white of exploding flashbulbs. Her white-gloved fingertips on her father's black-sleeved arm, the brief unchaste kiss, the nagging weight of the second ring, the cracked cake, the honeymoon in a downtown hotel room. Out on the bay the freighters were tipped with bits of lights, and the North Shore mountains were a dark mass against the last light in the sky. To the south were Kitsilano, the beaches, Point Grey. Straight ahead, west, were the islands, studs in the crawling sea. A rich man's view. His skin smelled of soap and smoke. She wept with the pain, expectedly.

An argument, this one brushed with malice sticky as tar. She had bought some books.

But they're second-hand, she said.

It was the bulk of them that seemed to aggravate him: ten books. Ten books! Before it was over he had reminded her of his meagre income, his miserable inheritance, his own worrisome health, his troubles over the house – when the lawyers advised him to sell, his mother had cried. Greedy, he said now. Women were greedy, also stubborn. They didn't know the value of a dollar. They were sentimental, they formed sentimental attachments to objects, they lacked a sense of fitness and proportion, they spent money like it was toy. She would have to take them back.

Not my books, she said. Oh, Buddy, not my books.

He was firm. He lectured her again, patiently repeating himself. If she did not take them back, he said, he would have no choice but to suspend her allowance. She was irresponsible, like a child, and spendthrift, and sulky. She saw it was his increased responsibilities at work that had given him this new taste for supervision, and determined to shred his new composure.

At least I don't send my friends to check up on you, she said.

He offered to.

Peretti, they meant, when she was still sick. He had returned one evening when her mother-in-law was at bridge, to tell her her husband would be working late, and to see if she needed anything.

No, thank you, she had said.

May I, he had started. Then, instead: How are you feeling?

Ever so much better, she said. It was true. The fever had broken, leaving her feeling weak and saintly, cool, a little thin at the edges but back on land, certainly.

Have I upset you?

They had been sitting across from each other in the living room. She had not made a move to light the lamps as the day waned, hoping he would take the hint, but darkness had fallen and he had stayed.

No, she said. Her voice seemed loud in the dark. His face wasn't clear. She said again, more softly, No.

That evening, I meant. In the kitchen.

No.

No, he repeated. Well. He sat forward and she wondered if he was gathering himself to leave, the way a bird gathers itself to launch. He said what she had been thinking: I can't see your face.

He wasn't checking up on you, anyway, her husband said. I don't send people to check up on you. That's quite a hell of a thing to say.

I suppose it is.

You suppose it is. What's got into you, anyway? You're getting damn hard to be around, you know that? You never used to be so, so –

It's your precious job. I suppose you think –

– anything to do with my job. Such a –

I'm bored, Buddy. I'm going out of my mind.

Such a bitch, frankly.

They stared at each other. Now they were somewhere.

Yes, well, she said. Suppose we do something about that.

Now you're just being silly, he said, because she was putting her coat on. From upstairs her mother-in-law was calling, Buddy? Buddy, what's going on?

It was a warm night, with a few white points of stars and shreds of high cloud, and a moon like a thumbprint. She had told him the truth and he had not even shrugged. Out of my mind, that was what she had said. It was the correct phrase. Stepping out of the front door, she felt she had left a small space for a larger one, a place without heat or pressure or constraint, and if she were careful she might remain there for a while, until she had completed certain tasks. Later she might have to come back to the world and to her own small self, but she had a window now.

⬥

You're joking, the butcher's boy said.

They sat in the café again, mid-morning this time, as passing

automobiles struck flares of light off the saltcellars, tipping the
boy's ears with a lurid translucence. They were the only customers. Behind the counter, the waitress swept. On the high
ceiling a pair of fans slowly wheeled, like the lazy noses of
planes, their big orbits telescoped down to her hand idly circling
a spoon through her coffee. Since the night of her decision she
had seemed to live within the gearwheels of a perfect watch.

Now the boy sat across from her, squinting in the strong light.
The sun cut a line across their table, cutting her off at the wrist,
painting her out with shade. I must be practically nothing to him,
she thought: a dim nearness, a voice only. She stayed back in it.

I couldn't do that, he said.

Well, you don't expect me to, do you?

She had him on the rack. He was trembling again, thoughts
written on his skin like a girl's.

Look at you blush, she said.

Don't you – doesn't your husband –

His fingers fidgeted with the detritus on the table between
them, a napkin, a sugar sachet. They could not keep coming to
this same café, she decided. The risk was too great. Peripherally
she sensed the waitress and for a moment felt a pulling tiredness, the eyes-closed colourlessness of despair. There were too
many details to keep in balance, too many pins and cogs. One
slip would jam the whole mechanism, flip her life to farce, or
worse. The boy, too, she saw, was hesitating. He thought himself
the hero of a grand passion, had not realized until a moment ago
that there could be humiliation in success as well as in failure.
She would have to work him for a while, like a dough.

I wouldn't ask you if I could do it myself. If there were another
way.

I'm too young.

Are you, suddenly?

The look he planted on her then.

It's easy, she murmured. You go into the drugstore. If there's a lady in there you buy a paper and go to another drugstore. When you find a good one you just go up to the man and ask. You say, I want –

The sachet tore in his fingers, sending a spray of sweetness across the table between them.

I want –

He reached across the table to cover her mouth with his hand. She pushed it away. Will you? she said.

He nodded.

Like an artist, she saw the prettier ways it might have been done. I can't eat, she might have said, I can't sleep, do you know how thoughts of you distract me? She might have seized his wrist, just now, and suckled the sugar from his fingers. But these were the cheap possibilities, the gaudy strips of celluloid to leave on the cutting room floor. Her style was colder. She was here at all because of that cold empty place. True, she might not have lied, might simply have taken what she needed from the cheerful mess in Buddy's bathroom drawer (he was constantly losing count, running out, constantly), but she needed the boy to see that he was capable of doing things for her, things he never expected of himself, things that might at first have seemed impossible.

The waitress was not the same one as the first time, but that was just luck.

I don't like this café, she said. Let's not come here any more.

Then there was the house to prepare.

In the bedroom her husband's parents had shared she remade the stripped mattress, swathing its faded, faintly stained cabbage roses in a snap and drift of white linen. She gathered up her mother-in-law's fripperies – a china goose-girl, a nosegay of dried primrose and clove, a toilet set, lipstickery, framed photographs of the baby Buddy – and hid them in the top drawer of the bureau. It would not matter if she put them back in the wrong places when the time came. She had moved them to dust, she would say, that was all. Anyone could run his finger along the windowsill and see that was true. They had set no assignation yet and as she moved around the room she felt pleasantly detached, mechanical, as though she were carrying out tasks which had been allotted to her but which of themselves meant nothing. Anyone watching her would see nothing out of the ordinary: a woman fixing a room. Even if she chose to go down and open the door to the basement (as she did now) and sit on the top step for a while, the most she could be accused of was curiosity. She had been sent down here once or twice to fetch pickles or a bucket, waving a hand in the absolute dark before her, swatting like a kitten for the string to the single bulb, and once her husband had hidden below in the crook of the unbanistered stairs and grabbed her before she'd found it, snatching her off her feet and down into the darkness with him. That had been a terrible thing to do. Now she sat dreamily in her kerchief, chin in hand, noting the essential (only one door in or out, that she sat in; no windows; concrete walls) and the inessential (her husband's old toys, train set, a bicycle, skis, preserves, steamer trunks emblazoned with great emblems of locks and corners decked like epaulettes, a mangle and rack). What harm, what crime, in looking? What crime in an act of imagination?

That night she served peaches and pears for dessert.

Are these my own? her mother-in-law asked.

Why, yes. You don't mind?

Her mother-in-law did not touch her spoon. Preserves are for winter, she said. It's almost May.

Have I done wrong?

Her mother-in-law lifted her eyes from the fruit and smiled and said softly, You greedy, wasteful girl, and started to cry.

⬥

Across a shaved lawn she could see a nurse conducting a game of croquet. The players tapped the balls with their mallets, distance gently disjointing sound's ball from action's socket, and stood back out of each other's way. The intense quiet gave it the aura of a championship match.

Anna!

The players looked up as one. She understood they had been soldiers, boys whose families could afford private care.

Her husband stood on the stone steps of the nearest building, waving her over. The sanatorium was several Victorian buildings set on rolling, discreetly gated grounds. You did not walk from one building to the next but rather took a small bus. In the farthest buildings there were some very sad cases but there were no bars on the windows here, and when she first escaped to this bench a young nurse had come trotting after her, offering to bring a cup of tea out to the lawn. There had been a tiny bit of a scene, inside.

The doctor would like to talk to us, he said, when she reached the portico.

How is she?

She wants a private room.

Inside a second time, then, where the halls smelled acceptably of floor wax and disinfectant. The ceilings were high and to the wall outside the doctor's office was stapled a large crucifix.

You didn't mind the little mix-up, I hope? the doctor said. Our patient expressly forbade –

Of course, her husband said.

You must not take it personally, the doctor told Anna, crinkling his face. One of the symptoms of this kind of breakdown is paranoia. Our patient will manifest a strong dislike of a loved one, often triggered by the most trivial incident. Naturally she would refuse to see you. In her current state she barely knows who you are.

She seemed quite rational just now, her husband said in a low voice.

Grieving is a complicated process, a mysterious process. You must think of it as the soul caring for itself.

Yes, of course, Anna said.

They walked back across the lawn to the bus stop.

Did you tell the doctor about the dessert? she asked.

I told him.

I didn't know it was his favourite. Your father.

Of course you didn't.

I wouldn't have put it in front of her if I'd known –

All right.

They watched the shuttle bus toil up the hill, so slowly that it seemed to run not on oil and gas but on a small child's winding.

Can you fix her house up? he said suddenly. Make it nice?

Her mind scuttled, a spider, reaching in every direction at once.

I just don't think you should sell it without her consent. It will be one more blow.

They sat in the car on the sandy grass verge of the dirt road watching the waves roll up the beach. Behind them loomed the ancient tangled forest of the University endowment lands. He had driven her here once when they were courting and then lost his nerve. Perhaps because of that first occasion it had become their holy talking place. He liked to trap her here on rainy

Sundays and talk about his dreams and plans for them, and when necessary to pick at such recalcitrant shoelace knots as arose in their lives. He liked to smoke out the open window and talk or just watch the rain through the windshield while she watched his profile, or curled obediently under his arm. He could never see the ugliness in the metal sea, the endlessly dripping trees. Often he would bring his camera and practise while she stayed in the car, curds of headache curling and thickening in her skull.

She could be in there a month, her husband said. I'm cutting corners as it is, putting her in a shared room, but there's no other way I can afford it.

What's the room like?

I didn't think it was bad. There's a curtain separating the beds. The other woman wasn't there. The nurse told me she lost a baby.

Oh.

(She wondered if that was the woman they had seen on their way upstairs, before the nurses stopped them, apologetically but firmly, and sent Anna back down; the quite young, dazed woman who had looked directly at Anna as though she recognized her and said, I'm cold.)

How is she?

She was only half-awake because of the medications. But just as I was leaving she said she wanted her own room. She was pretty clear about that.

Maybe she meant she wants to be home. In her own room with her own things.

You don't want her living with us, is that it?

She said nothing, was silent long enough for him to become repentant. Then she said, Let's go home.

Are we friends?

Buddy, please, let's go home.

I'm sorry. But I don't like arguing with you. It's all we seem to do any more.

Well, I don't like it either.

Truce?

She touched his cheek with her hand. It was enough, apparently.

What a lousy day, he said in a more normal voice, turning the key in the ignition.

The boy stood with his pants in his hands, hands pink to the wrist because she had sent him to wash them, they were so cold. He had smelled chokingly of aftershave and she had told him to wash that off too.

Have you got them? she had asked first thing, and he had laughed and pulled an envelope of prophylactics from his jacket pocket and tossed them to her, frightening her a little. She had expected certain things but not playfulness, not *happiness*. She had been reassured by his delivery boy's bicycle, its wheels glittering in rhythm with her thoughts as he walked it into the back shed as she had directed, but then his face had confused her.

Have you done this before? she asked.

Curiosity killed the cat.

He had actually said that, the very words.

They kissed for a long time in the kitchen. She had decided this would be the worst part, and therefore it was. There was no natural spark between them, no comfort. His hands were clumsy and cold. But even as she doubted curiosity quickened deep in her, a worm in the brain, and again it was as though she could look into darkness and see shining a single thread, a filament of a path through to the other side. If that was the way forward, she would go forward. She would do one thing and the next thing and see what happened then.

He pulled away from her, flushed, almost unrecognizable, and said something thickly that she didn't catch. When he repeated it she felt a great wincing contraction of pity coupled with an electric eagerness to proceed. The filament glowed white-hot along its length. She sent him to wash.

You're quiet this evening.

Am I?

Penny, he said. She held out her hand. He rolled his eyes, smiling, and dug in his pockets.

I've got a penny, Michael Peretti said.

She reached across the table and let him press it into her palm. Now I've got to deliver, she said. She felt less afraid of him now, even though he still held her hand a fraction too long, even under her husband's eyes.

I want my money's worth.

You'll get it, she said. I was thinking about the war.

Is she telling the truth, Pass?

How should I know? her husband said. Grinning, though. Earlier Peretti had enquired after her mother-in-law and expressed his concern like a gentleman. He had rested a hand on her husband's shoulder and asked for the name of her pavilion so he could send flowers. Did she have a favourite flower? Roses, her husband said apologetically, but he had taken it in stride. Now they were kidding a little in their old way – a first small sweet candy, bittersweet, after their long abstinence.

What about the war, then? he asked. What does she think of the war?

That it will be over soon.

She reads the newspapers.

Smiling: Sometimes she does.

And will we be better or worse off when it's over?

What a question, she said, and started to clear the table.

What were you really thinking about at supper this evening? her husband asked her later, after Peretti had gone. You were miles away.

Have you taken your pill?

Sitting in bed, he held up his water glass to toast her. She saw him in the mirror of her vanity, where she sat with her back to him, brushing her hair. When he set it down she saw the dim places where his fingerprints had clouded the glass.

Maybe you should sell the house, she said slowly. I've been thinking.

That's more like it. He looked up from his magazine, interested now.

I keep thinking about your mother, she said, wrinkling her brow. And those boys playing croquet. And how when I asked her to come to the house with me she always said she couldn't face it yet. I've been thinking she might be afraid of having to go back there and selling it might actually be a weight off her mind.

See, he said eagerly, slapping his magazine on his leg. That's just what –

Wait, though. My mind's been going round and round. I keep trying to juggle the best thing for you and the best thing for her –

– understand me. I –

Yes, she said. We'll have to show the house. I'll get it ready, like you asked me to.

Come here, he said.

Have you taken your pill?

There had been no pleasure in it, his eagerness, his breathing. She lay curled in the heavy warmth of her husband's pinning limbs, soft meat in his shell, and let images from the afternoon reappear. Fumes, nothing. Despite his cocky entrance he had

clearly not done anything of the kind before and between them
they had not even managed to warm the sheets. She had lain in
gooseflesh while he strained, with his skinny sharp knees and
skinny sharp elbows, his bitter little hip bones pestling her own.
The joke was how quickly he coated the reality of it, came to
believe he'd acquitted himself like a champion. Or perhaps
the joke was on her, the joke being that the prism of his senses
so refracted her own experience that he really had been as happy,
as shot with rainbows, all that hour, as he swore. Her husband
shifted beside her in sleep, managing to turn away and bring her
with him, so that their positions reversed and she pressed
against his back, their four ankles still tangled. If it were only
this half of him, the night half, the hot sweat of the marriage
bed, if only she could cut away what she wanted as though
cutting away the bad half of an orange. She would leave a trail of
halved people if she could, even (sleepy now, fonder now) keep
a small wedge of the boy to squeeze into her blander days. The
intensity that propelled him past caution, the way curiosity did
her: that tart concentrate. That she would keep.

Suddenly her days were full, dangerously full, glass after dark,
brimming glass she must carry across whitest carpet. The real
estate agent, a major's wife keeping the business warm, came
every day with the spare keys to prepare a lunch in her mother-
in-law's kitchen and drink tea from her mother-in-law's cups and
show prospective buyers what she referred to as the house's
points. (Some of her mother-in-law's wealthy crosstown friends
had decked themselves out in hats and gloves, as prospective
buyers, to keep an eye on the woman for poor Cora's sake, they
told Anna when they proposed the cabal, something they would
never have suggested had the agent been the major. Though

they enjoyed their tea the same either way by the number of cups, stained and grimy with sugar, left in the sink every evening.) And every evening, now, after this approximation of a working woman left, Anna arrived to clean – shoe prints on the floors, furniture out of place, smudges on walls and glass and brass, some fingerprints to wipe away, many more to leave. Her days were full, the house was full of prospective buyers known by their soiling, of her parents'-in-law's appalled ghosts. (She pictured them precisely where they had left themselves, *in extremis*: her father-in-law at the kitchen table breathless over a newspaper, her mother-in-law smiling at a spoon.)

There was the boy. When she explained he mustn't leave marks on her, she saw his eyes deepen at the thought, one which had not previously occurred to him. She saw she was damaging him but it was not to be helped.

Evidence: he grew braver. On the first of May he produced the little leaf of paper she had given him the first time they met in the café. He carried it everywhere, evidently, tucked inside his cigarette box. They had had a little connubial conversation about it, nude and cooling, had talked a little philosophy, aired a little cynicism there on the sheets. He had liked that. She began to get a sense of his life – the giddy younger sister, the family dog, the meaty meals, and his contentment with it all until he started reading certain books. He had been a happy child (she placed it, finally, that telltale lingering coarseness, that inclination to *laugh*), but now he claimed to recognize a fecklessness in his mother's sandwich doilies, a living death in his father's ruminant tranquility before the radio every evening. (The sister he loved and swallowed whole and would have died for, though he didn't know it and was as abominable to her as he knew how.) He read, he brooded, he suspected himself of a superior intellect. His grades slipped even lower. His friends smoked but

they did not read Sartre. He had no one to talk to about Sartre
and Marx and Turgenev, his salt licks, and then there was the business of girls and women, the torment of girls and women. After
he left her in the evenings, he returned to the store to help his
father slaughter chickens, and then he had homework, algebra,
and then to bed where – he claimed with a morose relish – he
couldn't sleep for thinking of her and their "impossible situation."

Her husband, too, worked into every evening now, a foot in
each job while the management decided where they liked him
better, setting type or taking pictures. At night they lay together,
jointly and severally exhausted, minds swirling with plans and
cold dregs of plans.

⌖

Buddy, that's wonderful.

Starting Monday. (He socked his fist repeatedly into his palm,
like a boy waiting on a baseball.) I'll be working directly under
Peretti now. And another five dollars a week, how about that?

You deserve it.

At first I didn't know what was going on. Tanner called me
into his office and there's Peretti at his elbow and both of them
looking grim as thunder. For a minute I thought it was that
Bonner business again, you remember?

He blushed a little just saying it, she noticed.

The next thing I know there's a glass in my hand and they're
toasting my future. I couldn't believe it.

It's wonderful news. Do you think –

Mm?

Wait. Do you think I could have my allowance back, in that
case? We can afford it now, can't we?

He let go.

I see, she said.

I told you how it was. It's not a matter of what we can afford or not afford. You have to show a little responsibility first. You must learn. I told you.

All right, you told me, she said.

The next evening they were invited to a party at the Tanners' in honour of her husband's promotion. They had quarrelled again in the car on the way over and when they got there he abandoned her at the door, riding into the big house on a swell of cheers when the other guests realized who it was. She hung back, allowing Mrs. Tanner to take her coat and congratulate her on her husband's good fortune.

Oh, we're thrilled, Anna said.

So you should be, dear, Mrs. Tanner said.

Knowing no one, she smiled and smiled and looked for small places where she could stand aside and watch the room. Someone brought her a drink, wet all over the outside of the glass, and talked to her. He must have got bored because she took a sip of her drink and when she looked again he was gone. So strong was her desire to be anywhere else that the room lost reality, thinned somehow, until normal behaviour seemed strange as anthropology. She knew it was necessary for these guests, these colleagues, to talk to one another; she knew it was necessary for their wives to smile and laugh and speak and be pleasant and set one another at ease. They greeted her but instinct moved them quickly away, as though from a vacuum they risked being sucked into. Far away, through layers and layers of glass, these good people lived their lives, but she was another species entirely, with her quick black smarts, her smiles reeking of theatre, and they knew it, and she knew it. Nothing came naturally. A merciful God would not let me know these things about myself, she thought. He wouldn't render His creation so clumsily and then give her a hawk's eye.

I hadn't taken you for a wallflower.

Am I?

Aren't you?

What did you take me for, then?

A collage of images assembled and disassembled in her mind in the moments of realizing who had taken her elbow and greeted her so familiarly: rinsing relief, first, at the familiar voice, and second the flaring realization that he was the one she should have chosen. He would have been willing, would have known what to do. In this reaction she saw the dimensions of her own loneliness, even as she found herself wondering if she had ever truly disliked him.

They're not used to a young man, Peretti was saying, nodding across the room to where her tall tow-headed husband stood in a clutch of women old enough to see a son in him.

He was desperate when the army wouldn't take him. People used to say things to him on the street, just walk up to him and call him a coward. To look at him you wouldn't know there was a thing wrong with him.

He almost didn't get this promotion because of that, Peretti said. Tanner wasn't sure he'd be able to take the strain.

He can take it.

Can you?

You ask very personal questions, Mr. Peretti.

Michael.

Michael.

I take a personal interest, he said. Is she enjoying herself?

Why, sure I am.

Is she happy?

Of course.

No, she isn't.

You do ask the most extraordinary questions.

I get excited when you lie, Michael Peretti said. Why is that?

Will you excuse me, she said, but he would not leave go her hand.

I know a friend of yours, by the way.

She was watching the Tanners.

Bumped into him, I should say. Boy on a bicycle, staring at your house. The last time I came for dinner.

Friend of mine? she said. I don't know any boys.

She was watching the Tanners bully a young reporter into another drink. Cat and dog, those Tanners, hot bark to icy purr, and every night they lay down together as though the rice was still in their hair. You could tell. They'd be bringing out cigars next. Peretti's thumb in her palm. Her mind everywhere.

You do, Michael Peretti said. Because I saw him at your mother-in-law's house also, one evening last week, going round back like he knew his business.

What were you doing there?

Expecting to find you alone.

Across the room her husband saw them standing together and held a hand up to Peretti, who did the same, like men saluting each other across railroad tracks. There's no sin in dreaming, is there? he murmured. I have an idea what her little life is like.

Do you?

A boy? he said. A child? Shame, Mrs. Pass.

I don't know what you're talking about.

She watched his broad back as he walked away from her, toward her husband, and shivered. Oh yes, he was definitely the one she should have used. She watched them meet in the centre of the room, shake hands, and trade places: the American to stand amongst the newspapermen, her husband to come to her side.

He was laughing still at something the other had said. When he reached her he said, Your face. What was Michael telling you?

Oh, she said. I'm in a black mood tonight. He was just trying to cheer me up.

Anna?

Sleep left her slowly, teasingly stripping its veils away. She had been dreaming that someone was crying, a great rhythmic wailing that made sense of something she had been struggling to understand. The last puzzle piece fell into place as she realized the sound was coming from her own mouth.

Baby, wake up.

She whimpered a little at being woken. The wail persisted. So it was not coming from her after all.

Something's happening, her husband said, his own face still creased with sleep as he winced at the morning light.

Air-raid sirens, that was the sound. She looked at the clock: four minutes after seven.

It's the war, she said, realizing. It's over.

They went downtown, like everyone else, it turned out. They took the streetcar, where the driver waved them on for free. The men were laughing and shaking hands all up and down the car, full of pep, and the girls were all dressed to the nines. Anna found herself next to a little waitress who was skipping her shift to go downtown and see the fun.

Well, I'd like to see him fire me over this, she kept saying, and Anna kept nodding as though she was intimate with the details. He can threaten every little bit he wants. *I've* got brothers just the same as anyone.

They'll be coming home soon? Anna said politely.

The waitress turned to the woman on her other side and said, I'd just like to see him fire me. I'd just like to see him try.

The streetcar made halting progress as cars surged by, honking and trailing strings of tin cans, with passengers leaning out the windows, cheering and waving. People without cars ran alongside the traffic, shaking cowbells, blowing whistles, beating pot lids, any noisemakers they could find. They weaved in and out of traffic, strangers beating out tattoos on the sides of the tram and kissing each other. A tribe of young boys who had clearly skipped school were behaving like Red Indians, with makeshift headdresses and feathers, whooping and stomping in a victory dance. Above it all the air-raid sirens persisted, keening peace.

At Hastings and Granville the streetcar stopped and the driver put everyone off. It was as though they had jumped into an ocean of sound: the car horns, the bells and whistles, a ragged refrain of "Roll Out the Barrel," and from the harbour the obstinate lowing of ships' horns. Faces flared and faded back into the crowd: men of business and their secretaries, newsboys determinedly hawking papers left over from the weekend. Looking up, Anna saw men and women leaning out of office windows and emptying their wastepaper baskets onto the revellers below. Then the air was full of paper, white scraps she picked from her hair – bank statements, tickertape, adding-machine paper, bills. More young boys were festooning the lamp standards with toilet tissue, and then the church bells began to ring. They forged upstream to Hastings and Howe, where office workers had formed a conga line and were dancing through the crowd, picking up length by the moment. Anna lost go of her husband's hand then and felt herself swept towards the whip-end of the dancers. A man behind her seized her hips and tried to manoeuvre her into the line. He nuzzled into her hair and licked at her ear, pressing her into the dancer in front of her, whose shoulders she had automatically taken to steady herself. Then Buddy was back, laughing and pulling her away.

All right? he said. She could not hear his voice but made out the words from the shape of his lips.

Fine, she said, and could not hear her own voice either.

He pushed her ahead of him after that, keeping a hand on her neck like a collar, so he wouldn't lose her again. She felt the skin of her throat go taut and slack, taut and slack, as he kneaded the back of her neck in his excitement.

As the morning wore on, the festivities became both more organized and more general. They wandered all over downtown, letting themselves be pushed by the crowd. Cars were draped with flags, now, Red Ensigns and Union Jacks, and the cathedrals had thrown open their doors for impromptu thanksgiving services. Crepe paper streamers replaced toilet paper in Maypole whirls around the lamps and in the trees, and one department store had hung enormous coloured likenesses of Mr. Churchill, Mr. Stalin, and President Roosevelt from their fourth-floor windows. But stores were largely closed, some with their windows nervously boarded over, and by noon many cafés were closed too, having run out of food.

My camera, Buddy said, stricken.

They were standing a ways up Granville Street, by the Birks clock, not far from where a woman had just fainted away from all the excitement. A photographer had appeared even before some men with a stretcher, a man who exchanged nods with her husband before going about his work, asking people to step back and give him a little room around the unconscious woman with the blouse skewed off over one shoulder.

That's Smith, her husband said, fretting now. You met him

at the Tanners', don't you remember? By God, I should be working too.

She thought for a moment, then took a single halting step and stumbled against him as though her legs had gone weak. She held a hand to her forehead and said wonderingly, Buddy?

Just the heat, that's all, her husband was saying a moment later to the knot of concerned passersby who had gathered round. He had got her to sit on the curb and was squatting next to her, fanning her with his big paddle of a hand. Saying: Just the heat and the excitement.

I should go home, she said.

He looked torn, then, as she had planned.

I heard some people saying the streetcars are running again, she said. We could split up, if you like. I'll just head home if you want to get your camera from the office.

I can't let you go alone, he said uncertainly, glancing at the man Smith, who had abandoned the unconscious woman and was now posing some pretty office girls with tambourines against a wall and snapping away while they stuck out their chests and giggled.

I'm fine now. I'll just go home, that's all. She took his hand and looked into his eyes and said seriously, I'm fine.

Go to Mother's house, he suggested. It's closer.

By the time she got to her mother-in-law's house it was mid-afternoon. The excitement in the streets grew sparser as she left downtown, though here and there she encountered a clutch of housewives listening to the radio on each other's front lawns and teenagers stuffing toilet tissue through the open windows of parked cars. When she saw the house at a distance her need for solitude broke like a fever. If she had to smile one more time or wave one more time, if she had to dance or sing, if she had to perform for one more person –

Finally, said a voice, as she fumbled her key in the front-door lock.

Baby and Buddy, Stephen said. My God.

Stop it.

He prodded her with a finger, the butcher's boy, like she was a cut of chicken. He tried to be sardonic but he had dog eyes. He had skipped school and come straight to the house this morning, he had said, as soon as he realized what day it was. He had been hurt, she could tell, that she had not automatically done the same. Hours he had waited, hiding in the shadow of the shed, with all that nonsense in his mind and his heart and his pants. Now it was early evening.

We can't meet here any more, she said. Outside another car sounded its horn.

I wish you had a car, she added, going up on her elbows.

He didn't look at her but his eyebrows went up. So do I, he told the ceiling, and she knew he was gazing on a world of private desires that did not touch her at all. But there was not supposed to be any such world.

We can't meet here any more, she said again, and then, Don't you know any nice girls at school?

Nice girls, he said. Sure, nice girls.

Outside a shrill white whistle sliced the air, followed by a bang and the sound of footsteps sprinting to silence. Kids, she said, and he: Fireworks.

Downstairs the front door slammed.

Anna? he breathed.

She mouthed, Get dressed.

Another explosion, so close that the room was briefly flooded with milk.

Anna! her husband called.

They dressed in furious silence. His shirt was grimy at the nape, and staleness wafted from the folds of her dress when she picked it off the floor. Theirs was a small story, a loveless cliché, with only a little bitter lust at the pith.

Anna! her husband called, his voice closer, bottom of the stairs.

Coming! she called.

I came to see how you are, he called. You didn't answer the phone.

You're going to help me with something, she whispered to the boy.

He nodded dumbly.

Don't come up! she called down to her husband. I'm coming! Put the kettle on, would you? Isn't it wonderful?

In the swarming silver point half-darkness she took a pair of white cotton gloves from the dresser and whispered, Put these on.

They glowed serenely on his hands, like mitts.

Take this, she said, handing him the china goose-girl.

Perplexed, he half smiled.

I'm going to go down there, she whispered. I'm going to turn him around so his back is to the stairs. You're not going to make a sound. You're going to wait by the turn in the stairs until you hear me say, That's fine. Then you're going to come all the way down.

My bike's still in the shed, he whispered doubtfully. I've got deliveries tomorrow, I can't leave it. You want me to use the front door?

I want you to hit him on the head as hard as you can.

He started shaking, and her whole body began to sparkle.

⬥

Here you are, he said.

They embraced. From outside came the sound of more fireworks, tripping a clatter of falling garbage cans and a dog's snatching bark, and farther away radios and car horns and, she heard now, cheers. His skin smelled of soap and smoke and was warm.

I've come to get you, he said. The paper wants me to stay out all night, but I wanted you to come. I want us to remember this together. Will you come?

Of course, she whispered.

Are you cold? He rubbed her back and bare arms. You're barefoot, he said, noticing. The kettle started to moan. Beneath the moaning she heard the stairs creak once.

I washed my stockings, she said. They're probably dry by now.

Over his shoulder she saw the boy's white face. He came down the last step and when she turned as though towards the kettle he raised the figurine and brought it down on her husband's head. It didn't break. Her husband half turned and caught a second blow on the temple. He stood still.

That's fine, she said.

What's wrong with it? the boy asked, meaning the figurine. The three of them looked at each other. A second later a goose fell from the figurine's foot and hit the floor. Her husband sank to his knees.

Hit him again, she said, but he tipped over then and lay still.

She had expected to feel different. She had expected some blood rush or clarity but it was simply the world in yet another possible arrangement. The kettle whistled until she stepped over and took it off the burner. The sound died sulkily.

Why didn't it break? she asked.

It did, the boy said, and a moment later a rain of china chips and shards poured from his hands. His grip had held it together.

Her husband moaned once but his eyes stayed closed.

We should make it look like a robbery, the boy said.

God bless the movies, she said. Get his wallet.

Outside another rocket exploded. They both ducked. My God, the boy said, laughing. You live, don't you?

He'd have done you worse.

He drew his foot back as though to kick the prone man, lips drawing back from his teeth simultaneously, as though foot and lip were drawn by a single marionette string, then abandoned the gesture and squatted down to peer at him. His head's going to hurt tomorrow, he said.

No it isn't.

She was rifling the kitchen drawers, leaving some ajar. The boy patted at the man's pants and withdrew a leather wallet and a vial of pills.

Now what?

Take the money out and drop it.

The wallet dropped by her husband's face, stirring a hair or two on his forehead. What do I do with this? the boy said, holding out some paper money.

Keep it.

What about these?

Give them to me.

What are you looking for?

Outside a radio came on loudly, dance music.

Go up and rob the bedroom, she said.

Shouldn't we leave?

Anna, her husband said in a low voice.

She found the twine. Hold him, she said.

As she worked she seemed to see their six hands like a knot of larval creatures writhing in a nest – the boy containing the man's weakly struggling hands between his own while she wound the twine around and around the fat white wrists.

They got him into the basement between them, though his weight got away from them at the bottom. He fell the last few stairs heavily and once again lay still, near a decorative iron drain plate set like a navel in the concrete floor. There was a slight slope all around it, as though it had been gently depressed by a giant fingertip, pulling the floor with it. A few milky chips of china still adhered to her husband's cheek from the dragging across the kitchen floor.

Get the light, she said. The boy jerked the string and squeezed past her to the kitchen. She stood for a moment looking down into the blackness.

Baby? her husband's voice said. She realized he could see her up above him, framed in silhouette by the light of the kitchen.

She suffered him a long look, then closed the door and threw the bolt.

Go up and rob the bedroom, she repeated, because the boy was staring at her.

She stood alone for a moment trying to enumerate the crimes committed so far. She didn't think breaking the figurine counted for anything. So there were the two blows, *assault*; tying the hands; and locking the door. That counted, probably. But these last two would be erased, they would not exist by tomorrow. He would probably sleep for a while now, her husband.

The boy returned with a few spiked flowers of her mother-in-law's jewellery, earrings and brooches, most of it paste, she knew, but for the one charm bracelet of horrible clanking sterling silver. She was probably wearing her rings.

Tomorrow you'll have to get rid of these, she said. Bury them or throw them in the ocean. Did you make a mess?

He nodded.

That's good. That's what a robber would have done.

Who's going to find him?

I am. Tomorrow.

Think he'll remember anything?

I don't think so, she said.

He'll think he was hallucinating.

She embraced him then, spontaneously, for the narrow earnest machinery of his thinking. He was still innocent though she was not. She had a black dye contained in her own skin and despite the past ten minutes or half-hour or whatever it had been he was still untouched, unstained by her. She knew he could still reconcile all they had done, so far, with self-defence, or passion. Perhaps they had escaped love only narrowly after all.

I have to go now, she said. There's one more thing I need you to do.

We can't both leave at the same time, he guessed.

Well. Yes. That's it. Now, listen.

Far away, below them, something glass smashed.

Jesus, the boy said, almost giggling.

Outside someone was sliding the loud radio's tuning dial, sucking down stripes of static and music and announcers proclaiming peace from the ether. Somewhere a string of rockets popped serially, like corn.

I need you to stay here tonight, she said. And just before you leave I need you to go down there and untie his hands. Take the string with you and get rid of it when you get rid of the jewellery. Make sure you get all the bits.

Oh Jesus, the boy said, finally realizing.

He'll be sleeping. You won't have to worry.

From below they heard another glass smash and an odd, high, muffled cry.

You took his pills, the boy said. He won't be sleeping. Why do you talk to me that way?

I've done things for you. I took risks, she said. Now it's your turn. You just have to be patient, that's all, and keep the lights off. It's not like you're alone. You can hear the radio even from here. You can just sit in here while you're waiting and listen to the good news. I'm not asking you to *do* anything. Just sit in a chair, that's all. Here.

She took a chair from the kitchen table and turned it to face the basement door.

Sit down, she said. Sitting down doesn't mean anything.

He sat down. His mouth had gone slack, spent elastic, and his eyes moved from her face to the door, back and forth.

All right? she said.

She walked out of the house then. A Catherine wheel arced into the sky from behind the houses opposite and spun in a fury of flung sparks and dripping tinsel. The revellers had moved, they were a street or two away now, and she could see no sign of them beyond the odd stray rocket above the roofs, though it seemed that throughout her walk home that pleasant warm May night they were always just around the next corner, for the sound of them accompanied her to her own threshold.

Inside the phone was ringing.

Ordinarily I would answer the phone, she thought.

It was her mother. Sweetheart, you're home! she said. Isn't it wonderful?

Yes, she said. Oh, yes.

Oh! Her mother was crying and laughing at the same time. We're just heading out, aren't we, darling? (Her father must have been standing nearby.) Are you alone? We'll come get you. Where's Buddy?

Well, I've been waiting for him. But they probably sent him out to take pictures. It wouldn't surprise me if I didn't see him tonight at all.

Didn't he call?

He probably did, she said. But I was out a little bit too.

Leave him a note, her mother said. Shall we come for you? You can't stay home on a night like this. What will you tell your children? You put your coat on and be waiting, we won't be ten minutes, will we, darling?

Yes, Mummy.

Maybe we'll see him down there.

Yes, I should think so, she said earnestly.

She hung up the phone and took her grocery pad and pencil and wrote, Dear Buddy I waited but now I have gone to see the celebrations with Mummy and Daddy. Isn't it wonderful? Love Anna.

She left the note on the kitchen table and went to wait on the sidewalk for her father's car like any girl on her way to a fancy party.

The next morning she woke late. Her husband was not beside her, no.

For a moment or two she stretched luxuriantly, feeling a sweetness in her limbs. Perhaps her husband had already woken and left while she lay in. A lazy puss her mother used to call her when she was younger. Lazy puss in the sun. But his pillow lay plump and uncreased beside her own.

Would she be concerned at this point? No. Probably she would decide to take a bath. Probably they would be keeping him busy at the paper, developing his photos from the night before. She smiled, rubbing between her fingers the familiar gritty texture of the bath salts, wondering how many of the fellows in the newsroom that morning had jaws that felt like this, in need of a proper shave, how many were yawning and grinning and bashful, exhausted and elated both. He would have got some marvellous shots. She herself had seen just a corner of all the goings-on, just a crumb really, in the restaurant her parents had finally settled on. They had worn paper hats and the owner had given them each a free glass of wine. The faces! So much kissing and singing and happiness. The three of them had sat apart a little, smiling politely, watching. It had been like being a girl again. Oh, but her father had been in a marvellous mood, insisting he wanted a pizza pie. They had laughed! But of course it had not been that kind of restaurant.

After her bath she dressed slowly, in a pale spring dress of eyelet cotton and a pair of stockings she had been hoarding for a happy day. She tidied the house and planned an elegant meal, soup and omelette, entirely out of leftovers. For once it was not a day for frugality but she didn't feel like going to the store and shopping as though it were any other day. She just didn't feel like it.

By mid-morning he had still not phoned.

The real estate agent phoned. Oh, no, Anna said. Oh, I'm so glad you thought to call. No, I don't think we'll need to today, do you? Gee. (She giggled.) Were you up as late as I was last night? I feel like a ghost. I should have called you, though, and told you not to bother. Well that's fine.

When she hung up a wave of nausea drove her to the sink where she leaned retching, but nothing came. She had forgotten about the agent. She had forgotten about breakfast too, though, and felt ever so much better once she'd had a bit of toast. Afterwards she listened to the radio and did some mending and pressing from her hamper. She made Buddy's white shirts very nice as always. By four o'clock she was wondering whether to start supper when the phone rang again, making her drop the iron. Her nerves, she admitted, were a little on edge.

On a normal day I would answer it, she had to remind herself. I will answer it.

Mrs. Pass, Michael Peretti said. Not disturbing your beauty sleep, I hope? Or your husband's?

No, she laughed. I guess not. I mean, I'm afraid Buddy's not home from work yet.

What work? No one's seen him since yesterday.

Isn't it wonderful news?

There was silence.

Isn't it wonderful news? About the war?

Did he come home yesterday?

Not for a minute! she said. But I guess you boys have been busy getting the story. I was a little surprised he didn't call, but he's explained to me about deadlines and getting the job done no matter what time of –

Yesterday, Mrs. Pass. Yesterday afternoon as he was leaving he said he was going to surprise you. He was going straight to your mother-in-law's house. Did he surprise you, Mrs. Pass?

Well, I guess not. He must have got there after I left.

Maybe he left you a note.

Maybe he did. Should I go over there and take a look?

What? Peretti's voice said. He wasn't speaking to her. *No. I don't know. Not yet. Fuck Tanner. Look, not now.* Mrs. Pass. Are you still there?

I'm here.

Shall I meet you at the house?

I don't suppose that's –

In half an hour. Twenty minutes.

That's very kind of you, but I really –

– outside. Will you –

I really don't –

But I do.

She saw it would be coy and unnatural to resist further and so said: All right, if it's so important to you. Do you know the address?

You know I know the address.

She hung up. He was insolent, that Michael Peretti.

The first full fat day of peacetime was a warm one, the sky lushly clouded, gardens rain-glutted and densely succulent. Like corpses in the gutters lay a few squibs from the night before. She stopped on the walk outside her mother-in-law's house and made a show of digging in her purse for her keys. There was nothing to see from the outside, nothing to smell or hear, no abnormalities at all until she arrived (lightly, trippingly, even) at the front door and found it unlocked. Consternation, yes, self-chastisement (was it her own silly fault, her own birdie-head that had forgotten to lock it?) and then something made her look back over her shoulder and there was her husband's car parked a little way up the street. She wrinkled her brow as though to say: Now that's odd.

Inside the house was silent. The soles of her feet began to prickle but she forced herself to stay in the character she had worn all day. I don't suppose I would call out, she thought. I would leave the door unlocked behind me because Mr. Peretti is coming and I would go to the kitchen and put the kettle on because Mr. Peretti is coming.

What's this? What's this?

I have seen the kitchen drawers ajar, I have seen the broken pottery on the floor, I have seen the chair pushed away from the other chairs and the door to the basement wide open. *Jesus, why open?* What am I doing? I am crying out but no sound comes. I am running to the basement door, crunching and kicking the shards a little more, I am hesitating, the darkness is utter, the silence, I am taking a first step down, swatting the void like a kitten for the string to the bulb, I am taking a second step but there is no string, it is caught around the bulb, *or some hand has clipped it off*, what hand, what hand? What am I doing? I am panicking, I am bravely panicking and pawing for the light string because *this house is not as I left it yesterday*, because *there has been a robbery* (oh!), because my husband's car is outside and the doors were open, doors that should have been closed were open to the world, and because *my fear is great*. Then her fingers found the string and she seized it and pulled and there was light.

What had been her husband lay as though sleeping, curled around the drain, mouth slightly open, hands – one behind him, one before – slightly darkened. With what a delicate brush had he been painted! The familiar caressed face, the line of the jaw, the chest so close to life, to breath! What a work of art!

What am I doing? she asked herself. I am seeing my husband apparently unconscious, caught unawares by a robber. I would approach, I am approaching, I am trying to say his name but my mouth would be dry, my mouth is dry, and no sound is coming. (Above her head she sensed Peretti on his way, the way a chess player senses time running out on the clock – a tiny figure growing slowly larger as he navigated the city, this taxi, that street, until he stood life-size before her, sprung from imagination to life, and she must act for him too.) For the first time she saw a faint glimmer on the floor around him, veins and droplets of silver moisture, thickish and still as mercury, and realized he had soiled himself (smell it), and vomited (his lips were silver); also that he was lying in glass, juice, and blood; for some of the glimmering substances she saw were moon-white mounds of pear. He must have found his feet briefly and flailed in the dark, her Don Quixote, at his mother's sweet summer preserves.

As she stood transfixed a single bright thread of liquid detached itself from the pool by his mouth and ran down into the drain and disappeared. She heard it dripping.

What am I doing? she asked herself. What have I done? But there was nothing more to do. It was a finished work.

Up the few stairs, across the kitchen a last time, down the dark hall, out the front door and into the light of the world, where with Swiss perfection Michael Peretti was stepping from a cab, the cab was pulling away, wheels speeding up and then slowing as, in his mirror, the driver saw a pretty little curly-haired bit of a thing run screaming from a house and collapse in his American fare's arms in a perfectly timed, exquisitely executed, and absolutely genuine dead faint.

⬦

She wrote:

This is, for me, the loveliest and saddest landscape in the world. It's here that the little prince appeared on earth, then disappeared.

Look closely at this landscape in order to be sure of recognizing it, if you travel one day in Africa, in the desert. And, if you happen to pass by there, I beg you, do not hurry, wait a little just under the star! If then a child comes to you, if he laughs, if he has golden hair, if he does not answer when you question him, you will guess who it is. Then be nice! Don't leave me so sad: quick, write me that he is returned . . .

Her mother looked in and read over her shoulder and said, Oh, the lamb, and hurried out, biting her lip.

She worked in her old bedroom at books her mother gave her – children's books, her own and some newer, like this, that her mother had clearly been stocking in the expectation of a grandchild. The curtains were drawn; she worked at her old table by fringed lamplight, filling a schoolgirl's ruled notebook with her rounded, softly pencilled hand. Now and then her mother brought soft foods on a tray, coddled eggs, bread-and-milk, and she ate. When her hand tired she lay down on the high narrow girl's bed, where sleep came easily and often. Her body seemed to suck unconsciousness from the air like oxygen.

She had awoken a few moments later, still – had not the action moved forward? apparently not – in the street. She had lain on the cabbie's coat, head and shoulders propped in the lap of a neighbour lady. The commotion had ferreted her out, as it had women in housedresses and curlers up and down the street. Now then, the woman had called sharply when she saw Anna's eyelids moving, and suddenly a rude finger had been inserted between her lips, prising them open, and she was gagging on *eau de vie*. About that time Peretti had returned.

Where do you live? he had asked one of the women.

She had pointed at a house.

Go the hell home.

He had ignored the abuse that followed and knelt down. Mrs. Pass, he had said. Anna.

But the women wouldn't have it.

Leave her alone.

Who *is* he?

Can't you see she's ill?

Don't let him touch her.

Cabbie, Peretti called.

The two men between them got her into the cab, where she sat with her hands in her lap. She could smell the liquor spilt on her dress. Far away she heard sirens. She leaned her head back and closed her eyes.

Has one of you got a blanket? she heard Peretti say. She's in shock.

I suppose you would know? someone said.

Stay away from there, Peretti called sharply. You, away from the house.

Hey, who are you, anyway? someone said. I've never seen you around here. Where do you get off giving people orders?

That's Cora's daughter-in-law, someone said.

Buddy's wife.

Who's *he*?

Anna, Peretti said again. She opened her eyes. He was leaning into the taxi, pressing a woollen blanket around her. The police are coming, he said in a low voice. I called from inside.

Yes.

Their eyes met briefly.

That wasn't necessary, he said.

Later she had given a statement at the police station. Such kindnesses she had received there, scalding sugary tea and a new blanket and condolences all round. She would turn her face away to cry very quietly and they would pause, waiting with their questions until she was able to continue. When it was over they led her back to the public rooms, where her apprised and pompously expressionless father was waiting to reclaim her.

Now, in the evenings, after her books and her little tray meals, she came downstairs and sat with him while he played the gramophone, the operas he loved. Her mother had been forbidden these sessions, it seemed, for she stayed in the kitchen, knitting. Perhaps her father thought he was inflicting a cure. He sat under the single lit lamp reading the papers, purposefully ignoring her, but if she rose he would say, Sit down, and she would have to sit. Long ago he had trained her not to interrupt his music. So she sat while a woman's voice like a searchlight pierced the room, lamenting this or that corkscrewing of fate. She would admit it was a beautiful voice, high and husked as a child's.

At the funeral white flocks of pollen funnelled in the air, adding to the usual mourning sounds the occasional discreet sneeze. Such a crowd! They had to a man followed to the grave-side, curiosity unslaked by the church service. No, that was unfair; there was scarcely a dry eye. She stood between her parents, tractably dressed that morning in her weeds, a black suit of her mother's that had a faint, unlaundered sweetness, and itched. A hat was found. Her mother wept modestly. Her father played army, remote and stoic. There were the sisters and cousins, unfamiliar without their earmuffs, bawling; there too was the rogue uncle, hair a shade blacker than she remembered from the ski trip, face a pudding. There were the Tanners, lean and flawless, curried by grooms, probably; there were his news-paper colleagues, the typesetters and photographers, oil and vinegar from the look of them. There was Peretti. Around the graveyard rose pigeons with stuttering wings. The sun was high, thin, and fine.

I have wrenched the world off its tracks, she thought, looking around the scene, as the breeze pushed at the black lace of her veil. As the service dragged on she made a game of shifting her chin this way and that, ever so slightly, enough to blot out various faces with the larger knots in the lace. Thinking: I made this, and this, and this.

Victory bunting still hung from the windows of the sanatorium, weather-stained and limp in the pale June sun. In the hospital grounds it seemed more like sere August, the grass cooked crisp and colourless under the piling heat. Probably, Anna thought, it would always feel more like the end of something here than the beginning. Keys *were* thrown away, sometimes; grass was not obliged to grow. Patients, nurses, doctors, visitors were nowhere in evidence, unless they had metamorphosed into the fat black flies that picked over the property, droning and hand-wringing, obsessives.

Please, the doctor said, indicating with the sweep of a hand that she was to precede him up the stairs.

How lovely! her mother-in-law said. Is Buddy here, too?

Cora, Anna said, taking a hesitant step into the sun-washed room.

Come in! I'm quite the princess in my tower up here all alone, aren't I, Doctor? I can't remember when I last had a visitor. Well, of course Buddy's not here, he's working, isn't he? I'm forgetting it's a weekday. But I'm so pleased you came to see me, dear.

She is better, Anna thought, seeing the quick glance take in the fact of her son's absence, check, and respond simply by boosting the wattage of her smile. The social graces had returned, flowing again with the juices of health. By the window she sat tatting, of all things – insects again, Anna thought, though spiders were not insects strictly, they had lungs and nervous systems. Horrible thought. But Cora had laid her shuttle aside and now they were pulling up chairs. The older woman clearly thought she knew what it was about: colouring faintly, she glanced at the doctor, at the floor, at Anna, smiling, and said, I owe you an apology, I believe, dear.

Oh, no. No.

My God they have had Talks, was what she was thinking.

I don't remember everything from – when I arrived, Cora said. But I know there was some strain between us and truly I regret it, truly I do. We're family, we have to stick together now. You're a lovely girl really. I don't know what came over me, though the doctor has explained –

She hesitated. The doctor nodded encouragingly. No doubt, Anna thought, he had rewritten the script for her, given her a version of herself she could even feel proud of, cant as ointment – a blossom of Greek myth here, a prickly thicket of medical jargon there – recasting her hatred as grief and letting her feel a little proud of herself, even, for what the depths of her love for her husband had driven her to. Here surely was a great-hearted love, one for the bards!

One thinks these things though one must not, Anna thought. Indeed, are they even lies? Is she not loving and repentant? I may dislike her, I do of course dislike her – the voice, the vinegary courtesies – but, poor Cora, she has woven her health up around herself like a bamboo pagoda, and here I come scything, again.

From down the hall came the sound of a wail, almost inhuman, or almost human. I will judge less, Anna thought, I will be more kind. Forecast by the sound of trotting footsteps, a nurse appeared in the doorway and said rather sharply, Doctor, for a moment, if you please.

Left alone, the two widows smiled tender, unfathomable smiles. Anna looked around the big room. The second bed was stripped and the other woman's personal effects were not in evidence.

She's gone, Cora said, following her gaze. The police came.

Anna saw the memory of it confused her, was part of that time she couldn't clearly remember. A sweet cloud troubled her eyes.

I heard the nurses say it was because of the baby. Do you suppose that's right?

I shouldn't think so, Anna said reassuringly, but with a quickening of the senses, remembering her suspicion that the woman must have killed it, thinking, *So she was caught*. You're looking wonderful, she added. Very rested.

I want to tell you the truth, Cora said, leaning forward slightly. I'm ashamed. I've heard so many stories in my weeks here, shocking hardships. I've even been volunteering a little in the kitchens, the doctor said it would be good for me and it has, but I see some of those boys who've come back from the war, I've talked to them a little, I sit with them sometimes and hold their hands, oh, it's been wonderful but terrible too, and I tell you I've learned shame. My troubles are nothing to what those boys have been through. I don't belong here.

The wailing ceased abruptly.

I'm quite ready to leave, she said. She was holding Anna's hand now, looking at her face.

Now then, the doctor said, returning.

I was just telling Anna, Cora said. I was even wondering. Is today my day?

The doctor glanced at Anna.

To leave, I mean.

The smile, the society manner, were gone. She had not – how could she have? – rehearsed this moment. Raw dignity this was. Dignity itself a scab on raw need. The thought pleased Anna, though not the expression of it. She tried to translate it into French, to see if it would sound more at home there. *La dignité est une croûte –*

Unfortunately, Mrs. Pass, the doctor said, taking charge when Anna didn't respond. Mrs. Pass, there's been an accident.

For a moment Anna saw Buddy clearly in his mother's innocent, perplexed face. The man looked out of the woman. Then the ghost vanished as Cora realized what was coming and resumed, quite desperately, her smile.

Her father it was who had arranged the funeral, who met with the lawyers and pulled Cora's house off the market until the police investigation was concluded, who went through Buddy's bills and files and papers, seated grandly at the dead man's desk and frowning at various shoeboxes she brought down from the bedroom cupboard, filled with receipts and notes and possibly important papers.

I suppose you knew about this, he said, extracting a portfolio of papers from one particular manila envelope.

What's that?

Insurance.

That's to do with the house, she said. I think.

He frowned at what he must have supposed was her ignorance, but said nothing. It was as though, in her widowhood, she had become an infant again, helpless and in need of protection, unworthy of even the gentlest reprimand. When the police came to the house to ask more questions, as they did more often now that she was past the first debilitating shock of her husband's death, he treated them with suspicion and minimal courtesy. He was affronted that they would not leave her alone. This, she saw, was both a rare manifestation of his love for her and a concern for his own name and honour now that she was, again, in his possession. When one young officer, fed up with his bullying, said he would prefer to interview Anna alone, her father threatened to call a lawyer.

Certainly, the officer said.

Still, she could not bring herself to worry. Stephen was the one they needed, and Stephen she felt sure of, though she could not have said exactly why. Her certainty came down to a few remembered images: his hands, trembling on the table in the café; the poem he had felt compelled to read to her, ears pinking predictably, from his school textbook. Also he had learned so much from the movies about chivalry in a fallen world. Once, after they made love, he had wept. What were the police, what was a parent, after that? He was her Alan Ladd, her John Garfield, her cynic with a cigarette, and underneath her Knight of the Rose.

We shall have to pay a visit to this insurer, her father was saying, as he turned the pages of the policy with a deliberately licked finger. I suppose you will have to accompany me, as the beneficiary.

She watched as he worked his way through Buddy's papers, touching finger to tongue to page, again and again, as though compelled to leave his own faint spoor on all that had been kept from him, until now.

Her strongest urge to confess came in the elevator on the way up to the insurance agency as her father pulled the wrought-iron cage door closed. The cage was a pattern of spear-like fleurs-de-lys. She wanted to tell him about the repairman, about the image of the stalled elevator car and what she had seen in it, the gilt and the abyss.

Mr. Pass, the tall secretary said before she had a chance to introduce him. Mrs. Pass. She nodded to them both, though her glance returned to Anna. A flickering of interest, appraisal. I'll just let Mr. Foster know you're here.

A boy who had been sitting in one corner of the waiting room reading a magazine glanced up at the name. Something about him snagged at her memory. Dark-eyed, pale, with a fine skin and legs like shoots. A private school boy, tie and briefcase and all. Did private school boys need insurance? They had many needs, obviously. He might have been fourteen but already his shoes, for instance, were enormous. Their eyes met briefly, but Anna turned away to fold back the veil pinned to her hat. She still wore her mother's good black wool suit.

Mrs. Pass? the secretary said, at the same moment as her father's impatient, Anna.

Ben Foster, the agent said, shaking hands with her father. Turning to her: My condolences for your loss, Mrs. Pass.

She recognized the boy then, in the desk photograph that was so clearly this good, dull man's cynosure and pride.

There were forms to fill out, a few questions. Her father answered everything. Anna was aware of a formality, a guardedness even, between the two men that had not been there the time she came alone, but her father pulled greyness from the gayest of men, she had seen it often enough. Still, while her father was engaged with the forms – reading every word, in his mulish way, before he would touch the proffered pen – the agent caught her eye and shook his head and said, I know it must be very hard.

Her eyes filled with tears and she permitted herself a single low, aching sound from the back of the throat in assent. Her father glanced up sharply, then returned to his papers.

Wordlessly, the agent pulled a clean handkerchief from the breast pocket of his suit and offered it to her across the desk. When she touched it to her cheeks and nose, it smelled faintly of laundering. In that moment she would have liked for him to understand.

I don't care about the money, she said.

Quiet, Anna, her father said. We know what's best for you.

She watched the agent's dislike for her father give way before the urge to live up to the unexpected thrill of that *we*. She saw he couldn't help it. He was an animal just like her father, with young of his own.

Usually no payments can be made prior to the conclusion of the police investigation, the agent said. But in this case – with Mrs. Pass being so young – well, I'm going to see what I can do.

Thank you, her father said.

The agent walked out into the waiting room with them. My son, John, he said to Anna.

You see, she thought. The boy shook hands like a proper puppet.

It's time for a new photograph, she said, eliciting the same frail, sweet smile from both father and son. The boy looked at his enormous feet.

He won't let me, the agent said.

What are you working on? she asked, for she saw he had swapped the magazine for a notebook, hastily slapped shut when they appeared.

Outrageous question, apparently! The boy flushed.

It's an opera, isn't it, John? the agent said encouragingly.

Anna.

Her father stood by the elevator, frowning. There were references in this conversation he didn't understand. Clearly, Anna knew, he believed his position was being undermined by some prior familiarity with the agent that she had not seen fit to reveal to him.

I'm sorry, the agent said softly, frowning. She thought perhaps he was embarrassed to be standing before her at such a time, a man with a child, when she had neither.

It's very nice to have met you, she told the boy.

It *is* an opera, he said urgently.

Stephen, that was who he reminded her of. Well, sure. She supposed any boy would do for that. This one was younger by a year or two, but the intensity was there. Perhaps they were all like that, perhaps it was all just puberty ripping through. As she readjusted her veil in the elevator, as the mechanism of winches and pulleys engaged, as they sank past the second floor and came to rest on the ground, she decided she had better check on Stephen just in case.

⊰◈⊱

Twenty-nine!

A pinch-faced woman stepped up to the counter, pinched out a smile, and pointed to a particular piece of fish. Like to like. The butcher held it out on a piece of brown paper, cropped tail limply dangling, for her inspection. She nodded.

Thirty!

A woman Anna's age – a sapped, milky blonde far gone with child – wanted sausage rolls.

A dozen, did you say?

Two dozen, she whispered, obviously mortified by her own appetites.

Two dozen, the butcher repeated loudly, busying himself. The woman's maternity dress looked home-sewn, a jersey sack with a poorly finished neck facing, complete with unintentional pleat where the machine had nipped a little extra fabric and she had not known what to do, Anna thought, and so had made the bunny-bright decision to ignore it, to believe it wouldn't show. She would be the kind who could make a decision about a belief. Obviously the whole wide world was new to this girl and she was coping as best she could.

Two dozen, the butcher said, placing the package on the counter. Thirty-one!

He was brusque but he at least did not slap the food around the way his son did. Usually when there were this many people waiting the son would appear but today the butcher simply worked a little faster. Though of course he was a delivery boy now, no longer his father's boy.

Thirty-two!

But then she could phone for a delivery, not to her mother's house of course, but to her own. She went there days now to clean, as she had once cleaned Cora's house, though nights she still spent in her parents' house, and would for the foreseeable future, into the fall at least. There was no way around that. The twenty-first of June it was, only. The butcher severed a portion of ground beef with a paddle and scooped it into the scale. The silver finger on the scale's clock face swung round and stopped, trembling, then snapped back as the butcher removed the meat and swung an increasingly lazy pendulum arc back and forth across the zero.

Thirty-three!

Thirty-three, Anna said, placing her ticket on the counter.

The eyes and voice, those were the easy conduits. You might have said, indeed, that the son stood clothed in the father, costumed in the older man's heavier flesh, peering out through his eyes, the particular tenor of his voice warped only slightly deeper by the thicker configuration of mouth, tongue, and throat. He was recognizably there.

As she watched him count and clip off her sausage links she said, You're busy today.

No rest for the wicked, he replied, not bothering to look up from his work. Thirty-four!

At the bungalow she placed her mesh bag in the icebox without unpacking it and immediately called the grocery store. While she waited she dusted. After about forty minutes came the knock at the front door.

Delivery, Stephen said.

Won't you come in? Just while I find my purse.

Seven twenty-nine.

He closed the door behind him and stood with a bag in each arm. Baking goods, she had ordered – flour, yeast, vanilla essence. It would all keep. So much for the neighbours.

In the kitchen he began unloading the bags on the table, checking each item off against his list. When she said his name he repeated, Seven twenty-nine. Or I could put it to your account. You'd have to sign here. Do you have an account with us?

Stephen.

You'd have to sign here.

Slowly understanding, she took the pen and signed where he pointed.

We have special delivery rates on Wednesdays, he said. Wednesday is always a good day to shop at Farrell's Fine Foods.

I'll remember that, she said gently.

There was a knock at the front door.

Why go out? the boy said.

She glanced from him to the door and back.

Why go out when you can stay and shop from the comfort of your own home?

Won't you excuse me?

We're open Monday through Saturday, the boy said.

She opened the front door.

Here is Mrs. Pass, Peretti said. Hello, Mrs. Pass.

He wore his camera case the way her husband had, slung across his back with a broad strap. They stepped together into the house, he forwards, she back, a dance step gone wrong.

You know you've left your bicycle in the yard, son? Peretti said to the boy. You should get a chain. You're asking to have it stolen the way you leave it lying around.

We're open Monday through Saturday, the boy said. Bakery specials on Saturdays.

You ought to be more careful, Peretti said.

Are you following me? Anna asked.

May I have a cup of tea?

She held her palm out in the direction of the kitchen, an automatic and absurdly polite gesture, as though to say she would offer it from her own hand on a silver salver momentarily. Then she walked Stephen back to the front door.

My Stephen, she said softly.

He walked down into the yard, picked up his bike, and rode away. She trailed a few steps after him.

Mrs. Pass, Peretti called behind her, from the doorway. Would you offer me that cup of tea, Mrs. Pass?

He sat at the table while she opened and closed cupboards, pulling out the tea things.

Is she planning to do some baking? he asked.

Christmas is coming.

Peretti laughed. Christmas is always coming, he agreed.

They sipped their tea from her best china like dowagers.

They found stains in the bed, Peretti said. Stains in the bed and a note in your handwriting, Mrs. Pass. On the bedside table. The police are waiting for you, at your parents' house. I got the call about an hour ago. An old friend at the station – I scratch his, he scratches mine –

A note? Anna said, honestly perplexed.

In French.

She held up the pretty pot and he pushed his cup toward her. There was no point behaving like a ferret.

I didn't help them, Peretti said. I just watched.

They keep you pretty well informed.

I keep myself informed. I've been tailing you for a while now, just waiting to see how this would play out. I suppose that boy has a name?

Bruce, she said promptly, and he laughed again.

I can't say I understand you, Mrs. Pass, he said. But I admire you like hell.

I can't imagine what happens next, she said.

$$2$$

He lay in bed, listening. Birds: birds stuttered and bubbled in the trees, fell off the branches, caught themselves in the air with a parachute snap of wings. Crows in their ratcheting language worried scraps. Gulls called out in misery. With a meaty thud the newspaper landed on the step. Cars sighed down First Avenue, two blocks over, down and away into the city, while directly below him his mother's slippers tapped the kitchen linoleum. Through the vent he could hear bacon and eggs hissing, hell in a pan. If you were Catholic you couldn't help thinking in pictures that way. He was not Catholic but many of the neighbourhood boys were Italian, and with little prompting they would explain volubly about hell. They had scared him once when he was a child, told him he would fry like bacon. He could still think of it sometimes and give himself a shiver. Bring home the bacon: that was what his father did. Every morning there was bacon in the pan, or ham, or sausages. They were fortunate to have meat when so many were doing without, in London, for instance. He saw the newsreels every Saturday afternoon at the cinema, and they had also discussed it at school, of course. In Latin class even they had discussed it, using a vocabulary gleaned from Caesar. Now Europe was relaxing from her recent convulsions, and though the Pacific theatre was still lively – he could not help imagining it in miniature, toy planes zooming over a bathtub sea studded with white knee-islands – it seemed unlikely he or his classmates would be needed by the time they were senior boys. That was a mixed blessing.

Now, John, his mother called. She had called him several times already.

A mixed blessing because he would have liked to heft a gun, to march with a loaded pack and uncover in himself some valour, rescue some comrade or girl and vanish back into the French mist before his name could be ascertained, or suggest some strategy to a superior officer that would save ten men in the face of two hundred. He would be taken before the general, he still in his muddy boots and with a cut above one eye, shown into some high gilt room in a commandeered Italian villa retrofitted for the administration of war. The great general sat behind a curly Duke's desk and in a voice like the purr of a Bentley said, I see from your strategy, Private Foster, you are acquainted with Caesar's exploits in Gaul – Yes, sir. – Well it's a rare pleasure to meet an educated man out here, you, Colonel, get this soldier a bandage, cigarette? – No, thank you, sir. – Very wise, that shows will. He would refuse as many honours as he decently could, though he could not decently forbid a dinner, a feast, for his unit, where the ten men would be feted and fed with boar and cranberries and champagne and small chocolates and brandy and tobacco; but he himself would melt away, as he always did, at the most reeling hour of hilarity, to walk through certain cold streets to a tall shuttered house of fantasmic repute, where a beautiful girl worked in rags as a maid, singing strange bewailing, bewitching melodies, a girl with a defect, some lisp or limp, that caused her to be overlooked by all but him. He would sit and sip some sweet burning nutty liquor and watch the girls and their customers, the drinking and singing and ongoing accumulating undress, and at some crucial point retire alone to his room, to an ascetic narrow bed. No one could understand –

John!

– why he chose to rent a room here of all places –

Let him sleep.

– he with all his bravery and dignity and quiet honour –

I already have let him sleep.

– until the girl slipped into his room without knocking –

Have you seen this? No, don't, love. Let him be.

– the whisper of skirts, the rasp of stockings, the pinpoint snap of hair clasps and other clasps –

I know he's awake. He's just shamming.

Knock first, at least.

He heard his mother's trudging step on the stairs, heard her open his door.

Nonsense, she said. Knocking in my own house. I know you're awake. Your breakfast is positively congealing.

It's holidays, Foster mumbled, flushed with sleep, hiding against the pillow.

Downstairs his father had the newspaper all over the breakfast table, and some on the floor. Usually he would look up and smile and say, No rest for the wicked, knowing Foster was not wicked, but today he said only, Look.

He went to stand at his father's elbow. Who is she?

Don't you remember?

A high-school yearbook photograph was blown up past sharpness on the front page of the paper, a photograph of a curly-haired girl with a precious, pushed-in face and an armful of roses, staring honestly and earnestly at nothing.

Aunt Trudy?

You met her in my office, don't you remember? Last week. Cass, look.

I already looked.

But John thought it was Trudy.

His mother did look then, and raised her eyebrows briefly in verdict. Trudy's face isn't so round, though, she said.

Still.

Yes.

The three of them stood for a moment, admiring the resemblance to his mother's younger sister. His eyes drifted up the page to the headline: GIRL, 22, AND BOY, 17, ARRESTED FOR MURDER. Beneath the girl's photograph was a much smaller one of a boy with a dark flop of hair and a shy, squinting grin. His face was tragic with acne. Even a cursory glance at the layout showed the editors' interest lay primarily with the girl.

You shook hands with her, John.

Ghoulish, his mother said. Stop it.

Did I?

The day of your recital.

I remember, he said slowly. He tried hard not to look at his hand because his father was watching his face. He looked sad.

Why was she in the office?

His father looked away. Some people believe she killed her husband for his life insurance, he said.

Don't you?

I didn't.

Eat your breakfasts now, both of you. Honestly, his mother said.

His interest lapped away a little when she brought a plate of redolent fried meat and potato to the table and set it in front of him. Food was his other great need at the moment.

Holidays, is it? his father said, folding the paper with care along its creases.

First day.

That's a fine feeling. What will you do with it, this first day?

He shrugged. Library.

Don't spend it all indoors. What are you working on?

Dad!

That reminds me, his mother said. I promised to phone Mrs. Agostino today and tell her if you wanted to continue your piano lessons for the summer. Do you?

He nodded hugely, chewing, and both his parents smiled.

Will you do some shopping for me on your way home?

Foster and his father pointed at each other and each said: You. This was their game.

John will do it, his mother said firmly.

I'm late, his father said. He stood by the table, hesitating, slapping his leg with the refolded newspaper. His mother stood to give him her quick harsh kiss and then sat back down to her black coffee.

I'm late, Cassie, his father said again.

Go then, his mother said.

A look passed between them – he saw it.

After his father left, he asked his mother what was wrong.

He wouldn't wait for the police, his mother said. He wanted to approve that girl's claim. It was Jim Hammond who smelled the rat.

He smiled at the slang term coming from her prim mother's mouth.

More coffee?

He held his mug out. Coffee was a conspiracy between them. His father disapproved, said he was too young for habits, but his mother loved it and had shared it with him since he was a baby.

Real coffee, sent by Aunt Trudy in Toronto. Aunt Trudy had a hush-hush job with access to all kinds of things. Coffee was the least of it, his father had said once, making his mother very angry, he didn't know why. Packages arrived with coffee and tins and small chocolates and silk stockings. Feel, John, real silk, his mother would say, and he was always happy to feel, the way his smooth fingers became rough, catching on the even smoother fabric, and the feeling this gave him in his hands and his belly. His mother liked that he wanted his piano lessons and appreciated good silk. His father liked to lean with the other fathers against the low fence around the school track and cheer him on at Saturday meets. He was no trouble at all, a little shy but only he himself worried about that. A good boy.

He could have left us the paper, he said. His mother began clearing the table.

Hush, she said. He needs it today. Are you going to Carnegie?

He nodded.

You can renew my book for me.

All right.

She gave him a shopping list and said, Now don't be late and don't forget anything. We're having the Hammonds to dinner tonight.

At the foot of the stairs he turned back and said, I guess he believed her.

What? his mother said. The girl in the paper? Yes, I suppose he did. Your father tends to believe people, she added dryly, more to herself than to him.

The luxury of dressing in his own clothes and not his school uniform displaced thoughts of the girl right until it was almost time for him to get off the streetcar at the big stone downtown library, columns and cupola, with his mother's book and his own notebook under his arm. He had been drifting along on the rhythms of the streetcar and the people sitting and standing around him, their snatched conversations, and the deep voice of the conductor calling the stops – Nanaimo, Commercial, Clark, Fraser – when a smartly dressed woman in a black hat standing by the doors glanced back over her shoulder, and he recalled the girl in the waiting room of his father's office last month had done a similar thing, shot him a glance back from under her pinned veil as the secretary led her through the door. *Mr. Foster will see you now*, the secretary had said, startling him with his own name, though of course it was his father she was taking the girl to see. He thought he might find a newspaper at Carnegie and read about what she had done. His hand had felt like a piece of meat this morning when he had tried not to look at it, for his father's sake, but now for the first time it prickled a little, a thrill he thought he might nurture into something bigger, something to dream on. He watched reluctantly as the chic woman stepped down to the street. Through the window he watched her walk around a corner and out of sight, white legs working like scissors.

Main Street, Main and Hastings, the conductor called.

In the library he found a quiet carrel and opened his notebook. He had been using the same notebook that day in his father's office. Idly he turned back the pages, trying to find what he had been working on when the girl had interrupted him. There had been a man with her too, he recalled suddenly, her own father possibly, a frightening, hatchet-headed man, not unlike Mr. Leavy at school, Mr. Leavy the history and geography master, who favoured Livy and the strap. Livy and Leavy, that was the joke. His school was strict but fair, generally, though some teachers were ruled more by the letter than the spirit, an expression he had read somewhere and liked. It was an expensive school, he knew that, involving a long daily commute from his East Vancouver home to the moneyed streets of the

West side, where the air was cleaner, the gardens more lush, and the leaves fell more neatly from the trees. Days when he was kept late after school, by fundraising for the war effort, or Math club, or practices with the track team, or Drama club (culminating, this year, in a public all-boy performance of *King Lear*, for which he had composed the incidental music, an Overture, Fantasia, Lament, and special sound effects representing the Heath), he would meet his father downtown and be driven the rest of the way home. Extra tutoring for his Latin final it had been that day, and it had paid off too, *Prima inter pares*, Mr. Pollit had murmured, handing back his paper yesterday with its red one hundred, and the other boys had grinned and shaken their heads and slapped his back and said, Trust Foster.

He opened his notebook to the sketch he had been working on, aria for alto, full orchestral score yet to be written. He composed the way Mrs. Agostino taught him to play the piano, shaping the line of the melody first and fleshing out the rest after. Filling in the flesh, Mrs. Agostino called it. In one of his fits of childish enthusiasm, which inevitably he regretted, he had confessed to his parents his plans for an opera, and now they encouraged him mercilessly, though the law remained their dearest dream for him. They made no bones about wanting to see him rise in the world. After the performance of *Lear* two weeks ago, he had met up with them in the school foyer, where they had been unusually subdued in the throng of boys and men and women in furs, though they had insisted on taking a little walk through the nearby streets before going home. The school was in a residential area. His mother had said, This old coat, and then fallen silent. The streets were familiar to him but his parents had gazed around like tourists.

That's the house I like, he had said finally, pointing at a filigreed blue one with a maple tree, just a thing to say, but relief had flared on their faces. He knew they wanted him to like good things, rich things, to aspire to them and work hard for them.

They caught up to two of his classmates, twins, walking home with their own parents and sister, and he felt obscurely ashamed. The brothers had played their parts very straight, not mincing or lisping in their dresses, but standing tall and cold, and terribly lacking in irony. Now they greeted him cheerfully, introduced him as the sound man, and he responded in kind – *Goneril, Regan* – but their cheerful voices rang falsely in the stern quiet of the dark street.

This coat, his mother said again, when they had moved on.

What does the father do? his own father asked.

He's a QC.

And then there was nothing left to say, all the way back to the car and all along the long drive home.

The aria he had started was pretty good. It began in the low register, an eerie, chromatic murmuring, then flared out in anguish. It was a deep woman's voice he heard most often in his head, and often composing was as easy for him as transcribing that voice. He listened, he heard, he copied down. People said he was gifted but he did not feel anything remarkable. All he had to do was go somewhere quiet, like the Carnegie, and the voice would come. No one looking at him would be able to tell he was not just doing sums, some doltish boy's summer school work. He sat quietly in his carrel, hair neatly combed, without affectation, not humming or tapping his foot. You would not know him for what he was at all unless you were looking right over his shoulder.

By early afternoon he was too hungry to continue. Around the corner from the library in a café he got a sandwich and a glass of milk and ate staring sleepily through the dirty glass, thinking this could become his summer routine. He chewed his sandwich like cud. Writing always left him feeling a little stupid and gutted. A curly-haired girl walked by and he realized he had forgotten to look for a newspaper in the library. But his father would probably bring the evening papers home, and it was not that important anyway.

When he got home his mother was still in the kitchen. Show me, she said.

He set the brown paper bag down on the table and pulled out items, all he had bought for her.

What's this? What's this, young man?

He smiled and snatched the little white bag of toffees off the table before she could get at it. My commission, he said. What's for dinner?

She made a grab for the bag but he held it over her head. He was the taller.

Fish, she said. Now give your tired old mother a sweet.

He proffered the bag and she pincered out a piece of the tan candy with finger and thumb, other fingers delicately fanned.

Did you have a good day?

He shrugged, morose suddenly.

All right, I'm not asking. Did you renew my book?

He pointed at it on the table, under the grocery bags. *Sewing for All Sizes*, it was called. He had glanced through it on the streetcar coming home, couldn't help himself. The varieties of woman were arresting.

It was on the radio today, that case, his mother said. I suppose one oughtn't to be shocked by anything any more.

How did she do it?

The husband needed some kind of medication. She locked him in the basement without it overnight. It seems that was all it took.

But why?

Oh, John, she said impatiently, turning away from him. Where are my potatoes?

He guessed that meant there was a man in it.

Only they weren't trash at all, his mother said, as though he had suggested they might be. They all came from Jericho.

Jericho was the neighbourhood of his school.

They all?

Well, the couple and the parents, his mother said, digging at potato eyes with the point of the peeler. His parents, I believe. And the – hand me the colander.

And the –?

Good people from good homes, she said, in a voice to close down the conversation. I'll never understand it.

He watched his mother for several minutes, then, her hands and face, as she pricked and dug at the soily-skinned potatoes. He knew her mind was not banal – she it was who had taught him to love Schubert and Beethoven and Brahms and Mahler – but that it worked on sealed levels, like a mine or a skyscraper, with some off-limits to him. The results – what came from her mouth – were often, therefore, less than spectacular.

Heavy steps sounded on the front porch.

Not already! his mother said, genuinely startled. She had been as far away as he, apparently.

Cassie?

In here, his mother called back, her voice rising petulant and thin over her own kitchen clatter. Go see them in, John, she added. Take Mrs. Hammond's coat and hang it nice and straight in the closet.

But when he stepped from the kitchen he saw only big Mr. Hammond and his own father, closing the front door behind them.

Who are you? Mr. Hammond demanded. I've never seen you before in my life. Where's that kid of yours, Ben?

His father smiled weakly.

That little kid you used to have.

May I take your coat, Mr. Hammond?

Not unless you're practising to be a butler. It's going to be law, though, isn't it? That's what your father tells me. How's the music? You still swinging?

Yes, he said, not sure.

That's what I like to hear. Say, why don't you show me your room?

What?

Model trains, airplanes, hockey sticks –

His father put a hand on his shoulder, drawing his attention away from Mr. Hammond's bombast. His father's face was pale and he had forced a sick smile.

I just need to talk to your mother privately a minute, son, he said quietly.

Where's Mrs. Hammond? he responded stupidly.

We need to talk some business tonight, Mr. Hammond said. Your Dad and me and your mother. I'll tell her you asked for her, though. She'll certainly appreciate that. So what do you say? Want to show me around? Christ, you've gotten tall, he added, following him to the foot of the stairs. Excuse me, so to speak. I guess it's been a few months since I've seen you. I guess your old man's tall.

My mom's pretty tall, too, he said agreeably, knowing his father would stand listening until they reached the second floor. She can sink a basketball.

Mr. Hammond barked a laugh. Can she? he said. I bet she can, too. Can she box?

I don't think so.

Good.

First came his parents' room, then the bathroom. His room was at the end of the hall on the right.

Tidy kid, huh, his father's friend said resignedly, looking around. Well. What's this?

Spaceship, he mumbled, of a colouring tacked to the wall. He was not yet a man. Was that his fault?

Nodding at a black case, like a black lunch box with a shiny latch and reinforced metal corners: What about that?

Oboe.

Jesus.

It's not mine, he said quickly. I just borrowed it from the school music room for the summer. To try it out.

He watched the big man's eyes rake over the room and stop on his corkboard, on a piece of staff paper pinned there. Ha, he said.

That's just something I was writing. Some music.

I know what a score is.

He waited, flushing. He had forgotten Mr. Hammond could read music.

Will you play this for me later?

It's not done.

I can see that.

It's almost done, he said defensively.

Mr. Hammond studied the notes a little longer, evidently trying to hear them in his head. He was frowning.

It doesn't really have a tune. It's more like a sequence of harmonies, of blocks of sound. It's a technique I was reading about.

Mr. Hammond was watching him, listening. He always wore warm cologne and expensive clothes. With a start the boy realized he was sitting on the narrow bed still wearing his camel's hair coat.

You know, the older man said, still watching him, I know both your parents pretty well. You are not what I would have expected them to produce.

I'm sorry, he said low, burning, meaning it.

That's not what I meant, son.

What –

The older man was nodding, looking around the room again. Did something happen?

The older man undid the buttons of his coat. Underneath he wore a blue suit. He touched the knot of his tie, as though to steady it, and frowned at a scuff on one shoe. He reached down and swept at it with a thumb. Then he looked up, almost negligently, and said, Your father was fired today.

The boy could hear the tick of the furnace, like a metronome, and behind that the alternate, inarticulate swells of his parents' voices – his father's brown, his mother's a watery cream – rising and falling in the kitchen. Mr. Hammond shifted his weight on the bed, crossed his legs the other way, making the floorboards creak. His own breath made a colourless sound, draw and release. Even with your fingers in your ears there was the low radio hum of blood in your own brain.

Why?

Your father made a mistake at work, Mr. Hammond said. He tried to bend the rules. Now, I don't want you getting mad at me. He errs on the wrong side, see? He figures it's better to let a few bum claims go than to risk turning down someone with a genuine need. That's a damn fine way of thinking. Only it's not the company's way. Are you listening to me?

He was listening, listening so hard he had turned his face away, the better to focus on the sound of the voice. Reluctantly, because of the distraction in it, he brought his eyes back to the man's face.

Your father works hard. He's going to find another job pretty quick. Only he's not cut out for insurance. Christ, there's no shame in that. We're a bunch of cold sons of bitches. We screw the widows and laugh. Your father doesn't have to be that.

Something happened, a soft folding over in his brain. Something opened out.

It was because of that girl, he said.

Mr. Hammond looked startled for a second. He realized his father's friend had been basking a little in the picture he had painted, not only of his father as a decent gentleman but of himself as a wise guy and a cynic and a tough, and he was not expecting the boy to turn corners in the conversation before he did.

The girl in the paper this morning, I mean. My mother said he approved her claim.

The man's face relaxed. That was just the last straw, he said. These things never turn on just one case. But it would have been bad publicity for the company, if it had come out later, after we'd paid out. You understand?

My mother said you were the one who – figured it out.

I smelled the rat, he said cheerfully, but his face changed colour a little.

How.

Take it easy, son.

How.

Intuition, he said, tapping his hairline with one finger. I was reviewing the file and I got a little spark off her.

My Dad didn't get a little spark.

That's enough, now, Mr. Hammond said easily, standing up. Foster realized the man was used to dealing with angry, confused people, not children but people who in anger would behave not much differently from children.

Will there be a trial?

Yes.

Will you have to testify?

Your father and I will together. We figured it out together. After I brought certain elements to his attention.

Have you met her?

Not yet.

I've met her, the boy said. Why were you reviewing my father's files?

Because the company asked me to.

Did my father ask you to?

Mr. Hammond laughed. Good boy, he said. Good for you. You're going to do all right. Well. What do you say we go downstairs and see what delicacy your mother's cooked up for us tonight?

It's fish.

Fish! Mr. Hammond said, as though that were a true revelation.

Fish and potatoes.

Slay me, Mr. Hammond said. They went downstairs.

His parents were sitting in the living room, sipping at clear drinks. Immediately his father rose and said, What can I get you?

Sit down, Mr. Hammond said, waving him off. I guess I can find my way around a bottle of gin as well as the next man. He turned to the boy and said, Martini?

Yes, please.

His mother, he saw, had been crying, but was composed now. She sat in her apron, holding her glass and smiling tiredly.

All right, my Cassie? Mr. Hammond said, taking her half-empty glass and handing her a full one. That was a funny thing for his father's friend to call his mother, but Mr. Hammond had always shown her a special courtly tenderness.

Martini, sir, he said, offering the boy a glass of tonic with an olive floating in it. He glanced at his father's face and back at the drink. The slick bobbing meat of the olive made him feel ill.

Sorry, Dad, he said quickly.

Good lad, his father said. We're just rallying.

When did they tell you? his mother asked.

At noon. It was very decently done. They waited until the office was practically empty.

Decent, his mother repeated.

Now, Cass.

I'm not, she said.

I want to apologize again, Mr. Hammond said. I've said this to Ben but I want to say to all of you how sorry I am I had to have any role in this. It was an awkward situation. Maybe I did the wrong thing. I want you to know I stressed my friendship with Ben, I told them straight out it was a hell of a thing for them to ask me to do.

That's enough, his father said.

I feel guilty as hell.

Over a few files? his father said with his faint sweet smile. Rather you than some fool.

Guilty that I couldn't tell you, I mean.

The boy's stomach growled loudly.

On that note, his father said, making everyone smile. I move we adjourn to the kitchen.

Seconded, the boy said, when no one else did, and he really did want to eat, though he hated having to be sporting about it.

What about another field? Mr. Hammond asked, taking a second helping of fish. They had been discussing jobs his father might seek, various insurance firms in the city that might be hiring, the pros and cons of each, and assorted gossip – this firm was a closed shop, that one was aggressively recruiting, and so on.

All through the meal he had thought of what Mr. Hammond said
about his father not being suited to insurance, and wondered why
he would play such a game. Now he saw the man was just being
patient, working his father round to a new way of thinking.

What other field? his father asked. He had eaten little but
drunk steadily. Foster watched the men's faces like a ball game.
Mr. Hammond must have judged his father to have reached a
point of optimum pliability, before the wine turned back round
and made him contentious.

What about sales?

Should I be a salesman, Cass? his father asked his mother.
Would you like that? Sample cases by the front door? Me walking
the streets every day selling – what am I selling, Jim?

Within a company, I meant. An office job, of course.

Encyclopedias, isn't it?

His mother put her fork down.

All right then, Mr. Hammond said. All right. Let me think.
You're a researcher, an investigator. Policeman?

Too old, his father said.

Ah. But – private dick.

The boy and his mother laughed. His father looked wounded,
then worried.

Hey, he said. Hey. That's a real possibility, isn't it? I mean,
I'm a shoo-in for that job. Hey!

Our man from Pinkerton's, the boy said, making his mother
laugh harder.

Stop it, now, his father said irritably.

It is a good idea, his mother said, sobering immediately. But
isn't that more of a big city job? How many firms would there be
in a town like Vancouver?

You'd be surprised, Mr. Hammond said. And I understand

it's not so glamorous, anyway. Missing persons, divorce. There's adultery everywhere.

His mother coloured.

I have years of experience, his father said carefully. I'll just have to put together a CV. References, of course –

His mother stood to clear the plates. Mr. Hammond cleared his throat and said, Wonderful, Cassie, wonderful.

We'll have coffee in the living room, if you like.

There's no alternative, Mr. Hammond said. This boy of yours has promised me a performance.

That's it, his father said, and the boy could see he was in deep water now, far out and on his own, trying to keep his head up, trying not to drown. Some music for dessert.

They waited for his mother to bring in coffee on a tray. Now, who's first? she said gaily, meaning she expected Mr. Hammond to play too.

The boy caught the man's eye and took his seat on the piano bench. The front legs were carved into paws so that he always felt he was facing into a maw, paddling at the teeth of some beast. As a toddler once he had trapped his fingers in the lid, probably the source of this fanciful dread. He disliked the instrument but understood he needed a fluency in it if he was to continue in composition.

Play your recital piece, his father said. That Brahms.

Brahms' Waltz in G-sharp Minor. He had last played the piece the day he met the girl in his father's office. Instead of going home after his father's interview with her they had driven to one of the cathedrals downtown, where Mrs. Agostino had entered him in a competition. Down there in the basement he had tied with three girls for third, a contemptible insult to all of them, he had thought at the time. A girl with a Russian name had taken the little gold-plated cup, her prettier sister the silver ribbon. Five of them played the same Brahms waltz; the pretty sister played Rachmaninoff. But the girl who won played the Brahms so well she might have been playing a different piece entirely. He heard lines and turns in the music when she played, buried counter-melodies brought out like gold and silver veins in a mine wall, that he had not noticed himself, in his own study of the piece. He felt humiliated and fascinated both. She had opened the work up like a book and taken out what she wanted. He had studied the score feverishly, in the car, all the way home.

You played it differently tonight, his mother said, when he lifted his hands from the keys. I heard a little thing I never heard before.

This, he said, fingering out the figure. He had cribbed it from the girl.

That's it, she said. It's very familiar, but I never noticed it.

It was always there.

It was and it wasn't, she said. You never played it quite like that.

I like that one, his father said. I haven't heard you play it since the recital. The evening –

Yes, he said.

You see, what I don't understand, his father said, turning abruptly to Mr. Hammond. What I don't understand –

All right, Ben, Mr. Hammond said.

No. She was just a girl. How do you look at a girl like that and think what you thought? How do you make that leap?

When the purchase and the claim are so close together, you investigate, Mr. Hammond said softly. You know that yourself. It's standard. I was just following procedure.

But *I got a little spark off her*, he had said earlier, the boy remembered. Which was the lie?

She was grieving, his father said. My God, Jim. You could see it in her face.

Now it's Mr. Hammond's turn, his mother said, sprightly-brightly.

After you.

No, not tonight, she said, her smile firming up a little.

His father shook his head, like a dog shaking off water, and said, Please, Cass.

The three of them looked at his father.

Please, his ruined father repeated.

His mother played her old standby, a Beethoven second movement she had learned as a girl and liked to soothe herself with. She would play it at twilight on Christmas Eve, waiting for his father to come home from work, aggravating the boy enormously with her sweet, affected melancholy. Once he had called it a chocolate, to hurt her, but she had only smiled. On those rare occasions when she was out and he was home he tried to play it himself, but its winding intricacies were beyond his sight-reading, and pride prevented him from giving it serious practice when she was around. She played it as well as she ever did, batting .500 on the ornaments and taking the tiger-purr bass line far too slowly, luxuriating in it too much. He hated the way classical music made otherwise intelligent people go gooey, willing to expose the worst parts of themselves, physically and spiritually. He suspected sex did something similar and feared that, too.

Beautiful, Cassie, Mr. Hammond said. With a feeling that was some dark, unsmiling cousin to amusement, he saw the man was genuinely moved.

Oh, stuff, his mother said. I'm rusty as old nails. I'm afraid my boys have heard that old piece far too many times.

Never too many, his father said fervently, nodding his head. Never too many.

That's a fine instrument you've got there.

A wedding gift from my parents. It keeps its tune very well. It was made specially for the West coast climate.

A piano built for the rain, Mr. Hammond said.

For the humidity, the boy said, and both his mother and Mr. Hammond laughed. He didn't know why.

Now then. His mother got up from the bench and smoothed down the front of her dress. Enough chocolates from old Europe. She shot the boy a wink. Give us something from the new world, Mr. Hammond.

Pearls before swine, I'm afraid, he said. That makes me the swine.

No, his father said.

Mr. Hammond dragged the leather bench back before he sat on it and worked the knobs until it was down as low as it would go. Then he played jazz, his playing as fast and strident as his mother's had been soft and unfocused. His mother started to clap along, but when neither he nor his father joined in she stopped. Mr. Hammond played on, oblivious, occasionally shifting the bench under himself with his exertions, until it was completely out of alignment with the instrument. His technique was fast and only occasionally sloppy. As the big man slapped and slaved away the boy realized for the first time it was possible to gain proficiency on an instrument with no conservatory training whatever. The world was full of treachery.

One of my favourite composers, Mr. Hammond said, stressing the last word a little, when he had finished. Mr. Duke Ellington.

That's not simple music at all, is it? his mother said.

He was classically trained.

They looked at the boy, who found he had spoken the thought aloud.

I read it in a book. He came from a wealthy family.

You're really making a study, aren't you? Mr. Hammond said. Maybe one day you'll be as big as him. Maybe one day we'll be sitting down in the parlour to play your work.

I doubt it, he said frankly.

That's right, Mr. Hammond said. I forgot you're with the avant-garde.

Not always.

I liked your *King Lear* music very much, his mother said, in a private voice just for him.

John never tells us what he's working on, do you, son? his father said. We find out when it's all over.

Like a strange physics, they were, each exerting a force he must fight or yield to. And he would be a moon amongst planets for a few years yet.

I want to hear that piece you were showing me upstairs, Mr. Hammond said. This, too, was treachery.

All right, the boy said.

Upstairs he unpinned the page of manuscript from his corkboard. His bedroom still held a faint thread of Mr. Hammond's cologne, and the bedspread was dented where the man had sat. He remembered the girl in his father's office had worn a scent, and spent a moment imagining it had been her, not Mr. Hammond, in his room an hour ago. The idea hit him so hard his face dipped, his body sang.

What are you working on? she had asked.

This *is* a treat, his mother said, when he went back downstairs, page in hand. The three adults sat up straighter.

Seven minutes later – he knew, had sat on a kitchen chair in front of the clock on the stove and sounded it out in his head –

he lifted his hands from the keyboard and put them in his lap. For a long moment there was no sound at all. Then he looked up and saw his mother was crying again.

I'm sorry, she said. I'm sorry.

What was that? Mr. Hammond said.

Through the stifling return of all the little sounds that plugged up the world, the breathing and fidgeting and white noise, he murmured: What I'm working on.

That's not what I was looking at upstairs.

No, he agreed. That was something else.

I thought you were going to play chords.

I changed my mind.

Jesus, Mr. Hammond said, more to himself than anyone. What *was* that.

He glanced at his father and saw that although his head remained lowered, in a posture of listening, he was staring at him.

John? he said.

I'm sorry, Daddy. It's what I hear.

That's all right, son, he said softly, without moving, as though the boy were some feral creature that could be frightened by a sudden movement.

Mr. Hammond left soon after. The boy watched him do a curious thing: at the door, as his father turned away to rummage in the closet for the camel's hair overcoat, Mr. Hammond caught his mother's eye and mouthed an apology. The boy saw it clearly, the soundless shapes of the words: *I'm sorry*. His mother did not react beyond a very slight shake of the head.

Here we are, his father said, handing over the expensive coat. He seemed suddenly very tired and did not pretend he wanted Mr. Hammond to stay.

We'll see you tomorrow, Ben, the big man said, and with a

start Foster realized his father faced the additional humiliation of working out the week, wrapping up his last few files. Somehow he had just assumed it would be a holiday for both of them for a few days, until his father found his next job.

Tomorrow, his father repeated. Good night.

Good night. Thank you, Cass.

Good night.

Keep in touch, Mr. Hammond said, a remark seemingly, strangely, directed at the boy.

Goodbye, he replied.

After the door closed the three of them stood for a moment, suspended.

I'll do the dishes, he offered.

His parents moved together towards the stairs, as though he were the adult who had released them from an habitual duty. Then they seemed to remember themselves and turned back to wish him good night.

Are you all right? his mother asked.

Fine.

It will all look better in the morning, his father said.

Sure.

Thank you for entertaining us tonight.

Guilt seeped sweetly in his chest. He said, I don't mean to be secretive.

You're not, his father said, surprised, and the boy saw he really believed this was true. So either he had been quite drunk or the remark had meant something else entirely.

What was that strange thing you played? his mother asked shyly. She was always tentative when she asked about his work, knowing he hated to talk about it.

Nothing.

She hesitated, then followed his father up the stairs.

After he finished the dishes he recovered the little bag of toffees his mother had squirrelled in her baking cupboard and the evening paper his father had left on the table next to his chair, and went up to bed. But when – lying on his belly, sheet pulled to his waist, mouth sweetly full – he finally unfolded the *Daily Province* on his pillow, he saw someone had neatly scissored out the lead article, leaving a frail empty square in the front page.

That was Monday. On Saturday he rode his bike ten blocks west, to a house with vegetables growing in the front garden. From the sidewalk he could hear the piano.

Yes, Mrs. Agostino said, when he crept by the open door of the studio, where a straight-haired girl sat weeping silently on the piano bench, to the waiting room. I see you, John.

When it was his turn, he explained that he would not be continuing his lessons through the summer after all.

Where is your mother? Mrs. Agostino asked.

He explained that his mother was busy at home.

I see, Mrs. Agostino said. A stroke had left one side of her face paralyzed, and her mouth hung ragged when she listened. She had a withered hand also, and taught from a chair across the room.

He was unsure whether he should take his usual place on the bench. He had not brought his books. From his pocket he took an envelope and said, My mother says this is for today.

With some difficulty Mrs. Agostino tore the envelope, put the money on the table, and unfolded the note.

Instead you are going to spend the summer exploring your interest in sports? she asked.

He said nothing.

There is money trouble at home?

His mother had instructed him not to speak of this.

Sit down.

I didn't bring my books.

Sit down.

His lesson lasted one hour. Scarlatti, Bartók. At two minutes to eleven he heard the front door. A student crept by to the waiting room.

Yes, the crippled woman said. I see you.

He stood up and said, Thank you, Mrs. Agostino. I've enjoyed my lessons.

All right, she said, glancing at the clock. You are a talented musician, though not at the piano. But you have an interesting ear.

Thank you.

You will come back in the fall?

I think so.

No, she corrected, shaking her head. I don't think so.

Outside he got back on his bike and wavered home. His mother had explained they would be living on a budget for a few weeks, just until his father was confirmed in another position. They would simply cut back on a few frivolities until that time.

Summer poured long and yellow and smooth, with its interminable days and brief hiding nights. Foster tried to continue his life in its old patterns. He wrote and read and drew and took the streetcar to the park and to the beach, and closer to home to the fairgrounds, where he sauntered among the roller coasters and the carousels, inhaling the rich prize stench of livestock.

After a day's work he liked to walk, anywhere where there were crowds, alone in his head but insulated from the sounds that came to him in quieter places.

One evening, early in August, he came home with his mouth still sticky from a five-penny wad of cotton candy, panting a little, a little dazed still, to find his father had got a job at an investigative agency.

Where? he repeated. The house seemed small and dazzlingly dim after a long white day in the sun, and the faint sugar-sickness that had been pleasant enough out of doors turned bilious when he stepped through the front door and smelled the supper he would be expected to put away, something thick with cheese. He had had to hide his need for sweet things ever since his mother had started watching the flow of pennies, and guilt added to his swelling discomfort. He thumbed surreptitiously, hard, at the corners of his mouth.

Ghent and Coutrell, his father repeated. I start Monday.

They're detectives?

Investigators, they call it.

They kept their voices carefully neutral.

That's great, the boy said.

Yes, his mother said, setting her empty glass down. She had left the olive in it, lolling on the bottom. When he was a boy he would beg her olives and she would give them to him, cool and plump with gin. The thought of putting the slick thing in his mouth now made him close his eyes with queasiness. Immediately he was back at the fairgrounds, listening to the harsh, glassy cadences of the carousel, watching a fatty blond woman throw darts for a teddy bear, watching children queuing for the Teacup, a tilting, spinning ride in cup-shaped cars; then a brief cooling walk through the cavernous exhibition hall to watch a horse auction, all but incomprehensible to him, and back outside to see teenagers older than himself in a screaming, preening knot, sending a flask from mouth to sucking mouth, the girls' red pursed lips, the boys' chapped and paler, swigging; and a carny hawking tickets for the freak show and the burlesque.

I'm fine, he replied to a question that broke through this film of thoughts.

Too much sun today, maybe, his mother said.

Where's the office?

Cordova, his father said, naming a brick-cobbled street in one of the oldest parts of the city core, in Gastown. From the street it looks like nothing, just a door and a stairway up to the second floor. It's all very discreet. I'll have a desk next to the secretary's for the first few weeks, but definitely an office by October. There's a printing firm next door and we're planning to take over that suite as soon as their lease is up. I'll have a proper office in there.

We, that was an off note. His father had never seemed pathetic before.

Here's the thing, though, son, his father continued. The firm's waiting on a contract with a department store, a big contract. If they get it, they'll be expanding and my job will be a lock. But until then I'm on probation, you see?

A department store?

Plainclothes security, his father explained. Six floors. Stores in three different locations. The contract is a cherry. They'll know in a few weeks.

His father in a brown suit, laying his hand on the arm of a teenage shoplifter. The carny in a hay-brown suit, laying his hand on the boy's arm. *Miss, if you'll come this way. Sir, this way for you, sir.* Caught.

What I'm trying to say, son, his father said. I'm just not going to be earning as much as I used to for a little while.

That's all right, the boy said, after a minute.

His parents exchanged a glance and he felt a surge of impatience. He reckoned he had seen as much as they ever had, after today. Vicious pride, swimming shame, both.

It's about your tuition at St. John and St. James, his father said.

But that was all wrong, of course. The boys who went there knew to call it Jack and Jim's.

It's not that you'll never go back, his father said. It's just that we need to be cautious for a few months, not commit ourselves to more than we can – not bite off more than we can chew.

The girl, the girl.

A year in the public system shouldn't set you back. It's not a big exam year for you, this next one, is it? And it's just for a year, a year at most. Maybe even by January. I know everything feels a little loose right now but we'll get it all nailed down again, you'll see.

Which school will I go to?

Aberdeen.

The boy closed his eyes and opened them. Aberdeen was where the Italian boys in the neighbourhood went, and the Chinese, and so on. Boys did not graduate from Aberdeen to become artists or musicians, or even lawyers. They became clerks, at best, if they became anything at all. So it was like that now.

We fall in their catchment area, his mother said quietly.

You'll be able to walk there, his father said. That'll make for a change. Maybe with the time you save getting there and back you'll even be able to take an after-school job. What would you say to that?

Eyes open: I'm old enough.

That would be something, wouldn't it, John? his father said. To be a working man like your old Dad?

Eyes closed: he saw again the inside of the tent, the hot pale light through the fawn-coloured canvas, and all the working men seated in docile rows at the front and standing at the back. He had stayed at the back.

Are you listening, John? his mother's voice said.

I could get a paper route. I already have a bike.

Good lad, his father said.

There had been a girl on the stage, a dark-haired girl dancing with one small breast already bared, so that he thought he would go mad.

You're not too disappointed?

What?

Pardon? his mother said.

Pardon?

You're not too disappointed about the school? You'll make new friends, won't you?

Sure. Sure I will.

There she was, almost washed out in a shaft of sun, a shaft like a spotlight through a hole in the roof of the tent. Like an overexposed photo she was, dancing in the middle of the day in a shaft of white sunlight that glittered with dust, white hands winding, staring honestly and earnestly at nothing.

We might just wait a few weeks with Mrs. Agostino also, his mother said. Instead of going back immediately in September, like we usually do.

There had been a giant and a dwarf too, but that was later.

John!

Yes, he said. It's all right. I don't mind, really.

Outside the tent had been a candy cart, and he had straight away bought a great puff of candy floss, stuffed his mouth full of it to resurrect that jolting surfeit of sweetness he had known in the tent. The candy was a pale imitation but when he found the

carny again to ask about the next show the man pretended not
to recognize him, and told him he was too young.

We've got a fine young man here, Cass, his father said.

I know it, his mother said.

On his paper route, now, every morning, as the final days of
summer flipped away, Foster paused beneath the pink sky to
inform himself of the progress of the murder investigation. His
father rarely brought the papers home any more so he tracked it
this way, between houses, the case bubbling along in the back
pages, awaiting the high heat of the trial in September. He spent
time over the girl's photograph, memorizing the pale, round
face and soft hands; he spent time over the details of the crime,
the French proverb and the basement grate and the delivery boy
from Farrell's Fine Foods. That she had chosen a boy over a
man – he went weak to think of it. Though Farrell's of course
was a fine place, spanking new, and on a fine wide avenue, three
blocks only from his old school. From the newspapers he con-
structed an image of the boy, Stephen, a delivery boy, like
himself now, only a year and a half older. The newspaper edito-
rials maintained she had used him, corrupted him, and he could
not truly be held responsible for whatever he might have done.
Foster thought that sounded right. He would have been dazzled,
as Foster himself had been dazzled in the tent at the fairgrounds,
dazzled and ashamed and painfully grateful all at once. Now he
was in jail, awaiting trial, probably still dreaming helplessly of
their – what? He didn't know the word for it. Rendezvous?
Sessions? Sometimes Foster would go so far as to close his eyes
and try to put himself in the other's place, to see the bricks and
bars while summoning the feel of her clothes – silk, surely – in
his hands. Then some sound would startle him, some dog's bark
or cry, recalling him to his duty, and he would bike on through
his own newly hateful neighbourhood – the cheap, scant trees,

feeble houses, washing hung in the gardens, and over it all the thin, rank, seedy pall of garbage – dismissing each paper with an angry, reckless toss.

One morning he recalled how, in his father's office that day, beneath the perfume, an unpleasant camphorous odour had emanated from her clothes. This, too, he savoured.

At home he took fiercely to the piano, rattling off the exercises that had so recently bored him, fighting Bach, fighting Beethoven, fighting Chopin, fighting Debussy, until he caught his mother furtively listening, hiding in doorways, sitting once at the turn in the stairs just out of his sight, and this angered him past speech. Her shy encouraging smiles drove him to his room and his notebooks, where no matter how much he wrote he couldn't clear his head. At night he dwelt feverishly on the girl from the fairgrounds, who merged in his imagination with the girl from the paper, until they were – for his purposes, at least – indistinguishable.

His new school, Aberdeen, was a sooty brick building with slits of windows, as though for archers. Inside students roamed in packs, sorted along the lines of race. There were girls everywhere. He had expected some immediate violence and was at first relieved.

At the office, where he had been told to register, they made him sit on a bench while they sorted some paperwork. After an hour he tapped on the window and the secretary's voice, tiny and disjointed through the glass, said, Are you still here?

No one's given me a room.

Two-o-seven, she said, without referring to anything. He thought she had made the number up on the spot.

The doors of two-o-seven were closed. He knocked.

Yes, a voice said.

The teacher was a woman, not old, with a bitter, pretty face, a wealth of carefully rolled blond hair, and a name, glimpsed on a metal plaque outside the door, he immediately forgot.

Yes.

Please, Miss, I was assigned to this class.

The room went quiet.

The teacher waited a heavy, deadpan beat before saying, Name?

Foster, Miss.

First name.

John, Miss.

Sit down, John.

Foster, Miss.

I beg your pardon, she said very quietly, and he saw she would be no help to him in the coming year.

I'm usually called Foster, Miss.

She took a minute to look at his clothes, moving her head so it was clear to those in the back row what she was doing. He was wearing last year's uniform: slacks and blazer and tie.

Do I know you?

I've transferred, Miss.

From which school?

St. John and St. James.

Run out of money, did we?

He heard, in his mind's ear, a ragged, surprised spasm of violins.

The teacher held up her left hand, palm towards herself, fingers splayed, and said, See this?

He wondered if she was going to hit him.

Learn my name.

The wedding ring, she meant, because he had called her Miss.

The lesson was French. Once he was seated and had been given a book he was able to relax a little. They were reviewing the parts of the family, mon père ma mère ma sœur mes frères ma tante mon oncle, and, for some reason, mes copains.

John, the teacher said. Combien as-tu de frères?

Je n'ai ni sœurs ni frères.

Again the class fell silent, down to the last fiddling and rustling of pages. His accent was better than hers.

Que fait ton père?

He hesitated.

Peter, she said. Que fait ton père?

Il est soldat.

Mario?

Il est magasinier.

Helen?

A Chinese girl said exceedingly softly, Mon père est malade. Il ne travaille pas.

The teacher met his eye again. Peut-être maintenant tu comprends la question. Que fait ton père?

Il est enquêteur.

En anglais. In English.

Private detective, he said.

The beating came during the lunch hour, behind the gymnasium. He recognized one or two of the boys by sight from the streets near his house.

Is she always such a battleship? he had asked one of them at the break, trying to be friendly. They had led him out back and kicked him until he couldn't get up. He understood it was not about the teacher.

By afternoon she had moved on to someone else.

Jean, you are wearing lipstick.

No, Mrs. Borsky.

The girl's real name, he surmised from her black and pink Italian prettiness, was not Jean, but something longer and prettier: Gianna, Giannina, Giovanna, Anna –

You are, Mrs. Borsky corrected. Where is your handkerchief?

They had been solving algebra problems, another class he found easy, though the others seemed to take it seriously enough, furrowing brows and breathing softly over the symbols, pencils poised but confoundedly still.

Here, Mrs. Borsky.

Wipe your mouth.

The girl dabbed her mouth with the cloth and held it up.

Wipe your mouth.

She wiped a little harder.

I don't allow sluts in my classroom, Jean, Mrs. Borsky said. Can you prove to me you're not a slut?

Tears started running down the girl's cheeks. She wiped until the wiping made her lips even more red than they were before, though the handkerchief showed nothing.

Go to the principal, Jean, Mrs. Borsky said.

The girl let out a howl, a few tumbling words not in English, and ran from the room. He touched the point of his cheek, gingerly, dabbed at it with his fingertip, feeling the lush bruise there.

After school they caught him again, this time for conversation.

Yes, Miss. No, Miss. Please, Miss. My father's a private detective.

Well, he is.

Bullshit. Your father got fired.

He studied the boy who had spoken but could not place him at all.

My mother says your mother is a snotty bitch, another said. In a mincing voice: My son's school, have you heard of it? My son's piano teacher, do you know her?

He realized his family had a public existence in the neighbourhood he had never suspected.

What's this? said a third, yanking at his tie. What's this?

They found a game, pulling his tie round to the back and
choking him with it. He experienced moments of pain accompanied by bursts of heightened hearing. As his vision started to
swarm he distinctly heard a rhythmic chanting that did not cor-
relate to the faces of the boys around him. He heard his own
blood and systems.

Mackenzie, someone said, and they scattered.

He went home. His mother clucked over his face but asked
surprisingly few questions. So she, too, had expected no less.

What are the academics like? his father asked him after
dinner.

Fine.

Comparable to the work you were doing last year?

Maybe a little easier.

It's only the first day, his mother said. They're just reviewing.

Any societies or teams? Did they make an announcement
about clubs day yet?

At his old school, boys would set up tables in the gymnasium one afternoon during first week, advertising the various
school activities – Math club, fencing, Drama club, rugby, and so
on. You got to skip class, to go and watch demonstrations and
sign up.

Maybe Aberdeen does things a little differently, his mother
said, when he didn't respond.

I know your mother won't like to hear me say this, his father
said. But it's important, these first few days, you give back as
good as you get. That way they'll learn to leave you alone.

His mother said nothing.

How's work? the boy asked.

There was no question of going to visit him in his office, the way he used to. He understood his father was experiencing some difficulties. He was distracted these days, and disinclined to talk.

His father shook his head. Coutrell's giving me grief, he said, addressing the boy's mother, as though she had asked the question. About those days I need off for the trial. He has to give them to me by law, but he's not happy about it.

When?

Starting Monday. They think it'll go all week.

All week, the boy said.

Why do they need you? his mother said. When they've got –

When they've got Jim Hammond? Good question. Why does anyone need anyone when the world has got Jim Hammond?

Ben.

You know what he's got me doing, Coutrell? The little camera he's given me? The marriages I'm hired to break up?

Ben.

They're going to crucify that little girl, his father said. They're going to make me drive in the nails.

I don't want to hear about it, she said harshly, and to the boy: Go to bed.

Slowly, because of the pain, he got himself under the blankets. His back ached, and he couldn't lie on his accustomed right side because of the tenderness around his swollen eye. He tried to summon up his usual fantasy, of the mysterious dark house and the girl with the limp, but it had evolved, with a kaleidoscope twist, into something at once darker and more familiar. This time he was in a grocery store, behind the butcher's counter, watching the girl from the newspaper walk toward him. Every moment she was near some new aspect of her broke over him like a wave – the brooch at the throat of her blouse, in the shape of an elaborately scrolled flower (borrowed from his mother), the length of the eyelashes (borrowed from pretty Jean), the hat (its shape painfully reconstructed from the blur of a newspaper photograph), the smell of camphor (most intimate of details, because it was the only one he owned). Though he savoured these things individually, they did not add up to a totality; he could not, in his mind's eye, look her full in the face. When he tried to roll over, some time later, and give himself to sleep, the pain brought tears to his eyes.

Every day at lunch and after school his classmates led him back behind the gymnasium, scattering only when some authority was sighted, some teacher. He would walk back home, after: alone and weak and milky, a walking aggregate of injuries. They would have to stop soon; they would never stop. It was absurd; it was deeply familiar.

On Monday morning he walked to school and then kept on walking. A few heads turned in the yard but no one cared to stop him. The pack had its habits, and mornings he was left alone.

He walked to Hastings Street, to his old stop, and waited with the businessmen for the number seven. He had never taken the streetcar this late before, and the light in the street seemed different, fatter and more sullied, disappointing. He touched his wristwatch through his sleeve but did not look at it. It started to rain.

What happened to you? someone asked him.

On the streetcar he dozed fitfully. He was sleeping badly for the first time in his life, and a warm, scraped, numb feeling often scrambled his consciousness so that he would come to at odd times throughout the day, belatedly realizing he had been gone.

Granville and Georgia, the conductor called, startling him so badly he wanted to cry. It was his stop.

It was raining in cold driving threads. By the time he reached the courthouse steps his chest and shoulders were dark with wet.

Dapper men, lawyers, hurried up the steps and through the doors.

Coming in? one of them called to him, holding the big door.

The first thing he saw, in the main hall, was his father and Mr. Hammond talking with two other men.

Which case? asked the man who had held the door for him.

He put a hand to his face, rubbed his forehead, turned away as much as he could. Mumbled: Pass.

Ah.

The murder case.

And are you with the bride or the groom?

Now the four men were moving off, up the curving staircase. He dropped to his knees, bowed his head over his shoelaces.

Yes, do that, the lawyer said amiably. I'll just be a moment.

The four men were gone. He watched the lawyer approach one of the big, uniformed men standing by the clerk's desk and ask him a few questions.

Room three-o-three, he said when he came back. I don't think they'll let you in, though.

Don't they have to?

What happened to your face?

The lawyer's expression was absolutely pleasant and careless. Foster said, Why won't they let me in?

What school do you go to?

St. John and St. James.

That's a fine school. Why aren't you there?

Why won't they let me in?

Right, the man said, unruffled. Well, for one thing, there are probably a lot of reporters and rubbernecks there ahead of you.

Foster thought about the word, a new one to him, then said, I'm not a rubberneck.

No, I don't think you are. For another thing, you're rather scruffy. The sheriffs, they're the men in the brown uniforms, like that one over there, they might look at you and think you look like trouble. Are you trouble?

The boy shook his head.

Three-o-three, the lawyer repeated, looking at his wristwatch. I have to go. You give it a try, though. You came all this way.

Thank you.

You're welcome.

He watched the lawyer trot towards the stairs, then followed him up to the third floor, where there was a thick crowd. He shouldered his way through, in the wake of the friendly lawyer, right up to the door of room three-o-three, where the man spoke a few words to the sheriff and was allowed in.

Full up, the sheriff said to the boy, barring his way. Through the open door he caught a glimpse of a crowded, restless, silent room. Just before the door closed the lawyer glanced back and winked.

He turned around and saw his father sitting not ten feet away, alone on a bench, staring at his feet.

He spent the rest of the day slowly pacing out the city block around the courthouse, hoping she might be allowed out for a breath of air, hoping not to round a corner and run into his father or Mr. Hammond. At two-thirty, he walked back down to Hastings Street, took the streetcar back to the East end, and walked home.

How was school? his mother asked.

Fine.

That evening his father went straight up to the bedroom and stayed there. His mother took him a meal on a tray.

He's got a screaming headache, she explained.

The next morning Foster left all but one of his papers in an alley and got to the streetcar stop while the sun was still coming up. He wore his school uniform. He was not afraid of bumping into his father or Mr. Hammond because he knew from the paper that they had both testified yesterday. Today it would be the murdered man's colleague from work.

He joined the lineup that had formed outside room three-o-three and waited there for an hour. Occasionally someone would speak a word or two to the sheriff and be admitted. The room seemed to be filling up but his line did not move at all. He watched a reporter show his credentials and go in.

Good morning, a familiar voice said.

Good morning, he replied. Faces turned sharply to look at him, at Foster. The friendly lawyer had some celebrity, clearly.

Better luck today, maybe, the lawyer said. Foster nodded. He watched the man greet the sheriff and go in.

Thank you, the sheriff called to the people waiting. That's all for today.

The line did not immediately disperse. Thinking these people knew something he didn't, he kept his place.

He saw another reporter hurry up to the door, speak a low word to the sheriff, and be admitted.

Thank you, the sheriff called again, over various protests and indignant fingers pointing after the man. That's it, folks, we're full up. You can read about it in the papers.

An old man in front of him began to make a speech about fairness and openness in judicial proceedings.

There's a rape downstairs, the sheriff said. In two-ten. It's almost empty. Only just started, I think.

The old man scowled and hurried away.

Foster stared at the closed door. They would have started by now. She was in there, probably not twenty yards from where he was standing, and the boy, too. He felt weak again, and closing his eyes found himself instantly in the hanging place between sleeping and waking. There had been a new photograph in the paper that morning, taken as she was led from the courthouse the day before, but her face had been obscured by a large hat. He had even touched it with his fingers, trying to push it back, to uncover her face.

He opened his eyes and went to where a knot of people stood trying to see through the window in the door, watched closely by the sheriff.

Where do the photographers go? Foster asked. To get them as they come out?

Scram, the sheriff said.

Who are you? one of the rubbernecks asked, temporarily diverted from the window. I saw Wilder talking to you.

I don't know who he is, Foster said, and the eager man said, Counsel for the defence. For her.

That evening, he overheard his mother telling his father that Mr. Coutrell from the office had called for him at home, asking when he was coming back to work. I thought you *were* at work yesterday, his mother said.

I was, his father said. That is, I was out following leads all day, so he wouldn't have seen me in the office. But I was working.

Well, he wants to see you in the office tomorrow, he says, for sure.

He will, his father said.

On the third day the friendly lawyer stopped again and said, Good morning.

I want to meet her, Foster said.

He saw the man have his habitual word with the sheriff at the door before he went in, saw the sheriff glance over at the boy and nod. His line advanced to the door, but when his turn came the sheriff held his arm out and said, Not you.

Tell me where the photographers go, he said.

Listen, punk, the sheriff said. Foster turned around and headed back towards the stairs. The line he had been standing in was still moving.

The alley, said the old man who had made the speech the day before, shuffling forward with the others.

Pardon?

The photographers. They wait in the alley. You won't see the boy, though, if you're a friend of his. They remand him here, in the cells. You'll only see her.

The old man went through the door. Foster went outside and stood in the mouth of the alley for six hours. After five hours men started to gather there, with sandwiches and cigarettes and bags of equipment. They joked loudly and cynically with each other but they ignored him, except for one who offered him a cigarette in a way obviously intended to amuse his colleagues. He declined.

A good, clean, healthy boy, the man said, and the others laughed.

By five to four the photographers, twenty or so, had gathered around a single doorway and were elbowing him out of their way. A car pulled into the alley and nosed slowly up to the waiting men. The courthouse door opened, tripping a flash; a man's head looked out and nodded at the waiting car. The car door opened. Foster went up on his toes, trying to see over the flashbulbs.

Piss off, the man behind him said, giving him a shove. He went down. Above his head the men began to surge and shout her name. Someone stepped on his hand, pinning it. He heard the snicketing of a hundred cameras, heard rather than saw the flowers of white light. Take it off, the men begged. He looked up and saw straight into her face, below the monstrous tilted hat, saw the soft black eyes, the vacant expression. Then she was in the car, the photographers were snapping lenses off cameras, and someone was helping him to his feet.

Sorry about that, said the man helping him up. You were in my shot.

He got home after his father.

You're late today, his mother said. Where have you been?

Band practice, he lied.

You never said anything about joining the band. That's wonderful. Ben, John's joined the band at school.

His father sat by the fireplace, clipping articles from the newspaper with his mother's big kitchen scissors. He lifted his head and said, That pleases me very much. You don't know. Which instrument?

I like the oboe, he said truthfully.

So do I, his father said, nodding, using the scissors like a seamstress with silk, just sliding cuts off the blade. Squares and columns of newsprint accumulated on the table at his elbow. His hands were black.

Ben, for heaven's sake, some others of us may want to read that too, his mother said, but his father carried on mutilating the paper just as though she hadn't spoken.

It didn't matter, though, because Foster saw the paper every morning and knew which way things were tending. The pair was down. The dead man's colleague from work, also a family friend, had testified that the girl had asked him to perform the task that had eventually fallen to the delivery boy, and had offered him whatever he might want in exchange. She had made it pretty clear, he said, what she meant by that. He had laughed her off, he said, and thought nothing more of it until her husband was found dead. The photograph in the newspaper showed the colleague to be a stocky man with salt and pepper hair, with a look that was truculent but not unamused. She must have been desperate, Foster thought. Sex in his imagination was tense but soft, his lips against the tendons of his own wrist, in a dim room that smelled unaccountably of Christmas baking. He could not imagine anyone enduring, let alone seeking, the embrace of the colleague.

He saw her twice more. The next day, a Thursday, he waited again in the alley with the photographers. This time he stood a little further back, out of the scrum. He wanted to call her name with the rest of them, to add his voice to that sound, but when she appeared he found he could not.

On Friday the jury began its deliberations. When he arrived, the alley was already full of reporters and photographers and others who had come to see. Cars slowed, stopped, and men got out; then after an hour or so word came that the police had cordoned off the street and were not letting anyone else near. He dared not leave his place to go and see for himself. Rumours rippled through the crowd that the city had shut down, that workers were leaning out of office windows in their shirt sleeves watching the scene around the courthouse, that traffic into and out of downtown was at a standstill, that they might have to wait well into the night.

At two someone brought word they had been found guilty and the judge was even at that moment sentencing them. Even before he had fully absorbed the words, Foster saw the door open and she was there, hands held awkwardly behind her back, flanked by two uniformed men. The crowd roared like Romans. A hand went up above the cameras, snatched her hat, and sailed it off into the sea of men, where it went down like an anchor. Flashbulbs exploded. She looked out over them once, squinting against the light, before they led her down the two or three steps and he lost sight of her.

At home he found his mother, his father, and Mr. Hammond in the living room, even though it was the middle of the afternoon. They fell silent when he entered, and he guessed he had interrupted an argument.

Ha! Mr. Hammond said. The prodigal returns.

Foster closed the door behind him.

We got a note from the school today, his mother said. They want to know where you've been.

Mr. Hammond winked broadly.

I cut, he said.

His father, he noticed, was slowly shaking his head, shaking his head, and didn't seem to have noticed his presence in the room.

Now, Cassie, Mr. Hammond said. You never told me he was such a rebel.

You must go to school, his mother said, without conviction.

Foster untied his shoelaces and hung his jacket on the tree by the door. He found himself trying to move as silently as possible, and wondered why.

That's some shiner, Mr. Hammond said. You need to put a steak on that.

Instead of going up to his room, Foster took a seat on the ottoman beside his mother's chair.

Your mother tells me you're having a hard time at school, Mr. Hammond said. What would you say about that?

Jim, she said.

Now, you see, Mr. Hammond said. This is what I mean. You have to let him answer for himself. You might as well hit him yourself as baby him, for all the good it's going to do. So you're cutting school, now, he continued, turning back to Foster. You've decided to run away from your problems.

No, Foster said.

I'll tell you God's truth, Mr. Hammond said. You're like a nephew to me. A son, hell, you're like a son. I held you in my arms before you could walk and I think of you in that way. It rips me up to see your face looking like that, and to know what you're going through with those animals in that dump of a school. But, by Christ, I'd be lying if I didn't say I thought it was good for you too.

Stop it, Jim, his mother said. Not now.

It'll toughen you up.

Jim.

All right, Ben? Mr. Hammond said in a loud voice, as though speaking to a child.

She can appeal, his father said, looking from face to face. Can't she?

He stood up and immediately toppled forward. Foster's mother and Mr. Hammond jumped up, one to each side, to steady him. The toe of his mother's shoe caught an empty bottle tucked beside his father's chair and sent it rolling. Foster realized his father was blind drunk.

Go ahead of us, John, his mother said. Open the doors.

Foster opened the doors to the hall and the bedroom while his mother and Mr. Hammond coaxed his father forward and half-pushed, half-dragged him up the stairs. At the door to the bedroom, Mr. Hammond hesitated.

Don't back out now, you, his mother said. You're the one who let him get like this.

Cassie.

He wouldn't have gone there today without you. You're the one who told him he had an obligation to see it through.

I happen to believe that's true.

Oh, you happen to believe, Foster's mother said. You happen to believe a lot of things, when it suits you. Get his shoes.

Foster watched from the doorway while they half-undressed his father, lying now on the made bed.

Next, a pot of strong coffee, Mr. Hammond said. He'll want it when he wakes up. I wouldn't mind some myself, and that's the truth. Come here, Cassie. Don't be angry. Tell her, sport, tell your mother not to be angry with an old friend of the family. I always mean to do the right thing.

Much later they sat in the kitchen, the three of them, with coffee, and crackers and cheese on a plate.

Oh, John, his mother said. This is hardly supper for a growing boy. I just can't seem to get my mind around anything right now. I suppose there are eggs.

I think Dad just called you.

Did he? His mother jumped up fretfully. Coming!

Across from him, Mr. Hammond set down his coffee cup and raised one of Foster's mother's good linen napkins to his lips. He watched Mr. Hammond smash a crag of cheese on a saltine with the flat of a knife, eat it in one bite, and prepare another.

A week is a lot of school to miss, Mr. Hammond said.

I'll catch up.

Oh, I know you will.

More casual pasting of crackers.

About the, the trial.

Not here, sport, Mr. Hammond said. It upsets your mother. You come to the office and I'll tell you what you want to know.

He offered Foster a cracker. The taste was thick, salty, exquisite. Foster closed his eyes.

Sure, you're all right, Mr. Hammond said.

Foster's mother came back down.

He's out like a light, she said. Maybe he was having a nightmare.
Or a sweet dream, Mr. Hammond said, winking at Foster.

Her sentence was imposed the following April, on schedule,
without appeal.

John, his father's old secretary said, with genuine warmth. I
almost didn't recognize you.

Johnny! Mr. Hammond said. My God, you're a monster.

Five foot ten, Foster said. How are you, Miss Craig?

Five ten! she said. And you've had a birthday, too, I think.

Back in March.

Fifteen years old, Miss Craig said. I can remember holding
you on my knee.

You'll embarrass him, Mary, Mr. Hammond said. And I believe
he's here on business. I won't have you embarrassing my clients.
Hold all my calls and send my appointments away.

All right, Mr. Hammond, she said, laughing and at the same
time running a finger down the page of her big book. Four
o'clock is your next.

Send them away, I tell you, Mr. Hammond said, glancing
from his wristwatch to the clock on the wall above Miss Craig's
desk, which said twenty after three.

Mr. Hammond had the office next door to the one that had
been his father's. Foster couldn't help glancing in as they passed.
A young man with a heavily Brylcreemed quiff of black hair was
pitching intently into the phone.

That's Laster, Mr. Hammond said. Is what he rhymes with.
He's doing fine.

He shut the door behind them and gestured toward a chair.

It's strange being here again, Foster said. Everything looks
smaller. I know I've sat in this chair a hundred times –

Spinning round and round, Mr. Hammond said. You made yourself throw up, once. You were about five.

My dad was here a long time.

Yes, Mr. Hammond said. Yes, he was. From the bottom of his file drawer he pulled a fifth of rye whisky, poured a shot into a paper cup, and took it into the hall, where Foster heard him top it up from the water cooler. He came back and shut the door again and sipped and grimaced.

At first I was able to help him out a lot, Mr. Hammond said. Little mistakes, little errors of judgment. Later it got harder to cover for him. He changed, too, over the years. He never used to take things so personally, your dad. By the end he felt sorry for everybody and it was pay, pay, pay. He stopped even going through the motions of investigating claims. You'd have thought this Pass girl was his own daughter.

Foster cleared his throat.

I'm surprised it took you so long, frankly. To come see me. I was a little hurt. I thought maybe you didn't trust me.

It wasn't that.

Mr. Hammond crumpled his empty paper cup and fired it over his shoulder, expertly nailing the trash can in the corner of the room. Foster told him about the job his mother had got, shelving books at the local library. She had also become obsessed with the variety, economy, and nutritive value of meatless soups.

Cassie, the older man said, laughing.

I just couldn't come here, right away, Foster said. I had to wait until –

Mr. Hammond nodded.

– over, I mean, at least for –

Now Mr. Hammond was shaking his head, meaning the same as the nod.

You saw, didn't you, Foster said. You went to see.

You know I did.

From the next room Foster could hear the young man who had replaced his father needling a client. Distantly a phone rang. Footsteps retreated to silence.

Dad was going to go, Foster said. He got permission and everything. Because of having to testify, and wanting to see it through. But he lost his nerve. That night was – well, I guess Dad probably told you. We all just sat there, waiting for midnight. You know my mother left the next morning?

Did she? Mr. Hammond said, very still suddenly.

To stay with her sister, in Toronto. My Aunt Trudy. She said Dad was more worried about a murderer than about his own family. She came back after a couple of weeks, though.

Mr. Hammond nodded. He looked over at the window for a moment, still nodding, then looked back and said, You've got your mother about you. He touched the corner of his eye and his bottom lip. Here, and here. I've always liked to see it.

Tell me.

What if I refuse?

Foster said nothing.

How are your grades?

Better, again.

School's better?

Foster nodded.

You got a girl?

Foster shook his head.

You will. You've already got a type, am I wrong?

The phone on Mr. Hammond's desk rang, but he ignored it, and after a moment it stopped.

I know what she had for her last meal, Foster said. They reported it in the paper. Chicken and rice pudding and tea. She wanted fresh strawberries, too, but it was too early in the season.

She had to eat her chicken with a spoon because they wouldn't let her have a knife.

I read that too, Mr. Hammond said.

It had been a mild night, fresh and damp, and a quick drive through empty streets. A guard posted at the door of the jail admitted him. He had assumed it would take place outside, in a courtyard perhaps, but the warden led him upstairs.

They brought a man in from Ontario, the warden said. If you can believe it. I heard they're paying him four hundred dollars.

His tone was bitter.

Would you have done it? Hammond asked.

I would not.

A dozen men were gathered in the hallway where the warden left him, a waiting area, he assumed. He recognized one or two faces from the courtroom – the husband's family, he guessed – and the girl's father, staring at the wall in front of him like a blind man. Others would be coroner's jurors, more witnesses. There was a clergyman, too, and a man in a particularly fine, dark suit who kept looking at the elevator door. It was the first time Hammond had noticed the elevator; the warden had brought him up the stairs.

At midnight guards came and asked them to move a few steps farther down the hall. The man in the fine suit opened the elevator cage and Hammond caught a glimpse of the retrofit inside.

But how will they know when it's over? the man beside him asked. If she's in the elevator shaft?

There's someone downstairs, another man said.

The doctor, a third said. The doctor's downstairs.

Two matrons brought her in, followed by the warden. She wore a dark dress and matching shoes and her hair was newly set. The clergyman stepped forward and began to murmur to her while one of the guards bound her hands in front of her with a leather strap. She looked at the assembled witnesses and for the first time showed signs of agitation, bringing her hands up as though to cover her breasts. The clergyman asked her to admit her guilt.

I don't want him here, she said. Why does he get to see?

Her father didn't turn his head when she spoke, didn't move, and after a moment's hesitation the men continued as though she hadn't spoken. In the elevator – a large one, fortunately – her legs were bound together with another strap, and her face covered with a black hood. While the clergyman read from the Bible the hangman placed the rope around her neck and adjusted it. When he sprang the trap she fell hard.

Clean, a man near Hammond murmured.

The newspapers would report it took her just eight minutes to die, though they left her for the full twenty.

After the last prayers and formalities, Hammond walked home. It was not quite one in the morning. He had got a thrill from the pageantry of it, the ritual; the sickness he had felt earlier had turned fizzy, a sparkling in his chest and the palms of his hands. He had felt a similar sensation when he had seen the straps and the hood. He understood this was not a fetish. At a certain point it was simply overwhelming to be alive.

Through the window Foster saw a car speed by, shattering the silver puddles on the road.

Why did you go? he asked.

Mr. Hammond laughed and said, Why are you here?

There was a tap at the door. Mr. Hammond, Miss Craig said. It's three fifty-five.

Thank you, Mary.

Foster turned away from the window. The big man was watching him, looking perhaps for his father's sick anguish in him.

It's fine, Foster said. I'm fine.

Mr. Hammond touched a few items on his desk, thoughtfully coaxing them into a finer alignment. He said, Well, I don't know that it is. I don't know that yet. Curiosity, Christ, I don't blame you. You couldn't have paid me to stay away. But I know you took things pretty hard, there, son, and you were a worry to your parents. I know that. Now I'll be damned if I know whether I've done the right thing here. Probably not. You won't tell your mother, now, will you, where you've been today? She doesn't need this on top of everything else. Give me your word, now.

Foster gave his word.

Find a nice girl at school. Mr. Hammond pointed a thick finger at him for emphasis. That's my advice. One step at a time. You'll get where you're going quick enough. No, don't thank me. I didn't do anything because you never came here at all, agreed?

Foster stood up and they shook hands.

I've messed you up now, Mr. Hammond said.

No.

Awkwardly, his father's friend pulled him from a handshake into a brief, fierce hug.

In the waiting room Miss Craig was chatting with a young couple, newlyweds probably. They looked awkward and eager to please, the man in a stiff, ill-fitting suit and the girl in a tight dress and hat with a tiny, coquettish veil.

Won't you please go right in, Miss Craig said, and the couple even smiled shyly at Foster as they passed him on the way to Mr. Hammond's office. The girl, a blonde, smelled supremely of lavender. He smiled back.

How is your father? Miss Craig asked.

Foster was looking around the waiting room. He had met her here, the once, under the old slat fan – had it been turning? – had spoken with her, touched her hand. With an effort he dragged his attention back to his father's old secretary.

He works in a department store, as a plainclothesman.

Gosh! she said, too brightly. Well. Well, you just tell him Mary wanted to be remembered to him. We all do miss him around here.

Thank you, Mary, Foster said. I'll tell him.

In the hallway he could take the stairs, or he could take the elevator.

What are you working on? she had asked.

As Mrs. Agostino predicted, he had not returned to his piano lessons, but had continued composing in secret, sounding his ideas out on the piano when both his parents were at work. The girl had never left him, but gradually his mercurial memories had hardened into stills. Those three last glimpses had become for him three attitudes of a religious icon: Anna the Sinner, Anna Agonistes, Anna Gloria. The girl and the work had merged in the delicate parts of his mind, until writing music had become his way – lush, private, barely articulate – of thinking about her. It would be an opera; it would make his name. Yet he had postponed any beginning firmer than sketches and a few general notes, knowing his talent was still too green. Sex, he would need to have had, and various other worldly experiences (he knew) before he would be ready to say in art everything she had meant to him.

The elevator dropped abruptly to his floor: red velvet, brazen gilt, black wrought iron bars. He opened the cage and stepped inside.

$$\left(3\right)$$

The door slammed behind her. Glitter of keys.

She spent the first few seconds arranging her clothes, retying the bow at her throat and straightening the seams on her stockings. They had rather rushed from the courtroom. She had glimpsed her father still sitting amidst the pandemonium, rock in the rapids, taking his medicine he would have called it. She was prepared not to see him again, old eyes gone dark with grief, waiting for her to take his hand. She was through with all that.

In those first moments, too, she saw the two insurance agents who had testified – the tall, thin sweet one she had met in the office in tired brown, and a slightly broader, shorter one in a suit of finest blue – shake hands with each other. The shorter one hacked laughter while the taller one bowed his head. They guarded the gates to someone's world, no doubt, but not hers. She was to hang, within the year.

Stephen they had led away through a different door, after the verdict and the sentences were read. She thought he would be all right. He was young, he had wept in court, he had apologized to God and his mother, he had done very well. She wondered if they would let him keep the little note that had been their undoing, or what would happen to it now. She thought of asking for it herself, to contemplate in her remaining days, but suspected they would deny any request of hers on principle.

Now, in her cell, she passed the time, as she often did at such between-times, standing with her back to the bars, eyes closed, face dipped, placing herself elsewhere: summoning in the cool underground gloom certain embers of sexual memories to warm herself over, or more often slipping into the plots of stories she had read, stepping through to those strange familiar rooms in her mind, and living there.

Later the sheriffs came to cuff her hands behind her back and lead her to a car parked in the alley behind the courthouse. When they threw open the alley door the light was blinding, daylight she thought, but her eyes would not adjust to the swarming brilliance of it. She hesitated on the top step while the photographers sighted her over the tops of their cameras, held up their silver flashbulbs, and called her name: a sound, to her ears, like a monstrous ocean, or the angry, wakening roar of applause.

ACKNOWLEDGEMENTS

My thanks to my agent, Denise Bukowski, and my editors, Ellen Seligman and Jennifer Lambert; thanks too to the Canada Council for the Arts. For information on the life and work of Charles Rennie Mackintosh I am particularly indebted to two books: Alan Crawford's *Charles Rennie Mackintosh* and Alistair Moffat's *Remembering Charles Rennie Mackintosh: An Illustrated Biography*. Any errors are mine.

Anna's books include *Le jeu de l'amour et du hasard* by Pierre de Marivaux, *Le mythe de Sisyphe* by Albert Camus, *Manon Lescaut* by Abbé Prévost, *Les liaisons dangereuses* by Choderlos de Laclos, and *Le Petit Prince* by Antoine de Saint-Exupéry. All translations are my own.